DANGER'S EMBRACE

My limbs felt inordinately heavy as I stood. Gathering my strength I started forward as the first drops of rain fell. Lightning cut a jagged path across the sky. I looked up, unaware of anyone near me until I heard the twigs snapping behind.

A hand shot out from behind an elm and grabbed my arm. I cried out in terror and stared at the gentleman before me.

"Free me!" I hissed, feeling dread in the pit of my stomach as his eyes wandered over me. His lips curved into a sardonic smile which sent chills running through me. The lightning flashed in the sky again, illuminating the severity of his handsome features.

"Are you a beggar or a gypsy? Who are you spying on?" he demanded harshly.

I shook my head, unable to speak. I could not hide my shivering and was surprised when he took off his coat to place it about my shoulders. I was about to thank him when I saw the ruby signet ring on his finger. It was the same design as my mother's pendant.

My heart began to pound as my eyes flew to his face. I tried to wet my dry lips, to swallow, but I could not.

The last thing I remember before fainting was his arms slipping around my waist as I fell toward him. . . .

THE
BLOODSTONE INHERITANCE

BY SERITA DEBORAH STEVENS

ZEBRA BOOKS
KENSINGTON PUBLISHING CORP.

ZEBRA BOOKS

are published by

Kensington Publishing Corp
475 Park Avenue South
New York, NY 10016

Second printing: November, 1992

Printed in the United States of America

Chapter One

The rain had stopped by late afternoon, but the sky was still overcast and gloomy, reflecting my feelings as I stepped from the train. In the last few hours of my journey I had felt an increasing chill and weakness. I hoped it was merely from apprehension and the unaccustomed train trip and not the first sign of illness.

Whatever was causing this pall on my senses, I had to continue my journey. I was determined to solve the mystery surrounding my birth.

Briefly, as if to give me some hope of elusive happiness, a rainbow appeared in the western sky. My spirits lifted as I stared at the greens, golds, and blues that faded into one another and seemed to point toward their treasure. I wondered if I would find my treasure here in Aberdeen. Did I dare hope I could be happy again?

The iron monster pulled to a screeching stop, nearly shaking me from the handle I held. I swayed for a moment and then caught my balance as the train vibrated about me, rather like a panting animal having run a race. I quickly lifted my case and other travel gear onto the wooden platform.

I was struck by the well kept appearance of the place. The fresh coat of paint still had the tangy odor of newness. I stepped into the waiting room and glanced about. It, too, had been made ready for passengers, yet I was the only passenger getting off here. Why did I see no caretaker or ticket manager about? I felt suddenly very alone, and a shiver ran through me.

With a sigh, I picked up my heavy travel cloak and portmanteau. Careful not to step onto the freshly painted boards, I walked the few steps down the wooden platform and out into the street. A wizened man appeared at the side window.

"Excuse me, sir," I said.

He stared at me. Did he not hear me? I stepped forward.

"Excuse me, sir?"

He pushed a square cap back on his head and continued to stare at me. I wet my lips as I tried to speak. "Could you direct me to Jerseyhurst?" I could see no sign of my mother's home from here, but she had said it wasn't far from the station because her father had not liked to take time traveling.

He glared at me a moment. Jerking a hand to the west, he slammed down the wooden shield of the window. I stared a moment at the barrier, startled. Then I turned in the direction he pointed. I saw nothing. In the east the sky was already darkening with the approaching twilight.

I glanced about in vain for some sort of conveyance.

Portmanteau at my side, I stood in the dirt road— muddied from the recent rain—and shielded my eyes. Nothing. No vehicle at all from which I could beg a ride. Well, I had made the choice to come without informing my cousins, and so I would suffer the consequences.

As I dragged my case along with me, I began to wish I had not been so impulsive in coming to visit my relatives without warning. I supposed I could have simply written Uncle Hayward of my mother's death, but then I would never have had the opportunity that presented itself now—to see the town where my mother grew up, to see my cousins, and yes, perhaps to see the father I had never known.

I would never have guessed Zebulon was not my father, had it not been for the letter. Though I still loved and respected him deeply, I was now determined to find my natural sire. It wasn't that Zebulon Larabee hadn't been everything I could have wanted in a father. He had. At moments like these, as I stared down the long empty road, I wished I had never found the half written, unsent letter in mother's corn husk mattress.

As I walked, I thought again of mother's letter. I hoped it would give me courage. The note had been dated shortly after my first birthday. I could recall the words as if the paper was in my hands before me.

My darling:
    I think it is your right to know you have a daughter. I have named her Elizabeth. Zebulon has been wonderful to me but I can't say I am sorry for what we did. I can only say I am sorry you didn't have the ability to be faithful to me.

The letter ended there, unsigned. Obviously, my mother had changed her mind and never sent it. I had no idea if any letter had been posted in its place or if my natural father knew of my existence. But it did not matter

9

if he knew about me or not; my own need to know him burned in me like the brand on a horse.

Since finding the letter, I had thought of little else. I prayed I would find out to whom the letter was addressed. I prayed my mother's family would give me some clue. Surely, they would know if she had been walking out with anyone, if she had been seriously in love with anyone.

A chill came over me from the rapidly cooling evening—or perhaps from my own heart. Had I been wrong to come searching?

Joshua Harmon certainly thought so. He had wanted me to wed him, to stay on the farm in Kansas with him, and to forget the letter ever existed—but I could not. I would not.

Dear Joshua. I would have to write him, to let him know of my safe arrival—if I did in fact arrive safely.

My arm ached as I continued to drag the case behind me. Momentarily, I let go to shake the blood into my arm. Once again, I looked about for a sign of human life—but I was alone.

It couldn't be all that much farther, I told myself. It seemed I would need all of the three weeks I had given myself to recover from this journey. I thought of the coming month ahead. I had told Joshua I would stay only three weeks and learn what I could of my mother's life in Aberdeen. If by then I had no inkling of my true parentage, I would return to Kansas, to Joshua and to the farm.

With a sigh, I looked down at the portmanteau again and flexed my fingers. It was growing heavier by the minute. I wet my lips. The two day train journey had been far more wearing than I cared to admit.

Lifting the case once more, I felt the ache in my

muscles. My whole body trembled. How much longer did I have to walk? I cursed myself for not asking more specific questions of that strange man. I wondered if he assumed I had transportation. Why hadn't I asked him? Why hadn't I done a lot of things, I wondered.

Shifting the battered brown case from one hand to the other, I paused to catch my breath once more at the top of a hilly incline. There seemed to be very few buildings around—only the lowering sky and the darkness of the wood by the unlit road. Trembling, I continued to walk.

Suddenly, the rainbow appeared again, and the light of the dying sun shone through it. By this light, I could see a house in the distance.

I stared, mouth slightly open at the imposing three-tiered structure. It sat at the edge of some woods, just as my mother had described it. That had to be Jerseyhurst! The columns in front were done Southern style as mother had told me, and I could see the lone oak which stood sentinel before the house, its branches waving in the evening breeze. My heart seemed to swell as I felt my mother's presence about me. This had been her home.

The returning cloud hung heavily over the house. I continued to stare at the building. A feeling of unease pervaded my senses. This was my heritage, these were my mother's people, but my mother had neither seen nor heard from them since she had run away twenty years before. How would they react to seeing the daughter who had caused her mother's death?

Tears came to my eyes as I realized, yes, I had done that. I had been driving the carriage when it overturned. I had survived but not my mother.

Well, I had made the decision to come. I would not turn back. Yet, the closer I came to the mansion, the more my apprehension grew. Obviously, no one would expect me. The house looked deserted with no lights or signs of life. Until now the possibility of no one's being at home had not occurred to me.

I wondered—could this dark abode really be the marvelous Jerseyhurst Mama had spoken so highly of with its wealth of oriental treasures from her father's China trade? A chill came over me as I stared at the silent walls.

Tears filled my eyes. The high neckline of my cherry poplin itched. Once again, I put the heavy bag down to rest. I looked back toward the station. No, I had to go on. Surely, there would be servants to let me in when I arrived. If not . . . well, I would think about the situation when it arose.

Except for the brook which ran by the old house, Mother had told me very little of Jerseyhurst, itself. I only knew the mansion I had just passed could not be the house since it lacked the southern columns I had been told to expect. I paused a moment again and stared at the lights which were on in this other place. My weariness nearly forced me to give in, and then I realized I had to go on because if I stopped, I probably would not want to continue.

During the last part of my pilgrimage, my breath had come quickly and with increasing pain. Only the determination which Mother had so often chided me about kept me moving. I would see Jerseyhurst again— and soon. Or so I prayed.

When I finally reached the wrought-iron gate with the "S" curled into the design, tears flooded my eyes. The entrance gate was locked. High up barbs precluded climbing—even had I the energy. There appeared to be no bell. Apparently Jerseyhurst did not have many callers.

"Damn!" I cursed, then looked quickly about to make sure none had heard.

Leaving my heavy bag at the fence, I circled the enclosure to seek out a side entrance. When I found none, I sniffled back tears and leaned against the locked gate, feeling my stomach tighten in fear. I had done the wrong thing by coming here, but it was too late to turn back now.

If only I had a place to sleep the night or some food. My head ached. It seemed ages since I had eaten. My stomach rumbled like the distant thunder now rolling across the sky. I stared up at the clouds as they moved steadily forward. I broke my morbid fascination with the sky as a harsh wind blew up behind, catching me at the back, causing me to cough fitfully.

Joshua had been right. I should not have come. He had tried hard to dissuade me but I would not listen.

I closed my eyes, feeling stinging tears of loneliness. Now that I was here I needed to decide what to do. Even sheltered under the tree as I was seemed precious little protection because the limbs were being whipped about now as in a frenzied dance.

I recalled the other house I had passed. It had been set further back from the road, closer to the woods. It seemed not to be as grand as Jerseyhurst but it promised warmth. If people lived there—and there had been lights—they could at least shelter me for the night. Perhaps if they were an old family they'd be able to tell me about Mother's family. Perhaps they would tell me why no one seemed to live here at Jerseyhurst.

I stared at the mansion before me, at the woods

13

behind me. I could hear the sound of water rushing in the distance. I knew it could only be the grand Mississippi for we had crossed it back and forth many times on the train.

Shivering again, I pulled the heavy cloak—my mother's cloak—around me tightly. My head felt hot and light. My vision blurred. I could see light at the distant house and knew I had to reach it before the storm reached me. Lightning flashed in the sky as if in answer to my worry.

I glanced down at my portmanteau. I would have to trust the universe and leave my belongings under the tree while I searched for other comforts.

As I started back on the road I had just traveled, I saw a gravel road cutting diagonally through the woods. It seemed to be a shorter way to the other house. Brambles scratched me as I struggled forward down the darkened path. Blackness seemed to close in ahead of me and behind me. The gravel part of the path ceased, but already deep into the woods, I had no desire to turn back, knowing I faced those brambles again. My head and back ached. Would I be forced to seek shelter huddled in the woods until daybreak?

I cursed my impulsive nature. I had started on this path without thinking, just as I had left Kansas without prior thought of writing ahead.

I breathed in and felt a sharp pain in my chest. The house couldn't be much further, I told myself.

Glancing down at my gown and pelisse, I saw the hems were muddied and torn. I was not a pretty sight—certainly not fit to call on family, much less on strangers.

But what other choice did I have?

When I finally caught sight of the house again, it seemed much further than I had expected. Much larger, too, from the back than from the front. Even from here, it was obviously bigger than Jerseyhurst. My breath caught in my lungs again as with an ache, I tried to think. Where had I made a wrong turn?

Turning about, I saw the foliage was more dense here than other places. The sound of the water was close and I knew I had to be close to the river edge. The green leaves swayed with the wind seeming to beckon me. I moved forward, thinking I could see the house—thinking . . . my heart leaped to my throat as I grabbed at the nearest branch and felt the ground disappear beneath me.

Terrified, I wondered if my screams would be heard. No, probably not. I continued to cling there a moment, hearing the creaking of the branch as it threatened to crack and drop me and it into the sound of the rushing waters which I now realized were below me.

My arms ached as I continued to clutch the limb of the tree, and then slowly, painfully, I pulled myself back onto firmer land.

For a few moments, I lay there gasping for breath, feeling the tears in my eyes, feeling the water on my face. As I forced myself to sit up, I saw the house again and realized that a huge chunk of land was missing here, that the cliff curved inward as if some giant had taken a handful of land out merely to spite me.

Touching my legs gingerly, I realized I was in one piece, but I was also without funds now for my reticule had gone the way I might have. Dizzily, I forced myself to look down but could not see it. No, not even I would be so rash as to climb down for it.

Tears burned my eyes. I was not only lost but penniless, as well. Perhaps death wouldn't be so terrible—not if it came swiftly, not if it enabled me to

15

rejoin my mother.

Then I took a deep breath and steadied myself. I could not go to my death without knowing who I was. I forced myself to move on.

It was possible now to see the back of the other mansion looming before me, but I knew I would have to rest before I continued on.

Spying a weeping willow near the clearing which led to the other home, I decided it would afford me some minimal shelter to catch hold of myself. I crawled beneath the draped leaves and leaned my head against the tree. Too much had happened to me in the past few weeks, too many disappointments. Life, I knew, could not be as miserable as it now seemed and yet . . . I bit my lower lip as I tried to think.

Without really seeing, I stared at my gown—at the way it looked. What would I say to these people? What would I tell them? What could I ask?

I was still trying to form my thoughts when the sound of footsteps vibrated on the gravel walkway leading toward the mansion. Someone was coming. Someone, I hoped, who could help me.

I wanted to call out but before I could, I heard a woman's high tinkling laughter, accompanied by the mellow baritone of her companion. I could not interrupt a tryst.

I pulled back into the shadow of the tree. It would be better, I decided, to wait a moment more—to gather my courage and head toward the front door of the house.

I laid my head on my arms to rest. The grass felt soft, if damp, beneath my cheek. I wanted to think things through again but, at the moment, it seemed too difficult. I tried to will myself to feel better, but without effect.

Finally, oblivion encompassed me.

Racking pain in my chest, in my arms, and the sound of thunder woke me.

The thunder came again. It was time to leave the shelter of the willow and attempt to speak to the people at the house. They would give me protection. They had to.

My limbs felt inordinately heavy as I stood. Gathering my strength, I started forward as the first drops of rain fell. Lightning cut a jagged path across the sky. I looked up, unaware of anyone near me until I heard the twigs snapping behind. I turned, not so much frightened as unsteady.

A narrow, white hand shot out from behind an elm, grabbing my arm. In a dream state, I stared at the gentleman before me. For just a moment, I found myself thinking he was the man who had called upon my mother a few days before her accident. When I forced myself to focus, I realized that our visitor had been portly and short, whereas this . . . this gentleman was taller than I and slender.

I attempted to pull away my hand, but he held me in a tight vice as I stared up at him. Despite the appearance of foppery—the perfectly creased tight trousers, cutaway frock coat, and gray spats—he was strong.

"Free me!" I hissed at him, feeling dread in the pit of my stomach as I stared at him, feeling his eyes wander over me. My mother had often warned me of such "gentlemen" who would take advantage of a lady.

I forced myself to meet his blue eyes again as a shiver went through me.

"Free me," I said again, not quite as hostile. "Please."

He did not do as I asked. He continued to stare at me. His lips curved into a smile which sent chills running

17

through me. With a free hand, he touched a damp curl on my cheek and pushed it back. The lightning flashed in the sky again at the same moment, causing me to gasp.

Once more, I tried to pull away but to no avail.

"Be still," he commanded, in a deep voice as he searched my face. I did not know what he was looking for, but I could suddenly no longer meet his eyes. Turning my own downward, I saw that his eyes matched the blue material of his coat. His hair was the color of straw at harvest time. I knew that how he looked made no difference to my situation and yet, I could not help but stare at him.

The fading light was just enough to show me the severity of his features. He was not what I would consider handsome, yet there was an air about him commanding respect.

I, too, would have liked some of that respect, but it seemed he did not think it was warranted because his eyes continued to roam me as if I was merely a piece of merchandise. Had I been free, I probably would have slapped him or . . . I noticed then that his cravat had been tied rather hastily. Had he been the one I had heard earlier?

"What are you doing here?" he asked. "What do you want?"

I wanted to speak but my mouth was not working at the same speed as my tired brain.

"Are you a beggar or a gypsy? Who are you spying on?" he asked as again he brushed away damp curls from my brow and again I felt my stomach tighten with that strange shiver. He only wanted to get a better look at me and when he did, I was sure he would see the resemblance to his neighbors.

18

If he saw the likeness, he made no mention of it. I realized then not only was my outfit out of date, torn, and muddied but I had no bonnet. It had gone the way of my reticule. I'm sure the dirt and mud on my skin must have made me look even stranger to him than my already sun-darkened complexion did. Well, it was not my fault I had helped in the fields. I glanced down at his white skin and wondered how dark he would be if he had to labor all day in the Kansas sun.

"I will ask once more before we fetch the constable." The vice on my wrist tightened. "Who are you?"

This time, I met his eyes. He might look the dandy, but he had strength beyond what he showed. My throat hurt. I tried to speak but no words came. I could only stare at his brilliant blue eyes and plead silently.

"Very well. We'll soon find out what you're up to." He began pulling me toward the house. True, I had wanted to go in there but not quite like this. Even healthy, I would not have been able to resist his force. Fatigued as I was, aching as I was, there was nothing I could do but passively follow.

Finally, I found my voice. "I won't say anything about before."

"What?" He turned and stared at me—anger was clear in his expression.

"I said I—"

"I know what you said, Chit. What do you mean by it? What did you see?"

His hands went onto my shoulders as he began to shake me. "Out with it! What did you see?"

I shook my head. The words fled me. Lightning again flashed in the night sky as thunder rumbled. We had reached a gazebo. He paused. With a glance toward the

19

house and then toward the threatening sky, he yanked me along. The white open-air cottage looked ghostly in the successive flashes of lightning.

The rain was coming down in earnest now. My captor evidently decided not to bother the run to the house. His fear for his suit was obviously not greater than his fear for what I had seen.

I winced with the creaking of the door as he yanked it open and pushed me inside the wooden structure along with him.

Releasing me only momentarily, he lit the lamp which hung by the door. There was room here for three or four people seated side by side. One of the benches was a swing which, from the sound of it, needed oil.

I shivered as my host directed me to one of the steadier seats and realized that my discomfort was not only from the wind whistling about us but from the intensity of his gaze. Blood rushed to my face and I felt the heat surrounding me.

The gazebo, I saw, was in the center of a garden maze. Well planted, it was effectively hidden from the main house by a series of trees. Should I scream—or require help—no one would know I was here.

My heart pounded again as I glanced at the man at my side. He was still watching me, studying me.

Vision blurred, I closed my eyes a moment and then opened them quickly. The light from the storm cast a halo about his golden hair, but I already knew he was no angel. A devil, possibly, but an angel—no.

Chills ran up my spine. I could not hide my shivering and was surprised when he took off his coat to place the jacket about my shoulders. I was about to speak—to thank him—when I saw the ruby signet ring on his finger. The ring was the same design as Mama's pendant.

Stunned now, I stared at the man differently this time. It was hard to connect what Mama had told me about her jolly red-haired brother and this man before me, yet he did wear the family ring.

Though I could no longer see the house, I glanced toward it now. Perhaps I had been mistaken. Perhaps this mansion was Jerseyhurst and not the other where I had originally trekked. Had my efforts at fighting the woods been in vain? Had my fears been for naught?

Realizing I did have a right to be here gave me more strength than I thought possible. It also brought relief. If I was wrong about matters, if this was the house, then I had no worry about shelter. It mattered only to tell this . . . gentleman. . . .

I shrugged the coat off of me in a valiant effort. Trying to keep my voice from quivering with fatigue and the other emotions welling up in me, I spoke.

"In answer to your question before." I could hear the trembling in my voice and felt it in my stomach, especially when I realized I now had his full attention. "Yes?"

"I am neither a spy nor a beggar, Cousin David."

I saw his blue eyes widen. Since we had entered the gazebo he had paid little attention to me except to give me his jacket and keep me from fleeing—which I would not have done anyway.

His hand loosened the pressure on mine, but he did not release me totally. He continued to stare now but differently than he had before. "Who are you?"

I swallowed the lump which had come to my throat.

"Elizabeth Ann Larabee," I stated simply. I felt sure this would be enough.

21

Before he could answer, the wind whipped the branches about us, so they thrashed the building and hit the roof of the gazebo. I felt like a child being punished for some naughty deed. It was as if God knew those terrible thoughts which had crossed my mind when I had first seen this man and was warning me away.

Chills went through me more violently this time. He adjusted the coat about my shoulders, and for that moment I was very grateful for his support.

"Elizabeth who?" His arm was about me now so that my head was cradled on his shoulder. It felt both natural and strange at the same time. I looked up into his eyes.

"Larabee," I forced myself to say. "Surely, Uncle Hayward has mentioned my mother—his sister."

The man who held me continued to stare at my face and once more touched my cheek. "This isn't Jersey-hurst, Miss Larabee. You've obviously become lost. This is Parkland. How you came by the woods I find baffling but you are not at your uncle's."

I wanted to explain, to ask him for shelter as I had originally planned but looking at him left me speechless.

"I am not your cousin, Miss Larabee."

My confusion must have showed. "But you're wearing the signet ring."

He glanced down at his smooth white hands and then at the ruby red ring. What a contrast between his pale skin and my own.

Shrugging, he smiled slightly. "The ring was a present from your cousin, David. My name is Peter Jason Parkisham."

My mouth must have dropped slightly for I was only aware now of my own heart beating as I stared at him in a way I had not before. I scarcely heard his question as he repeated again. "Why are you here—on my father's land?"

He was still watching me. I tried to gather my thoughts as I felt the shudder go through me. "I—my mother is dead."

"Ah." He raised a brow. "Funny, I wouldn't have thought you the type to be poor relation and beg on your family's inheritance."

"I am not!" I started to stand and dizzily sank back down. In my anger, I managed to yank my arm from his but still felt the pressure of his touch and his presence near me.

"Come. Come, my dear. It's obvious that's why you've come."

I glared at him. This time I found the energy to rise and walk to the door of the gazebo. Rain poured in on my face, but I didn't care. I didn't intend to leave, only to escape the scorn of his gaze. "I have only come to speak with my uncle. It's—a personal matter."

I turned back to face him now as I steeled myself for the rush of blood that was flooding me. "They weren't at home. At least, no one seemed about. I—had thought— your family might . . ." I glanced back again toward the woods where the branches were now being whipped into a frenzy. Again, I shivered and knew the thoughts I just had were evil.

I did not want to look at him, but he stood and pulled me to him. "Why you're burning with fever!"

I stared at him. Was it fever I burned with or the fires of my own hell being created?

"Come. Sit back down." He guided me back to the bench more gently than he did the first time. "You do have to admit my finding you under the willow, hiding as

23

you seemed to have been, was highly suspicious."

"I told you. I wanted shelter. I—"

"Ah, yes. Shelter from the storm." He glanced out as the clouds continued to pour their contents upon the land. "Tell me." His finger touched my lips. "What did you want to know from your uncle?"

I felt my green eyes go wide but I could not tell him. Not after hearing his name. Not after what Mama had told me about the Parkishams. I was suddenly aware of the stigma of my plight. I was a love child, and a person of his caliber would not want any involvement with one such as me.

Then another fear broke through my haze. Surely, I could not be this man's daughter? But could I be his sister? I wanted to pull away but had no strength to do so.

My stomach tightened even as I studied him. Could I be related to this smooth, dandified man who sat next to me now? Thinking of my mother brought more tears to my eyes. I was vaguely aware of his linen kerchief as it touched my face.

"Come. It can't be so bad."

I shook my head. It was impossible now to speak. All the strength seemed to have fled me. Having found a sanctuary, my body needed a rest and I could do little but heed it. I found my eyes closing as I leaned against him. I tried to open them, I tried to wet my dry lips, to swallow, but I could not. I felt the arms of Peter Parkisham holding me, comforting me. I felt myself being drawn to him in a way that left me confused and unsure—more unsure of myself than I had ever been before.

Chapter Two

Someone was crying. Maybe it was me. I felt Joshua—dear, strong Joshua—carrying me up the steps, to my room and to my bed. I had no fear of being dropped. Joshua was as strong as the ox who pulled his plows.

"Don't be sad," I told him, touching his ruddy, bearded cheek and finding it strangely smooth. "I've promised you. I will come back to you. I will come back just as soon as I've talked to my uncle. Please, Joshua, dearest, don't worry about me. You must understand how important it is for me to find out who I am."

"But who are you?" Joshua asked me. His features were fading in and out of focus as I tried to hold on to him. "Who are you?"

They were his words but it was not his husky voice. "My memory failed as I tried to picture the person who was speaking.

Struggling, I tried to speak but could not.

"What the hell is she doing here?" I heard.

Once more I attempted speech but failed. The buzz of voices receded and then grew louder as I struggled to see who was talking. I felt too weak. I wanted to answer—had to answer—the question.

With a great effort, I clenched my fist. "Father—I want my—father."

If anyone heard me, they gave no sign. I was aware of nothing but a slow rocking sensation such as I had felt on the train.

Yes. I was on the train. I could hear the whistle, the clanging of the bells. I put my hands to my ears, but I could not stop that deafening sound. The steam monster was pulling me away, taking me away from Joshua forever. I wanted to scream but the smoke clogged my lungs. It was almost impossible for me to breathe.

My head was lifted. I felt something cool being placed on my brow. The gray smoke clouds seemed to have passed. The wind was blowing them in another direction. I found suddenly I could breathe more easily.

I could hear someone reading a paper out loud. The missionaries were having trouble in China. I thought about my grandfather—Maxwell Swanson. He had been to China. He had also disinherited my mother. I wanted to think what I could say to him, but then I recalled Mother told me he had died some time ago. The speaker had gone on to read about President Harrison in Chicago. My mother had been to Chicago once. She had told me about it. But why hadn't Mother told me more about my father?

It was daylight when I opened my eyes and tried to focus. My vision blurred from tears as I thought once more of my mother.

The room seemed to be an odd-shaped triangle. The

walls were rose colored. Nearer, in a chair next to the bed, I saw the man whose voice haunted my feverish dreams.

I must have stared at him for several moments before I reached up to touch him. No words passed between us yet I felt a bond stronger than an iron shoe to a horse's hoof. I touched the trim blond mustache, the pale skin. He smiled at me and started to stand, looming over me.

I recoiled then, recalling parts of our meeting. He had called me a spy. What was he holding? Did it have anything to do with my quest?

I watched, my heart beating fast, as he took out his handkerchief—was he planning to strangle me? The fear made my heart pound. No, he wouldn't hurt me, he couldn't. His arm touched me. I wanted to pull back further but I could not move.

Instead of harming me as I feared, he dabbed the linen gently to my eyes, taking my tears away. The fresh linen smell reminded me of my mother. Why was he being so nice to me?

I knew the fever burned in me and I could not think, but I tried to recall all that had passed between us the other night. Why was I fearing him so?

"Where am I?" I asked, feeling my throat hurt. He stared at me. Hadn't he heard me? I tried to ask the question again but couldn't. His lips curved into a tender smile, and for the moment my fears were forgotten. His blue eyes watched me full of concern but he did not answer me.

I realized then he had not heard me. Once again, I tried to speak but my voice was weak. I sank back onto the pillows. The door opened and a plump girl with fair hair entered. Her green eyes were harder than emeralds and

27

narrowed as they watched him bending over me.

"How touching."

Peter Parkisham ignored the girl. Perhaps they were both part of my dreams, I thought. Perhaps none of this was happening.

I was not one to recall names well. It struck me how well I remembered his. I wanted to think of him as Mr. Parkisham but could not. He was Peter to me. My heart thumped wildly like a horse galloping. I recalled the storm and the way God had punished the branches—whipping them about—but I could not help the evil thoughts which came to my mind.

The girl disappeared from my view. Peter placed another cloth on my brow. I knew then the cool, soothing touch was his hand.

I closed my eyes again. It was too much effort for me to keep them open. I was still so tired. Someone was singing to me. Another reminder of Mother.

As if at a distance, I saw my mother standing next to Joshua. The sweet lullabies she sung drifted over the gulf separating us. I heard them as clearly as I saw her—the coal-black hair, just like my own, was streaming down my mother's back. Her Irish green eyes twinkled as they always had when she was excited; I knew she was excited now. I knew that, although she had kept so many secrets from me, she now blessed my quest.

I heard a sigh. It was mine. I was glad Mama no longer lay in the wet, cold Kansas grave. Tears came to my eyes. I could still feel the thick drops of water hanging in my hair.

On my final day in Kansas, it had rained. I had gone to say good-bye once more to my mother—to again ask for Mama's help in finding my father. Now, I knew Mama

28

would help me.

Something was not making sense to me. First I was saying good-bye to Mama one moment and then I was saying good-bye to Joshua. It was a dream. It had to be a dream because Joshua wasn't dead. Dear, sweet Joshua. I waved to him from the train and watched him frown. I wondered then why I hadn't tried to kiss him good-bye as well.

My sudden impulse to say good-bye must have been telepathic. He began to run toward me, loping down the track with that limp gait of his, running unevenly across the boards. I hoped the train wouldn't move away before he could reach me. Stretching out my arms I called, "Hurry, Joshua, hurry. Let me kiss you good-bye."

He contiued to run, blurring with speed as the engine started and the smoke began to pour forth. I couldn't see him any longer and felt an overwhelming sense of loss. Suddenly there was a slight pressure grazing my lips, a gentle touch of my hand. Joshua was there—even though I couldn't see him. I could feel him leaning over me.

Reaching my arms up and about his thick neck, I kissed his ruddy face and felt the roughness of his beard. I could see him again, standing on the platform, telling me that he didn't want me going, telling me that I had three weeks—no more. He would wait no longer than that.

I sank back on the wooden second class seat and felt the hardness beneath me. Joshua had kissed me. His lips touched mine. It was a kiss as he had never kissed me before. I felt my soul soaring. I felt so desolate as he disappeared. Was I making a mistake in trying to find my father? Was I making a mistake in leaving Joshua?

Even as he disappeared into the distance, I was

convinced he was not the Joshua I knew and loved. Had he changed—or had I?

From the low rays of the sun streaming in on my face, I realized it must be late afternoon. For a moment I just stared at the yellow beams cast by the sun on the floor and then at the odd-shaped room.

Blinking, I felt the softness of the bed beneath me as I tried to focus my thoughts. Was I at Parkland or Jerseyhurst? I recalled now in proper perspectives the events of my journey, the fight I had had with Joshua before leaving, and the meeting with Peter Parkisham.

After that, everything seemed to flow into the hazy world of memory. Closing my eyes again, I lay back on the pillow.

I became aware of the ticking of a grandfather clock downstairs. The striking indicated it was four in the afternoon. I knew it was sinful to be lying in bed so late in the day and yet, I felt too weak to move. There really didn't seem much to move for, did there?

Even as I lambasted myself for such slothful ideas, I felt the aching of my head. I obviously had been quite ill, but I hoped the worst of it was over.

Forcing my eyes to open once more, I stared at the faded pink rose clusters on the wallpaper above the wainscotting. The white lace curtains billowed out as a breeze blew them toward me and cooled my warm face. The bed was a narrow one and the quilt which covered me had been homemade. It reminded me of those my mother used to make. Maybe she had made this one. I touched it, wondering and hoping it would give me some clue.

The fireplace was small. My first reaction was that the

hearth was hardly adequate to keep the winter chill from the room. Then, I reminded myself, I would not be here for winter. Surely, my quest would be accomplished in a matter of days. Once done, I could return to Kansas and Joshua.

Or should I? For some time now I had not felt certain of Joshua's affections. Our last argument had proven to me he had changed and yet I could not pinpoint the change. Perhaps he was still upset at my refusal to sell him the farm. Whatever it was, the change seemed to have come about since my mother's death, and yet I could swear there were times before that when he had acted distant.

I sighed and continued to stare at the beam of light. Perhaps he was still worried about our future together. But he shouldn't be. There had been no man in my life but Joshua—until now. I closed my eyes and chided myself for such evil thoughts.

I resolved that I would handle my problem with Joshua when I returned with the answers to the questions now plaguing me. He was not the focus of this trip.

A fly buzzed about my head. I stared at it and turned to watch it land. The scratches on the wall looked like a child's attempt to print with a nail. A coat of paint had ineffectively covered it. Curiosity took hold.

Forcing myself into a sitting position, I stared at the markings. Still unable to read them, I traced the lines with my fingertips.

"I am Geo," it said.

"I am Geo," I repeated softly to myself as I sank back down onto the downy cushions. "I am Geo?" Who, I wondered, was Geo?

With difficulty I searched my memory for all Mama

31

had told me of her family. Georgiana? Could Geo mean Georgiana? That was my aunt's name. Why would she have scratched it here on the wall? If that was true, I had to be at Jerseyhurst.

I stared at the wall again as the sounds of angry voices returned to haunt me. Yes, I knew I must be at Jerseyhurst. I winced. It seemed the argument was about me. It seemed I was not a very welcome guest.

Well, I would make my position clear. I did not intend to stay here long. As soon as my questions were answered, as soon as I was well enough, I would return to Kansas or make other plans. I did not stay where I was not wanted.

Feeling a spasm of pain shoot through my chest, I clenched my fist. Obviously, I was not completely well yet. Joshua had been right about one thing. He predicted that my poor appetite over the last weeks and the train journey on top of that would make me ill.

In a moment, the pain subsided. Sweat was on my brow. No, I could not leave until I knew who I was. Then, I would go, no matter what the state of my health. Maybe I would even learn the facts today.

The room seemed to spin as I tried to sit up further. I was forced to return to a prone position and close my eyes once more.

I suppose I drifted off to sleep for another moment because when I opened my eyes this time, it was twilight. My attention was drawn to an oil lamp on the writing desk in the far corner.

This time I sat up. There was no pain at all. I was determined now to leave the bed and have someone know I was awake.

A wet cloth fell from my head and onto my lap. I had

not been aware of it before. Someone must have come in during the few moments I had returned to sleep.

Despite my weakness, I was determined to leave the bed. Pushing myself on my elbows, I stared out the window a moment and saw the cliff where I had lost my purse and nearly my life. Upright in the bed, I pulled an unfamiliar robe about me. I looked for my portmanteau and found it—at the end of my bed and open.

What right did they have to open my bag? What right did they have to search my belongings?

Angry, I jumped up. The dizziness struck me like a hard slap. There was barely time to grab the post of my bed to prevent myself from falling to the floor.

Suddenly, the room seemed filled with the presence of a huge black woman.

"Lordy!" she exclaimed as she caught me in her wide, pink palms and fairly lifted me off the ground before helping me back to bed. "Child!" she scolded. "Who told you t'get up?"

"No one. I wanted to. Have I been sick long?"

"Youse at Jerseyhurst, child."

I stared up into brown eyes as the questions spun through my brain. I knew without asking this had to be Tilly, my mother's old nurse. I had expected her to be older, but other than a few gray hairs, she seemed as spry as mother had been at half her age.

Knowing how much store Mama had put by Tilly's wisdom, I felt my spirits rise just having her about. If anyone could help me, she could. I couldn't count how many times Mama had told me stories of Tilly's folklore, of how Tilly had nursed Mama through illness after illness.

"Child," she said as she eased me back into bed, "you

33

been sick most on three days now. Had ol' Tilly worried. Mastuh Peter's been askin' 'bout you, too.''

Peter! I felt a strange elation knowing he had not been a dream, knowing he had been in the room. I also felt uncomfortable knowing he had seen me at my worst.

As I thought about my first meeting with him, I couldn't help but wonder again if he had been the one I had heard earlier with the woman. Did that mean I had a rival? My heart thumped wildly. I swallowed hard and realized that, if my fears were correct and if I was related to Peter, then I could be no rival to another woman.

"What of my aunt, my uncle, and my cousins?" I asked, forcing my mind away from the blond Apollo.

Tilly shrugged and tucked the covers about me. Now that I was back in bed, I realized how foolish it had been to get up so soon.

Without another word to me, Tilly went to the door. "Rose! Rose King! Git up here."

"Comin', Mama," came the faint cry.

Satisfied, Tilly turned her huge bulk toward me. Stepping back into the room, she said, "Gotta keep that girl busy or there be hanky-panky."

Even as Tilly finished her comment, I saw what she meant. The striking girl who entered was no more than seventeen, yet she had a worldly air about her. Her skin was the color of cream chocolate and her dark hair straighter than most darkies I had seen. Even as I studied her face, I could see her apron was awkwardly twisted as if it had been put on hastily.

"What you want, Mama?"

"Don't you give me no lip, girl!" Tilly's eyes flashed. "What were you doin'?" She eyed the untidy outfit.

34

"Nuthin', Mama."

Tilly snorted and lifted her large head. "Get some food for Miz Lizabeth here and tell Miz Terrah her cousin be awake."

"Yes, Mama." The girl lowered her eyes.

"Where's Mastuh David disappeared to?"

"Ah don't know, Mama." Rose gave me a slight smile. "I ain't seen him fer some time."

Rose turned and started to leave. I protested. "I can get up to eat. There's no need for her to bring food up here. At home, one had to be really sick for my mother to bring food into the bedroom. Surely I'm not ill anymore."

"No, miz." Tilly was exactly as Mother had described her—bossy, overbearing, and full of love. There was so much I wanted to ask about my mother's past, so much I wanted to know. Tilly was the person to ask. I was sure she would know who my real father was.

I started to speak and received a glare from the black nurse. Well, I thought as I shrugged and lay back, there would be time for my questions later.

Gratefully, I succumbed to the big woman's ministrations. It was nice to know I had at least one friend here. I watched as Tilly took the cloth which had fallen on the blanket. Dipping it into tepid water from the basin on the desk, she sponged off my brow and then assisted me with bathing the rest of my body.

There were several moments of silence before she asked, "Tell me 'bout your mama, child. Tell me what happened t'her?"

I saw tears in her eyes.

"Did she suffer?" she asked.

35

The lump came to my throat. "How did you—"

"Mastuh Peter." She glanced toward the window and Parkland. "He done tol' us when he carried you here."

I stared at her. "He carried me?"

I recalled my arms about someone's neck. I thought it had been Joshua. Flushing, I realized it must have been Peter. I cringed then as I realized, too, it must have been Peter I had kissed so fully. Of course, I had thought it was Joshua, but he didn't know that. What he must think of me!

"You've not answered me, child."

I stared at her a moment before responding. "No, I don't think she did suffer. The doctor said her death had been instantaneous. She was—" I paused as the scene returned with painful vividness to me. "She was thrown from our trap. The wheel had broken and—"

Tilly stiffened. "De wheel broke? You didn't know the wheel was bad?"

I shook my head. "No. It had seemed fine before then. The blacksmith was surprised."

I heard the intake of her breath. "Yes, he must have been. For sure." She put the washcloth down. "Well, it don't never mind. What be done, be done. Youse here now. That's all important." I wanted to ask her why she was questioning the wheel and then realized she probably wouldn't tell me.

"Tell me more 'bout your mama. I sure did miss her."

I wet my lips and began to speak of the memories of her, of Zebulon, of our good times and of our bad times. Even as I spoke, I sensed she wasn't totally listening to me. Neither was I totally listening to her responses. It was as if we were both playing a game of cat and mouse—

36

each wanting to hear the other's hidden messages.

She had dipped the washcloth in the basin once more and then stopped. Her eyes riveted on the dressing table where Rose had placed my silver brushes.

"Lordy! Those were you mama's!"

I nodded. She touched one. Her big hand caressed the silver engraving. They were one of the few things my mother had brought with her from this house when she had fled to marry Zebulon, and, along with the locket she had always worn around her neck, one of the few things I had saved from the sale of our effects. The bristles were worn with age but still strong enough to use, and I knew my mother had valued them.

Tilly continued to hold them. It seemed she was in a space faraway.

"They are lovely, aren't they?"

"Sure are," she said. "I be surprised to see them. I 'members the Christmas he—he gave them to her. Lordy, she were excited."

I held my breath. "Who, Tilly? Who gave my mother the brushes?"

Tilly stared vacantly ahead. Then recalling my presence, her eyes regained their focus. "I—forget now, child. It's been such a—long time." She patted my hand, absentmindedly touching her soft skin to mine. "'Scuze me, child. I'm gonna go see where that Rose is at."

"But you haven't answered my question!" I cried. "Who gave my mother those brushes?"

"I'm be gettin' old, child. There be a lot of things I be forgettin'." Her tone was wistful and sad. "Be a good baby and rest now. Tilly'll get you all better. Then youse can go back home."

"But I don't want to go home until I've found out who my father is."

Tilly stared at me a moment and sighed. She said nothing but closed the door after her, leaving me to look at the blank door. That door was a barrier, just as my questions were, dividing me from my family.

Chapter Three

By the time Tilly had brushed my hair into a loose bun, Rose had brought up a tray of food. Quietly, she placed it in front of the bed.

I glanced at the dishes: scrambled eggs flecked with cheese bits, creamy and light as my mother had made them. But, of course, my mother had learned from Tilly. There was also a hot buttered muffin and a steaming cup of cocoa. Despite the fact I had felt famished before, I found I suddenly had no desire to eat. Maybe it was the unanswered questions which had robbed me of my appetite.

"Rose." I glanced at the girl who had begun gathering up several of my dresses for cleaning and pressing. I saw my cherry poplin was not with them. Sadly, I thought it probably had been too torn to properly mend. I felt a slight grief since Mama had helped me make that dress myself out of a magazine pattern. It had always been one of my favorites.

The black girl dropped the dresses and gave me an obstinate stare—as if to say I had no right to ask her for anything. I was not going to let her intimidate me.

"Could I have more sugar for my cocoa?"

"More sugar?" Her nose seemed to turn up in the air. I wondered why she seemed to dislike me so. "Ain't it sweet 'nuf for you?"

Tilly reappeared at that moment. She was less agitated than when she had left, but her eyes were rimmed with red.

I was surprised at Rose's tone as she told her mother, "She wants more sugar!" The girl grinned.

I shouldn't have felt embarrassed, but I did. Feeling my defenses hackle up, I said, "Cocoa was the one thing Mama could never make right. She always burned it and used the extra sugar to hide the taste." I shrugged, feeling the flush come to my face. "I guess I've just gotten used to a sweeter taste."

Tilly nodded. "Sounds like my Maggie." She turned to her daughter, obviously angry. "Git her the sugar, Rose. Git it now."

Rose made a face as she left with my dresses.

Tilly sighed. "Sometimes that girl . . . I do wonder I even had her so late as I did. Most times it's like she not even be mine." Tilly forced a smile. "But I guess your mama thought that of you, too, at times." She tucked the covers about me. "I'll be back in no time, hear? So don't you try gettin' up."

I gave a reluctant nod. As Tilly departed my eyes went toward the scratched marks on the wall. Did they have anything to do with my questions? I would ask Tilly if my aunt could come up to talk with me. Maybe she would tell what Tilly was obviously reluctant to tell.

It was nearly ten minutes before Rose brought up the sugar. The cocoa was nearly cold, but I stirred in the sugar anyway. Tilly hadn't returned.

"How long have you been working here?" I asked, trying to engage her in conversation.

"What d'ya mean? I be been here since I were a baby."

"I mean," I said, flushing, "did you know my mother?"

Rose gave me a haughty glare. "Sure, I knew yer mama." She grinned. "Knew her through Mama's belly."

"Oh." I realized my mistake then. Rose couldn't be more than seventeen or eighteen. Since I was nearly in my twentieth year, my mother would have left before Rose had been born.

"Well, did you—uh—ever hear anything about my mother?"

"Sure." The girl grinned cockily. "Heard lots."

"Like?" I felt my heart beating faster. Was I going to learn the truth now?

"Like she ran away to wed your daddy 'cause she was too 'shamed to see her family."

"Nothing else?"

"No, miz. Nuthin' else."

I stared at the girl. Why was she smiling? I felt sure she was lying but couldn't prove it. I watched Rose move over to the old pine armoire which stood opposite the fireplace. Time had scarred the wood but inside it was roomy. As she opened the door, I could see how pitifully few the rest of my dresses seemed. I glanced down at the high-necked nightdress I wore. It was of better quality than I had ever seen. It was too big for me and I guessed it belonged to my cousin.

"Mama says I'm t'fix yer clothes." Rose removed two of the dresses. "Can't say as there's much t'fix. Looks as

41

if these 'ave been mended and mended." Rose gave me a look to let me know that I was a poor relation and she had no respect for me.

"There is nothing about my clothes that need mending." I glared at her. "They might need a pressing, but—"

Rose gave a sardonic smile. She shook her head. "No. You don't know Mama yet. She's pure hell if'n she don't git obeyed." Again, Rose smiled. I felt she was on the verge of saying something more, but the sound of footsteps echoing in the hall stopped her.

Rose's fingers touched my good lavender silk. "That all you got, right?"

Flushing, I nodded.

With a shrug, she bundled up my silk and my gingham-pleated sun-ray skirts I brought with me. Rose slammed the door behind her, leaving me very much alone.

Even as I lay there, I had the distinct feeling I was being watched, but no one came in—at least no one I saw. I shivered and realized I had not heard those footsteps again.

I must have dozed off several more times during the day but I did obey Tilly's orders and stayed in bed. I had to admit I felt much stronger than I had on my journey. I was getting anxious to meet my uncle and cousins. Why was it they had not come up to see me?

I told myself they must be busy with the household and their banking business, but I could not forget the blond girl who had come into the room when Peter had been with me. I knew her hatred was no dream.

Because I had slept so much during the day, I felt

42

myself grow restless as night came. After tossing and turning, I finally fell asleep only to be wakened by a harsh, piercing scream which echoed in my dreams.

Heart pounding, I sat up. I could feel my body cold with sweat. I could feel the terror within me. What had happened? Was it a nightmare of my own or had those screams been real?

The fear would not subside. I stayed where I was, still convinced someone might need help. I knew if I was afraid, I would want someone, anyone, to comfort me, even a stranger. I decided to leave my room and see what the commotion was about. If the halls were silent, then I would know it had been a dream.

Catching the bedpost, I felt myself sway dizzily for just a moment. Maybe this wasn't the best of ideas. I took a deep breath to steady myself. Eying my bed again, I told myself I didn't even know where the screams had come from. I didn't know if I could help or not.

Moonlight flitted through the room, dancing as the tree limbs waved in the wind of a gathering storm. I grabbed a chair as the distant roll of thunder unnerved me. Forcing myself to walk to the window. I took in a deep breath of the night air. The lawn which stretched out like a smooth carpet to the thick foliage of the trees and the cliff beyond seemed deserted. The shadows told me the time was late. Calming myself, I gathered my courage. Mama had always told me I was too impulsive, especially when it came to thinking I was of some help. I recalled the time when I had rescued the malformed kitten from drowning, only to watch it die several days later from its other disorders. She had told me sometimes it was best to leave things alone. But I couldn't leave someone alone who screamed.

I told myself I had no right to intrude, especially since I was a stranger here. I glanced longingly at my bed and probably would have returned when I heard the terrifying screams again. Whoever it was seemed to be in frightful agony. The least I could do was find some other member of the household and get them to help.

Not even bothering to throw on an additional robe, I fled my room.

It was in the hall and hearing the screams again that I realized I knew nothing at all about the structure of the house. How would I find the person who needed help? I took a deep breath and stared into the gloomy darkness. There was no rail nor any light near my room, though I could see some distant glowing gas lamps further ahead.

I realized the screams had come from below my room but where below?

Cursing to cover the fear I felt, I managed to reenter my own room, still lit with moonlight, and grab the candle from the nightstand. My hands trembled as I lit the small white stub with the sulfur match and smelled the odor. The light flickered a moment. I feared it would go out but it did not. Huge shadows danced about the room with the growing flame. I watched for a moment, then praying it would keep, I lifted the holder.

Armed with light, I returned to the hall. There were two sets of stairs. One near me, which obviously led up to the servants quarters, and the main staircase, carpet lined and wide enough for a princess.

Standing on the landing of the second floor, I stared down the hall. There was no indication which of the seven doors I needed to go toward. It seemed odd to me no one else in the household was about, that no one else had been disturbed by this scream. Was I dreaming? I pinched myself. No, I was very much awake and I heard those screams while I was awake.

I tried each door along the corridor. The light continued to flicker. Most of the doors were locked. I tried to determine where my help was needed but heard nothing.

Just as I was convinced the screams had been my imagination, I heard sobbing behind the last door. My anxiety and desire to help made me move without thinking. Turning the brass knob, I felt the coolness of the metal against my palm as the door silently opened on the hinges.

The light from my candle revealed a massive room three times the size of mine. Each end had a marble fireplace; heavy green drapes hung at the window. I wrinkled my nose. The unpleasant odor of urine and vomit made me want to retch.

Almost lost beside a four poster bed was the plump girl I had seen earlier. I stared at her a moment, realizing she was about my age. Perhaps a year or two older. Her pale blond curls were gathered loosely and tied with a green ribbon the color of her eyes.

Cradled in the girl's lap was the head of an older man bearing the chubby Swanson features. His red hair was streaked with brown and gray. I watched—almost horrified—as the girl continued to stroke his brow.

"Terrah. Terrah. Where is your mother? I want your mother, Terrah," he sobbed.

Even before I heard the girl coo, "Daddy, dear, don't cry," I felt my stomach turn. I knew with a sickening sensation the man being rocked was my Uncle Hayward. I thought of all Mother had told me about her brother—how big and strong he was, how he had protected her from so many things. Now, here he was, acting like a baby.

Embarrassed, I paused at the door without moving forward. Terrah glanced up and saw me. Her green eyes narrowed with hard contempt.

I recalled then how my cousin had come into the room during my illness. She had given me the same cold look. I met her stare, wondering why she disliked me when she knew so little about me.

I felt myself shivering under her continued stare.

"What are you doing here?" she said icily. "What do you want in this room? You weren't asked in."

"I—heard screams," I said taking a step forward. "I thought perhaps I could be of help. I've nursed many an animal on our farm through long nights and when my mother was ill—"

"My father is not an animal!" Terrah hissed.

"But I—"

Before I could continue my protestations, Hayward Swanson's bleary blue eyes focused on me. I was immediately conscious of my nightdress and of my hair tumbling down looking unkempt.

He struggled free of his daughter as he attempted to stand.

"Margaret! You're back! Oh, Meg! Meg, I've missed you so."

Terrah held him back with a force one would not think she had. "Daddy, darling, that's not Aunt Margaret. It's her daughter. It's Elizabeth, Daddy."

I stared at the man and brushed back the loose strands of hair from my brow, feeling my face flush. I believed he was drunk. I was glad Mama was not here to see this.

"Lizabeth?" he said in a childlike voice. "Lizabeth?"

I nodded and continued to stare at the man who had been only four years older than my mother. It was my grandfather who had gone to China and started the trade there, but according to my mother, it was her brother who had made the family fortunes in the banking business. It was hard to believe he had come to this.

"Poor Meg," he whimpered. Tears filled his eyes. "Poor Meg. Poor Andrew."

"Andrew?" I asked, hearing the name catch in my throat. "Who is Andrew?"

Terrah glared at me. "Now look what you've done. I don't know who Andrew is or was. Probably some dead child that my grandmother had." She turned her attention back to the older man. "Oh, Daddy, don't cry." I could hear the exasperation in her tone.

"Oh, poor Meg," he repeated.

I forced myself to speak. "Did you tell him of my mother's death?" I asked in a low voice.

Again, I felt the emerald stare upon me. "I most certainly did not. Daddy can only deal with so many upsets. I assumed you had told him. You're just country enough to do something like that."

I was flabbergasted at this accusation. "When would I have done that?"

Terrah didn't answer me as the old man continued to cry. "Daddy, it's all right. Stop crying, Daddy. I'll take care of you." The irritation in her tone rose.

Once again, she turned her attention to me. Her stare seemed to pierce my heart. "You're not needed here. You're not wanted here."

I took a deep breath and managed to regain my composure as I met her stare. "I may not be wanted, cousin, but I am here. Don't worry. I don't intend on staying long—only until I find out what I need to know—and manage to borrow some money."

"Money!" she fairly screamed. "I should have suspected."

I raised my voice over hers. "Money to get home with, since I lost my reticule over the cliff while trying to find my way here." She narrowed her eyes. I continued. "You will be rid of me only then."

Not waiting to hear her response, I turned and felt the sweep of the nightdress on the floor and saw the flicker of my candle. I was relieved to leave behind the stink, the hatred.

The window at the end of the hall was opened, probably because of the smell. I wondered how long my uncle had been sick and why he wasn't receiving proper care. Going to the ledge, I leaned on it gratefully as I inhaled the sweet freshness of the night air.

So many questions leaped to my mind. I wondered if I would be able to return to sleep, but as I made my way back to the third floor room, I found myself feeling exhausted.

The room was exactly as I had left it. I didn't know why I had thought it might not be.

Blowing out the candle, I pulled the quilt over me. My hand accidently touched that part of the wall where the scratches were. "I am Geo." I thought then about my uncle's crying. Was that what caused him to be in such a state? I know Mama's father had disapproved of spirits and all forms of drink. It surprised me that my uncle would have indulged so. Again, I was glad Mama wasn't here to see her brother's disgrace.

I woke as the first light of dawn streamed through my window. With a sigh I recalled what had transpired last night and why I felt so utterly lonely and empty.

It was not pleasant to know one was not wanted by one's family. I wondered if I should just pick up and return to Kansas as soon as I was fully healed.

However, if I returned I knew I would never learn the secret of my identity which had obsessed me for so many months. No, I had to stay, no matter what Terrah said. It was possible she was merely in a bad mood last night. Perhaps today she might apologize and retract her statements.

I realized that it must have been embarrassing for her to have me see her father like that. Surely, he could not be always so incapacitated. I was sure the secret of my uncle's melancholy was something she wanted to keep hidden. Well, I would reassure her. I would tell no one. The fact was, except for Peter Parkisham, I knew no one else in Aberdeen.

My eyes wandered once more toward the marked wall. I would ask about that today, I vowed. But still I continued to lie there feeling an inertia about me.

When I finally rose, I found the water in the basin was from yesterday. I disliked not having fresh water, but it was better than not having any at all. I had to admit after so many days of lying abed, I was surprised to feel so strong.

Going to the armoire, I realized Rose had not yet returned a large portion of my dresses. No doubt neither

49

she nor Tilly expected me to be getting up today, but I couldn't stay in this room any longer than I already had.

There were only two choices in the armoire which had not needed Rose's attention. My gray tabby—which I would be wearing for church—and one of my accordion-pleated muslin skirts. I did not think the puff blouse was the right one to wear with it, but at the moment I had little choice. Besides, I did not expect to meet anyone on my morning walk, and it would be foolish to have ruined my good dress strolling through the woods.

I found my leggings and my high lace shoes. As I bent to fasten them, dizziness came over me. But I was determined to do some exploring before I could be stopped by Tilly or by Terrah.

The quietness of the house told me no one was yet awake. It was just as well. As I left my small room, I wondered what my morning reception was going to be.

The warming rays of the sun made the oak bannister glow golden. Gently, I touched the wainscotting of the hall. It was so much nicer than my own room, but that was to be expected I supposed. I could see the wood had been polished with loving care and could feel the blue hall carpet springy under my feet. In this quiet atmosphere, it wasn't hard to imagine myself as mistress of this luxurious mansion. How would it have been if Mama had stayed in Aberdeen, if she had married the man who fathered me?

On the second floor, I hurried past the room where last night I had intruded. I did not want to think about my uncle's condition this morning. I wanted only to think about my quest and my mother. Thoughts of Peter Parkisham sprang to my consciousness, but I quickly dismissed them. I would have to avoid him at all costs while I was here. Tilly hinted to me that Peter and my cousin, Terrah, were nearly engaged. Even were he not related to me as I thought, I could not allow my feelings for him to surface.

Downstairs, I passed through the dim baronial dining room with its heavy red draperies and frowning picture of Grandfather Swanson above the fireplace mantel. I was glad I did not have to deal with him. My cousins and uncle would be enough!

The butler's pantry was lined with fine china and the silver. We had not had such finery in our home and it was impossible for me not to be impressed. I paused for a moment, again wondering how it would have been had Mama married here.

Because my aunt had been from the south and feared kitchen fires, the house had been built with the kitchen as a separate building connected via a walkway. I let myself out the door of the butler's pantry and hurried down the steps. It was still hard for me to reconcile what I knew of my uncle and his drive to make the family fortune with the pathetic creature I had seen last night. Sadness once more filled me, but I would talk with my uncle. Perhaps in a few days, he would be better.

Taking a deep breath of the crisp morning air, I forced away the evil thoughts which haunted me. With each breath, the cobwebs of my illness seemed to leave my mind. Life surged through me as I looked out over the expanse of lawn where the croquet hoops were set up and at the gravel paths, one which led to the east—and Parkland—and one to the west.

A bluebird sang and I felt joy at being alive, at having

reached Jerseyhurst safely, at knowing I would soon find out who my father had been.

Despite my cousin's attitude, I was confident I would get the knowledge I sought, and my mission would be successful. Yes, I would find my father and we would be friends. Whatever misunderstanding had parted him and my mother would be cleared up.

The bluebird chirped again. I took that as a good omen. Maybe I was being an idealistic dreamer as Mama had told me, but one didn't get anywhere without dreams.

Pausing at the entrance to the wooden path, I decided I had had enough of the Parkland manor to last me for some time. I would explore the direction to the west—being far more careful of my footing this time.

Even as I felt the softness of the ground beneath me, I could see the grass was still damp from dew. It didn't prevent me from wanting to kick off my boots, to feel the nubs of grass tickling my feet. It would have been easy to just run along the carpeted ground here and not explore the woods, but there was so much I wanted to see, so much I wanted to learn, and I did not have all the time I needed. I knew the three weeks I promised Joshua would go soon. I intended to know everything there was to know about my mother and her life here before making the decision to return to Kansas, before making the decision to marry Joshua.

I grabbed my skirts as I began to walk faster and faster and finally broke into a run. Jumping over several fallen logs and large puddles, it seemed to me this was a path seldom taken. That pleased me. I wanted to be alone when I explored the place where Mama's first home had been—the place she had lived before Jerseyhurst had been built.

Breathless, I was forced to pause a moment. I wondered if my father would be amenable to subsidizing Joshua in his farm. Ever since his accident the year before, farming had become harder for him and I knew any money would help him. Joshua had no head for mathematics but I kept books quite well. I knew things had been as hard for Joshua as they had been for us, yet he never complained. It would be interesting to see how he balanced his assets and liabilities.

A sadness came over me as I realized I had learned all my math ability from Zebulon and that I had kept the books of our farm since his death. Zebulon was a good man and I had loved him dearly. Even now it was hard for me to realize he was not my father. I had to remember that in order to keep my single-minded purpose of trying to find my real father.

I wondered if my mother had been happy on the farm. She had seemed so, but every so often I would catch her in wistful moments. It couldn't have been easy for her toiling over the fields on a farm or over the hot stove when she could have been a lady of a mansion like this.

My heart felt like lead. Did Mama love Zebulon? She would have had to love my father to have me.

I swallowed the pain I felt and wondered if Mama had ever felt the sorrow of her decision. Picking a pine cone, I crushed it in my palm and the fresh pungent scent came to me as tears came to my eyes. If I loved someone, I would never leave him. Even—even if I thought he was unfaithful to me, even if . . .

I grabbed another pine cone and felt the roughness tingling my palm. I pulled each section out one at a time as I thought of Joshua. Did I love him? Had I left him by coming here? No, of course I hadn't. I had come here only to find my father. I had promised Joshua I would return to him. Mama had never returned to her home here, to her love.

Nevertheless, I felt a sadness in me as I thought of Joshua. He was such a good man. But at times when he spoke, when we touched, when I allowed him those precious few kisses—I felt as if something was missing. That feeling had been so much stronger of late. For that reason I had been glad to get away from Kansas for a bit. I needed to decide whether marrying Joshua was the right thing to do. Mama would have wanted it. She adored Josh. But was it the best for me? Once again, thoughts of Peter Parkisham came to me.

I dismissed them. I was comfortable with Joshua, but perhaps it was because he was the only man I ever knew. He was the only man who had ever offered for me. Would I be a fool to pass Joshua up? Would he be terribly hurt if I didn't return to him or would he also think it for the best?

I sank down on a nearby log and listened to the hum and chatter of birds. Joshua had been upset when I had sold the farm, but I had needed to pay off those debts we had incurred in the last few years. I cracked the stem of a lilly of the valley growing wild at my feet and picked it up, inhaling the scent.

Yes, money was a problem for me now that my reticule was gone. I supposed I could wire Joshua and get him to send me money to return, but then I would be in his debt and I did not want that.

Twirling the flower in front of my nose, I stared out over the cliff here and listened to the rushing sound of the water below. Where would I go if I did not return to Kansas?

Maybe my father, assuming he was in town, assuming he would acknowledge me, would let me stay with him until I formed a plan of action for my future.

Thoughts continued to whirl about my mind as I stood and walked down the rest of the path. How quiet and peaceful the woods were, how free of the tension I felt at the house, and how unlike the wide, open flatlands of Kansas.

A blue jay flew past me, plucking something from a tree and continued on in the direction which I was going. I knew he was headed toward Mama's old house, just as I was. Even with the sadness enveloping me, I felt everything would work out. It had to. I counted on it.

Determined to be happy, I bent to pick more flowers. The buds were just opening. I tucked a pink bud behind my ear and knew it looked fetching with my masses of unbound hair. Yes, I should have done something with my hair before going out. It wasn't right I had not. But no one was about and no one would see me. I would be back before anyone was awake. Out here in the woods, I felt more at home and more at peace than I had felt for days. Perhaps it was the tension in the house, perhaps it was just having been ill. All I knew was now I was free.

It was just beyond the clearing I stopped. The sight of my mother's old house affected me more than I thought it would. The two stories were just a shell, the house having been burnt before Mama left Aberdeen. I felt more connected to her here than I did in the mansion of Jerseyhurst.

I stood for a moment more staring at the empty windows, at the burned bricks. If only they could speak to me. If there were any clues for me, I would find them here. The silence around seemed to renew my hope.

55

Carefully, I walked forward and stepped over the threshold.

Cursing, I felt my skirt tear on one of the loose nails there. Something else for Rose to repair for me.

I released myself from the hook and took one step and then another into what would have been the front parlor of the house. I felt the presence of my mother—her warmth and her loving. Taking a deep breath, I walked cautiously over the boards, careful not to catch my skirts again, not to trip over the charred or weathered remains of furniture left in the house. I could see scraps of paper from the flowered wallpaper which had covered the sitting room. Closing my eyes, I tried to picture it as my mother had described it—with elegant chairs in the formal living room, the piano—where she had practiced so many long hours, and the comfortable armchairs in the sitting room. I knew she had resented that piano when she had been forced to practice, just as I had resented it when she had forced me. However, during our lean times, the lessons she had given the town children had helped us survive.

I took another step into the room and stared out through the broken pane glass toward the road, which could just be seen. I couldn't help wondering who had been here in this parlor. What men had called and which of those men might be my father?

My foot crunched on something. I realized it was dried pieces of wallpaper that had fallen. I picked up a part of it and watched it curl in my hand.

A sound behind startled me. I turned. No one was there but my stomach tightened. Was someone out there? Had I been followed from the house?

I allowed the material to flutter to the ground and felt a

chill come over me. Glancing up the stairs, I decided not to continue my exploration here today. Perhaps at another time. For now, it seemed I had best return to the mansion.

Lost in my own thoughts, I forgot to lift my skirts as I stepped over the burnt threshold. My foot caught in the brick of the stoop and my dress hooked again on the nail which had already torn it. Letting out a cry, I stumbled forward over the uneven rocks, sprawling into the mud.

I lay there for a moment, stunned. Then, realizing only my pride was hurt, I stood to see what damage had been done. My long skirt had protected me but it was badly muddied.

Once more I thought I heard a noise coming from the wood.

"Hello? Is anyone there?"

No one answered. I hadn't expected anyone would. It was just my own active imagination or maybe one of the squirrels I had seen earlier.

Looking down at myself, I knew I could not return to the house dressed like this. Taking a deep breath, I stood still for a moment and tried to think. Mama had told me of a brook nearby—a secret hideaway she called it. She had mentioned how she had often swam there and met her special friends there. Until now I hadn't thought but I knew the special friend must have been my father. Had I been conceived by the brook?

Swallowing the pain of my thoughts, I headed in the direction of the forest behind the house where I assumed the brook had to be. It didn't take me long to hear the babbling of its water.

Elated, I hurried forward—not only to wash off the dirt but also I hoped to learn something of value there. I would wash out my stained dress here. Rose could never get this as clean as I could. Besides, I knew Rose would be judging me, just as my cousin already did. I did not wish to explain where I had gone this morning or why.

Of course, even if I washed it, the dress would never dry before I returned to the house, but at least it would be clean. I would merely ask Rose to press it later.

Even with the sound of the babbling brook singing to me, I made several wrong turns. There were a few moments when I feared I would again fall into an abyss— but I was wrong. Each time I paused, I would hear the murmur of the stream beckoning to me, calling me forth. It seemed almost as if the brook was as anxious to talk to me as I was to see it.

The murmur was getting louder. A joy like the laughing water seemed to flood me. I broke into a run only to be halted as I came to a fork in the road. Reeling from the quickness of my stop, I grasped the old oak tree at the side and felt the roughness of the bark scrape my skin. Breathless, I waited a moment and stared. There on the ground, stretched out under the trees, was a body.

From a distance, I could not see who it was or even if the person was alive. My heart beat wildly. I took a deep breath to steady myself and tiptoed forward. I could feel the blood rushing through me in fear as I tried to think of what to do. If the person were dead, I would have to run back to the house for help. If he were just injured—well, I did know some nursing from when I had helped Mama and when we had had sick animals, but I knew I would also have to return to the house for help.

I prayed the man was only asleep and yet, if he was, I did not want to risk waking him for fear of the consequences.

Taking several steps closer, I saw a slight movement under the blanket. A scream threatened to rise in me. At least I knew he was not dead, but was he hurt?

It was only when I was within a few feet of the body did I realize it was Peter Parkisham. My blood rushed to my face as I stared at him. I felt my heart in my throat. Why in the world had he chosen such a place to sleep? How odd to find him here.

Wetting my lips, I stood there, staring at him—I think for a good five minutes. I knew as long as he wasn't hurt I should hurry on and yet—I continued to stare at him. There was something about his face, his features— perhaps it was the scar on his cheek. I didn't know what it was but it fascinated me. He fascinated me. He belonged to a world I could never enter and yet we had a bond. I knew it and felt it. If only I knew exactly what that bond was.

As I continued to stare, I thought of how childlike and innocent he looked, and yet I did not think he had been so innocent the day of our first meeting.

Still, I smiled. His features were boyish now, with the lock of blond hair falling over his face. I felt the desire to hold and cuddle him as I might have a baby or perhaps one of my cats at home.

A cooling breeze blew through my hair. It felt for a moment like one of those damp compresses he had put on my brow when I had been ill. I wondered why he had been so nice to me.

Unable to take my eyes off him, I took a deep breath and tried to calm my emotions, to banish those evil thoughts circulating in my brain. After all, he was engaged to Terrah. Tilly hinted the official announcement would be made at the end of the summer. Tilly made it clear that when my cousin wanted something, she went after it like a bull breaking out of its pen.

Well, I would be here only a few weeks anyway. There was no sense in letting my heart get broken by some local Lothario and then mourn for it the rest of my life the way Mama had.

Besides, I swallowed hard and continued to stare, if what I suspected was true, if Peter really was my brother, then there was no way I could associate with him other than as a friend. A shudder passed through me. I longed to meet his father and the rest of his family to learn what I could of my mother and her life through their eyes.

A tear came to my eye. Turning, I walked quickly away, trying to be as silent and soft as I could. A twig snapped under my foot. Worried, I looked back. No, Peter was still asleep—or so it seemed.

After a few more moments of searching, I reached the wide brook. Seeing Peter had momentarily made me wonder if I wanted to continue, but since he was asleep, I decided to sit by the brook anyway.

Finding a suitable log, I sat down and felt my throat close. Had my mother sat on this very same log? I stared out over the crystal green water as it foamed and rushed toward the rocks, frothing white before it cascaded down. Around me the forest stillness was broken by morning sounds. The water was exactly as I had imagined it to be—cool, clean, and clear. Deep enough to swim in and yet not so deep one would fear drowning.

The water continued to murmur as it lapped the rocks, trying to coax me in with its little green tongues.

Responding to the silent command, I glanced quickly about to make sure I was indeed still alone. Then, hastily, I removed my boots and leggings. Placing them under a nearby elm, I grabbed a stick for support and edged myself slowly down the incline into the water.

I tied my skirts high so I would not trip here in the water and delicately put one foot into the gentle eddy. Quickly, I drew back, teeth chattering.

"Don't be a ninny!" I told myself. "It will be better when you get used to it."

Taking a deep breath, I stuck my foot out once more, holding onto the twig growing at the side—as if that would really keep me from the water. My foot stayed in a few moments more this time but quickly came out.

In frustration, I stared at the stain still on my dress. How was I going to get this clean if I didn't go into the water?

Pressing my lips in determination, I thrust ahead. This time I put both feet into the water and stood upright. The shock of the cold made me drop my skirts, totally soaking the hem. But then I supposed that was what I had wanted.

For several more moments, I stood there shivering until my feet gradually became used to the water. Then, realizing I was no longer cold, I lowered the rest of my body into the swirling waters. Covered to the waist, I began to scrub at the troublesome spots.

Nothing was happening.

I knew then I would probably have more luck if I took the dress off. Did I dare?

I glanced about. The area was still totally void of human life—or so it appeared. I couldn't help but recall Peter Parkisham lay not more than a moment's walk away. If he should come and see me—God only knew what would happen. I knew if I allowed my thoughts to continue I would be damned forever!

It took only a moment for me to climb back onto

shore. Wringing the brook's water from my skirt, I tiptoed back to the spot where I had seen Peter a few moments before.

I looked at his face, studying his long lashes, his smooth skin with just the shadow of a beard, and the boyish, tossed hair. From the depth of his breathing, it appeared as though he would sleep a good while longer. Would it be enough time for me to wash and return to Jerseyhurst unseen?

I decided it would. Turning, and determined to get this over with as soon as possible, I hurried back to the water's edge.

Once more the babbling brook tried to lure me in, and voices of the water nymphs seemed to call out to me. I could see why Mama had loved coming here, why she often spoke of it.

Pulling off my skirt and blouse, also stained in my fall, I lay my petticoat over a branch so it might dry while I was washing. I put the dress over my shoulder and headed back into the gentle waves—ready as the day I was born.

My thoughts turned to my mother. I imagined her swimming here, and I hoped I would not repeat her mistakes. I hoped I would not fall in love with someone unsuitable as she obviously had done.

It took but a moment more for me to again become accustomed to the coldness of the water. Once my body had warmed to it, I found myself enjoying the sensation of freedom as the water flowed about me. There were no restrictive bodices, no bands about my waist.

Now that I was used to the water it was easy to see why Mama had loved this pond so. How peaceful it was. How much more peaceful than the house. The tension I already felt at Jerseyhurst was something I did not like. I knew however long I stayed there I would be coming away to the quiet solitude of the brook.

The water reflected my features as I looked down into it. I realized how very pale my skin was, especially in contrast to my dark hair, which I now let fall unburdened to my waist. For a moment, I stood quietly, taking in my surroundings and listening to the morning cooing of the bluebirds. A robin, small and fat, landed on the branch above me, rustling leaves as it moved. I watched for a moment, feeling the water lap and swirl about my feet. Yes, this was an enchanted place.

The distant ringing of a bell as it sang through the air told me time was passing. It would not do for me to be here when Peter woke.

Deciding I had best get to the task at hand, I scrubbed my dress harder. The stains were stubborn. It took several moments before I was satisfied with the results. My hands were red from the effort. Wringing out the fabric, I waded back to shore.

The sun was higher now. However, out of the water I felt much colder. Goose bumps came to my skin. I hung the dress over the branches of a tree. I hoped it would dry enough for me to put it back on. I smoothed it with my hands and glanced toward the sun as it peered through the myriad of trees. Was it strong enough to dry my clothes?

Shivering, I decided I had time to return to the water a bit before returning to the house.

As if in response to my thought, a blue jay screeched, breaking the silence about me and shaking the leaves. For just that moment, I felt a frightening sense of loneliness as I stood naked and alone at the edge of the brook. It would have been lovely to have company—someone like Joshua—who would enjoy the beauty of the woods with me, the serenity of the spot.

I glanced toward the woods again, feeling the quickening of my heart. Peter was surely still asleep, I told myself, and it would be uncomfortable to be wearing wet clothes just now. Knowing it was an excuse, I returned to the water for a few moments of play.

As the stream covered me, my chattering stopped and I grew warm again. Smiling to myself, I wondered if Peter ever swam here. I wondered if—but no, I could not think such thoughts. Those were forbidden. If I thought of anyone, it should be Joshua. My poor dear Joshua back on the farm in Kansas. Why didn't we have quiet brooks like this near the farm?

I wondered if I shouldn't write and invite Joshua to visit here with me. It would be lovely to show him the brook, to show him that water came from places other than wells and one need not face a drought all the time or have to drill for water.

Touching the palm of my hands, I felt the soreness from the last time I had pumped the water up. I had even begged for water from our neighbor when our own well went dry. Recalling how awful it had felt not to wash for a whole week, to have the sand and dirt crusted on me, I quickly dunked my body into the water again. My hair floated above and about me.

Even though I was not a good swimmer, I knew I could never drown here in Mama's brook. Her spirit would protect me.

Head once more under water, I forced myself to open my eyes. I was surprised at how clearly I could see. The bottom was a golden sandy color lined with beautiful shells and stones. Grabbing one or two quickly, I could feel the tug of the current on my long hair.

When I could no longer hold my breath I surfaced. The wet hairs collected about my face, forcing me to sputter as I pushed them from my mouth and eyes. I had such a clean, exhilarated feeling, especially after having spent so many days in the sick room, that I was tempted to linger here the rest of the day.

I was about to make one more dive when my alert ears heard the crackling of brush. My heart came to my throat. Intently, my eyes scanned the shore and bushes. Turning quickly, I tried to see if there was anything or anyone about. My pulse raced. Was Peter awake? It couldn't be that late, could it?

Quickly, I sank into the water so that my body did not show as much. Shivering, I could only wonder if I had been seen. I knew the chill I was feeling was not from the water.

Tensely, I waited.

There were no other sounds. No movements. I felt myself relaxing. Perhaps it had been some wild animal. Perhaps a squirrel. There were several about.

I was sure that if Peter Parkisham had noticed me, he would be gentleman enough to go away and leave me alone. After all, it would be the courteous thing to do. Why then did I feel this forlorn disappointment? If Peter did come upon me . . . I grinned and then felt utter horror at my own reckless, sinful thoughts.

Quickly, I pushed the idea from my mind. I did not want to end up as my mother had. I did not want to give myself to any man before I was married, and yet, they did say that sort of evil often ran in the blood. If my mother had done it, was I not prone? I frowned.

Sighing, I knew it was time to head back to Jerseyhurst. I could not leave until I had done one more dive and picked up a few more shells. Who knew exactly when I would return to this brook or whether I'd have this chance again? Perhaps after I had collected another shell I would go check my skirt and blouse. It should be dry enough to wear without too much discomfort. Then, if I did see Mr. Parkisham on the path, I would simply curtsey as a proper young lady should and thank him for his assistance during my illness. If I said anything more to him, I knew my mother would turn over in her grave.

The time for thinking had passed. If I wanted to get back before the others woke, I had to get the shells now and then hurry.

Splashing the water high as I dived, I felt the pressure hit my stomach. Breathless, I sank down the sandy bottom and collected two more shells. The pink and purple ones were the most beautiful. I would put them on the mantel when I returned to Kansas. They would be a token of memory to my mother. Then I recalled the farmhouse was no longer mine.

Well, they would look nice on Joshua's mantel then.

Once again, I dived, hoping to gather another pair. I felt my hair shoot upward and outward with the current of the brook, and it fell into my eyes. I could not see, but suddenly I became aware of another presence in the water with me. Something touched my foot!

I gasped and tried to free myself from the vice. Trying to surface I found myself being pulled back under. Dropping the shells, I struggled, horrified.

Kicking with all my might, I managed to break free of whatever—whoever—held me. Breaking the surface of the water, I screamed at the top of my lungs.

Whoever it was—I did not want to think—had let me go. Without a moment's hesitation I swam to the shore and climbed out. I did not know if my attacker followed me. I heard only the beating of my heart as I ran for my clothes. I didn't want to look back, didn't want to think who it was, but my fear told me it had been Peter Parkisham. Oh, why did it have to be him? Was he disturbed? Was he . . .

I felt like a doe being chased by foxes as I jumped over trees and shrubs. My wet clothes were in my hands. My feet felt every rock, every pebble, as I continued to run. Branches scratched me as I veered from the trail and heard the footsteps behind me.

Breathless, I reached the fork in the road where I thought Peter had been earlier. Yes, it was empty. Quickly, I glanced around. It was the place. There was no doubt. Just as there was no doubt he was the one who had attacked me. Why, I did not know, but tears came to my eyes and my heart continued to thud.

Momentarily, my mind went blank as I searched for the proper path to lead me back to Jerseyhurst. Fear had made me forget. Panic flushed through me as I heard the vibrating sounds of footsteps behind me. He was following me!

Blindly, I chose the left path but my hesitation made me loose time. Behind me, I could hear the sounds of running coming closer and closer.

Hunting for some place to hide, for some shrub, I felt frantic. There had to be somewhere I could at least don my clothes and meet my attacker with dignity. There had to be.

The footsteps were too close. Weak from shortness of breath, I felt my lungs aching. There was no time to think as I put on my petticoat and slipped my still wet skirt and blouse on.

I heard the brush of leaves and the crash of twigs as he came by. Hiding behind the tree, I held my breath hoping he would run past me.

Eyes wide, I saw the passing figure. Was that Peter Parkisham? All I saw was the blond hair, but I knew with a sickening sensation it had to be he.

At least I was safe, I thought, as I leaned against the tree.

Too late, I recalled, I had forgotten my leggings and shoes under the brush by the brook. Well, I had no desire to return for them now.

Barefoot and angry, I made my way back toward the safety of my room at Jerseyhurst. How strange that I would be thinking of wanting to get back to Jerseyhurst when I had just moments ago been thinking of how wonderful the brook was.

Thank goodness no one saw me as I entered the house. At least, I didn't believe I had been seen. My feet were painfully aware of the lack of covering.

With the water in the jug, I hastily washed the dirt from the cuts and bruises on my feet. They hurt. Tears sprang to my eyes and I pressed my lips together. What hurt more, I think, was that I had been wrong about Peter Parkisham.

Peeling off my damp clothes, I lay them on the chair and returned to my nightdress. Falling into an exhausted sleep, I tried not to think of my fears.

Chapter Four

The late afternoon sun was low in the window when I woke once more. I was astounded at having slept so late, but then I guessed I was still recovering from my illness. My panic this morning had not helped. I still did not know if it was Peter or not, but it seemed he was the most logical choice.

It upset me. I did not think he would be one to attack a lady while bathing, and yet who else could it have been?

The knock on the door was like a pounding on my brain. It took me several moments before I could respond. "Who is it?"

I knew I sounded irritated, but I could not help myself.

"It's Rose, Miz Lizabeth."

"Come in!" I called to her, feeling unable to move from the bed. "Door's open." I laid my head back on the pillow to calm the pounding in my head. Mama used to get massive headaches but until now I had never suffered one. I could truly sympathize with her.

The door slowly creaked open, revealing Rose in the dim light of the hall. "Mama says youse not eaten all day.

Is you coming down t'dinner or do I bring up a tray?"

She entered the room without speaking further, without asking permission. I stared at her as she lit the small oil lamp. The room suddenly had an eerie glow to it, and I realized then just how late it must be.

"I'll dress and come down for dinner."

"You sure 'bout that?"

I nodded. "I wouldn't say so if I wasn't." I stared at her and decided to wait for Rose to go before getting up from the bed. Instead, she went to the door and bent down. Turning again toward me, she held out my boots and stockings. I stared at her.

"Where—where did you get those?"

"They are yours, then, Miz?"

I nodded, feeling a pain in my heart as I recalled the events of the morning. Reaching out for them I could see the trembling in my hands. "Where did you get them?" I asked again.

She brought the shoes and leggings over to me. Rose smiled as if she knew more than she was saying. "Why, they was left on the doorstep. They ain't Miz Terrah's so I 'sumed they be yours. I'll tell Mama youse be eatin' with the others. They always meet in the music parlor afore they go into supper. I 'spect you should be there, too."

"How soon?"

She shrugged. "Soon as you can, I 'magine. Miz Terrah hates to wait dinner for anybody." With another smile, she turned and disappeared.

I lay back down on my elbows, contemplating the shoes and looking at the room. How much, if anything, did Rose know of this morning? Had Peter told her he had seen me? Had the attack been planned? No, of course not. Who would have known I would go out walking? No one here knew my habits of liking to walk early in the morning.

With a determined sigh, I rose from the bed.

The water was fresh. Rose had obviously been in the room either during the morning when I had been gone or while I had slept. A shiver went through me. I did not like the way Rose slipped in and out of my room so easily and decided I would have to speak with Tilly about that.

I washed quickly and put on a fresh muslin gown for dinner. It was one of the light blue frocks Rose had recently cleaned. I had to admit, it looked better clean.

As my right foot went into the boot, I felt an uncomfortable pressure. Something was in the shoe!

Astonished, I pulled out the small piece of paper which had been curled up in the toe. Was Peter now trying to blackmail me or something? There was little I had he could want.

Both puzzled and curious, I uncrumpled the paper, tearing it open.

Several small colored stones and pink shells from the brook fell onto the floor. I stared at them. They were the ones I had been trying to gather when I had been attacked! Stunned, I could only leave them on the floor. There was no note. There was nothing to indicate who had sent them—but of course, I knew. It could only be Peter.

Furious with both him and myself, I crushed the paper. Going to the window, I threw it and the stones as far away as I could. I would not indulge myself in wishful thinking. The man was a fop with absolutely no gentlemanly integrity. I did not want to have anything to do with him, I told myself. Not anything at all.

I checked my appearance in the cracked mirror. The

skirt flared a bit too much in the back and the puffed sleeve on my blouse was not in proper style, but it would do for tonight. It gave me a decent appearance, and I hoped it would serve to impress my other cousin—and perhaps my uncle, if he came down for dinner.

Rose hadn't given me directions to the music parlor but I didn't think it would be too hard to find it. Feeling a definite unease, as if I was being watched by a pair of unseen eyes, I hurried from my room and down the long corridor toward the front stairs.

The house was filled with oppressive silence. Unlike the quiet calm I had felt this morning, it made me want to run away. However, I would never learn anything of my heart's desire if I left so hastily.

Still, I passed no servants in the hall nor any member of the family, which made me wonder where everyone was. Surely, if the dinner hour was approaching there should be others about.

The low gaslight shimmered in the hall, casting large shadows on the wall as I walked. I was aware of the rustling of my fresh petticoats and the spring of the carpet beneath my feet. My hand touched the well polished oak rail. Everything here seemed so new. Perhaps my uncle's fortune had recently increased. Considering his illness, it seemed strange, and yet I had no doubt many changes had been made here since the time my mother had lived here.

At the landing, I paused. The portrait of my grandfather Maxwell Swanson glared down at me. I could almost swear his eyes were staring at me, watching me. But of course it was ridiculous. Mother had always told me I had an active imagination and this proved it. Still, I could not help but notice his sour face. It was not a pleasant greeting for anyone. I hurried past the landing and onto the first floor. It still seemed as if the eyes were following me, disapproving of me for what my mother had done.

Perhaps it was just as well my dream of Peter Parkisham had been destroyed this morning. Who knew what would have happened otherwise? I did not want to think I had bad blood merely because my mother had done something many folks considered wrong and yet I had these feelings and sensations. They were strange to me but I could not censor them. It was just as well that I had promised Joshua I would stay only three weeks. Then, I would learn who my father was, return back to Kansas, and marry Joshua.

With a heavy heart, I realized Joshua did not excite the same feelings in my breast as Peter did, although I knew and trusted Joshua. I did not know Peter and perhaps I never would. With a sigh, I realized it was all a mystery to me.

Hurrying along the corridor, I wondered now where the music parlor was. Rose had not given me directions and I assumed I would not need them. My instincts would have to lead me.

Opening the first of the three doors, I was surprised at what a spacious room I found. Folding doors, which obviously collapsed, would provide ample entertainment room. I couldn't help but admire the richly hued oriental rug covering the floors, and the delicate Hepplewhite and Chippendale pieces.

In the middle of the room was a set of delicate Chinese vases. I assumed my grandfather had brought them back from his journey in the Orient. Gently, I touched the hand-painted silk fans which lined the walls. The smooth texture was a joy to my fingers as I admired the intricate work and detail of the dancers on the fans. I realized that if my mother stayed, she would have inherited much of this and shared it with her brother. I also knew that if she had taken any of it, it probably would have been sold to meet our debts.

The second room was much like the first. I opened the third door, but that darkened room did not seem to be the music parlor because it had not been cleaned for quite some time.

I stood in the hall, wondering what to do when I saw that in the second room there stood a grand square piano which I had overlooked in my haste. I did not think this could be the music parlor but it was the only place where there was a musical instrument and so I entered.

Lighting one of the gaslamps at the side, I turned to stare at the dark wood piano. Was this the one my mother had first learned to play on? She told me it had been saved from the fire at the small house.

Dust flew about as I raised the lid. I brushed off the bench and sat down. Coughing, I waited for the air to clear. I held my nose to avoid inhaling any more dust. The keys had yellowed with age.

Lightly my fingers touched the keys. Despite what Zebulon had said, mother had stressed I was a gentleman's daughter and should be raised as such. I never thought she was referring to anyone other than Zebulon—until now. Besides teaching me piano, Mother had also taught me fashions. I wondered now if she totally approved of my friendship with Joshua. She had liked him well enough as our neighbor. I stared at the silent keyboard. What would she have thought of Peter? What aspirations had she for me? Had she planned for me to come here to know my father? Would she have told me who he was had she lived?

Thinking of Joshua made me homesick. If only he were here with me, but much as I thought I loved him, I knew he would never have fit into this setting. Surely, he would have felt awkward.

Even as I felt awkward, I thought. Looking about the dim room again, I knew this could not be the place where we were to meet. Still, I did not leave the bench. The piano called out to me. Its vibrations seemed to speak to me, to beg me to play it.

Gently, I stroked the keys, feeling the smooth ivory yellowed keys, feeling the hard black sharps. The instrument was, no doubt, out of tune, yet I could probably still play melody on it, and melody would make me think of my mother.

It was as if my fingers were magically bonded to the keys. The excitement surging through me could not be denied.

Slowly, I pressed down. Dust rose. My nose tickled. It took quite a bit of effort to repress the urge to sneeze and yet I did. Continuing to stroke the keys, I tried to recall one of my mother's favorite lullabies. Playing softly, I allowed my voice to match that of the instrument.

My first tones were awkward. Although the piano had not been used for some time, the tones were sweet, nevertheless. It was almost as if it was thanking me for bringing it to life.

Within moments, I lost the hesitancy of my playing. I had lost my fear. I no longer heard the parts which were obviously out of tune. I could only think of my mother and her playing. It was a selection from Bach—one which mother used to practice each evening. The melancholy melody had suited her mood then and it suited mine now.

Lost in thought, concentrating on my finger motion, I was not aware of soft steps behind me until the large hands grabbed my shoulders.

Surprised, I dropped my hands from the keys. My reaction—jamming my elbow back—was instinctive. I heard the groan and spun about to face a chunky man, with a spotted complexion, doubled over. Burnished red hair extended over his hands, almost to his knuckles, and though he was not wearing the Swanson ring, I had no doubt this man was my cousin, David.

Standing, I approached him. "Did I hurt you? I am sorry."

He grinned. "Ah, I like women with spirit. I like your green eyes, too. What were you playing?"

I shrugged and glanced back at the piano. "Bach. It's something my mother taught me."

"It's unusual. Nice." He motioned with his thick hands toward the piano. "Terrah doesn't approve—" His words halted, as if he were in doubt as to what to say. I could smell the whiskey on his breath even from where I stood and felt my stomach cringe. His grin appeared more lopsided now. "She doesn't like music. My father is quite ill, you see."

I nodded, recalling last night. "I'm sorry. I had forgotten." I felt the blush rise as I glanced at him. It was obvious he had the same problem as his father.

"Quite all right. As long as Terrah doesn't hear you." He paused and picked up one of the Chinese vases in the room. It looked so incongruous in his large hand. "Actually, I've been waiting anxiously to meet you. I saw you walking this morning—" He left the sentence dangling and smiled at me. A chill went through me. Had he, too, followed me? I stared at him, wondering if he had witnessed the scene with Peter. Peter had been the only one I had seen at the brook. I swallowed hard as I stared at my new cousin.

Goosebumps went up my arms as David continued to smile at me. He looked away from my gaze and shrugged. "Perhaps you'll allow me to show you some paths you might enjoy the next time you wish to explore."

I stared at him and saw a strange light in his eyes. My stomach tightened. I knew he had seen me and I hated him for it. Maybe I was wrong about Peter.

"Well?"

He wasn't as drunk as I had thought. It seemed he also expected me to give him some sort of answer, but, stunned, I could at first only shake my head.

Finally, I found my voice. "Actually, I prefer walking alone."

"Oh?" He raised a bushy red brow; his forehead furrowed. He looked like pictures I had seen of Neanderthal man. There was a tension in the air. "You asked before how I expected you to respond to my hands on your shoulders, Cousin Lizzie, but I didn't answer you," he said, taking a step forward, closer to me.

I felt fear rising in me as I smelled the whiskey odor. One step back. He caught me in his paws and jerked me into his arms.

"David!" I screamed at him, pounding helplessly on his barrel chest. "Let me go! Let me go now!"

He laughed. His breath stank. "Come now, Lizzie. Don't you even want to kiss your cousin hello?"

His lips came down hard on mine. Revulsion curled the acid in my stomach. Pounding on his chest, I tried to free myself. He was obviously stronger than I, but perhaps the drink had affected his brain. Foolishly, he allowed my hands free. With all my might, I slapped him.

David blinked, stepping back. He released me and stared at me, stunned I had hit him. "I like my women spirited." He grinned. "Indeed, I do, and since you're our poor Kansas cousin, I would think some appreciation of our hospitality is in order." He grinned and then, seeing his sister at the door, rolled his eyes upward in mock horror.

"Hello, my dearest Terrah." He bowed low, his hand twisting into an Arabic salute. "Have you welcomed our new cousin, yet?"

"You're disgusting, David. Sometimes I think you're worse than father." She glared at me—as if I was at fault. "Who gave you permission to come in here? This room is normally locked."

I clenched my fist. The anger was rising in me but I forced myself to control it. "Well, it wasn't locked just now." I glanced back toward the piano. "I'm sorry if my playing disturbed you." I took a deep breath, mustering what dignity I could. "I was told to meet you here in the music room before dinner. I was looking for you when I found the piano."

"I don't know who told you to meet anyone here." She glanced sharply at her brother. "We do not meet in the music room or anywhere before dinner."

David flushed.

"Dinner is not for another hour and a half yet. We meet directly in the dining hall." With that, Terrah turned on her heel. Her stiff dress crackled as she moved.

Without glancing at David, I followed Terrah from the room. As I reached the door, I heard him say, "Don't worry, dear little cousin, we'll have plenty of time to

78

know each other." He laughed then; it was a drunken laugh that sent shivers through me.

Upset I hurried toward my room. As long as there was time before dinner, I wanted to explore the house which my mother had—for one year of her life—called home. But I wondered if I dared. Would David try to molest me again?

If he did, I doubted Terrah would do anything to help me. It seemed only Tilly understood my feelings and desires. Only Tilly would help me in this house of serpents. Tilly, however, was busy with dinner.

Anxiously, I returned to my room.

I did not want to be in a vulnerable position. I did not want David to have the chance to take advantage of me. My eyes lighted on the fireplace and the pokers there. I picked up the lightest one. It was well worn, iron and a comfortable weight. It could do enough damage to cool even David's ardor.

Confident, I left the wedge-shaped room. Earlier I had noted the back stairs which led upward—probably toward the storage rooms and servant quarters. A narrow set of stairs also led downward, but the way here was darker than one might expect and full of cobwebs. I decided not to go down but up. If there was anything left of my mother's belongings still in the house, it would most likely be in the storage.

Taking a deep breath, I started up the dark stairs. The wood was uneven here and warped as if it had been neglected for some time. Perhaps it had been neglected on purpose to discourage people from coming up here.

How could that be? I wasn't a frightened child. Didn't they know I would one day be coming to search for my mother's possessions? Besides, no one had really attempted to hide anything from me yet. I hadn't even asked questions of my cousins. Still, I did have the feeling they were not anxious to answer me or to assist in my quest.

Well, warped stairs or not, it would not dissuade me. I was determined to find out what I could about my mother's life here.

Taking another deep breath, I felt my heart race. Was it still my illness or was it fear coursing through me? I wondered suddenly what I would do when I had the information I sought. Could I just be satisfied to know who he was and leave this town?

Nearing the third floor, I noticed light filtered in from a round skylight in the center of the roof. A window was at the far end of the hall. Reaching the level floor, I stared. Rows upon rows of doors confronted me—all seemed to be locked. Did anyone live up here? I thought surely some of the servants would have been quartered here, but there was no indication of that.

The floor here was uncarpeted. My boots made a hollow knocking as I walked forward—or was that the loud pounding of my heart? I tried to tiptoe, still tasting the fear in my mouth. But the noise did not seem to lessen at all. I tried the doors again. Dust raised as I continued down the hall and I coughed violently.

When I managed my breath once more, I glanced about me. There was a haunted air of despair up here. It seemed to invade the dismal walls about me. No where could I see the evidence of wealth to be seen downstairs—no paintings, no carpets, no decorations of any kind.

I lit one of the candle stubs and noticed even they were spaced far apart.

Moving foward along the rows of closed doors, I felt a distinctly uneasy sensation. I clutched the poker tighter. Even without the threat of David, I was glad to have it.

I paused a moment directly under the skylight and looked up. The glass panes fascinated me. Was there any way to get up there? From where I stood, it was possible to glimpse the shadowy guard rail surrounding the circular glass, so I knew people could go up onto the roof. How? That was the question now, but I would answer it later.

Walking to each of the doors, stirring the dust, I tested each and found one unlocked. It stood at the end of the hall, just when my patience had become thin. The knob resisted me only momentarily and then it turned, creaking as it did so. The hinges groaned like a dying woman's screams. I saw my knuckles go white as I clutched the poker tighter—fearful of what I would find. But there was nothing frightening in this huge room. I peered into the dimness and realized my imagination had once more been overactive. The box lying in the center of the room could easily have been a coffin, but it was not. At least, I did not think it was.

It took several minutes for the dust to settle and for my heart to calm. Stepping forward, still holding the poker, I sneezed at the dust. There were boxes and bags, trunks and cases everywhere.

Suddenly something moved! Frightened, I let the metal clatter to the floor. The vibrations of the noise died but nothing else moved. I realized it was probably only a mouse. I continued cautiously through the narrow passage made by the boxes. I had nearly reached the center of the room when I became aware of the creaking door closing behind me—just in time.

Keeping my foot in the door, I reached out for an old hobbyhorse head. If there was a way into this room, there was a way out, but it wasn't a chance I wanted to take.

Awkwardly, I bent over, feeling the strain of my back muscles. Letting the poker take some of the weight, I felt my right hand close over the hobbyhorse stick. It was only as I stood upright again that I heard the slight hiss: My bodice had ripped.

"Damn!" I cursed. I wished now I had taken a moment to change my dress. Too late now.

Sneezing again at the dust which had been stirred up, I placed the hobbyhorse stick in the door. Then and only then did I feel safe to move on.

There were several other boxes lined along the passage but while looking at them had been my first intention, I now decided, seeing the door ahead of me, to go out onto the skylight. Later I would examine these boxes. They probably held most of the ghost of Jerseyhurst.

Picking up an old rag doll which had been thrust into one corner, I stared at it, wondering why it had no box home, wondering, too, how its eyes had come to be poked out. I touched the hollow cloth sockets. Could this have been Terrah's doing? I did not want to think my cousin capable of harming an innocent doll and yet . . .

Tears misted my eyes. I recalled the doll Zebulon had carved for me one day. How I had loved it. If only he had been my real father. Then I would never have come here.

Feeling the air stifle me, I quickly hurried toward the outer door which obviously led to the skylight.

I approached and yanked on the handle. The door seemed stuck. Frustrated, I pulled at the door with all my might. It wasn't until I used my hops as leverage that the door opened a bit—hinges crying loudly all the way.

Breathless, I stared at the narrow opening. Well, it was enough for me to get through. My dress would become dirtier, but since it was already ruined what difference did another spot make?

Holding my breath, I squeezed through.

Cool, fresh air greeted me, catching my curls and playing with them. Not wanting to take chances, I retrieved the rag doll and placed her as guard in the entrance. With the poker still in my hand, I stepped onto the wooden walkway. Quickly, I blinked as I tried to get used to the brightness up here. It really was beautiful, I realized. I could see for miles and miles.

Breathing deeply again, I turned slightly south, surveying my surroundings.

I felt the flush come to my face as I saw light reflecting off the brook. Could I have been observed from the house? Again, shame flooded me as I thought about the morning. I could see mother's old house, too, nestled quietly beneath the trees. Beyond and all around us, it seemed, was the mighty Mississippi—at times hidden by the valleys, and other times free and easy as the spirit of its name.

My eyes again returned to the brook and my fist clenched at my side. "Damn him!" I whispered.

Purposely, I turned in the other direction, but it seemed there was no escaping him. Parkland Manor was directly opposite me now, and I could see the majority of the forest track I had traveled my first day. From here the woodlands dividing the two properties seemed small but on my first night, it had been a wearisome walk.

With my eyes, I followed the path along the curve of the land and the shallow ravine. I did not recall that spot, but I did recall the missing chunk of land where I had lost my purse and nearly lost my life. My heart raced in fear as I again recalled those moments.

Was it possible to recover my reticule? I prayed so but I knew it would be difficult.

Forcing myself to remain calm, I continued to survey the forest, and, closer to me, the private gardens of the house. The early flowers were nosing their way up. Trees here were already spouting green leaves.

Still, I could not help but think of the cliff since it reminded me I was penniless and at the mercy of my cousins. My only alternative was finding my father. If I could not discover him, I would have to write to Joshua and ask him to lend me money for my return ticket home, but I did not want to do that. The drought last year had been bad for both of us. I frankly did not know how Joshua had survived, unless he had some hidden wealth he had not confessed to me. Nevertheless, my pride forbade me asking him for funds.

As I looked down, I felt suddenly dizzy. Clutching the rail until my knuckles were white, I felt my fact contort as a sudden wave of nausea attacked me. I waited a moment, forcing myself to take a deep breath. The agony slowly subsided. I did not know if it was from my illness or if I was, indeed, afraid of heights as Mother had been.

Daring myself, I looked down once more. It was a straight drop of four and half flights. My heart pounded. After my incident on the cliff, it wasn't hard to imagine falling through space here. I wet my lips and drew back. The pounding of my heart continued. I knew now why the creaking door sounded like the screams of a dying woman. I wondered how many had died here.

Shivering, I had just begun to retreat when the flash of a blue bombazine gown in the gardens below caught my attention.

I forced myself to lean forward slightly again. Yes, it was my cousin walking in the gardens of the house. She was with a man but it looked like neither David nor Peter. I stared at her and at him. Her head rested against his muscular shoulder in a loving gesture, but somehow I did not get the impression she loved him. In fact, I could imagine my cousin loved no one but herself.

As I continued to stare at his back, I could swear the man looked familiar but unless he turned, I could not see his face. I continued to stare and cursed my poor memory. Closing my eyes I tried to conjure up an image, but the only person who even came close to the image was Joshua.

My fascination with the scene below made me forget my earlier fears. Chancing discovery, I leaned forward slightly further. Instincts told me Terrah knew more about my family than she was telling me and that this man also knew. In fact, I could swear on my goose-bumped arms and active imagination that they spoke of me. I did not know what I could learn by watching, but I did know that seeing his hand on Terrah's breast, he could not be a gentleman.

The pair kissed passionately. Hatred surged through me as I once more thought of David's wet mouth on mine. I also felt hatred for Terrah as I realized she was not with her fiancé. Poor Peter. Did he know the type of woman he planned to marry? For one moment only, I wondered what it would be like to have Peter kissing me like that.

The pair moved further into the gardens. Not once did the man turn in my direction. Frustrated, I realized my discovery of Terrah's paramour would have to wait.

I drew back toward the door. I knew, even had I stood on the ground in front of them, they would not have noticed me.

The dying rays were already playing off the rocks by the brook. Darkness would soon follow. I knew it was time to leave the skylight and return to my room. I had to change for dinner. Even though there was no need to impress Terrah or David, I still wished to be on time.

As the outer door creaked shut behind me, I saw all was the same—except my footsteps were not the only ones in the dust of the narrow aisle. Large manish ones seemed to preempt my smaller ones. So David had followed me! The heaviness of the iron poker seemed comforting now. I wondered why David hadn't made himself known. Did David know what I had seen? If not, it seemed, we both had secrets.

Thoughtfully, I hurried toward the steps leading back to the third floor just as Tilly came lumbering up.

"Lordy Girl. Where you been?"

I glanced at my good gray tabby. The seam had ripped more than I had thought. My hair and face, I knew, were smudged with dirt and cobwebs.

"Examining my new home," I said, shrugging, meeting Tilly's eyes as I glanced back at the larger footsteps.

"Girl, this ain't no place for you to be. There ain't no place in this house as dusty as that, 'ceptin'—you went to the walk." It was more of an accusation than a question.

Not really knowing why, I felt rebuked. I nodded as I cast my eyes downward.

"Miz Lizabeth." Tilly gripped my hand tightly. "Don't you never go up there again. Never, do you hear?"

"But it's so beautiful."

"Honey, baby." Tilly's huge motherly arms engulfed

me. "That there be the place Miz Georgiana done fell and died."

"Georgiana? My aunt?"

Tilly nodded. "Don't nobody come up here since then."

"No wonder so many of the doors were locked and rusty."

"Promise me, baby. You won't go up there again."

I sighed and nodded. "Tilly, tell me. How did my aunt die?"

The wide lips clamped into a thin line.

"I shall go up there everyday until you tell me."

The huge brown eyes glared but there was more: There was fear. She glanced about as if expecting to see a ghost—or something equally terrible. This house held secrets far beyond my own questions. I waited for Tilly's answer as I felt the shivers go through me.

"Was she pushed or did she fall?"

Tilly's voice was soft, hushed so even the walls couldn't hear. "Iz don't know." Her face contorted with fear.

I recalled then my own fear. I wondered if I had been picking up the fear my aunt had felt. Wasn't it true ghosts could communicate feelings like that? "What a horrid way to die," I whispered.

"Promise me, baby. Promise me, youse never go near here again."

I nodded my response, feeling tears shimmering down my cheeks.

"Go wash n'change yer clothes. They'll be eatin' soon. Rose'll come and git yer dress."

"Yes. All right." There was a lump in my throat. In silence, the pair of us walked back down to the third floor where my own room was. At the door, I paused. "Was my aunt a prisoner in the room where I'm staying?"

The white and brown eyes rolled themselves heavenward. "Lordy, girl, you do ask them questions."

"Was she?"

There was another heavy sigh as tears filled Tilly's brown eyes. "Iz don' think you should talk 'bout it." She pursed her lips. "You're my Meg's girl. I don't want nuthin' t'happen t'you. Please, baby girl." She touched my hand. "Keeps your questions t'yerself and yer 'deas t'yer own, leastways 'til y'go."

"Don't worry, Tilly. I'll be careful." I bent to kiss her cheek. Then, turning, I disappeared into the room where my aunt had once been confined. I had to change for dinner.

Chapter Five

The huge dining room with its cathedral ceiling awed me. I walked in and looked up, feeling the hush I had felt the few times I had gone to church. Artificial light showed the dull reddish brown of the wainscotting and carpet.

I glanced toward the far end of the room, near the black marble fireplace where Terrah sat. The head of the table was empty and I assumed it was because my uncle was not yet well enough to join us.

There was another portrait of Grandfather Maxwell looking more disapproving than the first. The sconces on either side were low and cast light only on half his face. A shiver went through me as I felt his foreboding eyes upon me. I was glad he was not about for me to deal with as well. He had not approved of my mother's running off. He had not approved of her "wanton ways." I doubted he would have approved of me.

The empty place setting, which Terrah motioned for me to take, was directly across from her brother—a fact not pleasing to me. At least the table was wide enough so I did not have to suffer any physical contact with the man. Nevertheless, his stare and that secret smile of his was unnerving. I could not help wonder what he had seen this morning.

Could I have been wrong? Could it have been him attacking me—and not Peter? But no, Peter was the one who had returned my boots. Peter had been the one, I was sure, to put the colored stones in. It had to have been him. My heart felt heavy. I forced myself to look at my cousin. It was impossible for me not to wonder what he had done since our earlier parting. Had he once again followed me? Would he have thrown me off the sky walk had he the chance?

My stomach tightened. I stared at my plate of soup as I chided myself for my foolish fears, for letting them take control of me. There would be no reason for David to want to harm me—even if he was drunk.

As we began to eat, I noticed instead of the Canton chinaware, which I had seen earlier in the pantry, the table was set with chipped white day china from the kitchen.

"Tilly!" David bellowed, his face redder than the blacksmith's at the forge. "Tilly!" he screamed again.

My spoon was halfway to my mouth. I paused and replaced it in the bowl as I stared at him and then at Terrah.

Tilly appeared at the entrance to the butler's pantry. Her glare silently reproved him for his lack of manners.

Shamed for just a moment, he glanced down at his plate. Then, softening his tone, he looked up. "Tilly, tell me why the good dishes are not set." He grinned at me. "We're welcoming our new cousin."

"But Mastuh David—"

"I gave the order, David," Terrah said, giving us her sweet smile as she sipped her wine. "Knowing how poor Elizabeth's family was, I didn't want her to feel awkward about handling the good dishes."

I forced myself to keep calm. "That's kind of you, dear cousin." I returned her smile. "But it really wasn't necessary. If only you had asked, I would have told you. Mother set out the Haviland china at each dinner. She stressed I was the daughter of a gentleman and should be trained as such."

Terrah frowned but did not respond. A wave of satisfaction swept over me. I sensed I had won a battle, even if it was a small one. Maybe if I could win her over and show her I was not the country bumpkin she thought, she would give me the information I needed.

Terrah indicated we were to continue dinner. Feeling myself flush, I returned the spoon to my mouth, but I tasted little of the remaining duckling which Tilly had prepared. It remained to be seen if the next few dinners would see china or chipped plate.

As a larger family might, we took our coffee in the parlor. I couldn't help but note the furniture was slightly shabbier here than in the formal sitting room. Terrah allowed only three candles to be lit and the resulting light was dim. It gave me pause to think. I wondered if my cousins were more financially embarrassed than one might think.

I sipped my coffee slowly, letting the steam rise, as I savored the flavor. "When may I talk with my uncle?"

Terrah's jade eyes seemed to cut right through me. "Why do you need to talk with him?"

I felt my hackles rise. "I came here to talk with him. I want to know the identity of my father."

Terrah made a face. "Does that really matter? I should think you would be quite happy just to be alive. I know I, for one, should be shamed to my boots to learn I was born out of wedlock."

My throat tightened. "I was not born out of wedlock. Mother and Zebulon saw to that."

"What I mean is," Terrah said, waving her hand airily, "I would be mortified to know I really was somebody's bastard." She paused. "Besides, from all I hear, Zebulon was an excellent father to you."

I tried to calm my feelings and tell myself it was only natural curiosity on her part, that she meant no harm. Yet I myself did not believe her honeyed tones.

"Yes, as a matter of fact, Zebulon was wonderful. I would have been honored if he had been my true father, but I wish to know my real heritage. I have no desire to lay any claim to the man." I glanced first at Terrah and then at her brother. "I wish only to know who it is I come from." I took a deep breath. "So, I wish to speak with my uncle since he will probably know."

The light from the low fire glinted in Terrah's eyes making them hard, cold emerald green. "When he is ready, he will send for you."

She had scarcely put her cup back on her saucer when the startling scream made me bolt from my chair. Liquid spilled on my skirt.

"Georgiana! Georgiana!" His cry was a desperate one. I wondered if he imagined he saw his dead wife. A shiver passed through me as I thought of this afternoon. I wondered if he had had anything to do with her death.

Without glancing at me, Terrah grabbed one of the candles and hurried from the room. I had to admit the devotion to her father was commendable. Perhaps my cousin wasn't as cold and heartless as she seemed.

I looked about and saw David, too, had disappeared. Had he gone to help his sister or to spy on someone else— or maybe to keep Rose company?

Knowing I would not be welcome upstairs, I remained on the first floor, wandering into a book-lined room which had been closed earlier.

A catty-corner desk stood at the far end of the room. Even from here I could see that it was scattered with papers. I did not want to pry and so instead walked to the open french windows. Even so, the papers on the desk drew me to them. My instincts told me those papers would help me with my quest. How and why I did not know but I started forward.

It was obvious this room was an office, but whose? My uncle's? Why was the room open now when it had been locked earlier?

The evening light from the windows cast shadows about the room. I bit my lower lip, deciding whether I should go closer to the desk or not.

It was then I saw the huge leather-bound Bible standing on a wooden platform not far from the desk. The spine looked loose. I wondered how often it had been opened.

Crossing the carpeted room, I felt my heart in my mouth. If this was the family Bible, then it would have members of the family in it. I wondered if my mother's name and mine were mentioned. My blood rushed through me. I wondered if my father's name would be mentioned here, too.

My hand trembled as I opened the cover. The smooth leather had recently been oiled, but I could see the paper, itself, was probably far older than I was. My fingers touched the page of parchment as I stared at the ornate flower drawings on either side curling up the page.

Searching for my mother's name, I realized I was finding everyone in her family but her. Only as I was about to give up did I realize, yes, her name had been there—but crossed out. The thick vellum parchment had been torn with the effort. Was this done because of her elopement?

But surely, no one knew of her pregnancy.

I saw now, in smaller letters and with a different writing style, her name, Margaret Swanson Larabee, printed neatly below. I felt my eyes mist as I touched her name. Just next to her, in a large round handwriting, had been written Zebulon Larabee—and then mine. Someone had known about me. Someone had written us in. My uncle?

I glanced above it. There were no further screams. I wondered if he had been quieted from the nightmare he had had. I was sure if he wanted, he would be able to answer all my questions and then some. If only I could get to speak with him. If only. . . .

I noticed then the marker was in Deuteronomy. I started to turn toward the page it emphasized.

The sound of a creaking board behind startled me. I turned my head, prepared to greet whoever it was, to ask the questions on my mind, when I felt the force pulling me back off the ground. Struggling as best I could, I tasted the bile as it rose in my throat from the noxious odor. The heavy cloth was pressed to my nose and mouth. I continued to struggle against the effect of the chemical, but the arms holding the cloth also held me. Struggle was impossible. Blackness descended on me.

*   *   *

I woke to darkness again but knew I was in my own room—rather, in the wedge-shaped room at Jerseyhurst. My head ached. I tried to sit up and felt the nausea assail me once more. It was all I could do to find the bucket someone had placed beside my bed.

Closing my eyes again, I tried to move past the pain, to think of what had happened this evening. Why had someone drugged me like that? Had I been about to make some sort of discovery?

I inhaled and found even my breathing was painful. I knew whoever had carried me up the stairs had not been gentle.

Suddenly, the memory of the moment returned to me. It was like a flash of lightning before a storm. I recalled seeing a ring. Had it been Peter?

My heart told me no, but I knew what I had seen. I knew my cousin did not have his ring. At least, he had not been wearing it at dinner.

Tears came to my eyes, making the pain intensify. Why did Peter want to prevent me from finding out who my father was? Why had he even been in this house tonight—unless he had the sole mission of trying to stop me.

Slowly, I forced myself to rise again. This time, my stomach stayed settled.

Going to the window, I threw it open and inhaled the crisp night air. It seemed to revive me, to take away some of the grogginess. I stood there for a moment, looking out over the rolling land, looking out over the forest. The night sounds here were louder than I recalled from the night before. I was sure I could even hear the murmur of the Mississippi.

Once I felt somewhat better, I pulled my night robe on. Finding a candle, I lit it. The eerie shadows about me were frightening but not as frightening as what had happened to me earlier. I was more determined than before to find out what was in that Bible. Perhaps it had been left on the desk for a purpose. I did not know for sure. I only knew someone wanted to keep a secret from me.

The house creaked and moaned as it had—was it only this morning? Shivering, I pulled my robe closer about me as I felt a chill go through me. I did not know the time, but I could only guess it was very late.

At the far end of the hall, I saw a movement. Heart hammering, I stopped, pulling in toward a doorway. Sweat beaded my brow.

Then I cursed myself for my own stupidity. It had only been the curtains blowing in the breeze. Uttering a silent prayer of thankfulness, I continued my way down.

With every movement, with every sound, I felt my fear rise and my stomach tighten. I was sure that I would fail and let my weakness take over. I paused and tried to get control of myself. My blood was pounding my brain. I felt and heard my pulses. It was with great effort I forced myself to continue. Not even the dizzy sensation that I now felt—probably an aftereffect of the drug—would stop me. I was determined.

The first floor was as silent and cold as the second. With the taller ceilings, the shadows seemed even more ominous. I looked behind me, sure I was hearing sounds or steps. Perhaps it was just fear of what had happened before.

Reaching the door which I recalled was the study, I was frustrated to find it locked as it had first been earlier in the evening. I tried the knob once more. Then, I tried doors on either side. They, too, had been locked.

I cursed softly to myself. I would have to try again—perhaps tomorrow. I was going to read the family Bible. I was going to find out the secret of my heritage.

Disappointed, I returned to my room. There seemed little I could do this night, and my head was aching.

As I blew out the candle, I again saw the letters carved in the wall. Did the death of my aunt have anything to do with the Bible? With my own secret? I did not know, but my instincts told me they did.

I did not leave my room the following day but pleaded a recurrent feeling of illness. Whoever had dragged me away from the office knew I was not ill, but I did not care. I wanted to think, to plan, to decide what it was I had to do. My uncle was the first person I needed to speak with, but he seemed so incoherent and filled with drink, I wondered if he could even communicate his thoughts. Therefore, I had to alter my plans.

Tilly was solicitous of me during the day. I wondered if she understood the situation, but if she did, she gave no indication.

The next day was, I knew, the Sabbath. I would be expected to go to church with my family. At least, Tilly implied it. I wondered whether my cousins would dare attend the holy service, with the way they were treating me.

I sighed. No, they were not being evil, I told myself. They were trying to be pleasant—both of them. Or perhaps it was just one of them. I wish I knew who it was who had drugged me and then I would know how to proceed.

I dozed on and off the rest of the day.

Waking early on Sunday morning, I realized once again, I was up before the others. Quickly, I washed with the water still in the basin, just as I had done two days before. Only this time, I planned not to go toward the house and brook but toward Peter's. If he was about, I would confront him with my suspicions and see if he still wore the ring.

Having decided on my course of action, I hastily dressed in a gingham cotton dress and shawl. It was old but serviceable.

Downstairs once more, it was too much of a temptation not to try the office door once more. As I suspected, it was still locked. Well, whatever was in the office, I would find another time.

Letting myself out the back door, I held it so it would not slam.

It amazed me at how much freer I felt just being outside, just being away from the mansion.

Taking a deep breath, I felt my head clear as I looked in the direction of the wooded path. This time, I would know where I was going. This time, I would not make the mistake of the wrong turn. This time, I would reach Parkland Manor without losing anything, I told myself.

Even as I started on the path, however, I knew I was in danger of losing my heart. In fact, I feared I had already partially lost my heart to Peter Parkisham. I also feared he was part of this scheme to keep me from knowing who my real father was. I wondered—was I being naive? Did I really expect him to admit he had been the one in the library? The one at the brook? Did I really think he would tell me whatever he knew—just with my asking?

I had reached the gate which had barred my way the first night and heard the hinges creaking as I opened it. Shivers ran through me. For a moment more, I stood on the path and stared at the branches. I hoped my long sleeves would protect me more than they had the first night. It would take longer to go around by the road, and I glanced in that direction but decided I preferred the woods—dangerous as they were.

With light filtering in through the leaves, forming halos about several of the trees and shooting rays of morning sun onto the path, the woods looked more beautiful than I had seen them before. In fact, there was no hint of the menace I had felt the first night. Then, however, I had been lost and in dread of being out in the storm.

Lifting my skirts, I maneuvered my way over the fallen logs and branches. I realized in many ways I felt more lost than before. How could I be falling in love with someone I suspected was evil? How could I be falling in love with someone I suspected might even be related to me? Worse yet, how could I forget dear, loyal Joshua so easily?

Scarcely watching where I was going, I nearly repeated the same mistake I made the first night. Only by God's grace did I realize in time and pulled back. Heart pounding, I knew I had been thinking too much about Peter Parkisham and not about where I was walking. As my heart pounded, I walked away and promised myself I would ask both Terrah and Peter to put up some sort of gate there.

My face was flushed as I reached the clearing which started the Parkland lands. Staring out over the open area, I realized it was twice the space of Jerseyhurst. The gazebo, where we had taken shelter, stood proudly facing the hill and overlooking the cliffs of the Mississippi. It was just beyond the gazebo the land seemed to slope off and curve as it dropped again toward the river.

From the state of the grounds, it was obvious Parkland Manor was better kept and in a style more befitting the family's wealth than was Jerseyhurst. I wondered if Terrah was jealous.

Curious about the rest of the grounds—and suddenly dreading my hoped for meeting with Peter—I walked toward the gazebo. I wanted to see what the other part of the land looked like. I wanted to know if I could sense my mother's presence here as I had at the old house and the brook.

At the top of the hill, just near the gazebo, I paused. The view here was almost as breathtaking as the view from the widow's walk at Jerseyhurst. I could see for miles and miles as the Mississippi lazily snaked and curled its way down the riverbed. A breeze, soft and sweet, lifted the curls at the nape of my neck. For just a brief moment, I felt again like a child with a new toy. I recalled how Joshua and I had made hills of hay and how I used to love to run up them and tumble down the other side.

Unbidden laughter came to me. No one was about and I was going to run down this hill. I would, of course, stop at the end. Not thinking beyond the moment, I started my feet in motion, feeling the wind at my face and in my hair. It was a glorious, free feeling.

I scarcely heard the cry from Peter. In fact, I wasn't even aware of him until he grabbed my arm.

"My God! Stop! What do you think you're doing? If

you want to jump, then use the skylight like your aunt did."

I stared at him. "Jump? Who is jumping? You almost killed me just now. I'm not jumping, though I'm sure you and your people wouldn't mind."

His thick blond brows narrowed into almost one line. "Now what does that mean?"

The way he was looking at me nearly took my breath away. I fought to control the feelings raging inside of me. Quickly, I turned away, "I would have stopped over there, if you hadn't stopped me." I pointed and realized just how close we were to the edge of the cliff. Suddenly I was thankful for his presence but I would not admit it. He was being too smug, too self-centered.

"My dear Miss Swanson." A smile curved his lips. "There are other ways to enjoy one's self without endangering one's self like that." He waved his hand over the wide expanse of the view. "The cliff is *mur*derous." He emphasized the first syllable with a purr in his voice, and then he stared at me with an absorbing intensity in his eyes. "If you wish to survive at Jerseyhurst, you'll have to judge your adversaries with greater care."

I felt my green eyes widen as I stared up at him. "I told you, I was not jumping." I glanced down at his hand now. He did not wear the ring today but of course that didn't mean anything. My heart pounded. I tried to think of what I was going to say. I couldn't accuse him outright of trying to harm me, of hiding the secret of my father from me—could I? Mixed emotions flooded me. I saw he was impeccably dressed in tight trousers and a cutaway frock coat of pearl gray. Even the stiffness of his standing collar made him appear totally prudish and dandified. Only the unruliness of his blond hair, which refused to

101

stay equally parted, gave any hint of rebellion in him.

Was he ordered by someone else to harm me? Would he have accepted or refused? I continued to stare at him, to feel my own heart pounding like a blacksmith's hammer. They were sensations I had never experienced before. I could only recall how he had looked at the brook the other day, resting so peacefully and angelically.

I realized, he, too, was studying me in such a way that it made me more sure he had seen me at the brook and had attacked me. Like two shy children, neither of us said anything on the matter.

Trying to fight the annoying warmth surfacing in my body, a warmth I knew was being caused by his hand on my arms, I raised my chin higher. I would not allow myself to behave—I swallowed hard—as my mother did.

I raised my eyes to his. "You don't have to be concerned about me, Mr. Parkisham. I took care of the farm well enough when my mother was ill. I can take care of myself here."

His fingers touched my cheeks, causing the blood to rise in me, causing my heart to tremble. "There is quite a difference, Miss Swanson, between a farm in Kansas and a nest of vipers in Aberdeen."

"A nest of vipers?" My mouth was dry. "What—what do you mean?"

He smiled slightly, but the smile did not seem to reach his eyes. I saw him scrutinizing me as he had done before. "Just that you should be careful at Jerseyhurst. Your cousins are not happy at seeing you here."

"What do you know about my cousins? What do you know about my family? About my mother?"

Peter shrugged. He was still staring at me. "My family is what I know about—and they're concerned with

102

scandals. My father, Alexander Parkisham, is especially concerned. Since this happens to be Parkisham land you're on, since my father also owns a portion of Jerseyhurst land—"

He said no more for he must have seen my surprise. "I see Terrah didn't tell you all the facts."

I shook my head. "There is no reason she should. I don't care who owns what here. I told you once and I will tell you again: I came to Jerseyhurst to find out about my mother's past, to find out who my father is."

"I see. Your mother . . ." He tapped the tips of his elegant white hands together, "And your father."

His eyes were bluer than the lapis lazuli necklace Mother had once sold. Just the way he said those words made me think he knew something more than what he was telling me.

"Please, I must know. It's crucial to me. If you have any knowledge—"

Before I could continue the sentence, Peter Parkisham bent forward and kissed me on the brow. Stunned, I could only stare at him. He obviously took my lack of struggle as acquiescence on my part and put his lips to mine. An evil brew of thoughts stormed inside of me. I felt as if I were spinning through time and space, as if I were not here in Aberdeen but on some high clouds flying above the mountains and forests.

This time I did not need any drugs to make me feel faint. I knew I could have easily melted into his experienced arms, and yet I fought the feeling with all my might.

I forced myself to pull away. There was a part of me that was furious with Peter for taking his liberty with me and yet another part of me chided myself for being such

103

a prude. Peter's kiss had held a warmth and promise of something wonderful more to come, and had I not been so afraid of what the future might hold, I might have acted on impulse and given myself to him—then and there. It was only my mind chattering away which convinced me to hold back. He had tried to attack me at the brook and then again at the house. No, he could not be trusted with either my knowledge or my love.

Forcing my fury to come out, I glared at him. "I did not ask you for a kiss. I asked you if you had any knowledge."

Peter gave his casual shrug again. "The only knowledge I have is that you are a desirable young woman, and I wish to show you delights I am sure you've never experienced."

My mouth dropped open as I stared at him. "Tell me, would you be so crass in your proposition if I were a highfalutin lady like my cousin, Terrah? Just because I was raised on a farm—"

He took me into his arms a second time. This time his kiss was more forceful, his lips bruising, demanding. His tongue parted my lips, touching me as I had never been touched before. His arms stroked the muscles at the back of my neck and I found myself relaxing into his arms. I found, to my own horror, enjoyment in his kiss. His hands stroked my hair, sending shivers of anticipation through me. I wanted this moment to continue and yet— I had to stop it. I did not want what it would bring. I did not want to be falling in love with a man who had tried to harm me, who might easily be my brother.

"I have no desire to offend you, Miss Larabee." He gave a low bow. "I would have said the same to any woman I desired as much as I desire you." His fingers touched my tender lips, sending shivers through me. "I truly wish I had the answers to your questions, but I do not. Now, if you'll excuse me . . ."

I felt myself stiffen as he turned and began to walk away. Was he just going to leave me with those confused emotions? Oh, why hadn't mother confided in me? I glared at his disappearing figure.

I had expected the people of Aberdeen to be more sophisticated in the ways of the world, in the ways of fashion, but I had not expected them to be concerned with the possibility of scandal. It was a prosperous river town, but if his attitude was how one prospered, I was just as happy being a poor-relation cousin.

Peter's attitude was so typically dandyish. Had I something to throw at his back, I would have done so. As it was, my body felt strangely alive. It tingled with the pressure of his touch, with the momentary feeling of his closeness. I knew I could not be in love with someone like him. Love was not so complicated. You didn't love a man one moment and despise him the next. Love was—what I felt for Joshua.

From a distance there floated out the sound of church bells.

"Damn!" I cried out loud. Turning, I fled back along the path to Jerseyhurst. "Damn!" I said again, leaping over a fallen log in my way and not caring if I tore my skirt a second time. I could not be late for church. Not now.

Chapter Six

Tilly was in my room waiting as I ran in breathlessly.

"Where you been, girl? Don't you know the whole house been a searchin' fer you?"

"I'm—I'm sorry, Tilly. I just went for a walk and forgot about the time."

"Forgot? Forgot? You so perfect you can forgot yourself 'bout church?"

I flushed, recalling what had happened only moments ago. I was hardly perfect then. Strangely, I did not feel soiled as I had when David had touched me. Nevertheless, I knew the enjoyment from his kiss was wrong. I knew—relation or no—I had to stay away from Peter Parkisham. Even if he wasn't in this conspiracy to keep me from learning about my mother's past, I had to stay away from him.

"It will only take me a moment to dress, Tilly. Really, it will."

"It better. Miz Terrah don' like bein' late fer church. Youse t'leave the house in half hour exact."

I nodded and turned toward the pitcher of clean water

which the undermaid had just brought up. Stripping quickly, I began to wash. "I'll be ready, I promise."

Tilly grunted and left the room. Even as she closed the door behind her, my stomach growled. I had not eaten anything this morning and had eaten very little these past few days. Well, there was no time to think about food now.

I went to the dresser. My gray tabby had not yet been repaired, but my cherry silk and muslin were both in passable condition. The bunching around the neck could have been fresher and there was still a stain on one leg-of-mutton sleeve. Still, silk was the best I had for church. I had a moment of jealousy thinking of all the dresses Terrah must have to choose from, yet I did not think all of Terrah's money made my cousin's disposition any sweeter.

At least, I thought, unfolding the cotton chemise from my trunk at the foot of the bed, my underclothes would be fresh.

I had barely slipped into the dress when Tilly returned with a tray of food. My eyes widened. "How did you know what I wanted?"

"Honey, there ain't much youse can hide from ol' Tilly. I knew yer mother like the back of my hand. Assume youse a lot like her."

I felt my breath coming sharply. I was a lot like my mother, but I hoped there was one way in which I would be different.

Quickly, I ate the toast and eggs and drank the coffee while she waited to button me up. Shaking her head as she eyed the spot on my dress she said, "You should have better n'this for church. Rose is gonna get a whoppin'. She should've cleaned this right."

"Please Tilly. It's not her fault. I—believe it was just a

108

difficult spot. This is the dress I wore on my trip."

"And it was yer Mama's, too, weren't it? You cut it down."

I nodded. "I think I'd best hurry. I—Tilly, what do you know about Peter Parkisham?"

Tilly frowned. "I knows you should stay away from him. He's trouble with a capital *T*!" She quickly finished buttoning me and left the room before I could question her more.

I went downstairs, immediately following her. It surprised me to see Terrah and David already in the carriage. My cousin glared at me as if I had done the most odious thing. I felt myself flushing. Surely, she couldn't know about this morning.

"Haven't you a bonnet to wear, Elizabeth?"

I met her haughty eyes with an equal stare. "Of course I have a bonnet, but not for this dress."

"Then you shouldn't be wearing that dress. Don't you know? It's very low class not to wear a bonnet in church."

I stared at her. "No, I did not know."

She grinned at me with her superior smile. "Well, now you do. Tilly!" She clapped her hands. "Bring down my gray and cherry bonnet for my cousin to wear."

"But, Miz Terrah—"

"Do as I say, Tilly."

"Yes, Miz." Tilly disappeared back up the stairs. It was only as the housekeeper returned with the bonnet—one hopelessly out of fashion—that I realized what my cousin was up to. My dress was, of course, not in fashion, yet it was still stylish to a point with the trimmings and additions I had made. There was nothing which could make this bonnet acceptable.

"I'd rather not wear a bonnet than wear that."

Terrah stamped her foot childishly. I assumed it was her method of getting her way. "You must have a bonnet if you're going to church."

I shrugged. "Then I won't go to church. It won't be the first time."

Terrah stared at me, horrified. "You cannot remain in my house and not attend church. I would be the laughing stock of the community."

"Is that all you ever think about, cousin?" I glanced at Tilly. "Since my cousin wishes me to wear something, maybe you should bring down the black bonnet I wore for Mother's funeral. Living in this house, that would be fitting."

Terrah gasped. "You can't do that!"

"Why not?" I smiled sweetly at her, using her same honeyed tones. Two could play the same game.

"Because you—"

"Terrah, either I wear my own bonnet or I wear nothing. In my church, we did not need to keep our hair covered. It was sufficient we worshipped the Lord."

My cousin's eyes widened a moment. Then she backed down. Turning abruptly on the heel of her boot, arm on the strap, she said, "Get in the carriage. I don't want to be late."

Tilly was poker faced but as I passed her wearing the black bonnet, I saw her smile.

Inside the carriage, I was surprised to see my uncle huddled against the door and covered with a blanket.

He stared at me blankly as if he did not recall who I was. My heart went out to him. His rheumy blue eyes showed nothing of the handsome man which mother had described her brother to be. I glanced at my cousins and bit my lower lip.

While I would have loved to talk with Uncle Hayward, it seemed now was not the proper time. No, I would have to wait for a moment when we were alone. If that moment ever came.

The tension was strained as we drove toward the white spiral church. I almost asked if I could sit up with the driver, but I knew my cousin would definitely disapprove.

As it was, the drive was only a matter of ten minutes or so. The church was located at the end of a long and rather prosperous-looking street. I saw a bank, printing house, and several shops, not to mention boats tied up at the river dock.

I can't say I was surprised we were sitting in the front pew. Nor was I surprised to see Peter and his family sitting directly across from us.

I knew I should be listening to the prayers and the sermon, but all my thoughts dwelt on the wickedness of this morning, on how I had felt with his kiss, with his body pressed to mine.

Several times I saw him looking at me, smiling at me. My heart thumped—too loudly, I was sure. I would not acknowledge him. Despite my attention to Peter and the flush of my body, I could not help but notice the portly man who sat next to Peter. He looked familiar but for the life of me, I couldn't place him. Nor could I help notice the attractive woman and young child who sat on the other side of Peter.

I knew I should not have felt jealous, yet I did. Was he married as well as inciting me and philandering with

111

Terrah? I stared at Terrah and wondered what she was feeling and thinking. Still, from what I had seen of my cousin, I wouldn't put it past her to have an affair with a married man. No matter how much his touch might excite me, I could never consider such a dreadful thing.

I continued staring at the woman and little girl even as I heard the minister's fire and brimstone speech. The talk of how we should be grateful for small favors seemed directly aimed at me. I wondered if Terrah had told him about me, if Terrah had said she didn't feel I was appreciative enough of my stay at Jerseyhurst. I glanced at my cousin and decided it didn't matter what she thought—as long as I found out who my father was.

I was relieved when the service was over. So apparently was the little girl sitting with Peter. She ran outside as soon as the minister stepped down from the dais. I was tempted to follow her, but I knew I had to follow customs and trail out behind my cousin and the rest of the family.

Meekly, I did what was expected of me. Silently, I vowed I would come to this church as little as I could. I did not like the cold eyes of the minister, nor did I like the way he was looking at me.

It was our turn to shake hands at the door when I saw the little girl again. Horrified, I watched as she started to climb aboard the spirited bay, now prancing toward the post. My farming instincts told me this was not a horse to be played with. I felt my heart pounding as I watched her. Quickly, I glanced about. Where was Peter? Where was the girl's mother? She shouldn't be allowed to play like that.

112

Fear rose in my throat and knotted there as I moved quickly out of the line and heard the murmurs behind me. I knew I had committed a faux pas by not staying in line, not letting the minister shake my hand, but I couldn't let anything happen to the child. Even as I moved forward, the horse reared. I gasped. The child was grasping for dear life. Instinctively, I began to run, lifting my skirts as I did so. With my running, the horse began galloping faster. I began to fear I would never catch him.

A shout behind told me Peter was also running, but I was closer to the horse than he was.

I knew what I was about to do was daring and would injure me if I didn't do it right, yet I had no choice. The child was clinging to the mane and she was in danger. Nearly breathless, I made one final burst and lunged at the reins of the animal. For one fraction, my heart seemed to stop as I feared I had missed my hold and would be trampled by the pounding feet. Then, suddenly my pinkie finger caught in the leather bit strap.

Still, the horse galloped on. The rough hairs of the mane were hitting my face, making sight nearly impossible. I hung on for all my worth as I felt myself being dragged along the rough road. Tears came to my eyes and choked my throat. Now was the time for me to pray, not when I was in the stuffy church. The words would not form in my mouth, but I could only concentrate on my mother and recall the horses running away with her, of her hanging on for dear life, and her gruesome death as she became bloodied and trampled. Fear chilled me. I could not let go. I could not let the same thing or worse happen to this little girl. I could not let it happen to myself. My arms seemed about out of their sockets. I did not know how much longer I could go on. If I dropped now I would surely be trampled to death.

"Mother, please!" It was the only thing I could think of. It was the only prayer I could say.

As if by miracle, the horse snorted and began to slow. I continued to hang on, knowing to let loose now, even at this moment, would surely kill me. I could hear noises behind me but could concentrate only on the pain in my arms, on keeping my hold.

I felt a pull at the other side of the reins and saw Peter Parkisham grabbing onto the right side of the bit.

Finally, the horse stopped and snorted once more. Peter let go of his side and took the crying child into his arms. I was only vaguely aware of others running up, of the girl going in her mother's arms. Other hands touched mine.

"You can let go now, Elizabeth."

I realized I was still hanging on to the bridle, still gripping the horse's reins. With a sigh, I let go and felt Peter Parkisham put his arms about me. I let my tears go, cascading down my cheeks. For just a brief moment, I felt safe and content.

He carried me to my cousin's carriage even though I protested I could walk. "I doubt it," Peter replied. "You're probably sore as can be." He touched my face gently and it seemed, in front of everyone, he kissed my brow. I felt the flush creep up my face. I could almost imagine what my cousin and the rest of the town was thinking. "Never have I seen anyone run so fast."

"She could have been killed." I tried to keep my voice calm but his holding me was all I could think of now. My arms continued to clasp about his neck as his eyes narrowed. Our eyes met.

"Please, don't take such chances, Miss Swanson.

That's not to say I'm not glad you saved my niece—"

"She's your niece?"

"Yes, of course. What did you think?"

Again, a flush came over me. I shook my head, relieved I had been wrong—at least in this instance.

"I think you should have a greater care. There are enough problems for you to worry about at Jerseyhurst without creating others."

He let me down by the carriage. I wanted to ask him what he meant but now was not the time.

Terrah, David, and my uncle were already in the carriage waiting for me.

"Well, it's about time you returned. I might have known you would embarrass me in front of the minister and the whole community."

I glared at Terrah. "I don't call it an embarrassed thing to save someone's life."

Terrah snorted much as the horse had and rapped on the roof for the driver to start home.

I was probably lucky to be alive. Nevertheless, my arms ached and I was sore from where I had bumped along the path. David had wanted to carry me up to my room but, not trusting him, I had refused and hobbled up myself—only to find Tilly there waiting for me.

"Why did ya have t'run after dat horse?"

"Tilly, I'm surprised at you asking such a question. That little girl was in danger."

"Mastuh Peter would've gotten it. He came close for sure."

"He came close, but I reached it first."

"'Tain't right. 'Tain't ladylike. Youse most as

115

headstrong as your mama were. Youse better watch yerself with Miz Terrah. She be a good child, but she does have a temper. Miss Georgiana done say—" Tears came quickly to Tilly's cowlike eyes. She blinked them away. "Neber mind now. I gots permission fer you to have a bath."

"A bath? On Sabbath?"

"On Sabbath. Lordy, girl, you can't be presented at tea, the way you be. Not with Mr. Alex n' Mr. Peter n' all comin'."

The chills quickly covered my body. Peter was coming here. Not that he hadn't been here a million times before. I was sure the neighbors were constantly visiting, and yet it felt strange to have him coming here now.

What was I going to do? Each time I saw him seemed to drive the nails deeper into my heart as I realized there was no hope for my dreams. I had to stop seeing him. I had to prevent this attraction I was feeling for him. I knew if he continued to touch me, I would end up like my mother, only far worse.

The huge wooden tub was brought into the room and placed at the foot of the bed. I stepped in and felt the warmth burn at first. Then as I sank into the waters, I began to feel some relief from the pain.

Tilly's mouth set into a thin line as she watched me. "I knows I told youse 'bout Miz Terrah and Mistuh Peter bein' 'most engaged. I just wants to make sure youse knows it good."

I stared at her—about to protest my innocence. After all, Peter had kissed me. I hadn't flung myself at him, and she had been walking with another man. The understanding couldn't be that strong, or could it. It didn't make sense to me. Nor did it make sense the way Peter affected me.

116

I forced myself to look up into Tilly's caring face. "You don't have to worry about me, Tilly. I've a beau back home. I'll be returning to Joshua just as soon as I've talked to my uncle."

"What you say his name was?"

"Joshua. Joshua Harmon."

"Harumph!" Tilly grumbled. "That's what I thought you did say, baby child. Just you listen to ol' Tilly now. Men is—well men is not always what they seem."

"Oh, Joshua is. I've known him since childhood. He's a sweet fellow."

Tilly shrugged her massive shoulders. "Just you return to that sweet fellow back in Kansas afore it be too late."

"Too late for what?"

I rose from the water, and she helped me dry with a soft, fluffy towel. "Just you go afore too much happen. Give up your 'dea of findin' your father, baby girl. Won't do you no heap o'good if you ain't round to be with him."

A shiver ran through me. I turned to stare at her. "Tilly, you know more than you are letting on." The thick lips were now a thin line. "Tilly." My hands were on her shoulders. "I want to know. Who was my mother keeping company with?"

Her brow lifted. "Why, with Mastuh Zebulon. 'Course."

I took a deep breath, determined to win this battle of wits. "No, Tilly, I mean before that. My mother was pretty. She wasn't seeing only Zebulon. Wasn't there anyone special before Papa, I mean? It wasn't Zebulon who gave her the brushes. I know that."

Tilly shook her head. "It be so long ago. Iz don't 'member." Tears came quickly to her eyes, and she brushed them away as she picked up my cherry silk—

117

once more in need of cleaning. "Youse can't wear this t'tea. I'll find somethin' of Miz Terrah's or maybe of your mama's t'fit you."

She left the room before I could ask her anything more.

With just my dressing gown on, I walked to the window and looked out over the ravine and the cliff. Restlessly, I twisted my hands. My thoughts were a jumble of confusion. I wanted to get to know Peter Parkisham, and yet I did not trust him. How could the two go hand in hand? How could I be falling in love with someone who seemed not to have my best interests at heart?

I glanced at the woods again. They looked so green and peaceful in the sunlight. I wished right now I was out there, walking along the cliff, walking through the woods, as I had been this morning. I did not want to go to tea. I did not want to see Peter again, not after this morning.

The smile came unbidden to my lips. I wondered how he had felt being bested by a female this morning. Of course, it hadn't been a real contest. Anyone would have tried to save the girl, I told myself. I was just astounded it had been Peter. Apparently, he wasn't the dandy I believed him to be. In fact, he had run far faster than even Joshua could run.

Forcing my thoughts from Peter, I thought of Joshua. Including my journey, it had been nearly ten days since I had left him. I knew I should write but what could I say? That I had no information, that I was falling in love with someone else—someone whom I suspected might even be my half brother.

118

Twisting my hands, I paced again and decided the best thing would be to write and tell Joshua I planned on staying longer than the three weeks agreed upon. With the time nearly half done, I was nowhere near discovering what I wanted. I would not leave 'til I had.

Sitting at the small writing table, I took out the quill and ink. I would write Joshua now.

Even as I thought about it, my mind went blank. What exactly would I say? I nibbled the tip of the quill. Ink dropped in a huge splotch on the vellum. I grimaced. I did not like wasting paper, but I had to say my words perfectly so Joshua would not get the wrong impression.

Finally, I penned a simple note telling him I was staying longer and nothing else. If he had any arguments, I was sure they would come by return post. Wondering what was taking Tilly so long and feeling anxiety over my meeting with Alexander Parkisham, the man I suspected of being my father, I sealed the letter to Joshua with hot wax.

A knock at the door made me turn. "Come in, Tilly."

Immediately, the huge red figure of David filled my door.

"What do you want?" I spun about in my chair, grasping the edges of my robe tighter. "Get out of my room."

"You invited me in, cousin." He came boldly forward.

I clamped my hand over the ink well. It was the first thing I could grab. "I thought you were Tilly. Get out of here!" I ordered him once more.

He smiled at me. His crooked yellow-stained teeth showed. "All the better for me." With that he threw a dress on the bed. I hadn't even noticed him carrying

119

it before. "Actually, Terrah sent me with this for you."
He smiled again. The man was actually enjoying my
discomfort.

Grasping the ink well firmly, I stepped back, wishing
now I had the poker or even my gun.

He did not move from the bed where he stood. Hands
on his hips, he gave a lewd grin. "Tell me, little cousin,
have you ever had a man?"

I flushed, averting his steady gaze. Clenching my teeth
with anger surging through me, I said firmly, "I want you
to leave this room!" My voice quivered only slightly as I
hurled the bottle at him.

David ducked. The glass smashed against the opposite
wall, staining it just above the scratch marks. It was like
blood, dripping down. David took a step forward.

"I'll scream if you don't leave."

"No one will come. They'll think it's my father."

"Oh, yes they will," Tilly cried, entering the room
behind him. "Git outta here, Mastuh David. An don't
you come in 'gain, less you're invited!"

David glanced at Tilly and then at me. Grinning like a
death's-head, he gave a slight bow. "I was invited once,
Tilly. I will be again." Smiling again, he turned and
slammed the door behind him.

I stared at the vibrating wood. What was happening?
First Peter and now him; I shivered, fearing the great
attraction I held for these men was more than for just my
beauty. If only I knew who I really was; if only I knew
who my father really was.

Still numb, I was barely aware of Tilly's putting her
arms about me. The tears began to fall then.

"Honey, child, you've gotta learn t'be more careful
with Mastah David. He try to be a good boy but

sometimes, he find it hard."

"Dear Tilly," I sniffled. "I don't think you see evil in anyone."

She hugged me closer and rocked me a bit. "Try not to." Giving me a smothering hug, she left me with instructions I was not to open the door to anyone but the maid who could come to clean up the mess the ink had made. I had one hour, she said, to be in the formal parlor. It was two now. That was just one hour to think and prepare, to try and understand what exactly was happening to me.

Chapter Seven

I waited until I heard Tilly's footsteps fade away. Then quickly I dug my portmanteau out of the back of the armoire. Straining, feeling the ache and pull of still sore muscles, I lifted my case out. After a moment's search, I removed my father's revolver. The heavy weight in my hand gave me a secure feeling. It was so beautiful and smooth.

I recalled the evenings when Zebulon would sit in his chair, taking apart the gun, piece by piece, then cleaning and oiling it. It was he who had taught me to shoot.

Of course, I would never be as good as he, but at least if I had the gun with me no man would take me unawares—not David, not Peter.

It upset me that both Peter and David obviously thought lightly of me because I was a poor relation. David's obnoxiousness I could understand but Peter's made my heart want to cry.

I stared at the gun and felt a chill. Then, I carefully laid it in the drawer of my nightstand, hidden beneath a pile of linen chemises.

Taking a deep breath, I felt my heart still pounding. Yes, having the gun there, within reach of the bed, was the right thing.

Having relieved my anxiety I now glanced at the dress which had cost me so much trouble. It was a prune-colored taffeta with a cream-colored underskirt. The bustle showed it to be many years old and not as crisp as it should have been, but it was still more stylish than my cherry silk had been. I noticed, too, that the cuff edges of the prune dress were badly frayed. Then I noticed the distinct odor of cedar on the dress.

I sighed. Finding some rose talc, I sprinkled it liberally on the inside of the dress. It didn't totally take away the smell of cedar, but at least it made it better.

Slipping the gown over my head, I realized it would have been some time since my cousin had been slim enough to fit into this outfit.

I stared at the gown in the mirror. There had to be something I could do to make it more attractive. My glance fell on my nightdress. Did I have time? Well, I would make the time. Detaching the length of red ribbon from my nightgown, I patiently resewed it onto the exposed edges. As the grandfather clock boomed three, I did up the last bit of ribbon and hurried to put the dress back on. Just thinking of Peter made my lips and cheeks turn scarlet. Nevertheless, despite my fears that Peter's attention to me was based on other motives, and that he was not the gentleman he appeared to be, I still pinched my cheeks and wished for some rouge. I was sure Terrah had rouge. She was the type.

Twisting my hair back, I braided it so it would make me look older than my twenty years. I slammed the door behind me and took the steps two at a time. Only as I

124

reached the second landing, did I slow down to a more ladylike gait. Tilly would have a heart attack if she found me running.

The butler had just answered the door when I reached the first landing. I could see Peter as well as several others behind him, but my vision was obstructed by the glare from the colored glass above the hallway.

It wasn't until I stepped down a few steps that I saw the others: the man who had sat next to Peter at church, as well as two women, and the little girl. My glance returned to the older man. He looked so familiar but I couldn't place him. I swallowed the pain in my throat as I realized suddenly: This was Alexander. My heart pounded as I grasped the rail to steady myself. I knew he was the same man who had come to our farm a few months ago—just days before the accident which had killed my mother. Only now did I think of him. Could he have—done something? But no, I couldn't very well suspect a man of murder just because he had come to visit us. My skin prickled like a cat with an arched back. I hadn't liked the man then. I did not like him now.

As he came forth, his profile was exaggerated by the lights and shadows in the hall, making him look more menacing. I held myself still as the second shock of the moment hit me. He was the same man who had been in the gardens with Terrah. I was almost sure.

Taking a deep breath, I held the rail for stability. I continued to the ground floor.

"Oh, you look so pretty!" The little girl I had saved came forth and hugged my legs. I was formally introduced to her now as being Karen Waterford, daughter of Harriet, the stately younger woman with us. Harriet, it seemed, was Peter's sister and just recently had returned to town with the death of her husband.

Glad of the momentary diversion, I bent to embrace the girl. "Hello. All recovered from your ride this morning, I see."

Karen grimaced. Putting her hands behind her, she nodded and glanced toward her uncle.

Harriet approached me now. I noticed she looked nothing at all like Peter. She was dark where he was fair, and yet there was a similarity in manner. I was glad, indeed, she was a sister and not a competitor—and then I told myself how silly I was being. Peter would be here long after I had gone back to Kansas—or wherever I was headed. I was sure he would forget me quickly, despite his sweet words this morning.

"I don't think you've been properly thanked yet," Harriet said.

I forced myself to look at her and not at Peter. "Just seeing her safe is proper thanks." I smiled down at the girl still hugging my legs.

"Oh, but we must find some way to repay you."

"No," I said, trying to be firm. "I don't want any payment."

It was Peter who took the step forward now. His hand touched my hand so that I shivered. His meaning was obvious to me.

"You will have payment. I will see you do."

I felt myself flushing. I hoped no one else had caught his meaning as I had.

From her expression, I could tell Terrah was upset I had interrupted her. Glaring at me she continued making introductions. I turned my attention toward her. Mr. Alexander Parkisham held out his hand to me. I stared at him for a moment and wondered if I should speak;

curiosity forced me to say what was on my mind. "Did you enjoy your journey back to Illinois, Mr. Parkisham?"

The heavy pepper brows knitted together. His face was plumper than Peter's and had a simian aspect, I thought. There was, in fact, a marked difference between the two men. Peter held himself with a natural grace—like a lion, like someone who belonged in a position of wealth.

His father, on the other hand, seemed almost apish as he tried to make himself seem what he was not.

Mr. Parkisham still had not answered my question. It seemed as if he was staring at me in an effort to intimidate me.

"Tell me, what journey do you refer to, child? I make many journeys in my business."

I continued to stare back at him. Even the voice was the same. Yes, there was absolutely no doubt in my mind he was the same man. "Your trip home from Kansas. After you visited Mother and me."

He smiled at me, but it was a smile a snake might gave its victim before it's ready to bite. His eyes were blue like Karen's and Peter's. Unlike either of them his eyes remained icy.

"I'm afraid, Miss Larabee, you are quite mistaken. It's true. I did briefly know your mother when she lived here many years ago, but—" He shrugged. "I've never been West." His voice was firm in his denial. He lied. I knew he lied by the twitching of the muscle in his cheek.

Behind him a fluttery, frail woman with a birdlike voice emerged, as if from the woodwork, to agree with me.

"But Alexander, you did go West—once."

"Ella." He glared at her. "I have never been to Kansas.

That is what this young woman means."

Terrah broke in, placing her arm through the crook of Peter's elbow. "I believe our tea is getting cold. Shall we go in? We can discuss this later." She made a vague gesture, but I doubted the conversation would ever return to this topic—voluntarily.

Alexander Parkisham took his wife's arm. David reached for me, but I quickly moved away. He took Harriet's instead. Like a lost sheep, I tagged along holding onto little Karen. At least she was safe and wanting nothing more of me than to be my friend.

At the beginning of the tea, I was unable to take my eyes off Alexander, but I soon decided it would accomplish nothing. If, indeed, he had visited us; if indeed, he was my natural father—though I could scarcely believe my mother would fall in love with him—I had nothing to gain by exposing him here. No, I did not want any gain. All I wished for was to know who I was.

Trying to forget his presence, I forced myself to relax with Karen. We discussed the best type of tea for her doll to have.

"Uncle Peter says Lily likes jasmine tea.

I smiled at the little girl, realizing here was a side of Peter I hadn't seen, nor expected to see.

"Do you and your uncle often have tea parties?"

Karen's front teeth were missing. She returned my smile as she sucked in her breath. "Sometimes." She glanced at him wistfully. "When he's not with a lady."

I pressed my lips together, trying not to think of my feelings as I poured more tea for us. It would be typical of a dandy like Peter Parkisham to have several women hanging about him, even when he was supposedly ready to announce his engagement to my cousin. I felt a sharp pang as I glanced toward them sitting on the love seat together.

I hated myself for my thoughts. I hated Terrah for not being true to him.

As if he knew we were discussing him, Peter rose from the place next to Terrah and strolled over to me. "You are looking quite lovely this afternoon, Miss Larabee. I'm glad to see you've recovered from this morning."

Despite my aches, I nodded. Terrah bristled, almost as if she knew about our meeting by the cliff, about our kisses, as well as about the church incident. I felt myself redden. David, too, was watching me intently—but then he probably watched anything in a skirt.

Nodding slightly toward my cousins, I acknowledged Peter's comment with a turn of my head. I didn't trust myself to answer. I hated him for the mixed emotions he excited in me. If Alexander Parkisham was truly my father, then there could be nothing for us but friendship. I pressed my lips together and tried to forget how many times I had heard Mama mention the name Parkisham. There had to be a reason. If Alexander wasn't my father, then why did she have a light in her eyes every time the name was mentioned?

I glanced again toward Peter from under my dark lashes. One did not think of a friend the way I was thinking about Peter Parkisham! Even in the face of all he had done to annoy me, my thoughts constantly returned to him. It was maddening.

I looked down at the multi-hued carpet, feeling the color flood me. Harriet broke the silence. "Didn't you once have a piano? Why doesn't someone play?"

Terrah sipped her tea, replying coolly, "Ever since poor dear Mama died, we've given up music. Besides,

Cousin Elizabeth is also in mourning."

I gave Terrah an innocent smile. "Music doesn't bother me. Mother would be sad if she knew I had given up the joy of the melody for her sake."

David grinned. "Terrah, you know you couldn't stand Mama, and anyway it's been almost two years since she died."

It was my turn to stare at David. How could he speak to his sister with such little respect. It took only a few moments of studying him to realize that, despite the fact it was Sunday, my cousin was as drunk as his father.

Peter smiled, addressing me as he cocked his head. I could feel his eyes boldly assessing me. Was he, too, recalling our kiss this morning? A tingling sensation rose inside me.

"Terrah's playing leaves much to be desired. Do you play, Elizabeth?"

I swallowed hard and stared up at him, meeting his eyes. Why was my heart beating so loudly? This man was probably my brother! But then he didn't know.

"Well, do you?"

It was Alexander who spoke up now. "Your mother, I believe, used to play passably well."

"I—yes—she did play and—she taught me as well." My voice, I found, was not sounding like my own. It was as if I were not here. I could barely speak over the rushing of my blood. How in heaven's name could I be reacting this way?

"And just what did she teach you on?" Terrah sneered. "I thought you were poor."

I cast my eyes down. "We—were. Mother often took me when she taught lessons to her clients. I learned at the same time on their pianos, and then she also continued my lessons on an old piano we had at home. It had been given to us by a client who decided she did not have the talent to play."

"Well, then," Alexander said and slapped his knee in a very ungentlemanly fashion, "let's hear something." He glanced at Terrah, and even though his wife was in the room, he placed his hand over the back of the love seat where he sat near his mistress—for I could only interpret the gestures I had seen between them in this colored light. He shifted his body toward her, verifying my suspicions. "It has been a long time since there has been any gaiety in this house, Miss Swanson." He smiled at Terrah and I knew he was silently communicating something to her, but I did not know what. I only knew I felt uncomfortable with the pair of them. "You ought to have a ball to welcome your cousin to Aberdeen."

His lewd smile turned to me now, and I felt a shiver go up my spine. Was this his way of acknowledging me? Perhaps privately, he would meet with me and explain why he had done what he had, why he had not done the honorable thing and married Mother. I avoided his eyes for the moment.

Yes, I realized. I was a bit disappointed this man should be my father. I had hoped Mother would have had better taste. But I had to accept what obviously was. I decided then and there. I would not demand he acknowledge me publicly—not if he didn't want to. I would demand that he only tell me the truth about my heritage.

Beside me, I felt Peter stiffen at his father's suggestion of a ball. He had been staring at the fireplace—at the red and gold flames which merrily nibbled at the logs—and, without looking at me, took my hand. His movement shocked not only me but the company as well.

131

Peter smiled at his father, as if he knew what he was doing. I wished I was also privy to his plans. I wished I knew what the others in the room were thinking as well, but I could only guess.

Peter's voice was soft as he continued holding my hand. "I don't think it right for there to be a ball in Elizabeth's honor. Not with her mother so recently in the ground."

I started to protest. Although I suspected Alexander's motives for deciding this, it would be exciting to have a ball for me. I had never been to a formal ball and certainly had never had one just for me. The only time I had ever danced was at the county fairs and then only with Joshua.

Thinking of my dear friend made me flush with shame. How could he be so easily gone from my mind? I wondered if I could ever go back to being content with him.

"Peter, my boy," Alexander said, his eyes narrowing. His brows became a heavy, hairy line. "We have already discussed this privately. A ball in honor of Elizabeth isn't necessary. She needn't come if she feels it improper for her. That will remain up to her." He paused, smiling for my benefit again, eliciting my feeling of distrust for this man. His eyes returned to his son.

"I think a ball would be lovely," Terrah cut in. Her voice was breathless as a fragile flower.

"But of course, Parkland is more suited for such things. We could have it there, couldn't we, Alex?" She smiled at him with the sweetness of a rotten apple. "I think Elizabeth would enjoy it. Wouldn't you, dear?"

I pressed my lips together, not knowing what to reply. I knew Peter did not want this ball. I could tell from his eyes, from the way he was looking at me. The flush rose to my face. Did he expect me to make the decision for him?

He spoke before I could, but I still felt his eyes on me. "Very well." His voice was gruff. "I give my consent."

Inside, I felt my stomach quivering. The nausea threatened to rise up and drown me. Obviously, Peter was being forced into something he didn't want to do. I wished, if only for the sake of our being related, I could help him. But what could I do?

Alexander grunted and nodded. "Good. Why not hear some music now? Let's get into the spirit of things."

He stood along with Terrah who held out her hand for Peter to return to her side. Glancing at me for just a moment, he did so. I wished I could read his eyes and know his thoughts just then.

The triple doors, which divided the formal sitting room from the music parlor where I had been the other day, now creaked as David pulled them back. It had been here that David had found me the other night. Even with the others here, it still had unpleasant memories.

Terrah walked over and opened the french doors which led to the gardens. March sunshine came in weakly since it was already late in the afternoon, but it did something to dispel the stuffiness of the room. As she sat down again she pulled the red velvet cord violently to summon Tilly.

When the housekeeper appeared, Terrah gave her order. "Teas are to be served here from now on. After today, this room will be cleaned and aired regularly."

Tilly's wide face broke into a grin. Pleased with the change, she nodded. "Yes, miz." Glancing at me as if I had done magic, she nodded and disappeared.

I don't know how I got through the rest of the tea. Terrah made sure both Peter and Alexander were by her side the whole time. I wondered if Peter knew she and his father were—well, I could not be the one to make accusations. Nevertheless, I thought the situation rather odd.

I was thankful to retire to my room and have a rest before dinner. Despite the warm soak before the tea, my muscles still ached and probably would for several days. Sighing, I lay on my bed with just my cotton chemise. If only I could find out who my father was. If only I could leave.

I glanced at the letters on the wall again and gently touched them. I had the distinct feeling there was more to my aunt's death than I was being told. That didn't concern me, did it? Would knowing more about my aunt help me in my quest for finding my father? Did I dare just go over to the Parkisham's and confront Alexander?

My head ached at the thought. I did not want to do anything which would cause Peter any trouble, and somehow I felt my talking to his father would do that.

Once again, I traced the lines of the letters. What would my uncle have to say to me—when he was able to talk? Would he have answers for me?

I sat upright in the narrow bed as the idea came to me. He had been to church with us this morning. Did it mean he was now sober? He had been sullen but he had been sober. I wondered if he had stayed so this afternoon. Terrah had said that her father would send for me when he was ready to talk—but I doubted that.

134

Quickly, I slipped on my brown dress again. My first action had to be discovering where Terrah was. It would do no good for me to find my uncle and have Terrah come in when I was speaking with him.

Even the noise of my dress rustling as I walked seemed to bother me. I stopped first in one room and then the other on the first floor. There was no sign of her. Of course, she could be outside, but twilight was already upon us and I did not think she liked the outdoors at night.

It was in the library/office I found her—the same room where I had been looking at the Bible, the room where I had been drugged. I pressed my lips together as I thought of the moment again—of the ring which I was sure I had seen. Had it been Peter? But surely he had nothing to gain by helping my cousins keep the secret from me—or did he?

Terrah was studiously absorbed with some books. She almost looked human with the specs perched on her nose. I prayed she would be busy for the rest of the hour—at least.

I turned swiftly, hoping my dress did not make as loud a noise as I thought my heart did. I needed to be silent. I needed to speak with my uncle, *now*.

Stomach tight, I made my way back up to the second floor. I recalled where my uncle's room was and probably should have just gone in—but fear made me pause. I felt as if someone was watching me. But no, there were only the eyes from the picture of my grandfather.

Holding my breath I placed my hand on the doorknob and turned it ever so slightly. Locked! They had my uncle locked in his room.

My own heart thumped in fear. What was I to do now?

Softly, I knocked, hoping it would get me some response from the inside, hoping against hope he would be sober enough to speak with me now.

The hollow sound of my knock seemed to echo in the halls, and in my ears—or was that the pounding of my blood? I knew my uncle's knowledge was crucial to my quest. I knew my cousins were purposely keeping him from me. If only I could make them understand. All I wanted was the knowledge—nothing more. Did they fear I would do something to harm them?

There was no sound from inside the room. Swallowing a lump in my throat, I knocked once more. Was my uncle a prisoner of his daughter?

I did not like the thoughts which were circulating in my head. I rapped once more. Surely, Uncle Hayward was there. He had to be. He was too ill to go anywhere.

The voice behind me startled me and brought the sweat to my brow and the lump of fear to my throat. It was Terrah. "Can I help you, cousin? My father is asleep now. Did you want to see him about anything in particular?" She smiled at me like a viper ready to bite.

I felt the flush jump to my skin as I turned to face her. "If he is asleep, why is he locked in?"

Terrah stared at me as if I were a ghost. Her eyes seemed to drill through my heart. "What did you want to see him about? I'm in charge of this household. I can tell you anything you wish to know."

"Can you? Can you, really?" I questioned her boldly. "Then why haven't you? You know why I've come to Jerseyhurst. You know I want to learn about my mother's life here. If you have facts which affect me, then tell me."

"I have nothing to say to you about your mother. My

136

father has no memory of those days. He has been ill for quite some time now. He has forgotten about your mother."

"That's not true," I confronted her, pulling her back when she tried to turn away. "He called me Margaret the first night I saw him. He does remember her. I want to talk to him."

"I'm sorry. I can't let you disturb him. He's a sick man."

"Yes." I glared at her. "I've seen how sick he is. He has the same illness your brother does."

Her eyes narrowed. "I don't like hearing talk about David in such a tone. I have just told you. My father is asleep. He cannot be bothered."

"Then when can he speak with me?"

Terrah gave her apish smile and, shrugging, turned away from me.

"I will wait as long as it's necessary to speak with him."

Again, she smiled. "Your wait might be a longer wait than you wish for, Elizabeth." Lifting her skirts, she brushed past me.

The pit of my stomach curdled like sour milk. There seemed nothing I could do at this moment. Nothing.

Upset, I started back toward my room. I had to think this through. There had to be something I could do. If nothing else, I would talk to Alexander Parkisham. I was determined I would do whatever it took to find my heritage.

I watched as Terrah started down the stairs, and I glanced back toward my uncle's room. No, it didn't do any good to try to see him now. I would wait. My moment would come. It had to.

It surprised me to find the door of my room open. I did not think I had left it ajar. I paused a moment and glanced about. Could David have come here? I wanted something to protect myself with, but there was nothing about. Edging closer to the door, I decided I would check out what was happening for myself. If I saw him there, I would return downstairs for Tilly. If not, it would be silly for me to burden her with my fears.

My mouth opened in shock as I saw, indeed, there was someone in my room. It wasn't David.

Anger surged through me as I pulled open the door, banging it against the panels. "What do you think you're doing?" I confronted Rose King.

She jumped, obviously startled. Quickly she placed the gun back in the nightstand drawer.

"I were just cleanin', miz." She glanced downward, unable to meet my eyes. "Just cleanin' as Mama told me to do."

"Liar!" I shouted at her. "You're a liar." The color washed my face like a wave of angry heat. "Why are you in my room and by whose order? I know Tilly wouldn't have told you to clean on the Sabbath!"

Rose wailed. "I swear by my word, miz. Mama done said—"

Attempting to hold my temper was not easy. My voice must have sounded calmer than I felt as furious thoughts rushed through me. "Even if your mother did order my room cleaned on a Sunday, I don't want to see you snooping in my drawers again. Get out of here Rose King!"

"I weren't—"

Unable to speak further, I advanced toward her.

She obviously saw my fury and, flinching, she turned

138

and fled the room.

Clenching my fist, I took a deep breath and sank down on the bed. My head ached furiously. First it had been the confrontation with Terrah and now this with Rose. What was happening in this house?

I pulled open the drawer and took the gun out. Lovingly, I touched it. Damn Rose! What had she wanted in here? I sighed and stared at the weapon. I knew I would have to find another hiding place for the gun now.

The metal felt smooth in my hand. I doubted Rose had been looking for the gun or even knew how to use it, yet she now knew I had a weapon. I was sure it was not a subject which would remain a secret in this house for long.

Slowly, I turned about the room, looking for someplace new to hide it. Someplace where, should I need it, it would be easily accessible.

The fireplace was made of brick. I stepped forward, staring at it. At home, the fireplace had several loose stones. As a child, I had often concealed my treasures there. Would I also be lucky here?

Bending down a moment, I felt along the rough edges of various bricks. The gritty sand reminded me of home.

It took several moments and two broken nails to locate a stone just below the splintered wooden mantel.

Elated, I pulled the brick loose without problem. The space behind it was much bigger and deeper than I had imagined it would be. It was almost as if someone had dug it out.

Carefully, I wrapped the gun in the linen handkerchief left here by Peter. I thought it fitting he should be protecting me in some way since it seemed he was partially at fault for my problems. Staring at the cloth in my hand, I shivered. No, Peter was not to be trusted and yet—I bit my lower lip as I tried to tell myself the attacker could have been someone other than him. With a sigh, I placed the gun in the space. The fit was perfect.

I replaced the brick and counted the spaces once more before trying to take the gun out again—just to check. Yes, it would be safe there. But was I safe here?

My heart aching, I sank down on the bed again and closed the nightstand drawer.

Eyes closed, I lay back. Was finding my father so important to me? Maybe I should give in and go back. It wasn't even just the people, it was this house as well. It seemed to be closing in on me. My heart ached like those songs of betrayal and sadness Mother used to sing. I had not counted on such hostility. I had never assumed there would be any problems. Why couldn't the family just welcome me and tell me the truth?

If only I had the money, I would leave Jerseyhurst tomorrow. But at the moment, I had nothing. No, I had to wait and speak with my uncle.

The room was shadowy dark now. I lit the lamp, wondering why the house seemed so silent. Dipping my washcloth in the basin, I realized just how tiring this day had been for me. Was I still ill, as Tilly said? Had I dreamed the Bible? Or had I really fainted as Tilly suggested? I had been in the office/library several times since the other night, and there was no Bible on the table, nor anywhere to be seen in the room. Was it just my fervent wish to have information about my father which could cause hallucinations?

Feeling chilled, I pulled the window shut. Then, blowing out the lamp, I settled into the eiderdown comforter, still awake. I had no desire to eat dinner this

140

evening. Would Tilly come up and speak with me? She had—every night so far—come up to see me in the evenings, and I did want to speak with her, but yawning drowsily, I decided it would have to wait for tomorrow.

I had wanted sleep to come immediately, to drown my thoughts, but it did not. Every time I closed my eyes, I saw the face of Alexander Parkisham without his moustache—just as he had been when he had visited us in Kansas several months before. It had been him. I knew it had.

Finally frustrated and in need of talking, I found my dressing gown. It was already past ten at night, I knew from the clock in the hall. It surprised me that Tilly hadn't come up at all, hadn't worried and nagged me about my not coming down to eat.

I decided I couldn't wait to talk with Tilly. Sleep would not come until I had resolved the problem in my mind. I didn't know if she would be able to tell me if Alexander had been out of town, but at least she would tell me if he had been walking out with my mother when she lived here. Surely, as close as they had been—as much as my mother had spoken of her—Tilly had to have known who the man was who had captured my mother's heart. Even if Mother hadn't confided details to her—surely, she would be able to make an educated guess.

Maybe Tilly didn't realize just how important it was for me to know. Maybe she thought it was just a foolish whim. I knew Joshua thought so.

Once I had made Tilly understand my desperate need, once I had told her I needed to borrow money from my uncle to return home, and that I would leave immediately thereafter, maybe then she would tell me. Maybe Tilly, herself, had some money saved she could lend me.

Terrah was right about one thing. I didn't want to stay around here any longer than I had to. I didn't like my mother's family any more than they obviously liked me. If they knew of my need, I was sure my cousins would give me the loan—only to get rid of me. But I had to stand firm on the issue. I could not leave until I had talked to my uncle, or until I knew for a fact that Alexander Parkisham was indeed my father.

Striking a match, I smelled sulfur as I applied the light to the wick. The match was still burning, the flames flickered weakly as I heard the screams.

My pulse quickened. I dropped the candle as my stomach tightened. I had no moment to think before stamping out the flame with my foot. Lighting another match, I ignored the charred spot on the rug.

I took a deep breath and put the candle on the stand so I wouldn't drop it a second time. I wondered what exactly affected my uncle and caused him to scream so. I was tempted to go and comfort him, but I was sure Terrah would be taking care of him. Besides, I knew she would not let me speak with him now, and I had something far more important to do. I had to find Tilly. I had to talk to Tilly.

The hot tallow dripped on my shaking hand as I made my way up the dark stairs. Why had all the wall sconces been extinguished? I swallowed the lump of fear forming in my throat. How hollow my feet sounded on the steps. They seemed to be the only noise in this silent house!

It was hard for me to believe no one was around, and no one was awake. I would surely have heard people going to their bedrooms—wouldn't I have?

A feeling of terror washed over me like a tidal wave I could not control. My heart hammered as I stopped for a moment, thinking someone was behind me. I turned. There was only darkness. The dim light from my candle did not show far enough. Was it only my frightened heart which I was hearing and feeling? Why should I be frightened? There was no reason for me to fear Tilly, no reason for me to fear going to her.

I took a deep breath trying to steady my nerves. I knew some of my anxiety stemmed from that moment when I had been attacked in the library. Was I close to the truth? Obviously, I had been close to finding out something about my family. I was sure that was the reason. There was nothing for me to fear in talking to Tilly.

The creaking of boards above my head startled me. I glanced up and paused. The rhythm of the walk was light, as if there really wasn't any pressure at all—as if it was the ghost of my aunt walking. But no, of course, it couldn't be her. I didn't believe in ghosts.

I reached the third floor without further mishap, without further indication of being followed or watched. Still, the unease I felt was like a fire gathering strength. Each step I took was adding another log to the fire. Each breath I took was fanning the flames higher.

The corridor was much the same as it had been when I explored earlier, but now the moonlight danced on the dusty floor, making it more phantasmic. I could almost imagine that my aunt was here, dancing and twirling as mother had described her—a happy-go-lucky girl. I doubted if the woman who had been penned up in the room I was now occupying could have been happy in any way.

Did my aunt's death have anything to do with the secret this house protected? Did my aunt know my real father? Was knowledge the reason for her death?

I chided myself for being so silly and so conceited as to think everything revolved about me and my problems. I was sure there was more to this house than learning the identity of my father.

Nevertheless, thinking of my aunt, of her death, made my stomach tighten as if my corset was two wires tighter than usual. The pain was something I would have to deal with.

I felt a shiver go through me as I reached the room which I now knew to belong to Tilly and Rose. How bleak it was up here. It still surprised me to find them housed up here. I wondered how they tolerated it, but I guessed Terrah had given them little choice.

"Tilly," I called out as I rapped loudly on the door. "Tilly, I must speak with you."

There was no answer. I knocked again. The sound of my hand on the wood was like the sound of a woodpecker on a tree.

The silence persisted.

Frustrated, I was about to turn and go downstairs to seek her when the sound of movement from within made me stop. I rapped on the door again.

"Tilly? Are you there? Rose?"

I held my breath as the door opened. Rose stood there, blocking the entrance. The room behind her was in total darkness.

"Were you getting ready for bed? I'm sorry."

Rose shook her head.

I wet my lips. Even from the dim light of my candle, I could see she had obviously been crying. Momentarily, I felt a surge of compassion for the girl. It faded abruptly as Rose's sarcastic tone came forth just as sassy as it had in my room before.

"What do you want?"

I glanced at her, trying to understand what was happening. "I want to speak with your mother. Where is she?"

"Ain't here."

I sighed. I was going to get as much cooperation from her as from a snail on a log. I tried to look behind her. I was sure Tilly had to be inside.

"Rose," I whispered, "I won't tell her about the incident earlier. I merely want to talk with her about a different matter."

Rose glared at me. "Told you. She ain't here. If'n I see her, I'll say you wants her."

I clenched my fist. There didn't seem much more I could say or do at this point. Rose was adamant about not letting me into the room. I breathed deeply, trying to keep my temper from exploding as it had before. "Thank you, Rose, I would greatly appreciate it."

Rose closed the door deliberately before I could even turn away. I was about to move off but something made me wait a moment more. Did I hear crying?

I pressed my lips together in bewilderment. What should I do? Rose was obviously upset about something. Maybe Tilly had punished her for something. Knowing her, it was quite possible.

Without another moment's hesitation, I moved on. It didn't do any good for me to be standing here in my nightdress.

A feeling of evil and doom still seemed to oppress me as I walked down the stairs. Every so often I found myself glancing back. Yes, I still felt as if I were being followed, as if—but no one had been there except Rose.

The rest of the house was still silent as it had been

during my climb up here. The goose bumps I felt were like a whole army of insects had attacked me. Every shadow which fell on the wall from my candle made me jump with fright. I felt the same way as I had the day the doctor had come to the house in Kansas. The day of the accident when I had been forced to pace and wait outside, not knowing from one moment to the next if my mother would live or die. But no one was dying now—or were they?

By the time I reached my room, sweat had beaded my brow. I washed my face in the water remaining in my porcelain pitcher and dressed in a gingham work gown.

I didn't know why but my heart and soul seemed to cry out to me. I had to find Tilly. I had to talk with her tonight. It seemed until I did, sleep would elude me.

If for some reason I could not find her, then I would take a walk. I knew it was not considered wise to go out at night, but I hoped that walking to my mother's house in the clearing would somehow help to lighten the burden I was now feeling. Perhaps it would give me some measure of comfort.

The remains of the evening repast were still on the table. It surprised me Tilly would not have this cleared up. She was usually so prompt at that. Well, I couldn't think about messy tables now. She probably had found another duty to be more pressing.

Rapidly, I strode through the empty dining hall. The grandfather clock now bonged eleven. Again, I thought of how strange the silence was. No, I did not believe everyone could be asleep.

Absentmindedly, I picked up a roll from one of the baskets on the buffet and began to nibble at it. Maybe Rose was right. Tilly couldn't be up in the room there. If she were, the table would surely have been cleared. Where was she then?

Cutting through the butler's pantry, I saw the door was unlatched. Had Tilly gone out for a walk?

Although, I didn't think it possible, I was willing to explore it. I stepped out.

The cold night air hit me like a slap. I allowed the door to close behind me. The wind felt refreshing on my hot skin and its fingers combed through my hair. Until this moment, I had not thought about putting it up. Well, if I met anyone, they would have to understand I had not planned to go walking.

I took a deep breath as I heard the lock click into place behind me. I realized too late I was locked out. Now, I had to find Tilly. Two steps at a time, I hurried down the path.

I wondered now if I shouldn't have taken the gun with me. What if I met darling Cousin David? It could easily have been him following me.

Recalling my suspicion of the day before, I realized if Peter was involved in this scheme to keep me from learning about my father, than it could also have been him following me, as well. I didn't want to believe Peter capable of harming me, but what could I think? I had seen the ring of my attacker.

Momentarily, I debated about going on. Should I try to get the gun?

I turned, about to ring the bell to the darkened house, when I realized someone was on the path. Peter? David? I was too far away to tell.

My curiosity impelled me forward.

The scream of terror which followed that moment made me jump nearly out of my skin. This time, I knew the scream was not coming from my uncle. It was too loud to be coming from the inside.

Without further thought, I picked up my skirts and began to run toward the horrified sobs which came from the far end of the path. The cries were nearly as loud as the other screams.

It took me only a moment to recognize the girl on the path as one of Tilly's assistants. She ran toward me as if I was a savior.

"Oh, miss! Oh, miss!" She cried as she shook with fear. "It's Tilly, miss."

My mouth must have dropped open. I felt my heart sink to my stomach as if it were leaded down. "What do you mean?"

"There miss." The girl turned and pointed to what I had not been able to see before. Sickness welled up in my stomach. It wasn't necessary for the scullery girl to say more. The moonlight showed clearly on Tilly's massive body. There was no blood to speak of but her head was bent at a radical angle like the hook of a fishing pole. Her neck had been broken. I closed my eyes, trying not to feel the despair, trying to keep control of myself.

Shaking my head in utter disbelief, I fell to the ground beside the rapidly chilling body of my mother's nurse. Tears formed in my eyes and flowed down my cheeks as I cradled the heavy head in my lap. I rocked her as she had rocked me.

All I could think of now was—I was alone.

My only real friend at Jerseyhurst was dead. I had the sickening feeling that I had somehow caused her death. She had died protecting me.

Chapter Eight

I can't say I was surprised to find Peter standing behind me. Was he responsible for Tilly's death? I looked up into his eyes. No, I couldn't think he was, and yet he was here, wasn't he?

The tears were still in my eyes as Peter drew me to my feet.

"An accident?"

I sucked in my breath as I stared at him. "I don't know." Did he know anything about this? Was his innocence just a play to fool me?

"Come." He took my hand. "Let's go find Terrah. She'll have to make the necessary arrangements for the funeral. Does Rose know?"

I thought of the girl upstairs—her red-rimmed eyes. Yes, I was sure she knew. Why had she said nothing to me?

It was impossible now not to think of the story of my aunt. Had Tilly fallen or been pushed? It was impossible for me not to think of the widow's walk, of how Tilly had warned me of the danger. I did not think she would have gone up there without provocation.

"Where are you taking me?" I asked, realizing suddenly we were not headed back toward the house.

Peter leaned over and kissed my brow, exciting feelings in me I knew I had to suppress for my own sanity. How could I be feeling this after what I had just witnessed?

I tried to pull away but he looked me in the eyes and held me there like a mesmerist. "Terrah and David are over at Parkland," he told me. "Terrah said you were feeling ill from this morning and had gone to sleep. We did not want to bother you, especially since Terrah had business to discuss with my father."

"Oh." I swallowed hard, thinking of the silence of the house. Had I been suspicious for no reason? Then I realized with Tilly's death I had every reason to doubt both him and my cousins.

I stared at him again, trying to decide just how I was going to say this. There seemed no delicate way. Why did you come over just now, then? I mean, if you thought I was asleep."

His grin was like a little boy caught with his hand in a cookie jar. A lock of wheat-blond hair fell forward over his eyes. "I was hoping maybe you weren't really asleep yet. I felt the need to see you, to talk about this morning." He lowered his gaze. My heart pounded as if I had just run a ten mile race. "They were busy talking and didn't notice me leaving."

I swallowed hard. "You mean you would have come up to my room? That would be quite ungallant of you, sir." I pulled away, all the while feeling a tingling desire in me for his touch. It was madness. Pure madness.

Peter shrugged. "I've been in your room before."

150

"When?"

"During your illness. Didn't Tilly—" He stopped and looked back at where the body lay. "Come. We don't want to talk about this now. Let's get Terrah to come back here and see what must be done. I'm afraid I'll have to send one of my men to summon the constable. Father isn't going to like the bother."

"Yes, I recall." I grimaced. "Your father doesn't like scandal of any sort."

He helped me into the buggy which waited at the front of the house. I realized then my hair was unbound. It was not seemly for me to be seen in company—especially in male company in such a wanton fashion. Mr. Parkisham —I could not call him father yet until I was sure—did not approve of unconventional approaches. He would not approve of me with my hair down.

Quickly, I began to roll it up and hoped I could at least tie it behind. Peter put a hand on mine, stopping me.

"Don't," he said.

"Don't what?"

"Put your hair up. It's so much nicer down, so much more feminine."

"But I—"

"I've seen you before with it down."

So. He was admitting it. "At the brook, you mean?" I wished now I had the power to turn men to stone with my gaze, for I would have loved to do that with him.

"At the brook? No, I saw you with your hair down when you were ill."

I felt myself stiffen. "Are you telling me that you didn't attack me at the brook when I was swimming that day?"

His arm went about me. "I might have kissed you on

151

the cliff, Elizabeth, my dear girl, but I would never attack you."

"You did return my shoes, didn't you?"

He nodded. "I saw them there and thought you had been there and forgotten them. But I did not attack you."

The hurt expression on his face was vivid. Either he was telling me the truth and someone else had attacked me—of course, I wouldn't put it past my cousin—or Peter was lying about this and other things.

I sighed and allowed my hair to fall back. It was so hard to know who and what to believe.

He pulled the reins and the buggy started forward. I closed my eyes and tried to think. "What do you think happened to Tilly?"

Peter shrugged. "Her room is up there on the top floor, isn't it?"

I nodded. "But she's obviously had that room there for some time now. Surely, she would have been aware of the dangers."

He stopped the buggy a moment and faced me. "From what I heard Tilly has had several health problems lately. Terrah, herself, told me the doctor found a growth on her stomach. It's quite possible Tilly was in pain—more so than she was willing to admit. Perhaps she decided to end her life rather than have it be ended for her."

I shuddered. I could not envision Jerseyhurst without Tilly. I did not believe Tilly had been ill. Surely, she would have told someone. I sighed. No, I had not been as close to her as mother had. I could not have expected her to tell me—if she truly had been ill. Rose would have known, wouldn't she?

The only thing for me to do was to question the girl. As if Peter could read my mind, his hand covered mine. "I know since you've been here, Tilly has been a friend to you. I can understand, Elizabeth. Her illness and death must be a shock to you. But I would not pursue it further."

"What do you mean?"

Peter brought my hand to his lips as his eyes met mine. "I mean, don't ask any questions about her death. Leave her die in peace."

"But I can't do that. If she didn't die of her own accord, then the person responsible should be made to pay."

"Should but probably won't. Money talks, Elizabeth. It's something I've already discovered."

"Have you?" I pulled as far from him as I could. "Have you now?"

He gave an uncomfortable shrug. "Just listen to me, Elizabeth. I care about you. You might not believe this, but I do. I want nothing to happen to you."

I held my breath, feeling the pain in my heart. "You think my asking questions about Tilly's health will cause something to happen to me?"

Again, he shrugged. "I don't know. All I know is that your being here has upset a lot of people. I don't want you to leave and yet, perhaps it might be best if you considered returning home to Kansas, Elizabeth." He took my hand in his. I felt a shiver run through me. Why was he confusing me like this?

My spine stiffened. I was being bolder than I should be and I knew it. But I could not help the questions which formed.

"You know, you're more of a mystery to me than Tilly's death. I don't understand how you can say you care about me and yet want me to leave at the same time."

153

He stared at me with those eyes—bluer than the midnight.

"Tilly was my friend. She was also my mother's friend. If her death was not an accident, then I believe I have a moral obligation to find out what happened to her." The sadness welled up in me. Tears flooded my eyes. "I'm sorry. I can't believe she would have killed herself."

"So you don't intend to leave Aberdeen?"

I took a deep breath, feeling the sharp pain in my lungs as I inhaled, feeling the pressure as my blood rushed to my brain. I didn't know what I intended anymore.

Trying to steady myself, I closed my eyes. My voice was calmer than I had thought it could be. "I will stay here in Aberdeen until I learn who my real father is; until I find out what or who caused Tilly's death."

I didn't have to look at him to know Peter was staring at me disapprovingly. His voice was gruff. "You can't say I didn't try to warn you." Clucking his tongue, he shook the reins. The buggy jolted slightly and moved forward again.

I don't know how I got through the rest of the night. Terrah, of course, was duly surprised and astonished as was David. Were they acting or did Tilly's death truly come as a shock to them? It was hard to say. I knew to accuse my own family of murder was a harsh thing, but the only other choice I had was to accuse Peter. It seemed all too suspicious to me that he had been there at the house—coming to see me, as he said. It was impossible from the looks passing back and forth between Peter, Alexander, Terrah, and David not to know—something

154

was very much amiss in these two households.

It was Terrah's idea I go with Harriet to town several days later. Supposedly I was to see if there were any ready-made dresses I might want for my ball gown. If not, she had given me money to buy material. I was slightly taken aback by her sudden generosity. And I had to admit—it was exciting to think of getting a ready-made dress. Nevertheless, I could not help but question her motives.

Not knowing what else to do, I went along. Actually, I found myself looking forward to knowing Harriet. If Alexander Parkisham was my father, then Harriet was the sister I never had.

I glanced at her as we drove, the cart bumping along the dirt road as I held the reins loosely.

"I do wish you had allowed Peter or one of the men to drive us, Elizabeth," Harriet complained good-naturedly. "After all, it might be fine in Kansas for one to drive one's self, but here, my family has always been driven by servants—at least the women in the family."

"I told you. If I am to pick material for a dress or find a ready-made one, I don't want a man along."

Harriet shrugged. "I don't know other men, but we could have had Peter drive us. He does have excellent taste."

I felt myself flush with just the mention of his name. What in heaven's name was happening to me? My voice sounded strange, even to me. Yet, I had to speak. "It sounds to me as if you're extolling his good points too much. I'm sure he must have *some* faults."

"Oh, he does," little Karen piped up. "Grandpapa says—"

"Hush, Karen." Her mother turned about. "Elizabeth doesn't want to know about our private lives."

I felt my back stiffen. I did want to know about their private lives. I wanted to know everything about my new family. Maybe I was being hasty, but from what I had gathered so far, the Parkisham's were as much my family as the Swansons.

Harriet looked in my direction as if she expected me to answer. We had never grown beets back home, but I was beginning to think we had for my color here was constantly turning deep red.

"You're right, I don't," I mumbled. It didn't sound convincing to me. I wondered if it did to her. Well, as soon as Alexander Parkisham acknowledged me, she would understand my feelings. Certainly, I did not want her to think I was in love with her brother. I told myself such a thing was the farthest from my mind—wasn't it?

I maneuvered the trap into a space near the news office. On my wrist, the reticule which Uncle Hayward had pressed upon me felt uncomfortably heavy with money. I had to admit I was surprised to see him at breakfast, surprised he was informed who I was and what had occurred during the weekend—or most of what had occurred. The recovery he had made had been quick, but it was not hard to see the toll the illness had put on him. His eyes were weak and his body fragile. I tried several times during breakfast to get him alone and speak to him but someone was always around.

I wondered if Peter would tell me to buy a gown or material with the money, or if he would suggest I leave as he had done last night. I still could not understand his reactions to me. Did he suspect our relationship? Was he as wary as I?

Vague feelings of guilt assailed me. I really didn't want to buy this dress, nor did I want to attend the dinner on Thursday at the Parkishams'. My heart felt leaden. I had to attend. Since coming to Aberdeen I had learned precious little about my parentage. No, as much as I might detest it, this party would be important to me.

As the guilt feelings continued to assail me, I knew I also had to write to Joshua again. My three weeks were nearly up. Joshua wanted me to return. He expected me and I still didn't know what to do or where to go. Joshua had wanted me to return—with or without the knowledge I sought. How could I love anyone who didn't understand how important this was to me?

Well, if I conserved part of the money from the dress, I was sure that my uncle wouldn't mind. Of course, I would explain the circumstances to him. If only I could get him alone—in a lucid state. If only I could really talk to him about my mother and her life here.

I hopped out of the trap, unladylike, thinking of the miraculous recovery my uncle seemed to have made. Yet Terrah had told me again he claimed not to have any memory of the men my mother might have known.

The town of Aberdeen was larger than I expected it to be. I glanced down the street toward the docks where the boats paused on their way down the Mississippi. A huge steamboat was waiting for passengers, and I wondered what it would be like to ride on such a ship.

I looked again at the various shops lining the main street. Being a Mississippi River town, Aberdeen had twice the number of stores our town had. It was certainly as big as Galena—its upriver rival. On the one street alone, I counted two general stores, a millinery, hotel, jail, the bank which my uncle owned, and several fabric stores, some with ready-made dresses in the window. Again, I felt like a child in a candy store. All my dresses had been hand-me-downs from Mama or her clients or things we had made together. Never had I owned a new store-bought dress. I hoped we could find something.

A single sheet of newsprint had been taped to the wall of the news office. Like our own town, Aberdeen didn't distribute its news in great quantity.

"It is a bit primitive," Harriet said. "But they always post a copy here—for the benefit of those who can't afford the penny for the sheet." I glanced at her. To my way of thinking, Aberdeen was anything but primitive. Still, to someone who had lived in Chicago, as she had, I could imagine her feelings.

Harriet placed her arm through my elbow as she steered me toward the shopping area.

"I think you had best consider a ready-made dress, if we can find one you like. After all, a dressmaker can hardly do a decent dress in one day."

I shrugged. "I still don't see why my cherry silk isn't good enough. My gray tabby can be fixed—or—"

"Oh, Elizabeth, I saw those dresses in your armoire. You have to admit they are a bit old-fashioned. Besides, you might want to consider. Your mother's old lawyer will be there."

"My mother's lawyer?" It amazed me. Never had it occurred to me my mother would have had a lawyer. I felt the small bird of hope flutter in my heart.

"Well, I don't think he really was her lawyer, but I do know she saw him before she left town. At least so Father tells us. I believe she often talked over her problems with him since your grandfather was not the kind to encourage discussion. Anyway, I know he called at the Swanson home several times for her." Harriet blushed this time. "I mean not as a suitor but as a friend."

I nodded, trying to hide the joy I was feeling. This might be a breakthrough. "Is he—is he in town?"

Harriet shrugged. "I don't know." She smiled. "But I do know Peter has invited him to the dinner. We hope he'll be back from St. Louis then."

I felt my voice choke. "Peter's invited him?" My heart hammered. Was he really trying to help me or was it a ploy to keep me from learning more?

Harriet nodded. "It was Peter's idea. He thought Mr. McCrae would be able to set your mind at rest on various matters."

I didn't understand but nodded anyway.

Karen, who had been holding her mother's hand, suddenly broke free and ran into the street after a ball. Without looking at the passing carts and pony traps, she grabbed the bright object as both of us stared horrified. "Karen! Karen, come back here!"

The neighing of the horse as the bit was pulled startled us both. The horse and carriage pulled to a halt just short of the blond child.

Sobbing with relief, Harriet ran into the street. Scolding her daughter, she picked her up from the mud. A red-faced man, his skin spiderwebbed with small veins, stepped from the carriage.

"Harriet Dalton! Might have known it would be your daughter causing the problem."

Harriet stared up at the man. "Meredith? You're back from St. Louis."

He nodded. "My secretary sent me a telegram. Seems

159

your brother has somethin' special in mind. Told her it was imperative I be back in town by Thursday. Since I was done with my business—" He shrugged as Harriet smiled.

"Mr. McCrae, I'd like you to meet Elizabeth Larabee."

"Larabee—Larabee—Margaret Swanson's daughter." I stammered. "Yes, I'm Margaret Larabee's daughter." I felt the man's eyes focusing on me with great intensity. I studied him just as he studied me. His warm gray eyes were inviting, just the type to encourage secrets. I longed to talk with him now, but decided I would wait. Peter had invited him for Thursday and I would trust Peter—this time.

"Then you will be at Parkland for dinner on Thursday?" He continued to stare at me. "You are the lawyer who knew my mother?"

His thin lips curled into a smile as he continued to stare at me. His gray eyes twinkled. "That I am, lass. Yes, I will be at the dinner. I trust we will talk then."

He took my hand and patted it in the same way he patted little Karen's. "Glad the lass wasn't hurt. Better keep a watch on her, Harriet." Tipping his hat, he climbed back into the open carriage. "We'll see you on Thursday, then."

I turned and watched the vehicle driving down the street. "Why do you think he was staring at me, Harriet?"

Peter's sister shrugged. "Maybe he thinks you're pretty. You are, you know. Wish I had the hair and color you do. They say that Mr. McCrae had a real eye for women when he was younger. I wonder if he was attracted to your mother. They say men often pretend to be friends."

160

I stared at her now. "Are you suggesting he might have known my mother in another way than just friendship?" I blushed. My heart seemed to pound out of my chest. Had he called upon my mother? I did not find it hard to believe, and yet could Harriet be purposely throwing me off the track? I had made no secret of what I sought here. I was sure she knew what I wanted. I felt myself trembling. Could he be my father? The blood rushed to my face as I realized the truth. If he was my father, I had nothing but my own fears to keep me from Peter Parkisham's arms.

"Did he—really court my mother?"

Harriet grasped Karen's hand tighter to her. "I don't know if I would call it courting. Daddy and Uncle Andrew were both regular visitors as well."

The blood which had rushed to my face suddenly drained from it. There was another Parkisham. Was he my father? All these men in my mother's life were confusing me.

"Elizabeth? Are you all right?"

I nodded but scarcely was aware of it. "Tell me—about your uncle Andrew. Does he—look like your father?"

Harriet's laugh was like a hyena I had heard once in the zoo. "Father and Uncle Andrew? They are too completely different people. Of course, my uncle died many years ago. I bet you would have liked him—a lot more than you like my father."

My back stiffened. "What makes you think I don't like your father?"

She opened the door to the dressmaker's shop. "It's obvious. The way you stare at him. The way he stares at you."

I shivered. Did he suspect I was his daughter? Was it

161

possible that my father did know who I was but refused to acknowledge me? I clutched my reticule. My head was pounding. "Let's go in and see what we can find. Then, I believe I could use a cup of tea."

There was no one about when I returned to Jerseyhurst. Just as I was about to put the dress away, I heard another of my uncle's cries. Not knowing what to do yet curious about what was really happening to him, I quickly dropped my package and made my way to his room.

I had to admit, I was not surprised to find the door locked. "Uncle," I called out. "Uncle Hayward, it's me. Elizabeth. Please let me in."

The man inside continued to cry.

"Please, Uncle Hayward. I want to help you. Can you open the door?"

It was several moments before I heard the shuffle of feet and a voice, rough and coarse, cry out. "Can't. Can't open it."

I tried myself several times but to no avail, and then I saw the gold key on the ledge above the door. It seemed strange to me the key would be left there, but there was no doubt it was there for a purpose.

Inside, I could hear my uncle continue his crying.

My hand trembled as I touched the key to the door. Would this be the moment? Would I finally learn who I was and what had happened to my mother when she had lived here?

The lock clicking was like my own heart turning over. Almost immediately, as I opened the door, I was sorry. The stench was so strong that I didn't think I could even breathe.

162

Quickly, I went to the windows and opened one of them. Inhaling the fresh air, I turned and saw the shambles the room was in. It obviously had been a beautiful master bedroom at one time, but now drapes were torn, the bed was scratched, and empty whiskey bottles were lined against the wall.

"Uncle." I forced myself to advance toward the old man who looked nothing like the robust character my mother had described to me. He didn't even look half the man he had been at breakfast today when he had given me the money for the dress, when he had talked to his daughter about me. What had happened to change him so? To change him from the man he had been this morning? It was hard for me to believe he had again lost his memory of who I was, yet from the way he was staring at me, it would seem he no longer recognized me. He was even a shadow of what he had been in church the other day.

"Georgiana?"

Again, I had to hold my nose from the stink. I shook my head as I took another step toward the old man. "No, I'm not Georgiana. I'm your niece, Elizabeth. I'm Margaret's daughter."

"Margaret. Ah, Margaret." His already rheumy eyes took on a faraway look. "You shouldn't have left, Margaret. He didn't like it. He was very upset with you. You should have stayed and married him, Margaret."

My heart beat like a base drum as I felt the blood rush to my face. "Uncle, who is he? Is he still alive? Was he the one my mother was seeing?"

"Margaret, you shouldn't have left. The whole family was terribly upset with you. Papa even took you out of his will."

I forced myself to ignore the stink and moved forward

163

to my uncle. I took his weak hands in mine. Tears were in my eyes. "Uncle, this isn't Margaret. It's her daughter. Please. Tell me about the man you're referring to. Tell me his name." I paused. "Uncle, you must stop drinking. You must get better and help me. I need you. The bank needs you. Please." I could feel my voice breaking.

He seemed so hopeless. If only I could get him sober and keep him that way long enough for him to talk with me. If only I could get these bottles away from him.

My uncle looked at me blankly a moment and then it seemed as if he would speak. "Elizabeth. Elizabeth," he said, stroking my hair. "Elizabeth and her daddy. You look so much like your daddy. It's too bad."

"What's too bad?" I was on my knees now, holding his hand.

The door slammed open behind me. "It's too bad you've decided to come in here."

Quickly, I turned to find Terrah behind me. Her face was a study in rage.

I took a deep breath, trying not to inhale the smell. "I came in here to talk with my uncle."

"And I told you he wasn't well enough to see you."

"You've told me many things, cousin. That doesn't mean I believe them all. I want to know who my father was. I believe my uncle can tell me."

"Well he can't." She walked forward abruptly, the swish of her gown audible as she grabbed my arm and pulled me up. "You're going to upset my father and I won't have him upset."

As if on cue, my uncle began to cry softly. I glanced toward the old man. I had been so close.

I motioned toward the bottles of whiskey in the corner. "Is that how you keep him ill?"

Terrah laughed. "You really do have an imagination, cousin. Father has those bottles in the room for his— natural purpose. He's too ill often for a commode."

I stared at the bottles and then at her. She was lying, of course. She was keeping him drunk but why? It couldn't be just for me.

"I think you ought to leave now. My father needs his rest. It's all he can do to go to church on Sundays."

I glanced at my uncle. "Yes, I imagine you're right. It probably is quite difficult for him."

Standing away from her, I brushed my skirt off and turned back toward the door. "I will talk with him later. I promise you. I am not leaving here until I find out who my father is. If you think I intend to use the knowledge against you, Terrah, you're wrong. All I want to know is who I am. Then I shall be quite content to leave Jerseyhurst forever."

She stared at me. I could feel her eyes still upon me as I turned and departed.

Chapter Nine

I turned slightly and saw in the mirror the sparkle in my eyes brought out by the deep blue silk gauze of the blouse. My skirt was of a similar deep blue velvet trimmed with silver tinsel. I had even bought some new laced shoes. My hair was back from my forehead in a Grecian-style knot, which made me look far older than I was. Gently, I touched the matching shoulder cape. I felt absolutely beautiful. Of course, this was the first store-bought dress I had ever owned. I had been so lucky. There hadn't been many dresses in the shop, but this had been there, and it had been perfect. It hadn't even cost much. There was still money for me to use for my ticket, if it came to my leaving. Of course, I would tell my uncle about the excess money when I saw him, but as of today—two days after our interrupted conversation—I had not seen him since.

It bothered me my uncle was such a recluse, but I could not think of his problems now. Tonight, I had to concentrate on talking to the lawyer and finding out what I could at the Parkisham house.

The interior of the Parkisham's manor was as different from Jerseyhurst as the Taj Mahal was from a peasant's cottage. I had never, of course, seen either except in drawings, but it wasn't hard to imagine. I touched one of the polished wall carvings and felt the texture of the velvet. If Jerseyhurst was beautiful, this was ten times more so. The spacious rooms were baronial. There were easily twenty rooms here, with four parlors on the first floor alone. It took all my effort to keep myself from staring. If I had been my mother, in love with a man who owned such a fortune, I wouldn't know if I loved him for his money or for himself.

I immediately chided myself for thinking such mercenary thoughts. It wasn't right. Mother had done the right thing. Despite the agony of her death, her life had been peaceful. No, I could not imagine myself marrying just for money. I could not and would not think of anyone in those terms.

Peter stepped out of the largest parlor and immediately came over to me. His smile made my heart want to sing. I stared at him, at the tight beige waistcoat, cutaways, and the deeper brown jacket. I felt myself flush as my mind played its tricks on me—as I thought of the moment on the cliff when he had kissed me and pressed me to him. How could I even think such thoughts when I did not know where he stood? Or whose side he was on?

Taking my hand in his, and causing a shiver to go through me, he bowed. His lips touched my fingers and I knew, despite my suspicions, I wanted him to touch other

168

parts of me as well. It was a shameful thought and were I in church now, I would be saying several dozen Hail Marys.

"Welcome to Parkland, Miss Larabee," he said, smiling at me. Just the timbre of his voice set my nerves on edge. I nodded to him again, feeling the beets growing in their patch.

"Your cousins have already arrived, as you no doubt know. I was wondering what had happened to you."

"I—I didn't know they had left. I was just getting ready." Actually, I had known they were coming on ahead. They had refused to wait for me to finish my hair, though I had asked them politely to do so. I had been forced to walk over.

Once more he bent to kiss my hand—wasn't once enough to drive me insane? "Whatever the reason, I am glad you're here," he whispered to me. His blue eyes twinkled with merriment, and I did not know if he meant it or not. "You look ravishing, I might add."

I glanced down, not wanting to meet those devastating eyes of his. He could control me with one glance. I already knew my heart was pounding like a metronome at fast pace.

Peter held out his arm to me.

I stared at it, debating if I should take it or not.

"I promise," he said and laughed softly, "I won't bite you."

I still made no move.

"Elizabeth, I would like us to be friends. I am sorry if my behavior the other day offended you."

My voice seemed stuck in my throat. His behavior should have offended me, but all it had done was to confuse me. I couldn't be falling in love with my own

169

brother. It just wasn't possible. I forced myself to meet his eyes. The light from the Irish Waterford glass chandelier sparkled rainbows on his face. Was that another sign from the universe? I swallowed hard. No, he did not know of our possible relationship. He would not be doing this to me if he did.

It took an effort for me to place my arm through his.

I didn't know if I imagined it or if there really was music playing in the background as we began to walk down the hall toward the dining room where my cousins had already congregated.

Just touching him made my heart beat faster than it had. If being with him was heaven, then I wanted to die quickly, but I did not think dying would accomplish my purpose. I wet my lips and pressed them together as we entered the stately chamber. Peter Parkisham was engaged to my cousin, Terrah. Perhaps it hadn't officially been announced yet, but it would be soon. I was sure of that. Terrah was not the type to let things of such nature slide. For all purposes, he might just as well be my brother.

The Wedgewood china place setting was the latest from England. I recognized the pattern from a magazine I had seen in one of the homes of Mama's students. The goldware, too, was modern and indicative of the wealth surrounding us. I sat down and couldn't help notice the Waterford crystal nor the Irish linen tablecloth. Everything was so perfect here. Was this why Terrah wanted Peter?

I glanced toward her and then toward Alexander Parkisham. Sitting next to his wife, the birdlike and fragile Ella, the man seemed to have no sight for anyone except my cousin. I wondered why Terrah, being the conniver she obviously was, didn't simply get what she wanted from him.

As I glanced about to see if Mr. McCrae had come, I heard the fluttery tones of Ella Parkisham. "Oh, my dear, my dear. Harriet said you would look exquisite and she was right. She was so right. Weren't you, Harriet?" Without waiting for her daughter to reply, she continued. "I am really so glad you could come to my home for dinner. I mean, Alex says you will soon be leaving us, and I have heard so much about your dear mother. She really must have been a wonderful person. I feel as if I know her. I—"

Alexander Parkisham broke his attention from Terrah and glanced at his wife. "Enough of your chatter, Ella." His brows knitted together. "Elizabeth, I am glad you could come tonight. Peter has said you were anxious to see Parkland, and so I thought it fitting that you be a guest tonight."

I bit my lower lip as I avoided Peter's gaze. "I really didn't have much of a choice."

"Oh come. Come, my dear." Alexander took my hand and I felt my skin crawl at his touch. I could feel his strength and his determination, but I could also see his ruthlessness. All these skills, I was sure, had been needed to amass the fortune he needed for this home. But it should not be needed with family, or loved ones. How could I be related to this man? How could my mother have—no I did not want to think about it.

I was about to lean over and ask Harriet where the missing Mr. McCrae was when the door chimes rang again.

It was telling, I thought, that Alexander looked at Terrah before looking at his wife.

171

"Did you invite anyone else?"

"I did, Father," Peter spoke up. "Meredith McCrae. I met his assistant in town the other day and realized we haven't seen McCrae for quite some time. I thought it would be fitting he meet Elizabeth during her stay in Aberdeen. After all, he did know her mother."

Alexander cleared his throat. Terrah glared at Peter. Peter merely smiled at them both, and I felt my heart lift two steps. I did have a champion in Peter Parkisham. I was sure of his support. Why else would he have gone against his father and my cousin? I still did not know why but it didn't matter to me. At the moment, the only important thing was talking to the lawyer.

The doorbell rang again. "Well aren't you going to answer it?" David asked. Clearly, he was enjoying the game.

Mumbling under his breath, Peter excused himself and went to the door. I was surprised no servant had gone, but then I realized Alexander had shaken his head at the waiting butler. Apparently, Meredith McCrae was not the welcome guest Peter had hoped he would be. I watched Peter leave the room, feeling as if I had been deserted.

The little lawyer was exactly as I recalled him from our meeting on Tuesday. His smile was pleasant, but it also looked pasted on. He looked a little worried and not pleased at being here. Again, I noticed the spidery lines about his face. I was glad when he took the chair next to mine. I hoped I would be able to talk with him.

"Evening, McCrae," Alexander greeted the man.

McCrae turned to Alexander and nodded, then he smiled again. His eyes seemed to glow with the inner knowledge of one who knows who he is and where he is going. I envied him. I was sure now he had the knowledge

172

to help me. As he spoke, I noticed his voice was softer and calmer than it had been during our previous meeting. Were I not sitting so close, I could almost have sworn his mellow composure was due to drink. If he drank anything, I could understand it. Being with Alexander Parkisham was enough to unnerve anyone.

"I thank you for having me, Alexander."

Mr. Parkisham grunted. He motioned to the servant for the meal to start.

There was a moment of silence then, which fell over the room. I glanced at my plate and waited for the others to speak.

True to form, it was Peter who broke the silence. "Father," he asked, "what happened to the painting of Uncle Andrew which hung above the fireplace?"

Everyone at the table, myself included, turned to stare at the mediocre scene of river bluffs and boats which now hung above the fireplace.

"As I recall, it was an exceptional likeness," McCrae said.

Alexander took a deep breath and began pouring wine for his guests. "The portrait of my brother is—being cleaned."

Peter stared at his father. "Since when did the picture need cleaning, Father?"

There was an angry glare between father and son. I could not help but wonder what exactly was going on.

"It needed cleaning," Alex repeated again as he poured a full glass of wine for himself and for his mistress, forgetting about his wife until she pressed her glass to his.

"It was a good likeness," McCrae said again.

"I know it was," Alexander said gruffly. "You don't

have to tell me what my brother looked like. I know what he looked like. I also know far more about him than you people will ever care to know."

The tense silence was relieved only when the soup was served, and Harriet began to chatter about the local events at church. The feelings here were almost as thick as the pea soup in front of me. I wondered if I would ever cut through it, if I would ever learn the truth. When was Alexander going to talk to me alone?

The dinner was probably one of the most uncomfortable ones I had ever been to. Nothing seemed to go right, no one seemed at ease.

Several times when it appeared as if I would get to speak with Mr. McCrae alone, he would be called off— either by Alexander, Terrah, David, or by all three. Their determination to keep me from him made me even more anxious to speak with him.

Looking at him and talking with him, I no longer suspected he was my father—but I was certain he knew about my father or could at least accurately guess who the man was. Even as I thought it, I turned my attention to Alexander Parkisham.

He forced himself to smile, noticing my attention, but I saw those dark, thick brows frown. I saw the creases on his brow and the way he stared at Peter.

I would like to have said Peter championed me tonight as he had done earlier—but he did not. The rest of the evening was spent talking with Terrah or David, or of playing whist with his sister in the drawing room where we all retired.

My head was aching with a desire for sleep by the time

174

we returned to Jerseyhurst.

The memory of Tilly struck me as I prepared for bed. I thought of how she came up to speak to me each night, to tuck me in and talk to me of my mother. Tears came to my eyes. Rose had not said anything to me since her mother's death. It was almost as if the girl blamed me, but I had done nothing.

Washing my tears away with the water that was in my bowl, I decided I could wait no longer to make some move. The clock in the hall chimed quarter to midnight.

Along with Tilly's death I was also haunted by the mystery of the missing family Bible. I was sure I had seen it, but each time I found myself in the library/office, I looked hard, but there was no evidence of it. The book had to be there!

I had already taken my dress off, but I slipped it back on once more. My heart was pounding. I lit my candle and then reconsidering, blew it out. I had only lived in this house for a few weeks, but it was long enough to know my way downstairs. It would be best for me to make my way without any light.

With that thought, I took a deep breath to ease the fast pace of my heart. I opened the hall door and listened to the quietness. Wetting my lips, I couldn't help think the silence reminded me of the night I had discovered Tilly. Surely, there was no one else who would die tonight.

Other than the ticking of the clock, there appeared to be no movement in the house. Had Terrah and David already retired or were they waiting for me? Had Peter returned with them? I didn't think so, but then I didn't know what to believe anymore.

The shadows loomed thickly on the wall. My fear was drowning me, but with each step I struggled on further. I

175

would survive this and fight it. Shivers ran up my arms. I realized the chill came not only from within me but from the lack of heat in the house. Yes, there was no question that Parkisham Manor, despite its modest exterior, was a far superior house. Was it the money that my cousin was after? I wondered if she would leave Peter for me if she knew that I cared nothing for the other house.

It was not, of course, totally true. I would be a fool not to appreciate Jerseyhurst or Parkland, and yet to have a true love would be worth all the money.

I scolded myself. Once again I was thinking of Peter Parkisham as if we could be lovers when I knew we could not. How much more sinful could my thoughts be?

The swish of my dress was audible—at least to me—as I navigated the stairs. With each movement, I paused, wondering if I had been heard, wondering if someone was going to open a door and ask what I was doing at this time of night. I would, of course, say I needed a book from the library to read. I didn't know if they would believe me, but it was the only excuse I could think of.

Grandfather Maxwell's portrait stared down the stairs at me. Did I look like him or did I look more like my father's side of the family? I knew that neither David nor Terrah looked like him but they certainly had inherited his ruthlessness.

My mouth tasted sour. How could I hate my family so? I had looked forward to meeting my family for so long. I had looked forward to getting to know my cousins, and now it seemed as if I knew them more than I wanted to.

Breathless with anxiety, I stopped on the first floor landing. A door opened somewhere. The blood rushed to my ears. It seemed as if my heart would not silence itself. It seemed as if I would give myself away.

Relief flooded me as the noise stopped. Could my uncle be having another bad dream? After I had located the Bible, I would to go him and talk to him. Surely, Terrah couldn't keep me from him forever.

I waited in the shadows for yet another few moments. It seemed like a full hour to me, but I knew it could only be a few moments because the clock struck the hour. It had taken me fifteen minutes to make my way down to the first floor—fifteen terrifying minutes. The pulses in my neck seemed to jump out.

I felt a door open somewhere and cool air come in. I could see no one, however. After a slightly longer wait, I started forward once more.

The door was locked, as I had expected it would be.

Pulling a pin from my hair, I twisted it gently. I had heard this was a way to get into a room—but until I heard the lock catch, I had never thought it was possible to enter a room this way.

The door squeaked open. Once again, I was sure I would die on the spot from fear. But discovery did not come, as I had feared it would. The silence pervaded the house. Oh, yes, the creaks and groans continued, but then this was an old house.

I slid into the room. Only as I closed the door behind me for protection did I realize the room was cool. A window had been left open! How strange.

Quickly I closed it and glanced about again. Without light, I had some difficulty, but I was not about to put on the gas jet, nor was I about to light any candles. I glanced toward the heavy drapes. Did I dare open them at all? Would the light of the full moon help me? It would be a gamble.

Blood rushed through my body and knotted my

stomach. I felt a distinct pain there, but I could do nothing about it at this moment. I had to proceed. I knew my instincts were warning me, yet my desperate desire to learn who I was overrode my fears.

The drapes came back just a fraction, but it was enough so that I could see something of the room. The single thread of moonlight was like an opening in the heavens.

I glanced about and pushed the mutton sleeve of my dress up slightly higher. Turning, I saw the family Bible. I couldn't believe it was actually in the room.

Wasting no time, I pulled it over to the desk catty-corner to the window. I had to read it now. I would not let anything stop me. Horror caught in my throat and caused me to gag: The pages were missing. The Bible was here just as it had been before, but the front pages with the family charts were gone. Gone, too, was the marker.

It was difficult to keep the tears of frustration from my eyes.

With the drops still shimmering in my eyes, I turned the pages. I recalled there had been a marker in a section of Deuteronomy. Could I find that section? Could I locate it and understand what it meant?

Several times as I was turning the pages, I nearly dropped the heavy book.

Nothing in the fifth book of the Old Testament was making any sense to me. There were no indications of any marks.

With a sigh of disappointment, I closed the book. I would, I decided, at least mark down the sections which I had read. Maybe I could find another Bible in the house somewhere and read those sections over again. Maybe then I would be able to understand its importance.

I opened the desk drawer without thinking. Surely,

there had to be paper and some ink here.

I pulled forth several sheets. I was about to write on them when I realized they were not blank. On the back side were several rows of numbers.

Never had I liked math, but even I, who had done poorly at numbers, could see there was something off here. As I studied the sheet before me, I realized it had been taken from a ledger. Where? Which ledger?

My mouth was dry. Could this have anything to do with my uncle's being so ill? Could this have anything to do with the secret of my birth? No, I didn't think it was the latter, but it was quite possibly the former.

Eyes wide in amazement, I began to copy down the numbers on what surely seemed to be a clean piece of paper. Later I would go over the figures and check them. It seemed to me that there was something here I could use as leverage in my battle to find out who I was.

Replacing the pen and most of the paper where I had found it, I drew the drapes closed once more. How dark and eerie the room seemed without that one beam of moonlight. Still, it would not do for me to leave the drapes open. Everything had to be as it had been before.

I hurriedly put the Bible back on the shelf it had occupied. Those missing pages still bothered me, but I would find out all I needed to know in due time.

Swiftly, I walked to the door and closed it behind me. I heard the lock click into place.

With the paper tucked into my bosom, I swallowed my fear and made my way up the stairs and back to my wedge-shaped room.

I would add the columns up tonight, and tomorrow I

would have a talk with my cousin. If she felt she couldn't give me the information I needed, then I would bring these papers—whatever they represented—to the constable in town, or perhaps to Mr. McCrae. If anyone could help me, I felt he would. I would find who my father was, even if I had to be as ruthless as my cousins.

Chapter Ten

My room suddenly seemed smaller and more suffocating than it had ever felt before.

This time I had no hesitation in lighting a lamp. As I sat down at the desk to add the figures together, I realized these had to be from the bank. The numbers were lined up neatly, just like the bank ledgers I had seen at our Kansas bank. I continued staring at the page and noticed to my horror that on one page alone over three hundred dollars were missing from the bank funds. Had Terrah embezzled them? I didn't think David had done it. He seldom went near the bank.

Besides in the three weeks I had been here, I found David had no business sense. It was Terrah who controlled the funds in the house and doled out the money for her brother.

How much more had Terrah taken and what had she done with it? I knew her mother had left her an inheritance. Terrah herself had told me that. Surely, Jerseyhurst didn't take that much upkeep.

It was impossible not to think of my uncle. Not to

think of his wife's death and why he was now being plied with whiskey.

I stared at the figures again. If Terrah knew I had them, would it be enough for her to tell me the secret of my parentage?

There had to be something more than just hiding the name of the man from me. At one time, I would have been happy just to learn who he was and to meet him, if possible. Now I had other ideas. Now I wanted to know what the secret was they were so jealously guarding and why my uncle was being kept a prisoner in his room.

Reluctantly, I folded the papers. I would have to keep this in a safe place.

The idea occurred to me suddenly: I couldn't help but wonder whether these figures were enough of a persuasion to help me buy back my mother's farm. If I agreed to silence, would my cousin give me the money needed? Joshua would love for us to have mother's farm again, I was sure. He hadn't wanted me to sell it in the first place.

Thinking of Joshua made me think of Peter. I knew comparing the two was like comparing a raw, tart apple and a sweet apple pie. But I couldn't help comparing nonetheless.

Biting my lower lip, I glanced about the room. The only place I could hide this would be in the fireplace where my gun was now hidden.

Quickly, I crossed the room.

I had just taken out the brick when the knock at my door startled me. I hadn't thought anyone else in the house was awake.

"Yes. Yes, I'm coming." Reaching over, straining, I pushed the bed down so the springs sang. I hoped it told the other person I was just getting out of the bed.

Folding the paper once more, I placed it into the hollow space and turned once more as the knock came again. Quickly, I restuffed the brick into the hole. I was afraid the door had been opened. It hadn't. I couldn't help hear the beating of my heart.

Too late I realized that I was still wearing my dress. How was I going to pretend I had been to bed when I was still dressed?

"Who—who is it?" I asked as I hurriedly put on my dressing gown and tied it tightly, hoping my dress wouldn't show. At least, I could say that I had dressed just now.

"Rose, Miz Lizabeth."

I pulled the door opened and closed my robe tighter about me. I mistrusted her almost as much as I mistrusted my cousin. She stood there staring at me. I didn't know if she guessed anything, but she looked at me contemptuously as if she suspected something. I knew I had to be careful.

"What's wrong, Rose?" I said, realizing she wasn't going to speak.

"There be a fire in de town. Everybody be needed. Miss Terrah dun tol' me t'wake you. Theys have de cart outside."

I nodded. "I'll be right down." Turning, I quickly splashed water over my face. It took me longer than I expected to get out of my good dress and into one of my checked work ginghams, but I couldn't let anyone know I had not yet been to bed. I finished the buttons on my dress and grabbed a shawl. Then, taking the steps two at a time, I ran down the stairs and out to the main drive in front of the house.

As Rose had told me, the cart was there waiting. I was a bit surprised to see my uncle sitting there with the others, sober and awake. I stared at him, but he didn't seem to recall me.

It took a lot of effort for me to keep my silence. I longed to talk to him but, knowing my cousins were here, I said nothing. Wrapping my shawl closer about me, I stared out into the dark countryside.

It was only as we neared town that I realized David was not with us. My uncle noticed at the same time. It was the first time I had heard him speaking in his sober state. His voice was slightly higher than it had seemed before.

"I asked you where David was?" He repeated the question to Terrah.

"And I told you before, Papa." She acted like he was a child still on his leading strings. "David rode ahead." She turned to look at me as if I would somehow verify this for her.

Then I realized she was staring at me not because of what she said but because of what she was thinking. Her hand reached out to touch my curls before I could pull away. "You must be a remarkably light sleeper, Elizabeth. I know my curls always come undone at night."

"In fact, I am a light sleeper. I was so exhausted I clean forgot to take them down. I didn't even take time to run a comb through my hair just now. Do they look neat enough?" I forced myself to smile at her and hoped my excuse was taken. "I must have been the last one called."

My uncle glanced at his daughter as if to ask the same question—or maybe to ask just who I was. "You were," he mumbled. "Don't know why, but you were." I could have sworn, under his breath, I heard the name

Margaret, but I couldn't be certain.

He leaned out toward the driver, anxiously calling, "Hurry, William. Did they tell you what was burning?"

"No, suh." The black driver leaned down. "De runner didn't tell me."

Uncle Hayward leaned back in the buggy with a worried frown.

"Don't worry, Papa. We shall know soon enough." Terrah patted his hand.

"Can't help it. Had faith in your abilities when I was ill, but I think it's time for me to resume control of the bank."

"I know, Papa. David told me."

"Then you don't mind?"

Terrah gave a laugh. It sounded like what I imagined a banshee would. A shudder passed through me. "Why should I mind? I was just doing my duty as a good daughter. The care of the house more than takes up my time. Now that I'm to be married soon."

I felt the breath go out of me. I should have expected my cousin's control of the bank, but it came as a shock, nevertheless.

My uncle seemed not to hear the tension in Terrah's voice, but I certainly did. Terrah patted his hand, and I felt the lie in her actions.

The trap came to an abrupt halt. From the driver's seat, I heard William scream, "Mastuh Hayward, sir it's your bank!"

"No! Lord, no!" Uncle Hayward cried, as he scrambled out of the buggy, nearly falling into the muddy walk. He righted himself and then stumbled once more as he ran toward the burning building. Before anyone could reach him, he picked himself up from the ground and

185

continued running.

"Papa!" Terrah called. "Papa, wait for me."

My uncle paid no attention to her—to anyone. I saw him push through the crowds. He was intent on one thing: reaching his beloved bank.

"That stupid fool," Terrah cursed. "He'll get himself killed. William, go after him. See my father comes to no harm. I'll take care of the horses."

"Yes, ma'am," William cried, jumping down from his seat. He started out after Hayward Swanson while Terrah took the reins and handed them to one of the men. With Rose and myself in tow, she joined the women's group.

Sparks were flying everywhere, it seemed. Not only the bank but the surrounding buildings were on fire. Orders were being shouted, but no one seemed to hear. I froze as the scream of a girl nearby shocked me. A spark had hit her face. Without thinking, I dashed the bucket of water I had been carrying on her.

Several people glared at me. "We don't waste good water," one woman scolded me. Even with the heat, I blushed. "I'm—I'm sorry."

"Don't be sorry, just be careful." She handed me another bucket of water to pass along.

Another girl cried out. This time I waited and watched and someone slapped the sparks out.

I had to admit I was surprised a town the size of Aberdeen had no fire truck. Chicago had five. Even Galena had two.

Brushing the loose hair from my eyes, I swung the empty buckets back and the full ones forward. As I methodically continued my work, I realized a fire truck wouldn't have done much good anyway.

Someone cried out as the timber beam from the front

186

of the bank fell forward, splattering more sparks about. Even though I stood some distance away, I could still feel the intense heat and see the vibrations in the air as the fire radiated towards me. Sweating, I drew my hand over my brow. It seemed that our efforts were doing precious little to stop the fire.

I was keenly aware of my head aching, of the smoke irritating my lungs and nose, making me cough and sneeze. My eyes watered so badly that I could barely see. It was worse than grating onions on the farm. I would not stop. I would not let anyone else take my place in line. Terrah, it seemed, was working as hard as I was. Rose, too, was heaving those heavy buckets. Maybe the bank would be saved.

It was only then I recalled the column of figures I had copied down. Even as I handed the next water-filled bucket down the line, I knew the bank was doomed. I was sure the fire had been purposely set. There seemed little I could do about it at this moment except to watch and pray.

I continued to blink from the stinging smoke and the ashes flying about. Finally, I allowed one of the other women to take my place. My arms ached. The curls in my hair which Terrah had commented about earlier were gone. My hair, white from the ashes, was now hanging down about my shoulders.

Turning my head toward the river, I tried to catch a breath of the river breezes but to no avail.

The madness was all about me but I had to keep some sanity. Looking about, I realized Uncle Hayward had disappeared. I hadn't seen him since he left the carriage. Terrah might not be concerned about her father but I was.

187

The wind shifted again. The flames were beginning to die, but it was obvious the bank building was lost. All the outer walls had fallen. Most of the town now concentrated on the neighboring buildings, hoping to save them. I knew Uncle Hayward, if he was anything like my mother, would not give up so easily.

Determined to find him, I left the crowd and hurried toward the back of the bank. It was probably foolhardy but I had to find him. The passage which led to the rear entrance was extremely dark, despite the light from the fire. Yet it seemed the quickest route. It would be impossible for me to attempt the front door since too many people were milling about there. Besides, I was sure I had seen my uncle head in this direction as he had run from the buggy.

As carefully as I could, I made my way over stumbling blocks: cast-away objects, charred beams, and the like. I could only hope the back of the building was intact and that my instinct about my uncle was right. If not, I was uselessly risking my own life.

Coming closer, I could feel the heat growing stronger. I had seen no sign of my uncle. I had seen no sign of anyone.

"Hayward! Hayward Swanson!" I yelled at the top of my lungs.

As I feared, no answer came forth. Yet I continued to move. I could see the heat vibrating in waves about me now. My uncle was inside the back room of the bank. I knew he had to be. I knew that's where I would go if it was my business on fire. I would want to retrieve my records. Surely, my uncle would have thought the same thing.

Once inside the building, I felt the sweat drip down my brow. Flames still devoured the exterior of the building and the front.

A colorful square caught my attention. Bending down, I gave a gasp. This was the green cravat which David had worn at dinner. Fear now compounded my panic. I tucked the silk square into my pocket.

"Uncle Hayward!" I called out once more. "Uncle!"

I stepped forward into the blast of the flames and saw the bodies then: not just my uncle but Meredith McCrae as well. He lay atop my uncle's legs. It was as if he had fallen over my uncle on purpose—to prevent other damage.

"Mr. McCrae!" Heedless of my own danger now, I rushed forward as I tried to rouse both men.

My stomach sickened as my hand recoiled. The lawyer was already dead. His eyes stared upward at me with a glazed look that brought the bile to my throat.

From beneath Mr. McCrae, my uncle groaned.

"Uncle Hayward! Please. Get up. You have to get out of here. The bank's nearly gone!"

A coughing fit took hold of me. I forced myself to suppress it as I took his hand.

"I—I can't move," he whispered. "Help me."

Trying not to breathe the smoke-filled air, I managed to partially lift McCrae off my uncle's legs. I found I had no further strength to continue his rescue.

Tears came to my eyes. "Wait. I'll go get someone to help I'll—" My words were cut off by the crashing of a beam not ten feet away. Sparks flew; one alighted on the dead man. I smacked it out.

"Hurry!" my uncle whispered. "Hurry!"

I must have nodded but I wasn't aware of it. I ran out of the building, barely feeling the sparks that were falling on me. I had to help my uncle or I would feel responsible

189

for his death. I had to find someone. I knew I should have warned him of my discovery, but when could I have told him?

There was no time to think about that now or what might have happened if I had told him. I only knew I had to get some help.

The street was still crowded with people—everyone seemed busy.

"Please," I cried, going up to the first man I saw. "My uncle is injured. He needs help—"

The man pushed me away before I could finish my sentence. I saw then he was running to help with another fire that had started.

Frantically, I glanced about, running to approach another man, when I felt my arm caught. I looked up to see Peter.

"Where is he?"

"In the bank." The sob seemed torn from my throat. "The back of the bank. McCrae's there, too." My eyes watered and smarted with the smoke. "I—I can't get my uncle free."

"I'll find them."

"I'll come with you." I began to follow him back toward the bank's rear entrance.

"No." Peter pushed me aside. "You stay out here with the women where it's safe."

I shook my head, feeling the ashes fly into my mouth, feeling the heaviness of my hair and the heat all about me, smelling the burning leather from the dry goods store next to the bank."

"I'm coming with you, Peter. He's my uncle." Without another word to him, I ran ahead, avoiding his grasp.

I don't know how we got back into the bank. The flames were fiercer now and closer to where we stood. I bent over my uncle.

"McCrae's dead," Peter announced.

I felt the sob in my throat. "I know."

"I don't think he died from the fire." Peter pointed to the blood on his temple which I hadn't noticed before. I stared at the face of the dead man a moment. All I could think of was the scarf which was still weighing heavy in my mind—and of Tilly's death. The lump in my throat made me almost incapable of speech.

"Well come on, then. We don't have much time. Since you insisted on being here, you'd better help me move him out. Then we can free your uncle."

I nodded and took the lawyer's legs as Peter instructed me. This time, with his help, we succeeded in freeing my uncle, who was now unconscious.

As we carried Uncle Hayward out to the safety of the street, I felt the heat from the bank on my back as the flames devoured the rest of the room we had just left.

"Where are you going?" Peter asked me as I turned back.

"Mr. McCrae—"

Peter put a restraining hand on my elbow. "It's too late, Elizabeth."

I turned again toward the back room. Peter was right. A huge crash thundered about us as flying sparks shot upward. Flames went skyward and told me that Mr. McCrae's body had been consumed along with my uncle's bank.

Tears came to my eyes. The lump knotted my throat. I felt Peter's arm go around me. "He—he told me to come—to town—tomorrow—I mean, today. He was—I think he was going to tell me—about my—mother."

Even though Peter's arm was still about me, I sensed a change in him as he handed me a dry linen from his pocket.

I looked up into his eyes. The wall of flames had divided us from the rest of the people on the street.

It was as if we were in our separate world.

"You know something, don't you, Peter?" My voice was barely audible above the roar of the fire and the crowd.

Peter gave a slight nod. "I suspect something but I can't tell you about it until I've checked it out further. I wouldn't want you to build your hopes up for nothing."

I broke away from him. The linen cravat which he had just given me was also green—like the one I had in my pocket—just like the one David had been wearing. Surely, Peter, too, wasn't involved.

Anxious now to check my proof, I touched my pocket.

"The scarf! The green scarf is gone!" I turned about, looking on the ground beside me. "Have you seen it?"

Peter stared at me and shook his head. Before he could say another word, I had run back down the alley into the inferno of the burning bank.

I saw the green cravat there. It had dropped out of my possession and settled on a charred smoldering log. Barely able to breath or to see, I bent to retrieve it. I would need this, along with the set of figures, if I was to stay alive. If my cousins were willing to kill Tilly and McCrae, I couldn't hope they would consider to spare me. They wanted something but so did I. If they would tell me who my father was, I would gladly give them back my information about the bank.

Even as I tucked the scarf back into my pocket, my

MORE PASSION AND ADVENTURE AWAIT... YOUR TRIP TO A BIG ADVENTUROUS WORLD BEGINS WHEN YOU ACCEPT YOUR FIRST 4 NOVELS ABSOLUTELY *FREE* (AN $18.00 VALUE)

Accept your Free gift and start to experience more of the passion and adventure you like in a historical romance novel. Each Zebra novel is filled with proud men, spirited women and tempestuous love that you'll remember long after you turn the last page.

Zebra Historical Romances are the finest novels of their kind. They are written by authors who really know how to weave tales of romance and adventure in the historical settings you love. You'll feel like you've actually gone back in time with the thrilling stories that each Zebra novel offers.

GET YOUR FREE GIFT WITH THE START OF YOUR HOME SUBSCRIPTION

Our readers tell us that these books sell out very fast in book stores and often they miss the newest titles. So Zebra has made arrangements for you to receive the four newest novels published each month.

You'll be guaranteed that you'll never miss a title, and home delivery is so convenient. And to show you just how easy it is to get Zebra Historical Romances, we'll send you your first 4 books absolutely FREE! Our gift to you just for trying our home subscription service.

BIG SAVINGS AND FREE HOME DELIVERY

Each month, you'll receive the four newest titles as soon as they are published. You'll probably receive them even before the bookstores do. What's more, you may preview these exciting novels free for 10 days. If you like them as much as we think you will, just pay the low preferred subscriber's price of just $3.75 each. *You'll save $3.00 each month off the publisher's price.* AND, your savings are even greater because there are never any shipping, handling or other hidden charges—FREE Home Delivery. Of course you can return any shipment within 10 days for full credit, no questions asked. There is no minimum number of books you must buy.

hackles rose. I felt danger about me and it wasn't from the fire. My heart hammered as I started to turn. Too late. I felt the blow which hit me, but I saw nothing of my attacker. Only the smell of burning skin and burning papers, only the sound of the crackling wood and shooting flames came to me as I faded into unconsciousness.

Chapter Eleven

Aware of a jolting movement and of a sharp pain in my head, I opened my eyes. Above me, I could see the brilliance of the stars and wisps of clouds as they drifted across the moon. As the cart moved, I realized I was lying in an open wagon, away from the burning town.

I tried to sit up. A shadow loomed over me.

"Be still, Elizabeth. You've had a nasty fall."

"But I—" It hadn't been a fall and I wanted to tell him so. Then, I saw the green linen cravat he still wore. It was the same one he had given me before, the same one I had seen on the bank floor. I felt my body stiffen.

"Are you in pain? We'll get you to the house as soon as possible and I'll send one of the men for the doctor."

Tears came to my eyes but I shook my head. My pain was not physical. My pain was wondering if Peter was the one to attack me.

"What happened to the town and the bank? Where's Terrah, my uncle, and—David?"

"Don't talk, Elizabeth. Don't worry about them.

Everyone's safe." He touched my cheek softly. "I'm afraid the fire destroyed the bank and several of the surrounding buildings. Thank God, I found you before the fire trapped you." He put his hand in mine. I allowed it to rest there, but my suspicions would not rest.

"You're lucky Peter reached you when he did."

I raised my head slightly, despite the insistence from Peter that I not move. I recognized Harriet riding up front.

"Whatever made you go back in like that?" she questioned.

"I—"

Peter put a finger to my lips. "Harriet, you two can talk later." He adjusted the cloak about my shoulders and put his arm about me—taking away one chill but causing another. "We'll be at Parkland soon. Dr. Groton said he'd drop in as soon as he's tended your uncle."

"I hope you don't mind staying with us, dear Elizabeth," Harriet said. "Peter felt Terrah would have plenty to do caring for her father, especially now with Tilly gone. So we're bringing you to Parkland."

I nodded slightly. It was comforting to know my uncle, at least, was safe. Before I drifted off to sleep again, I thought of the green scarf.

When next I opened my eyes, I was in a room with a white canopy over the bed. The sun was shining, and it was hard to believe anything evil had happened the night before. The room was twice the size of mine at Jerseyhurst. I glanced at the peaceful Chinese waterfall scene over my bed and another on the far wall. It seemed the Parkisham family had also been big in the China trade

196

as well. Turning, I felt a slight pain in my neck. Peter sat in the rocker at my side, sleeping. I stared at him a moment, not wanting to wake him. He seemed so peaceful and childlike, so totally incapable of what I suspected.

He must have been aware of my attention for he opened his eyes and smiled at me. "Thank God you're awake. Oh, Elizabeth, I've been so worried about you. So very worried."

"Where am I?" My voice sounded hoarse.

"You're in Harriet's old room. How do you feel?"

I stared blankly at him. I still did not know how much I could trust him, and yet my feelings for him were growing despite what I feared.

Putting my hand to my aching head, I felt several bandages there. "I—I'm better, I think." I struggled to right myself on my elbows.

"No. No, don't move." Peter's hands went to my shoulders and gently pushed me back onto the massive feather pillows behind me. "The doctor says you really shouldn't be moving much yet. You had a nasty blow."

"Yes, I'm sure I did." I stared at him now, trying to take in every feature, trying to see if he was lying to me or not. "Did you really rescue me?"

"Of course, I did." He bent down at the bedside and took my hand in his. "Oh, Elizabeth," he groaned, "you don't know how I felt when I thought I had lost you."

I turned slightly and stared into his deep blue eyes. His sincerity engulfed me like a soft misty cloud. No, he could not have been the one to attack me—unless he had done it to help Terrah. Why were these anxieties confusing me?

His thumb was caressing my palm. "What made you do

such a mad thing? If you had been killed—" He paused, his voice was tight. "You were already unconscious from the smoke when I found you. A beam had fallen on your head."

I wet my lips. So that was the official story—a beam had fallen on me. I took a deep breath, feeling the searing of my lungs as I inhaled. I decided against my better judgment that I was going to trust him.

Swallowing the lump in my throat, I said, "It wasn't the smoke which affected me, nor the beam."

"Well what then?"

"It was—" I paused and again looked into his eyes. I had to trust someone and since Tilly wasn't here . . . "It was a man, I think. Someone," I said, glancing down at the comforter about my legs, "who wanted me silenced."

"Silenced? Whatever for?" Peter let my hand drop. He pulled away now. He stared at me, hurt as a betrayed animal. "You're saying you suspect me? Elizabeth! My feelings for you are—what reason would I have hitting you? I don't even know why you went back."

Tears shimmered in my eyes. My vision blurred. The pain in my throat made it almost impossible for me to speak. "No, Peter," I sighed. "I don't think it was you. But you were the only one who knew I was going back."

He frowned. "Elizabeth, the whole town saw you running back." He bent down next to me again. "Elizabeth, I tell you. I would never hurt you." The tears came to his eyes this time. "I almost went crazy when I thought you might be dead. I think ever since the moment I found you trespassing in the garden, I wanted to be with you. I guess that's why I was so rough with you that day. Elizabeth, say you forgive my faults—all my faults. I want to—" He touched me. Despite my

198

suspicions, a warm glow went through me.

"Elizabeth, I think I love you. You have a spirit and a loveliness about you which has me captured."

It was my turn to be startled now. I felt my eyes widen. "But you and Terrah—"

"Terrah be damned! I don't love Terrah. I love you. I think I've loved you since you first came into my life. It's my father who wants Terrah. Her marriage to me would merely have been Father's way of having his mistress safely under the same roof as his wife."

I was aghast. "Why, how could you allow yourself to be used for such a scheme? Why?"

Peter hung his head in a boyish fashion. He was like a child being reprimanded. He refused to meet my eyes but his hand still touched mine. With a sigh, he said, "It's a long story, my love. One day, perhaps after we're wed, I'll tell you."

I felt the lump in my throat more acutely than ever before. The acid seemed to come up into my stomach. How I wanted to be with him and yet even if he was innocent of all I suspected, even if I could trust him, I still had other fears. My voice was strained as I spoke again. "Then I guess I'll never know the story, Peter. I don't love you," I lied.

He stared at me, with a shocked disbelief. There was surprise and hurt in his voice, in his eyes. "You responded when I kissed you."

I blushed hotly, recalling the shame of my passion the other day. I nodded. "Yes, I did. But—" Frantically I searched for a reason. "I'm already promised to Joshua, back home."

"A farmer! I can give you twice what he'll give you. Besides, he can't love you as I do if he let you out of

199

his life."

I tried to think. "Joshua didn't let me out of his life. I came here to find my father. I intend to return to Kansas soon."

"You don't love him. I can see it in your eyes."

I sighed and felt the tears within me forming. He was right. I didn't love Joshua the way I was beginning to love Peter and yet, I did have a great deal of affection for Joshua. Besides, I had promised him I would return. I stared at Peter now, trying to see into his eyes, trying to understand him. This protestation couldn't be a play on his part, and yet didn't he have the same suspicions about his father as I did? Did he really want to marry me? I found it hard to believe, despite my affection for him because of my own fears. I found it hard to believe he didn't have the same worry about our being related. Hadn't it even occurred to him?

"At the fire, you told me you knew something. What was that?"

"I'd rather not discuss it now. Elizabeth, I love you. I want you."

I stared at him, feeling like I was betraying myself, but it could not be helped. Until I knew Alexander Parkisham was not my father, I would have to deny the feelings I was having for Peter.

He touched his lips to my brow. "Maybe you didn't understand, my sweet. I want to marry you. I want to take you away from here."

I stared at him. So that was the plan. He was to woo me away from Aberdeen so I couldn't find out about my father, so I couldn't tell anyone about my suspicions with the bank and my cousins.

"No, Peter, I cannot marry you. It's impossible." The

tears brimmed over like a waterfall. "Please, don't talk about this again."

He put his hand to my cheek. "I won't promise anything. I will ask you again when you are well."

"Peter, if your father has made his plans, if you have agreed, then he must have some hold on you. It's useless to talk. He'll disapprove and nothing you can say will change things—even if you are willing to go against him."

"You don't understand, I allowed him to control me this long because until now I had nothing really worth fighting for. Now I do. Elizabeth, please."

My answer was delayed by Harriet's entrance into the room. Immediately the room seemed sunnier and brighter with her cheerfulness. Harriet brought a calm tranquility with her.

Her infectious laugh made me smile. "I knew I would find you here, Peter." She turned to me. "I hope he hasn't been bothering you, Elizabeth, dear. If he has, let me know. My dear brother can be a pest at times. I shall get rid of him, if you want."

I shook my head. "He's not been a bother. But—" I glanced about the room, thinking of a way to get rid of him. My eyes focused on the flowered wallpaper and the chintz curtains blowing in the breeze. "My head is aching some." I turned to face the wall. I didn't want to see Peter's eyes; I knew he was staring at me.

The silence for those few moments unnerved me. Finally, I turned back.

"Come on, Peter. Let's leave our guest alone. Why don't you go down and bring her some breakfast from the kitchen? Then you can have Carrey go for the doctor to check her out again."

I swung my legs over the bed. "Oh, Peter doesn't have to bring up a tray. I'm quite fine. I can go down to eat." Barely had my feet touched the floor when the dizziness washed over me. There was barely time to grab the newel post as Peter rushed back toward me. His strong arms supported me.

His eyes met mine. "You aren't going anywhere, Elizabeth. Not until you promise you'll be mine." He bent and kissed my ear. I didn't know if Harriet saw or not, but I felt myself flush all over. "We must talk about this later."

I swallowed hard. "There is nothing to talk about, Peter."

"I disagree." He placed me back on the bed. I watched as first Harriet left and then he turned to go.

Trying to be firmer, I repeated, "*There is nothing more to talk about, Peter.*"

His shoulders were hunched over like a man who had lost his world. I felt his depression as keenly as I felt my own, but until I knew who my father was, I could not commit myself to Peter—or anyone.

Later in the day, little Karen came up to see me. "Want to play a game of cards?"

I nodded my assent.

"Good. At least someone will play with me. Mommy's busy and Uncle Peter's being silly."

"What do you mean?"

She sighed and put her hands on her hips. "Well he's moping and carrying on." Her chin jutted out and she smiled. "Like I am when I can't have a toy that I want."

I stared at the child a moment, amazed at her insight. Maybe that's all I was for Peter—a toy. Yes, I was a toy he

202

couldn't have. With his looks and his money I was sure he could have any toy in town or the surrounding countryside. My refusal to succumb to his charms meant he wanted me all the more.

"You're probably right," I told Karen. "He probably is acting like a child without his toy. I bet he'll get better soon, though."

She sighed. "I sure hope so. He plays the best tea time." Hopping on the bed, she confided in me, "I think Grandpa is sending him away for a couple of days. I heard them having an argument just now."

I wet my lips and tried not to show any real concern. "Well, I hope whatever they're arguing about is solved soon."

"So do I." She pulled out the cards. "I hope you don't cheat at cards like Uncle David always does."

Smiling at her, I tousled her hair. "Tell me. When you play with Uncle Peter, does he cheat?"

She pressed her lips together seriously. "I'm sure he must." Her hands went to her hips. "But I've never caught him at it."

I took a deep breath. So either Peter was absolutely honest or the most dangerously clever of the lot.

Two days later, I was well enough to return to Jerseyhurst. I was relieved Harriet had kept her word. Peter had stayed away from the room. Yet I also felt lost at not having seen him. I told myself it was better this way, but I didn't know for sure.

Immediately when I entered the hall at my family's home, I felt the tension in the air. Terrah swooped down the stairs in the grand manner to greet me. For the benefit of the servants, I guessed, she kissed me on both cheeks.

"I'm so glad you're not injured." She smiled at me. I felt hatred oozing through her.

David, too, pretended happiness at seeing me. Embracing me roughly, he picked me up and spun me about. "How wonderful you look, cousin." He laughed as he pinched me and caught my hand before I could slap him. "The smoke you inhaled has done wonders for your complexion. I shall have to recommend it to all of Terrah's friends."

"I doubt you'll have many people to mention it to, then." I smiled sweetly, returning Terrah's affection. "Thank you for the compliment, David. I believe, however, it wasn't the smoke but the tender care I received over at the Parkisham's and the way Peter waited on me constantly which made the difference."

I paused and glanced at Terrah. I hoped the full impact of my words would slip in as a letter opener, slightly dulled at the edges. I might be playing a dangerous game, but I wanted Terrah to know she no longer held Peter as totally as she had thought. She merely continued with her pasted smile.

Glancing upward toward the second floor, I asked, "Is my uncle up and about? I should like to see him."

Again, I felt the hatred coming from Terrah. She glared at me. "Daddy is resting. He was not as fortunate as you. I am told we have you to thank for saving his life." Again, she smiled at me. Again, I felt the falseness. She was like a rotten apple with a skin that was perfect and beautiful, hiding the poison within.

I turned to her, knowing she really hadn't wanted her

204

father saved. "No, actually, I did little. It was Mr. McCrae who really saved his life—and Peter." I brushed past my cousins, feeling their hatred pierce my back. "Perhaps since he can't see me now, you can arrange for me to have a horse. I'd like to go into town."

"Into town?" Both echoed their concern at the same time. I doubted if the concern was really for me.

"Are you sure you're quite well?" Terrah asked, entirely too solicitously.

I nodded. "I am well enough." Then I took a deep breath and paused. I probably was foolish to tell them this, but my own desire to gloat seemed to overtake my own survival instincts. "When he dined with us at the Parkisham's, Mr. McCrae mentioned he has some papers belonging to my mother in his safe. I was to have—" I said, pausing, seeing the face of the dead man confronting me, and swallowed my sorrow, "picked them up the following day but . . ." I left the sentence hanging. We all knew about the fire.

The color flushed Terrah's apple cheeks. "I'm afraid the smoke has affected more than your complexion, Elizabeth. Mr. McCrae is dead."

My heart hammered. Just the way she said it made me believe she knew more about his death than she should have. I felt the heaviness in my heart.

"I know he's dead, Terrah," I said, looking at David so that my cousin would know he, too, was not innocent. "His clerk, however, is very much alive."

"How do you know he has a clerk?"

"Harriet told me. Peter left a message with the clerk for McCrae to come to dinner. Surely, the clerk must still be there, winding up Mr. McCrae's affairs."

Terrah frowned but said nothing as I ran up the stairs

now toward the familiar wedge room before either of my cousins could say anything more.

The town had indeed suffered from the fire. The row of buildings which had been near the bank were now a charred ruin. Bits of timber and black rubble were strewn about the lot, but even only after three days it was possible to see workmen beginning to rebuild.

I had to admit I was surprised Terrah had given in so easily to my demand for a horse. True, it had been two hours or more before I was free to ride, but no other obstacles had presented themselves once I had taken the animal.

I had been wary but alert on the road, almost expecting to have some accident on the way, but no unusual occurrence, except a rabbit sprinting across the road and frightening the horse, had marred my journey. It hadn't been hard for me to control the horse again. I realized quickly that this horse was not an easy one to ride. Had they hoped something would happen to me? I didn't know.

As I approached the main walkway near the shops, I confessed a nervousness. What was the lawyer's clerk going to have for me? Would it tell me who my father was? Or had that died with Meredith McCrae? If only my uncle could recall the past. I shivered, realizing my only other alternative was to confront Alexander Parkisham.

I did not want to do that until I had exhausted all other options. Just the thought of speaking to the man in a room alone made my stomach curdle.

Heart hammering, I jumped down off the horse. With one last glance at the burned bank, I stepped onto the wooden sidewalk. I owed it to Mr. McCrae, if not to myself, to find out my hidden parentage and the reason, if there was one, why he had died.

A man wearing a green silk cravat passed me on the street. For a moment, I paused. My blood seemed to freeze. He looked familiar—with his blond hair and husky build. No, it couldn't be Joshua. I shook my head cursing my too active imagination. Joshua was back in Kansas. He would never leave the farm. He couldn't. Perhaps it was just my own feeling of guilt for not having gone home at the end of three weeks as I had promised. Perhaps, it was my own tug of war as I tried to think of him and found myself thinking of Peter Parkisham, instead.

I told myself it was seeing the green cravat that had startled me into thought. I couldn't help recalling the one I had found and lost in the alley. I knew it couldn't be the same one, yet the presence served to remind me of what had happened. There was more here at stake than just my parentage which Terrah and David seemed determined to keep hidden from me. I was sure it had something to do with the rows of numbers I had copied the other night, but they didn't yet know I had the information.

Or did they? Fear made my body tremble. I hadn't checked the place where the gun was for several days. I wouldn't put it past my cousins to search my room while I was gone or while I had been at the Parkishams'. The blood rushed to my ears, pounding in my lungs and heart. I would find out the truth—not only as it pertained to me but as it pertained to my uncle, my aunt, Tilly, and Mr. McCrae.

Hitching the horse to a street pole, I surveyed the scene for the moment. The lawyer's sign swung directly above the dress shop where I had bought the gown for the dinner. Was it an omen? My hands tightened on the rein. I would never know until I walked into the office.

Crowds of people milled about me, more than I had ever seen before. I realized a boat had just docked, and since the fire had destroyed the town, it was now almost a curiosity stop. I heard a whisper and turned, thinking for a moment they were speaking about me. But no, the couple behind me were pointing to the bank. I had to get over these irrational fears. No one would try to hurt me in the light of day, would they?

Putting my hand on the railing, I noticed the splintered wood. Pressing my lips together, I wondered if it was some kind of omen—that I should forever be splintered and not know who my true father was. I pressed my lips together in determination. No, I had to see the clerk. I had to find out what it was my mother had given Meredith McCrae.

I wasn't feeling as well as I had told my cousins. In fact, just climbing the few steps to the first landing nearly made me breathless. I would go on.

Taking one step at a time, I forced myself to take several deep breaths and calm down so I would not appear too anxious.

Stepping into the waiting room, I couldn't say I was impressed with the offices—at least with the outer office. The faded green wallpaper was peeling, the desk was scarred, and papers were piled high in corners about the room as well as on the desk.

A young boy, wearing specs, studiously copied page after page. He seemed not to notice me. He seemed not to notice anything but what he was doing.

I cleared my throat.

The startled boy glanced up. "Oh, miss. Oh, pardon me. I didn't know you were there."

I nodded. "Yes, I could see you were engrossed in your work. Are you, rather were you Mr. McCrae's clerk?"

The boy nodded. His eyes seemed to mist.

"He said he had some papers for me to see. Papers my mother had given him. I assumed you would have them."

"Oh no, miss. Not me. His partner, Lawyer Dunn'd have those. He be takin' care of all Mr. McCrae's matters."

I winced as a sharp needle of fear jabbed my heart. Taking a deep breath, I said, "Very well. Would you tell Mr. Dunn that Miss Larabee is here to see him?"

I could hear the scratch of his pen as he wrote down my name on a scrap of paper. He looked up again and pushed the glasses back on his nose. "You are a client of his, aren't you, miss? I only just started working for Mr. Dunn and I—"

I took a deep breath, trying to steady my nerves. "No. I am not a client of Mr. Dunn's."

His face brightened. "Then you belonged to Mr. McCrae?"

"You might say so." I could hear my voice trembling. "I've already told you. Before his death, Mr. McCrae had indicated to me he had some papers of value to me. He wanted me to come by and—"

The boy scratched his head. "Strange. There were another lady, miss, not an hour since. Told me near enough the same thing."

"Oh?" My blood chilled. Could I be jumping to conclusions?

The boy verified my fears almost immediately. "Dare say, her name was Larabee, too."

My heart pounded fast now as I felt the color drain from my face. "Oh?"

"I weren't payin' much attention then, but—yer sure ya didn't come along or send yer sister."

"No," I felt my back stiffen. "I did not come by. This is my first visit to these offices and I have no sister."

"Oh." The clerk stared at me, fixed his nose specs again and shrugged. "Well, I'll tell Mr. Dunn y'er here. Maybe I were mistaken."

He left the office, then. I was alone with my thoughts. Surely, Terrah wouldn't have tried to impersonate me.

I would think Terrah would be too well known in town for her to try impersonating me, for her to make anyone believe she was Elizabeth Larabee.

I closed my eyes and tried to think. I had seen Terrah from the window in my wedge room, walking in the gardens with Alexander, not a half hour before I rode out. There would scarcely have been time for my cousin to ride to town, talk with Mr. Dunn, and ride back.

My heart was in my mouth; either the clerk was mistaken or Terrah had found someone to play her part. Fervently, I hoped it was the former.

A flushed clerk emerged from the inner office. "Mr. Dunn'll see ya, miss."

Nodding to the boy, I swept past him and into the office of Harold Dunn.

as ......
th...
b...
t...
well

Chapter Twelve

The large room which I was ushered into was richly decorated in dark wainscotting. A thick Turkish rug of rich red covered the floor. Bookcases of walnut with glass covers extended to the ceiling. Books seemed to spill out of them, and every square inch of wall had books.

I blinked as I tried to adjust my eyes to the dimmer light.

The room contained two desks but of these, only the larger one was occupied.

A tall, skeletal man, who reminded me of Washington Irving's Ichabod Crane, came forth to greet me, extending a bony hand. I took his hand and accepted the chair he offered me. His grip was dry—as Isaiah's bone must have been rising from the valley of death—I thought humorously of the sermon this week.

They must have made quite a pair, I thought, trying to see the humor in the situation as I imagined the round, red-faced man with his spidery veined face and this gaunt giant.

"Miss Larabee?" His voice had a high-pitched squeak

like a door improperly oiled. It sent shivers up my spine. His eyes, too large for his thin face, shifted uneasily and seemed to bulge out. I knew he was examining me, just as I was him.

"You are Miss Larabee."

"Yes, sir." I nodded. "I am Elizabeth Ann Larabee."

"Daughter of the late Margaret Swanson Larabee?"

Again, I nodded. "Yes, sir." I felt the color drain from my face. "Is there something wrong? You do have the papers which Mr. McCrae promised me."

Mr. Dunn swallowed hard and cleared his throat. "Pray, miss—"

"Larabee," I filled in.

"Um, yes." He cleared his throat again and stared at me as he pushed his horn-rimmed glasses up on his nose. "You definitely are Miss Elizabeth Larabee?"

What was going on here? I took a deep breath. "Yes, Mr. Dunn, I am. Mr. McCrae knew who I was. He attended a dinner party the night before he died. He told me to present myself here the following day since he had papers for me from my mother. Unfortunately, circumstances prevented my coming immediately after the fire. I'm sorry I couldn't be present at the memorial service."

"And just what were those circumstances which prevented you?" His heavy hooded eyes narrowed. I flushed, recalling the pain I had felt at Peter's possible betrayal. "I, too, was caught in the fire. My burns were slight."

Looking up into the man's face, I noticed how much more pale he looked than before.

"Well, I've come for those papers now."

Harold Dunn went from deathly white to beet red. Once more he cleared his throat. "Well, um—there is some problem here."

"What type of problem?" I could hear the fly buzzing about the room. The office seemed sweltering at that moment.

Mr. Dunn turned away from me and opened his desk drawer. Folding himself into the leather chair, he sat down. Still, he did not look at me. "I—um—suppose you can prove who you are. Who you say you are, I mean. It is logical to assume you could prove it."

I stared at him. It was my turn to be caught off guard. I hadn't brought anything which would prove I was Margaret's daughter. I hadn't thought it would be necessary. The only things I owned of my mother's were back at Jerseyhurst—the brushes and her locket. I continued to stare at him. Never had it entered my mind that I would have to prove who I was. Not once I had safely reached the lawyer.

I opened and closed my palms as I tried to think. My stomach tightened and my nerves felt on edge. If I didn't keep a careful control on my feelings, I knew I was bound to start crying in a moment, and I couldn't let myself get carried away with the emotion. It would not convince him. My heart was racing like a train along a track. "You will just have to take my word, Mr. Dunn. I don't have anything here. There is something back at my cousin's— a locket which belonged to my mother. I did not think you would doubt my word and so did not bring it, but I assure you, if you wish to have your clerk go back for it—"

Mr. Dunn reddened momentarily and glanced away. "I do not think it will be necessary for such measures."

For a brief moment, I felt some relief. Then I saw him open the desk drawer. He removed something on a chain

213

and held it up. "Is this what you would claim as your link?"

I gasped. In his open palm lay the silver locket which Mama had given me. I stared at it, speechless. Blood rushed to my temples like surf pounding the shore.

"My mother's locket. Where—where did you get it?" Tears threatened my eyes as my stomach churned rapidly.

I reached for the locket, but he pulled it back.

"What are you doing? The locket belongs to me."

"So you say." He put it back into the drawer and closed the drawer with a final click. It was a click on the door of my grave. My mouth went dry, my throat ached.

"Yes! Yes, I do say. That is mine!"

He sighed and stared at me, adjusting his specs once more. "I am sorry, my dear, whoever you are. I would like to believe you, in fact, I do believe you, but not an hour since a young woman, also calling herself Elizabeth Larabee, presented herself to me. She gave me the locket as proof. I did merely what my partner requested."

"What did he request?" My throat was dry as I stared not at him but at the desk which held my locket. I felt so alone and so helpless. Even if Mr. Dunn believed me, the papers Mama had given Meredith McCrae were gone.

Clearing his throat again, the lawyer again looked down. His voice was barely audible in the cavernous room. "He bade me, if anything happened to him, to give Miss Larabee her mother's papers." He made a clucking sound with his tongue. "But as I live and breathe, I never expected anything like this."

"And what of my locket?"

"I'm sorry. I can only return it to the young woman who presented it to me. She has said she will return for it

214

in a fortnight's time."

A fortnight. I was to have left town by then.

I stared ahead numbly. Terrah had won this time.

A glimmer of hope occurred to me. "Did she say where she lived?"

"Why yes. She lived with her cousins, the Swansons."

I could barely swallow my hatred. I continued to stare at the man until I realized he was standing, offering me his hand again, urging me out.

Trembling, I stood. My knees felt weak.

"May I ask what was in those papers?" he asked.

"I'm—I'm not really sure." I felt numb inside and could barely think.

He cleared his throat again. "Must be important for two such beautiful young women to want them so badly."

"Yes." I nodded, not even thinking of the action. "They must be." My voice sounded toneless. I had lost.

He still held out his hand. "Thank you, Mr. Dunn. You've been most—kind." I shivered and left the plush office without a backward glance.

I was vaguely aware of the stairs as I went down them toward the horse, but for all I knew I could have been walking in quicksand.

I had lost—or had I?

By the time I reached the horse, anger had taken the place of shock. I knew now what Rose had been searching for the other day. I knew now what I had to do. My confrontation with Alexander Parkisham could not be put off any longer.

Mounting the horse, I nudged his side, urging him faster and faster until I was within sight of Parkland, the

Parkisham manor. My anger urged me on. I would not be played with again. I would know about those papers. I would know who my father was.

Only as I saw the columns of the mansion did I slow. Only then did I pause to think about what I would say.

It had taken me less time to reach Parkland than I thought. My anger sped me on for I continued nudging the horse.

Breathless, I dismounted. I knew my face was flushed. I wondered if I shouldn't wait a moment to calm down, but I knew if I waited I would lose my nerve. I had to know now. I gripped the riding crop and then let it drop. All my anger was stored up for dealing with—with my father.

The idea stuck in my craw. I still could not believe he could be my father. I still could not believe my mother would have been with this man.

Squaring my shoulders, I took a deep breath and walked up the front steps. I turned to see one of the black servants taking my horse. Was I expected? My heart hammered like an anvil as I realized my moves were probably being watched—by whom? David? Peter?

My pride was at stake. I couldn't turn back. I wouldn't turn back.

I had barely knocked before the door opened. The butler frowned at me. I couldn't believe it. My heart was going faster than the horse Karen had so wildly ridden at the church. I was surprised I was even able to speak.

"Mr. Parkisham." My throat was dry. "Is he at home?"

The servant nodded. "He be in the parlor, miss. Shall I

announce you?"

I wet my lips. "No. No, it's not necessary. I believe he's expecting me."

The man nodded as if acknowledging my fears.

I forced myself to smile my thanks as I walked down the hall feeling the silence all about me. How many times had my mother walked down this same hall? How different the house seemed from the day of the dinner. How different it was from those few days when I was here recuperating. Of course, I didn't have to see Alexander Parkisham then. Now I was finally coming to terms with my worst fears.

Never had I dreamed when I left the house this morning that I would be back so soon—nor under such a pretense.

The pulses at my temples were pounding. How could I even think to talk? I could feel the sweat on my hands; I could feel the sweat beading on my brow and dripping down the center of my dress.

Taking out a linen handkerchief, I winced, realizing it was one Peter had given me. Quickly, I dabbed away the sweat. I could not let Mr. Parkisham see my nervousness. I was sure father or not, he would take advantage of it. And if he was not my father, why hadn't he told me anything before?

For a long and silent moment I stood outside the parlor door, checking out both ways of the hall to make sure no one else was about, to make sure no one was spying on me. Was I being ridiculous? My throat was dry. I tried to swallow but could not.

Even with the moment of calm, I found myself unable to move. I continued to stand by the door, paralyzed from fear. Did I really want to hear the truth now? Maybe he wasn't even in there? Maybe—I heard the movement of the chair and I knew I had no other choice.

My hand was on the knob. I should have knocked, but I knew if I did, I would lose the momentum building up in me. Besides, once I announced myself, he could easily refuse to see me. If I was already in the room, he would not refuse me.

Slowly, I turned the knob. The door opened with the slightest of noise. My heart and the pounding of my blood seemed to be making more noise than the door.

Feeling the sweat again on my brow, I wet my lips. Quickly, I stepped in and closed the door behind me. I focused my eyes on the huge swivel leather chair which faced the fireplace. The room was larger than I had expected it to be, even knowing the proportions of the house. It was twice the size of the lawyer's office and that had been large. My focus returned to the leather chair. I knew Alexander Parkisham sat there. He said nothing and neither did I.

Finally, still facing the fire, he spoke. "Terrah, my dearest, you've returned."

"No, Terrah hasn't returned." My voice was a high squeak. Blast! I did not want him to know how nervous I was.

I heard the spin of the chair as it turned toward me. His face whitened. "Who let you in unannounced?"

I forced myself to meet his eyes. Could it be he hadn't been expecting me?

Taking a step forward, I gave a tremulous smile. "I let myself in." I calmly sat down in the chair opposite his desk. "You should be more careful of greeting people sight unseen like you had. What if it had been your wife coming in just now?"

218

His nostrils flared. "I'm not the dolt you may think me, Miss Larabee. My wife is visiting her sister for the next few days. Harriet is running the house at the moment—and she always knocks."

"Oh? To make sure you're alone?"

"What do you want here?" His eyebrows met into one heavy line. He was trying to intimidate me, I was sure. I could feel myself trembling inside but I would not let him know my fears.

"What do you think I want?" I asked, giving myself time to think.

"Peter isn't here at the moment. I sent him to town."

I felt the color drain from my face. Peter had been in town when I was. I knew he couldn't have impersonated me, yet it was impossible for me not to think he might have had something to do with it.

"I haven't come to see Peter. I've come to see you, Mr. Parkisham—or should I say *Father*?"

There was an unnerving silence before Alexander's eyes widened. He let out a laugh which sounded almost like a gun retort.

"And just what makes you think I'm your father?"

"Someone is."

"Well, I should hope so." Lines creased the thick jowls on Alexander Parkisham's face, making him look even more like a monkey.

"You are my father," I stated simply.

He gave me a smile. "What gives me the honor? I thought Zebulon Larabee had the dubious claim of siring you."

I flushed. "He didn't. You know he didn't. You know I came to Aberdeen to find out who my real father was."

"Tell me what difference it would make to your life—

knowing who you are. Even if you were my daughter, and I am not saying you are, what would you expect to gain from me?"

"Why, nothing."

He stared at me. "Nothing. I find it highly suspicious. Why would you come all the way here just to get a simple acknowledgement? Why not just write then?"

"Because I wanted to meet the man who swept my mother off her feet. I wanted to know who my father is." I flushed and stammered. He was getting the better of me in this confrontation, and I didn't know what to say or how to turn it about. I tried to calm my nerves. Digging my hands into the sides of the chair, I managed to steady my voice. "I believe you know a great deal more about me than you profess to know. I believe you know who my father is. I believe you are he."

He laughed again. It was unnerving me. I knew he wanted to upset me, but it was difficult for me to keep the upper hand. I had already known he was a master manipulator. Now I was seeing him in action.

"Tell me, Elizabeth. How did you come to the conclusion giving me the honor of being your father? McCrae visited your mother several times as well. Why not choose him?"

My mouth was dry. I didn't know how to answer. I didn't know if he was involved with McCrae's murder, or if it had just been my cousin. Maybe it had been an accident after all, and I was making more of it than was necessary.

"My mother mentioned the name Parkisham to me several times. She spoke of it with fondness. It was only when I arrived—"

"You mean when you saw the fortunes of the

220

family—" he cut in.

I forced myself to keep calm. I knew I was not after his fortune, even if he did not. "It was only after I arrived, I realized it had to be you. As to Mr. McCrae—" I shrugged, feeling the pain in my heart. I took a deep breath. "Mr. McCrae is now dead. I cannot talk to him anymore." I felt the rise and fall of my chest, felt the sweat dripping down me and heard the blood rushing in my ear as the time clicked away. "Mr. McCrae told me he had some papers in his office for me. Because he is dead, I had to speak with his partner, Mr. Dunn, today."

"Oh? And did those papers tell you I was your father?"

I shook my head and glared at him. "No. They did not. I have not read the papers."

"Why not? I would think you'd be dying to read them."

He was laughing at me and I hated him for it—but if he was my father, at least I could end my quest.

"I couldn't read the papers, Mr. Parkisham. You see someone impersonated me and reached Mr. Dunn before I could. Someone else has those papers. I believe they have information about my parents. I also believe that you have the papers or know who has them."

The force of my anger caused me to stand. I took a step toward him. He remained calmly seated in his chair, lighting a cigar and puffing away, filling the air with smoke as he blew out.

"Would you like to search my desk? I know nothing at all of your precious papers."

"I didn't say you had them on you. I believe you're far too clever for that."

He nodded, acknowledging my compliment. "You believe I am too clever to have your papers on me, yet you believe I have taken them. What proof have you?"

My fists opened and closed in anger. "None." I did not like the amused tone of his voice. In fact at this moment, I truly hated him. Had I Zebulon's gun with me, I would have shot him in a minute.

My voice was low when I continued. "You were in Kansas two days before my mother died. You denied it earlier in front of your wife, but you can't deny it to me. Both you and my cousins know why I am here. I can only conclude you are keeping something more from me than just the name of my father. I can only assume you are my father and for some reason refuse to admit it."

He puffed away and smiled once more. "Perhaps I am. What of it?" The stained yellow of his teeth showed now. "What then, my dear?"

I gripped the wood of the chair harder. How I hated him for mocking me! How I hated myself for not doing something to show him I cared nothing for him or his mistress. My temples pulsated like one of the African drums hanging here in his study. The wooden mask could easily have been my face as I tried to hide my disappointment. My head ached now. I could barely think.

"If you are my father, I ask you to acknowledge me formally."

"And then? I suppose you want money, Miss Larabee. Money to buy your silence. It is not the most elegant thing you know, to acknowledge one has a bastard child."

I gasped at the word. I had to admit, this was the first time I had ever thought of myself as a bastard. Love child, maybe. Bastard, no.

I stared at him, not really hearing what he was saying. My throat was dry. I licked my lips. Was I finally at the truth?

He continued his puffing, continued blowing his smoke rings about me.

"You're saying you are my father?" The moment lengthened as the blood seemed to sing in my ears. The pause continued.

Alexander spun about in his chair and stood to face me. "No, my dear, Miss Larabee. I am sorry to disappoint you. I am not your father." He waited a moment more for the information to sink in.

"But you were in Kansas."

"Yes," he nodded, inhaling, "I was in Kansas." He relit the cigar which had gone out. "Your mother wrote asking for help. I went out to see what could be done."

"I don't believe you. She never told me of any help you gave. I had to sell the farm because of our debts. What help did you give us?" There were tears in my eyes now; I hated crying, especially in front of him, but at least the anger was better than numbness.

He continued puffing and smiling obnoxiously. It was making me ill to look at him, to think about him.

"You have to believe me. You have no choice. Perhaps—" He was watching me closely now. "Perhaps if your mother had looked at me, I might have been your father. But I was never good enough for her." His nostrils flared slightly. "It wasn't until she needed money I became good enough to associate with her. As to your debts, Elizabeth Larabee, they would have been far more burdensome had I not stepped in."

I stared at him. I felt stunned and unable to respond. I wanted him to say more but a soft knock at the door stopped further conversation.

With a warning glance at me, he said, "Yes, Harriet,

love, come in."

"I've brought your tea, Father." Harriet entered the room, her back toward me. She was carrying a silver tray laden with tea items. As she turned, I saw her eyes widen. "Why Elizabeth. How nice to see you so quickly? Are you all right?"

I nodded, wondering if the stress showed on my face.

"Shall I bring another cup, Father?"

There was an uncomfortable moment of silence. "No, Harriet. Elizabeth was just leaving." He continued puffing at his cigar while Harriet stood there.

"Damn it! Pour the stuff! I hate cold tea."

"I—"

"What are you staring at Harriet?" He turned in his chair and glanced at his daughter. Glowering at her, he seemed to communicate something which I could not read.

I, too, looked where Harriet's gaze was focused. The portrait of the man there looked similar to Alexander, yet there was a kindness and a gentleness about his features which I could never imagine on Alexander Parkisham.

Harriet glanced at me then. I felt myself flush uncomfortably. "Is something wrong?" I asked, hesitantly.

I didn't know if Harriet was going to answer me or not. Her father again demanded. "I said, pour my tea!"

"Yes, Father." Bending her head slightly, Harriet poured out the hot liquid, and then added milk and sugar, stirring it as if her father were an invalid and could do nothing for himself.

"Now be gone!"

She pressed her lips together and nodded. Quickly, she left the room, closing the door behind her.

I stood there a moment more, studying the painting and wondering what it was I found so fascinating. Alexander Parkisham had turned his chair about once more to face the fire.

Finally, realizing he had forgotten me, I cleared my throat. "Well?"

He spun the chair about again. The smoke from the cigar now circled his face. For a moment his head seemed to have detached from his body. "I thought you had gone."

"I won't leave until I have an answer."

"You have one."

"Then if you aren't my father, who is?" My throat was hoarse with the effort of talking.

"What makes you think I know more than I've told you?"

The smoke continued to circle about him.

I sighed. "The papers. The papers which Mr. McCrae had from my mother. They must have said something."

Alexander Parkisham spread his hands. The cigar dangled from his mouth. "If you see your precious papers here or anywhere, you have my permission to read them. I see nothing." He adjusted the cigar. The stink of it was making me feel nauseated. "Tell me, Miss Larabee. Why is it so vital for you to know your natural father? Isn't it good enough that you had a decent man like Zebulon Larabee to claim you?" He paused and took out his billfold. "What if I offered you not only passage money back home but a goodly sum, as well. Enough to buy back your mother's farm, if you want, and for a comfortable life thereafter."

It was my turn to knit my brows together. I could feel my hands trembling as I again clutched the edge of the

225

chair. "If you're not my father," I said, my voice lower than it should have been, "why would you give me this money? Why would you pay me to leave?" I stared at him, trying to understand what was going on.

"Let us just say it was the personal affection I held for your mother."

"Why do you want me gone?"

Alexander Parkisham shrugged. "My dear Elizabeth. There is nothing for you in Aberdeen. You'd be far happier with your own people back in Kansas. Terrah tells me of a boy you left behind. In fact, I believe I met him in Kansas, didn't I? Joshua—something."

"You leave Joshua out of this! As to my leaving, with or without money, I shan't go until I know the contents of my mother's papers. I also insist on knowing why you want me away. Get me those papers back. Then I'll think about leaving."

I knew I couldn't get any farther with the man. I knew I had to get out of the room before I began to question my own sanity.

Even as I slammed the parlor door behind me, I heard his voice chasing after me. "You are playing a very dangerous game, Elizabeth Larabee. A very dangerous game."

I ran out the back of the house, hearing his words behind me, hearing them haunt me. Was the game I was playing too dangerous? Was I getting in over my head? I didn't know. I knew only I could not turn back without losing my pride, not without finding out about my father, Tilly, and Mr. McCrae. Too many things had happened since my coming to Jerseyhurst. Too many things prevented me from leaving.

Chapter Thirteen

Forgetting I had come on horseback, I ran down the path toward the ravine. The safety of the forest which separated these two evil houses was the sanctuary I sought.

Breathless, I paused at the willow where I had sought shelter the first night. Here I stopped again and sank under the covering leaves. I wanted to be alone. I wanted to think. I wanted no one about me, and yet I felt so lonely.

I allowed my tears to flow as I hugged my knees to my chest, like a child. I wished now I was back home in Kansas. I wished I had never found that letter, never come to Jerseyhurst. If only Joshua were here to hold me and comfort me. If only I wasn't so totally alone. Shivering, I sniffled. I could feel the coolness of the late afternoon coming about me, but I did not want to move.

My instincts told me that it would be wise to accept Alexander Parkisham's offer, to leave Illinois and this mess of the Swansons and Parkishams. But how could I go without solving the mystery of who I was? Didn't anyone understand this passionate need in me to learn my heritage? I didn't care if I was a bastard. I didn't care about the stigma it gave me. I only cared about the knowledge; I only cared about seeing the injustice I had experienced here taken care of in a legitimate way.

Tears again veiled my vision. My sobs sounded like soft moans from my aching throat. I had been stupid to think that my mother's family, which had ignored us for twenty years, would suddenly welcome me with open arms.

The sound of footsteps on the path made my breath come short. I inhaled sharply and waited. I did not want to be discovered here. As quietly as I could, I tried to pull back.

It was too late. The curtain of leaves parted. My heart quickened as I saw Peter. The green leaves on his blond hair rested like a Grecian laurel. He stood there a moment, staring at me.

For just a moment I stared back at him and then stood. My pulses beat uncomfortably fast in his presence. I could not let myself be drawn into his charms. I could not let myself act foolishly as my mother had.

I took two steps toward the opening in the leaves, starting to run. I should have known I couldn't run from my feelings.

Peter must have known, too, for he grabbed my wrist, catching me. "Wait." Peter entered the sanctuary of the leaves, letting the willow branches fall about him, hiding us. Suddenly, we two were alone in our own private world. "When I heard the sounds, I thought there might be some wounded animal."

"Well, I'm no animal."

His hand gripped my elbow, much the same way he had

the first night. "My sweet Elizabeth, you have won my heart as a small kitten might. And it's obvious you have been crying. Please." He touched a finger to my tear-stained cheek. "Tell me what's wrong?"

I shook my head trying to deny his question, and the feelings which were building in me. "No. Nothing." I attempted to evade his grasp.

"Do you know, I have never asked you permission to call you by your Christian name. For all we've shared already." He dropped his eyes. "Have I your permission?"

His request caught me by surprise. I nodded. Sometimes, he truly startled me. I wondered if I would ever really know him and understand him, the way I knew and understood Joshua. I was again surprised as he bent forward. I didn't move but felt my heart racing as he kissed me on the brow, sending shivers down my spine.

"Please, Peter." I tried to pull away.

"No. I will not let you go. You must tell me what's wrong. I want to help you, if I can. I want to be with you, Elizabeth." His arms were about me now, pressing me close to him so I could feel his warmth and the hard leanness of his body. His lips now came down on my brow once more. "You mustn't leave me. Ever. It would—it would destroy me." His voice was husky. I felt myself falling under his spell.

His hands touched my neck as his lips continued to graze my face. This was wrong, and yet I was not protesting as I should.

"Please, tell me what troubles you. Let me do something for you. Let me help you."

I felt my desire burning within me like a fire which could not be extinguished. What was I to do? His soft

229

voice was insistent as his lips which traveled my face and neck, my eyelids and throat. I was shuddering now, but it wasn't from terror. My fear was of what my own body told me. How could this one moment with Peter make me forget all my mother's teachings, all her sorrows?

"Peter."

"Don't talk yet." His breath was hot as his lips melted onto mine. "I love you, Elizabeth. Truly, I do." There was an urgency in his voice I had never heard before as he continued to hold me close.

His lips parted mine, and I felt myself responding despite my desire to stay chaste.

I was scarcely aware of sinking back down onto the grassy knoll, of his hands unbuttoning the back of my dress.

It took a huge effort for me to pull away. He touched my face again as I stared into his blue eyes. "You love me, too, don't you?" he asked.

Mutely, I nodded.

His lips grazed mine once more. "Darling, I know you just met with Alexander. I know he wants you to leave Aberdeen, but Elizabeth, you can't take his offer seriously. You can't leave. Not when I've just found you. Not when he's lying to you."

My heart hammered as my whole body shivered. "What do you mean, he's lying to me?"

"You're cold, my darling. Let me warm you." He kissed me again, pressing me to him as I felt the fires stir in me. My resistance was melting, but I could not give myself to Peter. Not with what I suspected.

Once more I managed to push myself away.

"Darling, I know why it is you rejected me earlier. Joshua had nothing to do with it."

I stared at him.

"Elizabeth, you are not his daughter."

I stared at Peter again, my mouth slightly open. "How do you know?"

"Because I love you too much."

His burning mouth bruised mine, making me aware of the passion building in me, aware of my own desire to be in his arms, to belong to him—no matter how evil my desire was.

"Even if it was true, dearest," he whispered, his voice so low I could barely hear, "it wouldn't matter." He kissed my throat once more, sending those delicious shivers down my spine. "I am not his son."

"What!" I pulled back now as my eyes grew wide. "But—"

Peter pulled me back to him. His eyes met mine. "That was the problem, wasn't it? You thought we were brother and sister."

I continued to stare at him. Then I slowly nodded.

With his free hand, he pushed the loose hair from my brow. "Darling, I must confess this to you, before I declare myself again." He paused. "My true father is—was—a convict. The man, I declare, I don't even know his name, had escaped from the sheriff when going to trial. He was, of course, caught and returned to prison." His voice broke then, forcing me to turn to him, making my heart melt.

I took his head, pressing it against my breast. "Don't go on, Peter. Don't torture yourself." It was easy enough for me to understand what had happened.

Peter shook his head. His voice trembled as he continued. "He raped my mother, Elizabeth. I—I am the result. Alex Parkisham married my mother to prevent

231

her from facing the shame. Though I'm sure the money from her father didn't hurt since Alexander had none of his own. It wasn't until my uncle died that he came into the full inheritance." Peter gave a sour laugh. "I guess my convict father accounts for my bad blood."

"But you call him 'Father.'"

Peter gave a sad smile. "Very few know the secret. My mother told me only last year. It was when I refused to marry Terrah for him." He frowned. "He threatened to tell the town about me. My life is too good here. I never before thought I could tolerate being cut off from the Parkisham money, but since I've met you." He paused again. "Elizabeth, I can tolerate almost anything if I'm with you."

He looked down at me. I realized I had said little since he had started speaking. He continued to hold me. "Does it matter to you, Elizabeth?"

"Oh, Peter." I forced myself to smile at him. "It seems how can you ask." I sniffled. "But surely people wouldn't hold the fact of your mother's rape against you."

Peter frowned. "You don't know the people of Aberdeen. I can't let anyone know. It's not the same as you. I mean I don't believe Alexander is your father—but whoever he is, he can't be as bad as a convict. Still, being a bastard is still a bastard."

He leaned over and kissed me tenderly. I felt my whole body tremble. I responded to his kiss this time—thankful he was not my brother.

I melted into his arms and allowed all my fears and worries to momentarily dissolve as I returned his kiss. He was here to comfort me. Joshua was not.

I knew what I wanted was wrong. I knew my mother's

blood was stirring within me. Yet, I could not deny what I was feeling.

Slowly, his hands roamed my body, making me feel more alive than ever before, making me feel as if I were a bird soaring free. I returned his kisses wantonly, knowing that I was probably making a fool of myself and yet I felt sure he felt the same as I did.

For just a moment, a warning echoed in my brain. Did Peter aid Terrah in killing Tilly? Did he attack me in the bank? Did he know who my real father was? He claimed not. As much as I wanted and desired him, there was still the nagging mistrust which invaded my precious love.

I was not aware of my bodice undone until I felt Peter's mouth on my breast. His tongue was causing warm sensations to flood me. They were sensations I had never before experienced, and yet even as I felt myself giving into him, I had to pull back.

"Darling. Darling Elizabeth. Whatever is wrong?"

I shook my head, unable to speak.

"What?" He kissed my brow, his hand stroking my breasts, making my nipples harden, causing my skin to tingle as I never thought it would. "I love you, Elizabeth. Truly, I do."

"Then if you love me, tell me who my father is."

"Oh, my precious sweet. If I knew, I would tell you immediately."

His eyes were sincere. I wanted to believe him and yet I couldn't. "What was the secret you said you were going to tell me the night of the fire?"

"Secret?" He paled a moment and stared at me. "I—I don't recall saying anything."

I could feel myself stiffen. "You did." I glared at him then. "I wonder if you don't know of the papers, too? Did you help someone impersonate me and steal them as well?"

"What are you talking about, Elizabeth?" He was obviously mystified. Or was he acting?

I told him then about the visit to the lawyer, Harold Dunn, about the woman who impersonated me.

"Well, it couldn't have been Terrah. She's too well known," Peter said. "I can't imagine it could be anyone else."

"Can't you? There must be someone whom your father—whom Alexander—or Terrah paid to impersonate me. Those papers have to be somewhere."

"Oh, Elizabeth," he sighed. "Darling, knowing who my father was just brought me trouble. Why don't you forget your search? Why don't you and I run away together?"

Tears came to my eyes. I pulled the bodice back on and began to button my dress again. "If you love me, you'll help me find my father. I won't leave Illinois until I find out the truth, until I know also the story of poor Tilly and of Mr. McCrae."

Peter reached out and tried to hold me. I shook my head. Tears were now streaming down my cheeks. How could I love anyone who didn't understand my desire to find out who I was?

I fled from Peter and from the willow. This time I remembered my horse. Going back to the front of the house, I took my horse from the black slave who still held it.

My vision was veiled with my tears as I rode the short distance back to Jerseyhurst. I had to find out who I was. I had to find those papers—and soon.

*   *   *

I reached the wedge-shaped room without seeing anyone from the household. I was glad for that, glad I didn't have to see my cousins gloating over their victory.

I lay on the bed as I tried to calm myself. Emotions whirled about inside me. I had to admit I was beginning to regret having come, but who was to know the viper's nest I would be opening? Who would have guessed my mother's family would turn so totally against me?

I rested for several hours, not closing my eyes but just staring up at the wall, staring at the markings made by my aunt. She had been killed, just as Tilly had. I was sure of it. I was also sure my cousins had their hand in all the deaths which had occurred since I had come. Was I next? Would they stoop so low? A shiver ran through me. I knew I had to protect myself. I knew the paper with the numbers I copied was one of my few insurances.

My heart was heavy as I raised myself from the bed. After first checking that the door was securely locked, I went to the fireplace.

For just a brief second my memory blanked. I could not recall behind which brick my treasures lay. Sweat broke out on my brow. If I had lost those, I might just as well have lost my life.

Frantically, I began tugging at several bricks. None moved. I turned away from the fireplace and began to pace. Then, once more, I stared at the fireplace. The number came to me as if unbidden. Six by six. That was the formula I had used.

I forced myself to take a deep breath, to calm the pounding in my brain. How I wished I had one of Tilly's powders to take away the pain. Counting to thirty-six, I placed my hand on the proper brick.

My heart sang with relief as it pulled apart.

Then I stared. Was the space empty? Panic engulfed

me. It couldn't be gone.

Nervously, I put my hand into the hole only to realize the gun and paper had just been pushed farther back, probably when I had hurriedly dressed for the fire. A laugh of relief escaped me as I pulled out my precious items. I felt the heavy weight of the gun again and kissed the paper with the numbers. Yes, both were fine. Both were going to help me get safely away from Jerseyhurst. Both were going to make sure my cousins told me who my true father was.

Thankful, I replaced the gun and my notes in the hole once more, sealing it carefully. I stepped back from the wall. No one could tell anything was amiss there.

My stomach gave an unexpected grumble. I realized then that I had eaten little since breakfast. I had been too preoccupied when in town to purchase food and had certainly not eaten anything since my confrontation with Alexander Parkisham.

I could smell cooking odors from below. I wondered why I hadn't been summoned to dinner or hadn't heard anyone calling.

Washing with the tepid water in my bowl, I freshened my face and straightened my dress. Head high, I started down the stairs.

At the door to the dining room, I halted and merely stared. It was as I had expected. My cousins were seated there, eating as carefree as one might imagine. But what startled me even more was the presence of Peter and Harriet at the table as well.

Peter smiled at me. Quickly, he pulled out a chair next to him. I continued to stand and stare.

"We wondered when you would rouse yourself and come downstairs," Terrah said sweetly. "Knowing you

236

were still partially recovering, we didn't want to wake you from your deep sleep."

I glared at her. Deep sleep my eye! I had not been sleeping and well she knew! Anger flushed me, but I held my tongue and decided not to say anything at this moment.

"You do feel better, don't you?" Harriet questioned, concerned as ever.

I forced myself to smile politely and nod. "Oh, indeed yes. The ride I had this afternoon did wonders for me. I learned quite a bit in town which helped me to understand several things." I glanced first at Terrah and then at David. I knew I was being vague, but I hoped it was enough to set them on edge. For all they knew, Mr. Dunn might have read the letters before handing them over to the imposter. I wanted them to think he had told me what I sought. I realized, of course, Terrah would have conferred with Alexander Parkisham but my bragging was worth a try.

If I had expected a reaction from my cousins, I received none. Only Harriet seemed flushed. I couldn't help wonder, too, if she was in on this scheme with them.

I took my chair on the opposite side of the table—away from Peter. Just having him dine at Terrah's table and not even ask me felt like a betrayal. How could I love anyone who didn't even protect my interests?

"So did you speak with McCrae's partner?" David asked, picking up on my words.

"Of course. He and I had a long talk. In fact, I shall prepare to leave when he sends the originals along. Apparently, he had given the first copy to someone else."

Peter leaned across the table and took my hand. "You are not leaving Aberdeen, Elizabeth. Certainly not until after the ball. Your cousins wouldn't hear of such a thing."

I was surprised at his reaction—in public, with Terrah staring at him. I tried to move my hand from under his and felt myself redden, but he would not release me.

"You promise you will stay."

I glanced at Terrah. Peter did, too. There was a brief moment of total silence in the room before she gave a slight nod.

"Of course, you must stay. The ball is in your honor. It wouldn't be right for you to depart before then."

Peter squeezed my hand. "You see. Everyone wants you to stay."

I took a deep breath and then turned my head away from him. I wish I could understand what was happening. I knew my cousins did not want me. Did Peter now have some hold over them? Had it anything to do with the papers? I pressed my lips together. "Very well."

Peter smiled and slowly let go of my hand. As soon as my hand was free, I drew back and clasped my hands together under the table, waiting to be served, feeling my skin burning from Peter's touch.

There was an uncomfortable moment of silence as the maid brought in my dinner. The whitefish was heavy with a French sauce, not the type I enjoyed, but at least it was food and I did need food to think. I couldn't help notice the good Haviland dishes were being served. But then of course, it was for Peter and Harriet.

I said little during the rest of the meal, eating only enough to keep up my strength as the others, especially Harriet and Terrah, chattered about me.

238

The others finished long before I did, but since I was the last one, I felt uncomfortable making them wait for me and yet, it was their fault for not calling me. I took two more bites of the meal and then stood, going into the parlor for coffee with them.

Peter grabbed my arm as we walked down the hall. I was sure that Terrah and David were watching him, but he didn't seem to care.

"What's this foolish notion about leaving? You can't leave. Not when we're so close to finding out who your father is."

I stared at him. My feelings were so confused. I wanted to love him, I wanted to give myself to him and to believe him. But how could I when I found him dining here constantly, when I found him talking with Terrah all the time? Yet now it seemed he wanted to help me. Could it all be a hoax he and Terrah were playing on me?

"Peter, wasn't it you who told me just the other night—" My voice choked. "When we found Tilly's body. You said I should not ask too many questions. You said I should leave as soon as possible."

"That was before," he hissed. "Before I realized how much I love you. Elizabeth, please." There were tears in his eyes; his voice seemed to choke. "Believe me."

The others had already reached the parlor, and the maid was pouring the coffee. "If you love me, then help me find the papers your fiancé stole. Help me find out who my real father is."

"What do you think I'm doing? I can't be too obvious, my precious. I must let Alexander and Terrah believe—"

Terrah looked back at us, as if she knew we were discussing her and yet, she could not have heard. Had this conversation been planned between them before I came down?

I sucked in my lower lip. I knew even if he couldn't help me find the papers, even if he was involved with Terrah, I would still love him. I knew now that he could not be my brother, no matter who my father was. Yet, I knew my heart had to be hard. I had to find out who my father was, even if it meant denying my love for him.

We had to part. We had to join the others, or Terrah would become angry. I was sure she already knew what we were talking about, yet, I wanted to give her nothing more to comment on.

"I will do all I can, Elizabeth. You have my solemn word," he whispered. "Meet me later—near your mother's burned-out house."

I swallowed and nodded. I would meet him later as long as my cousins didn't stop me.

It didn't take long for me to find an excuse and depart the company for my own solitude.

Lighting the lamp. I sat at my desk and began to write down what few notes I could recall from both my mother's memories and what I had learned here. Oh, if only I could speak with my uncle.

I cursed myself for not taking advantage of getting the information from him when I had the chance. I had been timid then. I had been scared of Terrah, but no more. Neither she nor David could threaten me as long as I knew about the bank. I only wished I still had the green silk, but then having seen Peter's and the one belonging to the other gentleman, I had no real proof that I had found David's.

Even as I continued to write, I felt the hairs on the back of my neck rise.

I was sure that if I noted down my thoughts and impressions, I would be able to make some sense of things, but it still remained a jumble to me. No solution showed itself.

With pen and ink in front of me, I stared at the paper. I nibbled the tip of the feather. Nothing further came to me.

I realized then that the silence about me was intense. Even though the window was open, I could hear nothing of the evening life outside. Surely, there should be birds or a murmur of the great river. But there was nothing.

I cocked my head and listened harder. The house, too, was deathly silent. I drew a deep breath. Was I going insane? Was the search for my father driving me into a hell of my own making? I had never been given to fanciful fears, but now it seemed I was allowing them to take over.

The extraordinary silence about me seemed to deepen. With it came a sense of cold. I seemed to be in a space apart, removed to where no human touch, no human voice could reach me. Indeed, I felt an utter aloneness and despair. It seemed as if my spirits would never lift. I was totally isolated here.

The stillness deepened still further. It seemed rather that I could hear every quick beat, every pulse of my body. A vague terror began to possess me and I fought against its insidious influence.

Maybe my father, too, had been a convict. Maybe my father had been—no—it couldn't be my own uncle! Yet, didn't one go insane when things like that happened? I tried to calm myself. My fears were totally irrational, but

I could not help them.

Bending my head down over the paper, which I had set out only a moment before, I tried to force myself to write, but my hand would not move.

I stared at the offending limb. The fear gathered in my throat like a lump that was immovable.

The cold once more swept over me. I was again drawn to the markings on the wall. My aunt's name. My aunt would somehow give me the answers. I shivered violently. Not all the fire in the world could have warmed me now.

It took several moments for me to regain control of my nerves. Finally, I began to write once more, putting down in sequence all that had happened this day. I was sure there was little chance of me forgetting it, and yet, it seemed the right thing to do.

Swallowing hard, I turned in my chair. My hair again seemed to rise as I had the distinct feeling of being watched. No one was about.

After one more quick glance of the room, I finished my notes and hid them along with my gun behind the rock.

I lay down on my bed then, knowing that if I was to meet Peter later, I would have to rest. The fear of the last few moments had drained me. Yes, it had been irrational. I knew my mother would never have—have made love with anyone but her heart's desire, and yet I could not deny my uncle's own guilt-ridden cries nor could I deny my own desperate fears.

Chapter Fourteen

I had barely lay down when the key turned and the door opened. I was shocked at the invasion of my privacy. Terrah stood there, framed by the wood of the door. She was like a picture of one of those cheerful Dutch housewives. Yet she was, however, anything but cheerful.

"Don't you ever knock?"

"I do when the company demands it," she responded, as she pranced in and sat down on the one chair I had. "I think it's time we had a talk."

I could feel my heart pounding loudly. After the unnerving experience I had just had, Terrah was not someone I wished to see. "About what?" My stomach tightened.

"Peter."

My mouth went dry. "What about him?" I sat up abruptly.

"I don't like the way you're encouraging his advances."

"I—" I glanced down at the comforter, recalling this

afternoon. "I am not encouraging him. If anything I am discouraging him."

"They why does he pursue you?"

I met her eyes this time. What I knew about her sickened me. I did not even want to claim her family, but I had no choice. She was my cousin. "Perhaps it is because he can't reach me as he reaches you."

She glared at me.

"Peter is mine. He is going to marry me."

"Yes, I know. So that Alexander Parkisham can have his mistress and his wife both residing at Parkland at the same time. How very convenient! Have you ever thought of Peter in this matter?"

She didn't even flinch. "He shouldn't have told you that. His father won't be pleased."

"Oh, do you know which prison his father's in?"

She reddened.

"Yes, he told me that, as well. So my own fear of Alexander being my father—even if it is true—and I pray it is not, affects nothing. That is, if I choose to allow Peter's desires."

Terrah stood now. Her dress swished ominously as she walked the few steps toward the bed where I still sat. "We are playing games, Elizabeth. To a point, I find them enjoyable, but they are becoming tedious. You are becoming tedious." She paused. "Peter doesn't love you. He's playing a game with you, just as he plays with all the women in town. I tolerate it because I know him. I've grown up with him and lived with him."

I pressed my lips together and said nothing.

Seeing that it had no effect on me, she continued. "He'll tire of you soon. He knows when he marries me, he'll get half of Alexander's fortune and my stock in the bank. I doubt you could do as well for him." She smiled at me. "Peter likes the good life. He always has and he always will. A pretty skirt is just a passing thing for him."

I shrugged, pretending not to care. "I might be a passing fancy for Peter Parkisham. Nevertheless, I wonder if he really knows about you. All about you, I mean."

Her eyes hardened like emeralds ready to cut me. The apple color in her cheeks heightened to ripeness. "You yourself just told me Peter knows about my relationship with his adopted father."

My heart was beating loudly. Every instinct in me was telling me to keep my silence, but I could not. Her attack on me goaded me on.

"Does he know of the money missing from the bank?"

If eyes could have shot daggers, I am sure I would have been dead.

"What money?"

"Does he know the fire wasn't started by accident?"

Her voice was menacing. "Just what are you saying? I think you had better explain yourself."

I didn't like the way she was towering over me. I stood up from the bed and walked toward the door, indicating that I wanted her to leave. Using the door as my support, I managed to get out my words with bravado.

"I frankly don't care who Peter marries." It was a lie, but I had to say it. "I do care, however, about who my father is. I told you when I first arrived, Terrah, I am going to find out. I refuse to leave here until I do."

I didn't think I could see hatred any deeper than I had already seen. Even though I kept my calm, inwardly I was trembling.

"Then don't leave." She smiled at me, using her

245

sweetest smile. "Stay as long as you want. Stay forever, if you want."

Turning, she swept out of my small room. The sound of her silk dress rustled like a rattlesnake about to attack as she moved along the floor and swiftly down the hall.

I don't know how I had the strength to keep standing. I didn't know how I had the strength to lock the door and return to my bed.

It took several moments for my heart to stop racing. Yes, I was afraid of Terrah and of David, too. I bit my lower lip. Would it help any to tell Peter what I knew? Could I trust him? I still didn't know exactly where he stood.

Closing my eyes, I prayed fervently that he had been able to locate the papers, that he could tell me who my father was, or give me some clues not yet discovered. Then and only then could I trust him.

It was ironic, I knew. The more determined they were to keep me from knowing, the more determined I was becoming.

I waited until I could hear nothing from the household. I knew silence meant little, considering all which had transpired in the past. However, it was at least a sign that I could attempt to leave the house.

The chemise I had been wearing was now sticky with perspiration. Quickly, I changed and donned a fresh one along with a black bombazine dress. Even as I put it on, I realized it was the same one I had worn for the funeral, but it was the best one to wear if I wanted to leave the house this night without being seen. I also hoped the dark color would hide my figure from anyone who might decide to be watching me. Besides, Peter had not seen me in this. I hoped he would like it.

It was true. I trusted no one in this household. No one—not even myself. I knew given the chance, I would betray my own ideals and those Mama had instilled in me for the desire and love of Peter Parkisham.

There was more than just a handsome face there. In spite of his foppish dress, in spite of what I suspected him of, there was also a gentleness within him, a sweetness which I knew I could share. Even thinking of him made me shiver, but it was so wrong. Look at what had happened to my mother. I doubted Peter would marry me—no matter what his good intentions. I doubted it, and yet I wanted him so much.

It seemed the boards creaked with every step I took in the hall. I hadn't been this frightened even when I had forced my way into the study and found the numbers.

How I reached the first floor without a candle, without tripping, I'll never know. Shadows from the dying fires loomed on the walls about me as if to warn me of evil but I would not, could not think of the evil. I could only think of Peter and what it would mean to see him.

The truth was that I was becoming almost as obsessed with him as I was with finding out who my father was.

Carefully, I unlatched the door and opened it, hearing the squeak and feeling the cool evening breeze upon my face. I should have brought a lamp to use for the woods, at least, but the thought hadn't occurred to me earlier. Now, it was too late. I was not about to return to my room. I would just go on without it. If the Lord meant for me to reach the burned house in safety then I would.

I stayed on the steps a moment, listening to the crickets of the night, listening to the other sounds about me, smelling the sweetness of the night jasmine and wondering if all the sounds I now heard were natural. I had to assume they were.

The door closed behind me. I took several steps onto the gravel path. Through the thin material of my shoes I could feel the hardness of the rocks. Strange how I had not noticed the firmness of the ground before. Momentarily, I thought of not taking the gravel path, fearing the noise might be too much, but recalling how I had become lost the first day, I did not want to take the same chance.

I turned back one more time to stare at the house. My mouth was dry. Every nerve of my being seemed to be shaking. Did I know what I was doing? What if Peter didn't have the information I wanted from him? Would I be strong enough to refuse him yet a second time in the same day?

The house behind me was dark but that meant nothing. It was with relief my feet touched the grass which began the wooded part of the path. My figure would at least be covered by the leaves and trees.

An owl hooted. I jumped nearly out of my skin.

I told myself Peter would protect me—but would he? I still wondered if he had rescued me from the fire or if he had delivered the blow to my head.

Thinking of the fire made my head ache. I wet my lips as I felt my utter confusion. How could I be in love with someone who I mistrusted so?

Even as I forced myself to continue on the path, I recalled how I had privately condemned my mother for her actions. It had been the first day I had learned the truth. I had lied to people when they had asked if being a bastard had upset me. Indeed, it had. I lifted my skirts and hurried along the wooded road toward Peter.

Twigs and leaves crunched beneath my feet. Again, I felt them more keenly than I had ever felt anything before. I should not feel guilty nor ashamed for this meeting. I had done nothing wrong. Were it not for my cousins forcing me to seek other means of finding information, I would not even be meeting Peter. Or so I told myself.

I was in quite a state when I finally reached the clearing where the old house stood. The light of the half moon shone on it. The ghostly arms of the decayed walls seemed to rise to the sky, beckoning me with a fatal persuasion.

I stood there staring at the burned structure. Having seen the building by the daylight, I was amazed at how different it looked now. Did I truly want to go in there? Did I truly want to risk my future by meeting Peter tonight? I felt almost like one of those showboat gamblers who had sauntered off the boat at the docks the other day in Aberdeen. Happiness for me, at this moment, seemed elusive and beyond the moon. Even my mother's pendant was gone. My whole life seemed to be changing in such a short space of time.

Even as I continued to stare at the structure I knew I had gone too far already. I had to see the night through. It would remain to be seen if I succumbed to my desire for Peter, if I allowed the devil inside me to surface, but I would at least meet Peter and talk with him.

The moonlight shone on me as I stepped forward into the clearing. At this moment, I felt more naked than I had when I had stepped from the pond. I shivered.

No sounds came from the house. I had not before wondered if Peter would meet me. Now, for the first time

249

the fear occurred to me. Suppose he could not find those papers. Perhaps he wouldn't come at all.

Well, I was here. I would go in and see if Peter was here. There could be no evil about this house, itself, no matter how gloomy it looked. My mother had lived—and loved—here. Surely, her spirit would protect me.

Carefully, I stepped over the broken stones and the charred remains where I had tripped once before. The moonlight seemed brighter inside as the rays shone on the remains of the flowered wallpaper.

I took a deep breath. Did I dare call out Peter's name? If he were here, why didn't he say anything?

I took several steps forward. Sounds seemed to echo here more than they did back at Jerseyhurst. The blood rushed to my head. I walked quickly to where the stairs were.

Glancing about one more time, I placed my foot on the first step. My heart went to my throat as I felt my weight sag the step. Peter couldn't be upstairs, I thought. He would never have gotten past this step.

I feared the step would break and quickly put my weight on the next one. To my relief, this one held. The cold bannister which I held onto didn't feel any steadier than the steps, yet I could see now there were markings in the dust of the steps. Footprints?

It was hard to tell in the dim light.

A moment later, I heard my name being called. I couldn't see where it was coming from, but I recognized the voice. My heart sang. "Peter? Where are you?"

He leaned down over the railing of the second floor. "Up here."

"How did you get there?" I motioned to the step which had nearly broken with my weight.

He laughed softly. "When one is a member of the Parkisham family, one learns to tread carefully."

I stared at him a moment.

"Come on. Come up."

Still I did not move. "Did you find the papers?"

"I found something."

"What?"

Even in the dim light I could see that cocky grin of his. Hating him for teasing me and yet wanting to be with him, I placed my foot on the next rung. It held. I moved forward again.

Becoming confident, I placed both my feet on the next step. It was a mistake. I felt the wood weaken beneath me almost before I could cry out.

Immediately Peter ran down the steps, carefully avoiding certain ones. I hadn't been hurt, only stunned as I fell back. Before I could protest, Peter picked me up in his arms and carried me back up the stairs. I was surprised, with our combined weights, that the stairs held.

"I told you, my love, you must be careful who and what you trust here."

He was right. I had never mistrusted until my mother's death, and now everyone was a source of suspicion. "Does that mean even you?"

Peter didn't answer but merely continued carrying me.

When finally he laid me down on a blanket in one of the upper rooms which had not been damaged by the fire, he kissed my brow. "I love you, Elizabeth. I mean to marry you. I hope you trust me, though I know you have reason not to."

I stared at him. He knew I had reasons. Was he then admitting he had attacked me at the pond? In the house?

251

At the bank? I could barely speak for the fear and anger that were surging through me.

"Darling, it's true I allowed my father to manipulate me into this marriage with Terrah, but no more. I promise you. No more. You are my only concern now."

Still I stared up into his blue eyes. I was aware of the warmth of his body as he held me close, but I was also aware of a chill deep within me. "Peter," I started to speak and found the words choked in my throat.

"No more talk now." He leaned over and kissed me. As his lips met mine, I felt myself resisting only a moment before I gave into the swell of desire which was flooding over me and heating my body. I felt my blood pounding in my chest now and in my brain. I feared myself and my reactions to this man almost as much as I feared him.

How could one who appeared so wonderful and sweet be someone who could harm me? I had to trust someone, I told myself. I had to put myself into his arms and trust him.

His tongue probed my mouth, and I tasted his sweetness as he pressed himself closer to me on the floor. Heat surged through me. I tried to think but found my thoughts hazy. All my being was centered on the pleasure of his touch as his hands roamed my body. All my mind was centered on him.

I felt his hands touching me, opening the bodice of my dress, touching me, kissing my breasts, exciting me by the gentle pressure of his tongue and mouth sucking at my nipples. A heady surge of excitement trembled through me to the core of my womanhood. I had no idea what I was doing or why, but my hands went to the back of his head as I massaged his neck.

Our lips met again and we pressed tighter together,

252

attempting to merge into oneness. Was this right? I didn't know but it felt right. Yet the power of my emotions scared me.

With a tremendous effort, I pulled away.

"Peter, please, you must tell me. What of the papers? Did you find out anything? Was your father the one who arranged to have them taken?"

He let go of me and glanced toward the window. "I'm sorry, Elizabeth. I could do nothing this quickly. I have my suspicions, but I haven't been able to prove them."

"Peter! You told me you would have some answers for me."

He touched my cheek with his hand. I saw the sadness in his eyes. "Elizabeth, I'm sorry. I tried."

"Oh, Peter. Don't you understand how much this means to me?"

He looked up now. I was surprised to see tears in his eyes. It touched me in a way nothing he had done yet touched me. Leaning over he kissed my brow.

"I do understand. I tried to find out. Alexander wouldn't tell me."

I stared at him, astonished now at his directness. I shouldn't have been because he was certainly bold enough with me, and yet I knew, despite his boldness, how much he feared Alexander.

"Yes, I went to his study immediately after I returned from Jerseyhurst."

"And?" I couldn't believe he was keeping me in suspense like this.

"Well, Alexander is not your father. I know for a fact."

"How do you know?"

"Because he's sterile."

I stared at Peter. "I know about you, but what about Harriet?"

He shook his head. "Mother's daughter by her first marriage."

I felt the news go to my head like wine. Alexander Parkisham was sterile. "Are you sure he wasn't just telling you this to lead you off? He obviously knew you were going to tell me."

Peter shook his head, some of his blond locks falling forward into his eyes. "I couldn't resist brushing them away. "No, I suspected Alexander's problem long before this, but he confirmed it tonight."

"How?"

Peter merely smiled. "Trust me. It's true. I believe him. Mother and he no longer sleep in the same room, but certainly Terrah would have become *enceinte* by now."

"But, Peter, he was the most logical choice. If he isn't my father, who is?"

Peter's lips grazed my brow. "I don't know, my love, but I promise, I will do all I can to help you find out. I know how much this means to you."

He spoke with such sincerity that I had to believe him. I wanted to believe him.

Once again our lips met. This time I allowed myself to feel the passion I had for this man.

I probably should have resisted and I do admit that thoughts of my mother again came to my mind as I realized suddenly I wore nothing but my chemise. Yet somehow it felt so perfect. Even if Peter didn't marry me as he promised he would, I knew I loved him and had to be one with him. I knew I would never forgive myself if I didn't take this moment to be his. Who knew if we would again have a time like this? Who knew if Terrah wouldn't do something horrendous to part us?

Just thinking of my cousin made me shudder. I pushed myself deeper into Peter's willing arms, forcing myself to think only of him.

I realized suddenly that I knew nothing of what was about to happen. I knew nothing of what to do. I glanced up at Peter, suddenly frightened.

He must have sensed what I was going through because he again kissed my brow and smoothed his hands over my back. "Never fear, my darling Elizabeth. It will be wonderful, I assure you."

I trembled inside. As much as I wanted him, I did not feel the same sureness. Although Mother had never told me anything, always saying she would explain things when the time was right, I had heard stories from a few of the girls in town. I didn't know if they had ever done it. All I knew was that they said one often bled copiously and that if you were not married to the man you did it with, you might die for the sin of it.

I swallowed my fear. My mother hadn't died and I was living proof that she had done it before she had wed. Nor had she wed the man she had lain with.

Still, I couldn't stop my trembling.

Peter put his jacket about me. I glanced toward the door, wondering now if I should pull away, wondering if I shouldn't stop all this and return to the house before it was too late, before I regretted everything.

I laid my head against Peter's strong shoulders. His hand was on my breast as he lowered his mouth to kiss me there. He was naked now as I was. I felt his arms go about me.

"Do you know how beautiful you are, Elizabeth? Do you know how much I want you and love you?"

I stared at him. Suddenly, I found it hard to believe. Tears came to my eyes. Why would he want me over my cousin? She had all the money, all the power.

Peter was talking to me, soothing away my fears. "I promise you. We can run away. Tonight, if you like. We can be in Galena by the morning and be married by a judge there."

I stared at him. Sniffling, I wiped my tears on his linen kerchief. "You mean that, don't you?"

"Oh, Elizabeth. Would I tell you I loved you if I didn't?"

I swallowed the lump clogging my throat and felt the acid churning in my stomach. "I don't know. I've heard that some men say they do, when they don't."

In protest, his lips met mine. I felt as if I were being devoured, as if I were being eaten alive and loving every moment of it. My arms went about his neck again as I stifled my tears. I pressed myself to him feeling his hardness but not daring to look toward it.

His lips touched my earlobes, sending wave after wave of pleasure through me. It was like nothing I had ever experienced before.

"Now," he whispered into my hair. "Was that the kiss of a man who is lying?"

Having never been kissed by anyone but Joshua, I didn't know if I was qualified to answer but I shook my head. "I believe you, Peter. I love you. I only wish—I knew who I was."

His kisses stirred me again. "Don't you understand, Elizabeth? I don't care who you are. All I care about is you."

"But—"

"No buts." His hands were rougher than I expected them to be as they stroked and tantalized my nerves, touching every part of me, touching all my being. His mouth once more centered on my nipples. I gasped, as the fire within me spread.

I was barely aware of his hands as they continued their magic on me, bringing me closer and closer to him.

My own arms dug into his hairy back as I kissed him more fiercely than I had ever kissed before. I would not think of the rightness of this. I would think only of the beauty and the joy, I told myself.

I was sure my mother could not have wanted my father more than I wanted Peter, and yet I doubted I would have the courage to pull away, as much as my fear continued to control me. I felt the blood rushing through me, alive as I had never been alive. He touched the mound at the top of my legs. I quivered as a taut bowstring.

For the very first time I stared at his manhood. I knew no other word for it. I continued to stare astonished. "Surely, you can't mean—"

Peter said nothing but smiled as his mouth found mine.

Yes, I was afraid at that moment but in his arms, so warm and so loving, I felt safe.

His fingers pressed me apart, stimulating my nerves until I felt a peculiar wetness.

Gently, Peter pushed me backward on the blanket. His jacket fell from my shoulders but I scarcely noticed it. I was conscious only of him and of his arms. I thought of nothing then but our love.

I gasped as he entered me. I cried out in pleasure and pain, but he quickly covered my mouth with his as he pressed himself to me, kissing me so wonderfully and deeply.

Barely aware of what I was doing, I lifted my legs so they rose up to his back. The pain had gone and now there was only a different kind of pleasure. I hung onto Peter as he rocked within me, giving me a rush of pleasure and warmth that I had never imagined.

I heard his heavy breathing mingle with my groans as I felt myself rushing faster and faster. It seemed as if I was going to crash, but I knew I would not. I knew I was safe with Peter. I knew our treasure lay in becoming one, in crashing into each other's souls and never leaving the other.

The final moment was better than I ever anticipated. It was as if together we had gone to heaven and returned. How could Mother have left the man she loved? How could I ever leave Peter?

I kissed his brow as he lay there, panting deeply on top of me. I brushed the damp hair from his head and felt his teeth on my lobes.

"You're not hurt are you, my sweet?"

I shook my head. "No. Just—just worried. I mean I—" I glanced down as he rolled off. There was some blood but only a little.

Peter laughed deeply. "The stories women tell each other sometimes amaze me."

I stared at him. "You mean, you know the stories? How? Have you taken other women?"

"Elizabeth, my precious one, I've not been a monk. Besides, one of us had to know how to do it."

Peter kissed my lips and chuckled softly at my naïveté. He brushed his hands against my breasts, causing me to feel that peculiar tingling again. "Elizabeth, darling, there has been no one since you have come into my life and there will be no other than you. Does that satisfy you?"

He drew me against him once more. We had a moment's peaceful silence, listening to the night sounds outside the room. I was able to pretend for those few seconds that we lived in a world all our own, that this was our own home and we were already happily wed. But even as I thought it, I knew it was not so.

"Well, my sweet, will you come away with me tonight?"

I looked up into his eyes. They seemed bluer than ever now. "Peter, how can you ask me to leave? You told me you understood my desire to find out my father. But your question is selfish."

"You're right. It is selfish, but I ask it because I love you. Because I want to care for you and take care of you." He kissed my lips. "Elizabeth, you should not stay here. These past few weeks should have told you so."

I shook my head. "These past few weeks have only made me more determined than ever to find out who my father is. You were the one at dinner tonight who made the fuss about my not leaving."

I grabbed my dress and chemise from off the floor. Quickly, I dressed. "I must get back to the house before they suspect anything."

He stared at me. "Elizabeth, please. You have to understand. They are not playing at children's hoops here. You, yourself, told me you suspected Tilly's death and Mr. McCrae's. Alexander is determined you are not to learn the answers you seek. I found out his determination only tonight."

"What do you mean? What exactly did you find out?"

"Elizabeth, I can't talk about it. Only trust me, my love, and depart this town. I promise you, you won't be sorry leaving with me."

I pressed my lips together. "But if they are so determined to keep the secret from me, then it's all the more reason I should know."

I had already dressed and was now pulling on my boots. He began doing the same.

"Oh, Elizabeth. I won't always be around to protect you." I stared at him but did not express my fear that he seldom protected me in the past. "Will I see you tomorrow?" he asked.

"Will you continue trying to find out what you can for me?"

He sighed. "I don't think it's wise."

I shrugged. The pain inside my heart was cutting deep, but I could not let him know it. He had to help me, but he had to help willingly. If he loved me.

He seemed to read my mind. "If you loved me, you would leave with me now. There are other ways of learning who you father is besides endangering your own life."

"What other?" I glared at him. "Even if I wrote letters, they wouldn't answer them. I tried talking with my uncle, but now he cannot talk. On the contrary, Peter, if *you* loved *me*, you would do all you could to help me."

He drew me into his arms again. I was fully dressed now, but it did nothing to delete the pleasure and the memory of our bodies as they had touched and joined only moments before.

"Will I see you tomorrow?" he asked once more. "Will you help me?"

"Yes." He sighed. "I will help you."

I raised myself up on my tiptoes and kissed him. "Then I will see you tomorrow night here."

His lips met mine for the final time that night, and I tasted both his tears and sadness, as well as his joy.

Chapter Fifteen

I don't know how I got back to my room that night. I seemed to have flown for I recalled nothing of my trek back through the woods.

Peter had wanted to walk with me, but I did not think the idea a good one—just in case someone saw us.

The downstairs door was unlatched as I had left it. After being careful to fix it as before, I lifted my skirts and made my way up the back steps. I didn't know why I hadn't used these before. They were closer to my room and farther from the rest of the household.

The darkness frightened me for a moment. As I peered up into the blackness at the top of the stairs, I had the distinct impression I was being watched. I could see no one there, but the feeling was strong.

Goose bumps on my skin quickly overrode the wonderful feeling I had had just now with Peter. I drew back and decided I would investigate the stairs by daylight. For now, I would return the way I had come—up the main stairs.

Still conscious of being followed, I took the stairs two

at a time. Grandfather Maxwell's picture seemed to stare ominously at me as I passed it. I knew he would not have approved of what I had done this night for he had not approved of my mother's wanton ways. Still, I hoped he would have understood my determination to find my father. Mother had told me Grandfather had been nothing if not determined. I had inherited his stubborn qualities.

My heart pounded unceasingly, as if I had been running miles. It took nearly an hour after I lay in bed to calm down. I could not help thinking about Peter, about the warmth of his body next to mine and the sweet pleasure he had given me.

I fell asleep dreaming of Peter and woke up the following morning, thinking of him as well. Sitting up in the bed, however, I found my sheet somewhat stained. I could only stare at it. Was this God's punishment, truly? Was I to die for a few moments of pleasure?

Unable to think clearly, I stripped the sheet from the bed and washed myself as best I could. Tears were in my eyes and choking my throat.

It took some time before I realized the bleeding had stopped and that what was on the sheet only remained from the night before.

Relieved, I bundled the sheet up. I would have to get a new set of linens from Rose—and that would not be easy. I supposed I could tell her that it was my monthly time. But what would I do when that came? No, I would have to wash the sheet myself—later.

I was glad to see that my cousins had left the breakfast table already. The food was nearly cold, but I was too hungry to care.

Just as I was going out the back door with the bundled sheet, having decided I would take it to the pond to wash, I heard Terrah behind me.

"Going out?"

"Isn't that obvious?" I turned toward her. She was watching me with such intensity it was impossible for me not to wonder—did she know? Was there something about my presence now which told her I was Peter's lover?

"What's in the bundle?"

"Nothing." I made to push past her and out the door.

"If you're staying in my house, I have a right to know what your plans are. After all, Elizabeth, you are my guest. I wouldn't want any harm to come to you."

Her smile seemed sincere and for just the briefest of moments I was taken in.

"Actually," she said sweetly, "I had hoped you would have some time today to help me plan the ball we are to have at Parkland."

I stared at her, realizing her motive was to dig in that she and Peter would be announcing their engagement.

Never good at lying, it was impossible for me to hide my smile. Peter would not announce his engagement to her. Surely, long before the next three weeks were up, I would have learned who my father was—I felt so close to it now—and Peter and I would be away from here.

"Of course I'll help you, Terrah." I paused. "After I return from my walk."

Trying to act as confident as I could, I pushed the rest of the way past her and out the door. I grasped the dirty sheet as close to me as I could, not wanting anything to be seen. I didn't know if she suspected anything or not, but

265

if I had to, I was sure I could make up some story.

I was not surprised to find Peter sleeping in the same place he had been the first time I had come upon him. This time I had no fear of waking him.

Bending down at his side, I stroked his soft hair until he opened his eyes.

"I am in heaven or I am dreaming." He smiled, kissing my hand.

I laughed. It was the first laugh in many days and, just being with him, I was able to forget the hostility and tension at Jerseyhurst. I forgot everything but my love for Peter.

He pulled me down so that our lips met. Immediately, I felt the hunger for him which had consumed me last night.

"How did you find me here?" he asked, when we had managed to break away from our kiss.

"I didn't." I smiled and touched his cheek. "I came out here only to wash my sheet."

"Why? Rose and the maids there can take care of—" He stared at me. "Oh, yes. I understand." He took the bundle from me and dropped it into the water, tying it to a limb so that the current would clean it.

His hands went to my hair, pulling down the pins so that my tresses tumbled to my waist. "You should keep it like this always. When we're married—"

I looked up at him and cut off his words with a deep kiss. I did not want him to make promises to me which might not be kept.

Now that Pandora's box had been opened, I felt free to express the feelings pent up inside. Not even aware I was doing it, I pulled Peter down upon me. His eyes seemed to twinkle.

"What have I done to you?" He sighed, tumbling in the grass with me.

"You have shown me into the paths of evil," I said and laughed, "and for that you have to suffer." Still carefree, I slipped from his grasp and quickly stripped my clothes off. It was, of course, not what a proper young lady should be doing, but since we had loved and would love again, I felt my inhibitions flowing away with the current.

Just as Peter was about to grab me, I laughingly jumped away from him and dived into the brook. The water was cold, but I knew Peter would soon follow me in to warm me up.

Cursing me for being a wanton little hussy, he quickly stripped off his cravat, waistcoat, and cutaways.

I stared at him. Seeing him by night was one thing; seeing him by day was another. It was enough to take my breath away. I couldn't believe, couldn't understand how he had entered and become part of me. But he had and once more he drew me to him as he stepped into the water with me. Holding me, he caressed me. The yearning for oneness with him grew inside me.

Yet, once more a nagging doubt surfaced. I feared our joy would not last as we both wished, and I was determined we should take the pleasure as we could. I wanted to carry the memory of Peter with me—no matter where I went. If it meant carrying his seed, as well, then so be it. It would not be the first time in my family for such an event.

In the buoyancy of the water, his hands slid over me, exciting my every nerve as he nibbled my earlobes and let his fingers explore my intimate depths. I strained against him, knowing how deeply I wanted him, knowing how I longed to be joined with him.

My own hands instinctively touched and stroked him as he was doing me. I heard his groans as they mingled with mine. How different it was here than on the floor of the burned-out house. Here we floated in ecstasy on our own private clouds as the water swirled and swished about us.

Even before we joined, even before he took me to heaven, I knew no matter what happened, there would never be anyone in the world for me but Peter Parkisham. It was as if we had been drawn together from the start, as if my coming to Aberdeen had been not to find my father but to find him.

Once more I gasped as I felt his hardness slide smoothly into me. My arms went about him as we kissed deeply, and I thrilled to feel his movement inside me. My legs floated up about his waist, holding him tightly. He was part of me now and forever more.

The current guided us and orchestrated our movements as we reached for the stars. We culminated our pleasure at the same glorious moment, writhing and splashing in ecstasy.

After several moments of happy quietude, staring contentedly into his beautiful eyes, I remembered my promise to help Terrah.

Reluctantly, I drew Peter back onto the shore. He showed me how to hang the sheet on the branches and promised he would watch out for it.

It was an effort for me to dress, for me to know I would be leaving him for even a moment, and yet I had to. It would not do for my cousins to know what transpired between Peter and myself, even though I wanted to shout his love from the rooftops.

Sitting on the rock a moment, I finally asked him the question which had nagged at me all day.

"Why is it you sleep outdoors here?"

Peter grimaced. "I often do when I have arguments with Alexander. I don't especially like the house or him. I feel sorry for my mother, but she refuses to leave him, so all I can do is leave as I can."

"But you don't work at all?"

He grinned. "At times, it does become necessary. Yes."

I pressed my lips together and looked toward the brook. Again I wondered how it was I had fallen in love with someone like him when Joshua was so good, so strong, when Joshua worked constantly and cared nothing for the frivolity that made up Peter's life.

His hand touched my cheek. "You're worried that I could not support you in the proper style, darling, is that it?"

I shrugged and then nodded. I could feel the tears in my eyes. I was crying for my lost feelings, for Joshua, and for the confusion which was once again consuming me.

His lips were gentle and sweet on my brow. "Have no fear, my precious. I have money of my own and I will work or do whatever is necessary to support us. You will have the life of a queen as my wife."

I forced myself to smile, to hug him, but I still could not help wondering if indeed I would ever be able to marry him.

He continued to kneel there in front of me. "Are you sure you don't want to leave with me today? I could get a carriage and we could be gone within the hour."

I sighed and looked at him. "Give me two weeks more. I promise you. If nothing has come to light about who my real father is, I will leave with you."

"Oh, Elizabeth, Elizabeth. I promise. You will not be sorry."

I stood and made ready to return to Jerseyhurst. I knew I could never be sorry for my love of Peter.

Terrah was in the study as I passed on my way back to my room. I had hoped she wouldn't notice me but she looked up just as I walked by.

"Well, did you have a good walk?"

I paused, feeling the panic in my throat. Then I nodded. I knew my hair was wet but she said nothing, even though she stared at me.

"I trust I can count on your help now."

"Can I count on yours?"

Terrah glared at me. "I have told you once, and I will tell you again, I know nothing at all of who your father is."

"Then let me speak with my uncle. Surely, he is recovered from the blow he received at the fire."

"What makes you think that? Who told you?"

"No one had to tell me. Do I speak with him?"

Terrah gave me one of her sweet smiles. "Well, it's possible by the time the ball comes, he'll be better. I can let you speak with him then."

I stared at her. Did she know of Peter's proposal? Had she somehow learned of Peter's wanting me to leave town with him; but how could she—unless he himself told her! My heart constricted like a sponge. No, I would not believe, could not believe Peter would have betrayed me like that.

270

"You want me to stay for the ball?" I asked uncertainly.

"But, of course! Didn't I say so last night? After all, it will be your first. I couldn't deprive you of such an experience."

I stared at her. "I thought you wanted to get rid of me. Certainly, your neighbor, Mr. Parkisham, doesn't want me around."

"Alex? That's not true. He has a great deal of affection for you, cousin. As I do. After all, you are Margaret's daughter. Margaret was his dear friend. Alexander wouldn't dream of doing anything but helping you, and I do so want you to stay."

I frowned. I did not trust either Terrah or Alexander, but until I knew what they were planning, I would have to go along with it. "Very well. I will wait and talk with my uncle later."

She smiled at me. I didn't know if I should be happy or not with our arrangement for me to see my uncle, but I did need to find out who my father was.

Returning to my room, I changed and in the mirror glanced at my naked body. No, there were no signs I could see of my lovemaking with Peter. How could she tell? Was I just being silly? I sucked in my lip, feeling panic rise up in me. I hoped I was.

Chapter Sixteen

There really wasn't much help that Terrah needed, and I wondered why she had even called me to assist her. But I did what I could to write out the lists she asked. Since we were working in the study, I couldn't help but wonder about the missing pages from the family Bible. Though I had found the list of numbers from the bank that night, I had never discovered the information which I was sure the Bible would give me.

It was nearly time for tea when I noticed Terrah staring at me. "You look tired, Elizabeth. Have you been sleeping well?"

I pressed my lips together. "Now that you mention it, I haven't. On several nights, I've heard cries in the hall. I know it can't be my uncle now. Is there something wrong with Rose?"

Terrah stared at me. "You would have to ask her that." She started toward the door and then turned. "Perhaps you would like to rest a bit before dinner. Peter and his family will be coming over again tonight."

I stared at her, not asking anything nor saying

anything. I wondered if she was inviting the Parkishams purposely to annoy me.

Finally, I found my voice. "Yes, I believe I shall go up for a bit."

Terrah nodded and smiled at me. I felt my stomach turning. She had to be planning something. If only I knew what.

I stood as if to leave the room but hoped to stay a few moments more to resume my search for the book. Terrah must have guessed my thoughts, however, for she continued to stand sentry at the door.

There was no choice but for me to leave the room.

I had not been back in my wedge room more than five moments before the knock on the door startled me.

"Who is it?" I rose from the bed.

"Me, miss." Rose King opened the door. She came into the room carrying two packages. "These be just delivered for you from town."

I stared at the boxes. I hadn't ordered anything. "Are you sure they're for me?"

"Sure am." She nodded.

"Do you know who sent them?"

Rose shook her head. "Don't know. Just a boy came and brought them, miss."

I saw she was smiling slightly. I was sure she knew more than she was telling me, but I couldn't outright accuse her of lying. She continued to stand there, probably hoping I would open the packages. I wasn't about to give her the satisfaction.

Finally she turned in a huff and left the room.

I stared at the boxes on my bed for several moments. Were they presents from Peter? Yes, that was what they had to be. I smiled to myself as I opened the biggest box first.

My heart leaped to my throat. I felt as if a knife had been stuck into my ribs. Inside the box was a black dress—the same high neck-style dress my mother had been buried in. Unlike my own bombazine, Mother's dress had mutton sleeves and ruffled hems, as she had always liked. I tried to swallow my fear. Who could have sent this? Who could have known the fashion of dress Mama would have worn at the funeral. No one here had been at the funeral.

My hands shaking, I opened the second box. I had expected it to be a bonnet or perhaps boots. It took all my effort to stifle the scream which rose to my throat. Inside this box was a wreath of black flowers—exactly like those which had been on my mother's grave.

I had stopped the scream, but I couldn't stop the tears nor the trembling which overtook me as I now sank onto the bed. I could only stare at the dress and the flowers. It was obviously a warning to me, but for the life of me, I did not know who would have known these things about my mother unless—unless Alexander Parkisham had come back and been at the funeral. But surely, I had seen him once. I would have recognized him again. No, I didn't think it could be he. I had no doubt that he and my cousin were somehow behind all this and yet there had to be someone else.

My nerve temporarily deserted me, but when I could look at the wreath again, I managed to pick it up and toss it out the window. I watched a moment and saw it land at the edge of the ravine. Later, I would go down and kick it over the edge. For now, I hadn't the strength.

The dress still lay on the bed. I had no idea what to do with it. I certainly did not plan to wear it.

Placing the cover back on the box, I threw it into the back of the armoire. I would think about it later.

I took the box which had held the wreath and was about to throw it out the window as well when I saw the white linen handkerchief tucked in one corner. It was hard to tell if it had been put there on purpose or if it had been left there by accident.

My curiosity got control of me. I pulled the linen out. The letter P was clearly embroidered on the linen. With a sickening feeling, I stared at it. Peter's handkerchief. I knew it belonged to him. Surely, he couldn't be behind this cruel joke—or could he? I realized with a sinking heart how very little I knew of this man I professed to love. No, it could not be Peter. I did not want to believe it.

I glanced about the room, searching for some sort of answer and silently praying to my mother for help. My eyes came to rest on my silver brushes. Tilly immediately came to my mind. Both she and my uncle had mentioned the Parkisham fellow, who else could it be but Alexander? Was Peter lying to me to save his own hide? What had Alexander promised him?

My heart was heavy. Even if I wanted to leave now, I had to stay. I had to find out what had happened; I had to learn who my father was—even if it meant my death.

I believe I did sleep but it was not a peaceful rest. I dreamed of Joshua and wondered what he was doing without me. The walls of the room seemed to be squeezing in on me. I wanted to be with Peter, to love and trust him, but how could I when things like this happened? I wanted to be true to my promise to Joshua, but how could I when I felt as I did about Peter?

I dressed for dinner in a simple yellow poplin with small bits of lace on the puffed sleeves and flounce. It was not a dress I favored because the neck was high and scratchy, but it was one of the few good ones I still owned.

How I remained silent through dinner, politely passing the food as if nothing had happened, I don't know. No one spoke to me, which was just as well for I felt I should have burst out crying had I been forced to make a reply. It was not like me to be such a coward, and yet things were simply getting to be too much.

It was difficult to admit I should have stayed in Kansas. Had I done so, lives would have been spared. But it was too late for me to return now. It had all gone too far.

Peter grabbed my arm as we were going into the parlor. I didn't know if anyone saw us, but he seemed not to care.

"What's wrong? You've said nary a word during dinner, my sweet."

"What should I say?" I stared at him. "That I'm glad you're making a fool of yourself over Terrah?"

"What?"

"Or perhaps I should have just returned this to you." I handed him the linen handkerchief which had been in the box.

He stared at it. "Where did you get this? It was a gift from Harriet."

"Where indeed! Why don't you ask the boy who delivered the black wreath?"

"What!"

He seemed astonished. It was easy to believe that he truly knew nothing of the gifts I had received earlier.

"Tell me, Elizabeth. What happened this afternoon? I demand to know! If someone has sent you a black wreath, it is either a monstrous joke or—" He grasped me fully by the shoulders. I knew we should go into the parlor and not let the others know we were in the hall talking and yet, his concern touched me. "Please my sweet. I don't like this at all. You must leave with me. The sooner the better."

I swallowed hard. I wondered what his reaction would be if I told him about the dress as well. Slowly, I shook my head. "We had best go in, Peter. It does not look good for us to be out here so long."

"Elizabeth—"

I turned and faced him fully now, looking up into the blue eyes that I so loved. "I cannot leave yet. I've told you. Give me two weeks. Then—I will consider it."

"Elizabeth. The ball is in three weeks. We must be well away from here before then."

I shrugged my shoulders. How I wanted him to sweep me up into his arms and take me away as he wanted, as he promised, but I didn't have the nerve to go back on my promise to myself. "I don't have a choice. I must have more time. I must find out what I can."

It was Harriet, coming out, who drew us apart. "You're being missed, Peter. I understand you want to speak with Elizabeth, but this is neither the time nor the place."

I nodded toward her. Did I detect a coolness from her? I wondered suddenly if she wasn't the one who impersonated me. I stared at her for a moment but said nothing about my suspicions.

Peter frowned. Touching my hand briefly, he started toward the parlor door. "Tonight," he whispered to me.

I wanted to say no, but my heart would not allow it. I would meet him this night and as many nights as I could.

That night I lay in the darkness, staring up at the moon and the aerola of brightness about it. Was it a good omen for me?

Silently, I dressed and started out.

This time my progress was halted by the noise of other steps above me. Rose? No, I didn't think it was she. Since Tilly's death, she had taken a room down below, supposedly because it was easier to light the kitchen fires in the morning. I felt sure it had something to do with her mother's death.

Peter would be waiting for me at the old house, and yet I couldn't leave without finding out who was walking upstairs. My hand touched the cold bannister and I stared up into the darkness.

With one foot on the upper step, I felt the chill penetrate me like a cold knife. There was crying. Soft moans and crying. My lips were dry. I wet them as I tried to decide what to do. Should I find out what was happening up there or should I hurry on to Peter? I didn't think that the person crying would be able to tell me anything about my father and yet—I didn't know.

It took but a moment more for me to decide. If someone was in trouble, I had to help them. I doubted anyone else in this house would.

Quickly, I returned to my room and fetched my lamp. If anyone saw me, I had a legitimate excuse for being up on the third floor.

I was soon thankful I had taken the light for, although I had been up here once before by daylight, it appeared much more menacing and haunting in the darkness.

My heart was racing by the time I reached the top floor. I had heard no more cryng, and yet I knew the sounds had come from there. Once more I felt the coldness surround me.

As quietly as I could, I walked to each door and listened. Nothing. No one was speaking; no one was making noise of any kind. Was I going insane?

I glanced up to the skylight and gasped. There seemed to be someone out there, someone standing on the roof.

Without any other thought, I ran to the door which led to the outside. It was locked. I began to shake it. Once more I heard the crying, but now it seemed to be coming from above. My heart was in my mouth as I saw the figure above me disappear. No. No, it couldn't be. There couldn't be another death here.

There was no way for me to find out who or what had been on top of the roof without running downstairs and outside to where I had found Tilly's body. Grasping the lantern, I flew down the steps so that the light in front of me shadowed its ghostly figures on the wall.

I wanted to call out for Terrah, for David, for anyone, and yet I did not. I feared if they found me out and dressed they would suspect I had done more than just investigate the crying I had heard. Besides, how did I know one of them hadn't been up there causing the death of the figure I had seen? How did I know anything about the people here at Jerseyhurst?

I probably should have been worried, but I took none of my usual precautions. I even allowed the door to slam, allowed my footsteps to be heard. All I knew was my fear and desire to aid whomever I had seen above. All I knew was there could be no more deaths because of me.

I stood there at the path directly below the walkway and gasped. Nothing. There was no body there, nothing to indicate that I had seen anything out of the ordinary.

Stepping closer, I looked about. It was inconceivable that I should have seen someone jump and there should be no one there.

The hairs at the back of my neck once more prickled.

The wreath which I had thrown out of the windows earlier and the black dress which I had hidden in my closet were both out on the walk below me—as if to tell me that I would soon take the plunge from the widow's walk.

I stared at it for a moment and then I fainted.

Peter was standing over me when I opened my eyes. He was holding my head in his lap.

"Darling, are you all right?"

I sat up slowly. Then I nodded. Other than the shock, I was fine. I glanced about, meaning to show him the dress and wreath—but they were gone.

"Peter, I—why did you come here?"

"Why else? I was worried when you didn't show. I didn't want anything to happen to you."

"Did you think something might?" I wanted so badly to trust him, and yet it was odd he should be the one to come find me, that the items which had so stunned me should have vanished.

"You saw nothing but me here. No one else was about?"

He shook his head. "You were on the ground here. I thought maybe something had happened to you."

I took a deep breath. "Something did." I proceeded to tell him what I had seen. Perhaps it was wrong to trust him, but I had to get my fears out somehow.

"Oh, my sweet darling. Someone is playing tricks and I don't like them." His lips met mine. "Please, Elizabeth. Allow me to take you away from here."

I glanced about furtively. We were taking a chance meeting and talking, kissing so close to the house as we

281

were. I feared for him—and myself.

Slipping my hand into his, I was glad of his strength. I realized that I needed him—body and soul—more than I had ever needed anything before.

We walked silently into the forest to the old house. There, Peter's hands touched me, exciting me. He seemed as hungry for me as I was for him, and yet, I still had my fears.

It took Peter only moments of tender touching for me to once more be in his spell and forget my fright of the few moments before. He had a power over me which I didn't understand. I wanted to be with him and him only.

I allowed myself to fall asleep in his comforting warm arms, and we made love again before parting from our secret place. I was sure Terrah had to know about us. After all, who else could have arranged what I had seen tonight? Yet, there was no one on the path to the house, no one waiting for me in the house itself.

Reaching my room, I washed myself and tumbled into bed. Tomorrow, I would confront my cousin. Tomorrow, I would again explore the third floor and find out who or what it was I had seen.

Chapter Seventeen

I slept late the next morning. Washing with tepid water, I dressed quickly in a seersucker blouse and skirt. Fastening my boots, I cursed my clumsy fingers. Finally, I was ready.

I could smell the odor of freshly baked rolls as I neared the dining room. Tears came to my eyes as I thought of the rolls Tilly would have made. I opened the door and found Terrah at the head of the table with David alongside of her. They had been laughing about something but stopped when they saw me. I flushed. It was impossible not to feel that I was the cause of their laughter.

"You're up early, Elizabeth," Terrah said and nodded.

I stiffened. "Not any earlier than usual." I sipped at the chocolate which the maid poured me and wondered how to broach the subject of the wreath and dress. Neither of us said anything. I picked up the fork to take a bite of egg when the maid came in—holding the wreath.

The metal of the fork clattered onto my plate. I stared

at the black flowers and then glanced at Terrah.

"Have you a secret admirer, cousin?" David asked. I could hear the laughter in his voice.

A chill went through me. I stared at him a moment and then looked at Terrah. "Yes, I believe I do. But then you must know about the flowers, Terrah, and the dress, too."

"Oh, did you buy a new store dress? My, my, aren't we becoming citified. Two new store dresses in a month."

I felt the anger surging through me. "I did not buy another dress. This was given to me by the same person, I suspect, who gave me the flowers. I believe you know more about my *gifts* than you are telling me."

Terrah shrugged. "I know of no one—except maybe Peter—who is as devoted to you as that. I can well imagine him giving you such expensive gifts but other than him . . ." She smiled.

The maid continued to stand there. "Miss, what shall I do with this?"

Terrah looked at me and remained silent. "You may destroy it," I said coldly. "Burn it. The dress, too, wherever it is." I threw my serviette on the table, stood, and left the room. I could feel both my cousins staring at me.

After I left the dining room, I went up to the third floor. There was absolutely no indication of the person I had supposedly seen last night. I was beginning to doubt what I had seen. Frustrated, I checked each door. None of them would open. Not even the door to the widow's walk was open.

I cursed.

Tears came to my eyes. I had to find out something and soon. The longer I stayed in this house, the more I felt

284

the danger. Peter was right. The incident last night had been meant as a warning. I would have to be careful. My cousins obviously felt threatened. Was I close to some answers?

Just as I started down the stairs, I heard the strange cry again. This time the sounds were distinct. It couldn't be a baby crying, and yet it sounded like it was. I went to the third floor where Rose had stayed with her mother.

Like the others, it was locked. I couldn't help wonder. Was there a baby here? The sounds stopped immediately. No, it was not my imagination.

I had pulled a hairpin out to open the door when I felt the presence of someone standing near me. Looking up, I saw David a few feet away, grinning.

"Looking for something?"

"Yes, I heard crying. I thought someone might need help." I stared directly back at him. "What's behind this door?"

"What's behind the door?" He swaggered forward, staring at me lewdly. My stomach tightened. I stood and took a step back. "Behind the door, dear Elizabeth, is Rose's cat."

He withdrew a set of keys. The door swung open easily. As David said, curled in a basket lay a cat and two kittens. A gray and white one—no bigger than my palm—mewed and climbed up on my skirt. I picked it up. My heart melted for it.

"Why do you keep it locked up here?"

He shrugged. "Because."

That wasn't enough of an answer. I didn't truly believe that a kitten had made the noises I had heard. David didn't appear concerned with what I believed. Grabbing my wrist, he pulled me toward him. Not having my gun with me, I did the next best thing.

Throwing the tiny kitten in his face, I heard his scream as the claws scratched him. At least, he let go of me. I ran downstairs, nearly tripping. Catching my breath, I heard him coming after me. I continued running and didn't stop until I reached the path to the old house.

I took refuge in the upstairs room where Peter and I met. It seemed odd, but this was the only place I felt safe. My heart continued to beat erratically for several hours. I had no idea what to do. I recalled then that I had not written to Joshua in several days. It was odd I should think of him at this moment when I was in fear of my life, but perhaps it was meant to calm me. I knew Joshua expected me back in Kansas long before this and I would have to return there to him shortly because there seemed no hope for my future here with Peter. Yet, after these few meetings with Peter, my heart told me, I did not belong with Joshua. Just where I did belong was a question for which I had no answer.

I stayed in the old house until long past dinner. I didn't want to face my cousins—either of them. I kept expecting to see one of them on the path, yet no one came. Surely, David knew where I was hiding. Knowing my cousins, I felt sure both knew of my relationship with Peter. I realized then how foolish I was to have come here. David could easily corner me—or even Terrah. I could be killed here and no one but Peter would ever think to look for me here. Would he look, and would my mother's presence here be enough to protect me?

I lay down on the blanket still on the hard floor. I thought again about leaving the old house but lethargy had set in. I had slept poorly the night before, and a desire for sleep now overtook me. I closed my eyes, meaning to doze for only a moment before returning to Jerseyhurst, before making my decision to pack and leave for—wherever it would be I would go—but I slept longer than I planned.

Darkness was falling when Peter found me. It didn't surprise me that I dreamed of him, nor did it surprise me to feel his lips on mine as I woke.

"My precious. It's all right."

Startled from sleep, I stared at him, confused. "How did you know David had been bothering me?"

"David?" He frowned. "I thought you were hiding from Terrah. She's been searching all day for you."

I shook my head. I had no idea what my cousin wanted me for, but I really didn't care since it couldn't be anything good.

"Well, you don't have to worry about David for the moment." I sat upright. "Why not? He's been a nuisance to me from the moment I've come."

"Alexander has sent him to New Orleans for a few days."

"What?" I stared at Peter. "Why? How? What do you mean?"

"When Alexander bought your grandfather's shipping business, David began to work for him. It was with the understanding David and Harriet would marry when she felt recovered from her widowhood." He smiled slightly. "So far after three years, she's shown no indication of being ready for a second marriage. I can't say I blame her with David as the groom."

I frowned. I didn't know David worked, nor did I realize how closely Harriet was tied to this. It was a part of the puzzle but only a part. I wish I had all the pieces to put together, but I did not.

"I don't blame her either." I pulled away and stood, brushing my skirt off.

Peter smiled, understandingly. "I told my father I was leaving and not coming back until after his precious party—if he didn't stop David from bothering you."

"But you're—I mean we're—leaving anyway. Aren't we?"

"Of course." He kissed my brow and drew me close to him. "But I couldn't very well tell him, could I?" He drew me up and, while we both wanted very much to stay here in our private world, we knew the time passed too swiftly.

"So what did Terrah want me for?" I looked up into Peter's perfect eyes. Did I see something hidden there? He paused a moment before responding.

"She said she was worried about you. She said you acted strangely at breakfast, and she thought you might be ill."

I gave an unladylike snort. "You can't tell me my cousin worries about me!"

Peter shrugged. "She says she does."

I grimaced. Straightening my gown, I prepared to return to the house. "Peter, what am I going to do?"

"Do?" His lips brushed my neck, making the shivers go down my spine. "You're coming away as my bride."

I sighed but said nothing. Instead, I quietly followed him back to Jerseyhurst.

The house was silent as I entered behind him. I expected to see Terrah waiting in the dining room to greet me, but there was no one there. Daring convention, he gave me a quick kiss on the cheek which made my heart race. "Peter, please. Not here." Quickly, I looked about. There seemed to be no one, but I had been fooled before.

He smiled and nodded, touching his fingers to my lips. "The fun comes when it's forbidden," he whispered as his mouth once more met mine.

This time I could not deny him nor myself. I only hoped Terrah was asleep and David truly gone. I wanted Peter all to myself without worrying about my cousins, without worrying about who I truly was.

The two weeks passed more quickly than I anticipated. It worried me I had not heard from Joshua. Peter also worried me. He had become bolder and more declarative of his love for me. I feared my cousin would object, or that Alexander would do something to keep us apart. But nothing happened. My love and affection for Peter continued to grow, but so did my doubts. If he was sincere in wanting to help me learn who my father was, if he truly was promised to marry Terrah, then why did neither of them say anything?

Even if Peter was telling the truth—and he swore each time we met he wanted to take me away, to return to Kansas with me or take me elsewhere—I wondered if he would fit in anywhere but here. He seemed so attached to life in Aberdeen. How would he leave? How would he ever fit on the farm?

No, it seemed history was going to repeat itself. Like my mother, I was doomed to part from my love. But if I had a child from our passionate play, I vowed I would tell her who she was the day she was born. No one should have to go through the hell I was now suffering.

As deep as my love was growing, even deeper was my frustration. I found out little more than I knew already. Despite what Peter had said, I suspected that Alexander

Parkisham was my father. If he wasn't, then he held the secret as to who my father was. Mother had mentioned his name too often for them to have been merely friends.

I continued to search for the family Bible, but it remained swallowed up by the evil forces which reigned at Jerseyhurst.

I remember it was the fourth day of the fourth week of my uninvited stay that I met with Peter again. It surprised me that he had gotten away for the day, but he said nothing about the subject and I was loathe to bring it up. I knew our movements were probably being watched, but I no longer cared. Perhaps he felt the same way. We picnicked on the banks of the brook, laughing at the foolish items he had packed for food. If he had such trouble taking care of himself how would he ever take care of me? We made love sweetly, fiercely, our bodies all but fusing into one.

Kissing him with all the love and passion I felt, I said good-bye to him for the afternoon.

I stood and took his hands as he tried to keep me. I shook my head. "No, I cannot stay."

"Later then?"

He was so pleading, so sweet. How could I deny him? How could I deny myself? I nodded, yet each time I left him, I had the hideous feeling it would be the last time we would meet. So far, neither Terrah nor David, who had returned the other day, had said anything to me, but I was sure they both knew how I spent my time. The smile Rose gave me every time she saw me told me she knew, too. Perhaps she was the one who did most of the spying.

Lifting my skirts so they would not become soiled with the mud puddles, I stepped over fallen logs and glanced back at him once more. My heart seemed to swell as a wave of love washed over it.

I let myself into the house and noticed the quiet. I had passed Rose in the kitchen, baking for the party, so I knew she would not be around, but the other maids and servants should have been. I stepped into the dining hall.

Every time I returned from being with Peter, I expected to find Terrah, to have her confront me. It made me nervous that she did not. Surprisingly, she seemed especially polite to me lately.

Could it be Terrah was consumed with the plans for her ball? It bothered me that my cousin seemed so oblivious, almost as if she had some secret plan. Perhaps she knew that no matter what happened, Peter would give into the pressures and marry her.

She smiled at me as I passed the library where she was making lists. My mouth went dry at the thought of her marrying Peter.

Just this afternoon, when we had consummated our passion, he had whispered, "I love only you. An engagement is not like a marriage. Father and Terrah may talk all they please. It's you I shall have. It's you I shall marry." But I was beginning to suspect he protested too much.

Still hungry after Peter's less than hearty packed lunch, I hoped there would be food in the kitchen. Instead of food I found Rose putting away dishes. I did not consider myself a coward, but at that moment, I suddenly lost my appetite. The black girl stared contemptuously at me, causing my heart to skip a beat. Yes, she knew! I waited a moment, wondering if she would say something, but she did not. As calmly as I could, I nodded a greeting and left the kitchen.

Of all the family and servants, only Rose outwardly

showed herself hostile to me. I didn't understand why the girl disliked me so. It should be the other way around. After all, I still didn't know how the lawyer had gotten mother's locket, who had given it to him. Nor did I know where the papers had gone. Rose was probably involved, though she would not have been the one to impersonate me.

I sighed. I still had learned nothing more of the deaths of Tilly or Mr. McCrae. My shoulders felt heavy with the weight. If only I could understand how everything was related.

Climbing the steps to my room, I longed to believe Peter's protests that he knew nothing—but could I? Was my avid hunger for him overtaking my better sense?

On the second floor, at the door to my room, I paused. I heard Rose as she continued to move downstairs. I knew Terrah was busy, but where was David? It had been nearly two weeks since I had tried to search upstairs. Did I dare try again? I doubted they would think to look for me now.

Softly as possible, I started up the stairs. There were no sounds of crying—kitten or human. My heart hammered louder now than it did when I escaped the house for my midnight visits to Peter.

I paused on the steps and looked up at the skylight, remembering the vision I had seen. Had it been a hoax? Or the ghost of my aunt?

A noise below startled me. Someone was coming up. I froze on the steps a moment. The sounds stopped. I realized the importance of my continuing the search. If my life was in danger then I wanted to know why. The sooner I found out what I wanted to know, the sooner Peter and I could leave.

I took two more steps. I wondered whether Mr. McCrae had learned of the embezzlement somehow, or if his murder had been related only to the secret of my father? Had he been about to tell my uncle?

I had seen my uncle up and about several times in the past few days, but he carried such a blank look on his face when he saw me that it frightened me. I doubted if he recalled the night of the bank fire. He certainly did not recall me.

I found it implausible that my cousin would kill for three hundred dollars. I was sure more was at stake than just the small amount of money. "If only I had more clues," I whispered out loud.

I reached the third floor. There was someone up here. There had to be. The feeling I had was the same each time. It wasn't just a knowledge that someone watched me. It was a sensation of hatred. I glanced about uneasily before moving forward.

I touched the door handle to Rose's old room. They couldn't have the kittens in there today. I noted the coldness of the metal. As usual, the door was locked.

It surprised me to see that the widow's walk door was open. The door creaked open only partway. I guessed it was blocked by trunks. Squeezing through the narrow opening, I held my breath, careful not to tear my dress a second time. The hobby horse stick was in reach. I used it to prop open the door. It was an easy matter to wedge the door, but it was not so easy moving through the rows of trunks and boxes. I stared at the items in the dim light. It appeared things had been moved since I had last been up here.

As my eyes became accustomed to the light, I gasped. A book! Heedless now of the dirt and dust, I leaned forward.

Could it be the family Bible?

I felt the flush and joy of discovery. But as I picked up the vellum-bound pages, I immediately knew by the weight and size that this could not be the book I sought. My disappointment keen, I tucked it into my pocket. I would examine it outside and hope it had something to tell me.

It looked like someone had been up here, reading the book and had probably forgotten to put it back. Who could have been up here? Terrah? Rose? I closed the flap of the box where it seemed to have come from. There were no other books within.

There was something else different about the storage area, too, but I could not grasp what it was. A feeling of closeness and suffocation suddenly attacked me. I felt a strong need for air. The door to the walk stood directly in front of me. I would be careful. I would not get near the edge, I told myself. Once more, I glanced about and wondered what was different about the room, but the answer did not come to me.

Proceeding out onto the parapet, I took a deep breath and viewed the beauty of the cliffs, bluffs, and river before me. Turning eastward, I glimpsed the brook. Even thinking of Peter made my body tingle from the memory of his touch. How I wished I were with him now.

With a stab of anxiety, I realized that Peter and I could have been seen at the brook from here. I bit my lower lip. Well, there was little I could do about that now.

Taking a tentative step forward onto the walkway, I glanced about. Leaning forward on the rail, I gasped as part of the rail came loose in my hand! My mind spun as I tried to think, and I grabbed the nearest section of the rail, scratching myself, tearing my dress, as I saved myself from falling below as Tilly had.

Breathless, I inched back toward the wall. I was unable to look at the ground below. I only knew I had a close call with death. My heart raced as I stared at the gap in the rail. It had been cut. I was sure of it. The edges were too smooth. Terrah? Was I assigning too much to her? No, I thought not. She was capable of far worse evil. I wondered then if this was where Tilly had fallen.

Standing, trying to be brave, I forced myself to glance down. Dizziness assailed me. Quickly, I stepped back, hearing the rush of my blood. Yes, it must have been from here. I forced myself to inch forward again. It was impossible not to recall seeing Tilly on the path just below.

Leaning against the wall, I remembered again how Tilly had been afraid of this walkway, how she had warned me. If she had fallen from here, then she had to have been forced. Unsure of my own stability, not wanting to look again at the open space of rail, I turned and prepared to go back to my room.

The door from the storage room opened in front of me.

My heart dropped as Terrah stepped out, smiling. She had probably been spying on me as I came up here.

There was precious little room on the walkway, but I stepped back, nevertheless. I feared Terrah more than I feared the heights and the chance of falling.

Terrah continued smiling at me. "I thought I'd find you up here. See anything interesting?"

I shook my head, unable to speak.

"What's wrong, Elizabeth? Why do you look so worried? I have no intention of harming you."

Her words were the same sweet maple syrup she had poured out since I had come.

"Why did you follow me?"

"Follow you?" Her emerald green eyes went wide in pretense of innocence. "I didn't follow you, Cousin Elizabeth. I only came up to see the view. I often come up here. It's lovely, isn't it? On sunny days, one can see clear to the town—and in other directions as well."

She took a deep breath and turned in the direction of the old house. I knew then she had seen Peter and me. The thought caught like a hard candy in my throat. The purple silk Terrah wore rustled in the breeze.

"You like it up here, too?" Terrah asked. Her eyes studied my features. I nodded, not wanting to turn my back on her.

Silence filled the air as she continued staring. "Oh, I almost forgot." She gave me one of her coy smiles reserved usually only for her male friends. "You have a visitor downstairs."

"I do?" I grasped the sturdy part of the rail as the breeze blew my curls into my eyes. "Who?"

Terrah shrugged. She moved closer to me. For just a moment I thought she would push me toward the hole on the rail. Her plump pink lips curled with satisfaction as she saw the fear I couldn't hide. "Go down and see. I'm not your social secretary. I believe Rose put him in the common parlor."

I clenched my fist but forced myself to smile pleasantly. Warily, I eased past my cousin. "Thank you for taking the trouble to come up and tell me."

"Oh." Terrah smiled at me like a cat ready to eat the mouse. "No trouble."

The door creaked again as I left the widow's walk. Not until I reached the second floor did I pause to glance back. My heart continued to race.

In my own room, I quickly repaired my hair and changed to my gray tabby, discovering the book which I had found upstairs and meant to read. I stared at the aged pages. This was my aunt's diary. Why was it up there in the storage room?

The prickles ran up my spine. Was my finding it truly an accident or had it been placed there purposely for me? And who would have put it there? I had made no secret of my going up to investigate, nevertheless, I found it hard to believe anyone here wanted to help me. I placed the book in the nightstand drawer, determined to read it later.

If I did have a visitor then I wanted to look proper. For the life of me, I could not think who it might be. I knew Peter wouldn't dare come to courting me or announce himself as my suitor. Even if he did, Rose would never put him into the common parlor. Could it be—might it be Lawyer Dunn? My heart skipped a beat as I hoped the man would have news for me about my mother's letters.

Glancing in the mirror, I pinched my cheeks. The bones there were far too high and my chin much too narrow. I sighed and wondered what Peter saw in me. My skin was darker than it should be. That was from all those hours in the Kansas sun. I didn't have the white milky complexion which Terrah did. How could he call me pretty?

I smoothed the line of my dress and left the room. The only way I would know about the visitor would be to go down there for myself.

The parlor seemed empty as it had been the first day, and for just a moment I wondered if it wasn't another trick. But as I moved forward, I saw a slight movement from the large floral armchair.

My mouth dropped open as surprise caught me unaware. Grasping the back of another chair for support, I managed to recover myself.

"Joshua! What are you doing here?"

My dear friend stood, hanging his head slightly. He was holding his hat in his hand and twirling it by the brim. "Hello, Beth." He kept his eyes cast downward toward his big feet. "Aren't you glad to see me?"

I stared at him. It was impossible not to compare my short, ungainly friend to the tall, graceful Peter, whom I had left only a few hours ago.

"Of course I am, Josh." I took a step forward. "But why have you come? I wrote you that I would be staying longer. I—"

"I know, Beth." He refused to meet my gaze; he continued to look toward his handmade shoes. "That's why I've come. Your uncle wrote—"

"My uncle wrote to you?" I stared at the paper which Joshua held out. I found it hard to believe my uncle had written anything. Knowing my cousins, they had probably written in his place.

"He said there was a young man courting you and—"

"That's not true!" I cried out, trying to defend myself. "No one is courting me here. I told you, I came to find out who I am. Who my father was." Besides, you could hardly call my relationship with Peter courting, I told myself. He had given me no presents, he had asked no permission of my family to see me and— I realized I wasn't listening to Joshua.

"But Beth, you've been here more than a month now. You promised me three weeks and you've hardly written at all."

I flushed. I had written him twice, but I probably should have written more. "But Joshua, my uncle's been ill. I've—I've been helping to care for him. He hasn't been able to remember yet—"

"Nor will he for some time," Terrah said, as she stepped into the parlor. She had changed her dress to an aqua-blue taffeta with light blue bows and a square cut bodice which revealed more white bosom than I thought proper for day wear. Her mutton sleeves made her appear more slender than she was. It was impossible not to notice the way Joshua stared transfixed at her.

Stepping forward, she smiled her sugary smile and held out her hand. "Hello, Mr. Harmon. I'm so glad to meet you. My cousin has spoken so much about you. I'm thrilled you could join us for awhile." I glanced quickly at Terrah and then at Joshua. Had I missed something?

"I do hope you'll extend your visit and stay with us until the ball. It will only be another week or so."

Joshua flushed a deep red and nodded. "If Beth doesn't mind, I—"

He glanced at me. Guilt gnawed at my stomach. I truly did love Joshua. He was a good man, yet why had my uncle or cousins written to him? Did they really think it would stop me from seeing Peter? I hoped it would not, but I did not know how Peter would react. I realized suddenly how little I really knew about Peter. Our physical love was only part of him; I wanted to know all about him. Looking at Joshua I knew I wanted to know Peter in a way I had never wanted to know Joshua.

Still, Joshua had been a good friend to me and to Mother all these years. I took his hand into mine. I would continue to remain his friend for as long as he allowed me. Reaching on my tiptoes, I gave him a slight kiss on the cheek—so different from the kisses I gave Peter. Yet Joshua thought we were engaged. I knew I would have to tell him of my true feelings soon. Perhaps this afternoon. Meanwhile, he deserved a kiss, at least. "Of course I want you to stay as long as I do. I mean, if my cousins don't object."

"Of course we don't object, Elizabeth. Any friend of yours is a friend of ours. There's plenty of room at Jerseyhurst."

"I'll say!" Joshua whistled in awe as he glanced about the parlor.

He still held his hat in his hands. I turned my attention to Terrah. I did not like the way she smiled at him. I remembered then, it was David who usually brought the post back and forth from town. They would have gotten Joshua's address from my letters.

I supposed it really didn't matter whether my uncle or David had written. What mattered was their invitation for him to come. I could only speculate on the reason.

As I turned my attention to Joshua's firmly set jaw, I saw again the way he looked at Terrah. Immediately, I felt as if part of my heart had been sliced away. True, I loved Peter in a way I could never love Joshua, and yet Joshua was almost a brother to me. My affection for him could never be replaced by Peter's love. I did not want him to be hurt by Terrah. I could only hope to warn him of my cousin's nature before she led him astray.

Even as the idea came to me, I knew there would be precious little I could do. Devotion shone from Joshua's eyes. Terrah devoured the affection like a queen bee expecting royal service. No, Joshua would have to see my cousin and her actions for himself. I only hoped he

300

wouldn't be too hurt when he found out the type of person she truly was.

"Terrah, I believe Joshua looks tired. Perhaps you can have Rose show him to his room."

Terrah grinned at me maliciously. "Oh, there's no need to bother Rose. I'll show him myself."

Like a puppy following a new master, Joshua left the room after her. I stared at them, my mouth open slightly. Had I been this oblivious with Peter?

I watched them go, feeling a deep sadness well up in me.

Confusion once again took hold of me. I owed Joshua so much and yet—now I knew love, I knew Joshua could not replace Peter. Yet in so many ways he bested Peter. Peter had an extravagant, boisterous nature. I had never once heard Joshua brag about anything. Then there was Joshua's devotion to the farm and to the way he had been so helpful to me during Mother's final illness; his concern for me and his desire not to have me come here, not to have me hurt. Of course, Peter, too, said he didn't want to see me hurt. Thinking of the pair of them was confusing me even more now.

Wondering what to do, I wandered into the study. It surprised me that Terrah had left the door open, but then I realized she would not have hidden anything of value here. Did she guess I already had information which could harm her? Could I, did I, dare use it to keep her from hurting Joshua? A frown creased my brow. Maybe I should just take Joshua and return to Kansas now. That would mean giving up my desire to find out who my father was. Tears came to my eyes. As much as I liked Joshua, I couldn't give up my desire to learn who I was. I wondered then if my cousins had been hoping I would

301

take Joshua home with me. Was that the reason for Terrah's sudden charm? I knew already my friend was not the type of man she liked, and yet she was acting as if he was the joy of her life.

It was all so puzzling, but there was nothing I could do right now. I picked up a book and stared at it but couldn't read.

Finally, I forced myself to go upstairs. I had to talk to Joshua. I had to make him understand how my feelings had changed.

I was surprised he had been put on the second floor as one of the honored guests. His room was twice the size of mine and had a larger fireplace, too. But then I knew what my cousins thought of me. I also knew what they thought of Joshua. I glanced at the blue chintz curtains which blew in the afternoon breeze and at the brightness and lightness of the room.

Joshua lay alone on the large bed, but I could smell Terrah's perfume lingering here.

I cleared my throat once. Joshua simply stared up toward the ceiling.

Finally, he spoke. "Your cousin sure is some lady."

"Yes." I cleared my throat again. "Joshua, I am so fond of you. And I've promised myself to you. But if you want—if you think it wise, we can break it off." Once again, the tears stung my eyes and tightened my voice. I had not thought this would be so difficult.

Joshua made no response other than to sigh. He held one of Terrah's flowers in his hands. I realized as soon as I saw them they were the fake flowers from the vase in the parlor. I hated her for what she was doing to him more than I hated her for what she was doing to me. Mother had prepared me somewhat for the ways of "a

302

gentleman's house"—though I would hardly call my cousins gentle folk—but Joshua was only a country boy. I feared he would be at her beck and call now.

Without waiting for him to say anything else, I turned and walked from the room. I decided then to return to the brook. Seeing the water might help me calm my thoughts and make a rational decision.

I should be relieved Joshua no longer wanted to marry me.

But would he again want to wed me—after he had seen Terrah for a few days, after he knew about her what I knew? Was I sure it was right to continue seeing Peter? Certainly, my cousins couldn't have planned *this* to happen.

Tears now streamed from my eyes. Whatever they had planned, it now played havoc with my emotions. I did love Peter, but I doubted he would marry me. I put my hands to my eyes. What a mess I had made of things. I wished now with all my heart that I had never found the letter, had never come here. But I had come and it was too late to turn back.

Staring at the water in the calm brook, I knew that if it meant giving up Peter, I would have to take Joshua back to Kansas. I would have to get him away from Terrah's spell. I didn't understand how she could have woven her magic over him so quickly. But she had.

For the first time I glanced toward the brook, noticing the water covered with a scum. A dead fish floated in the water. I stared at the bloated body and felt a chill go through me.

Another warning to me? Had someone—besides Peter—known that we were going to be here this morning? Horrified, I continued to stare as once more my doubts about Peter came up. Someone had purposely destroyed the fish because of me? I found it hard to believe Peter would do something like this, and yet he was the one who had planned this morning at the brook. It seemed my worries were true.

Lost in my own thoughts and fears, I didn't hear the noise of the approaching footsteps until they were directly behind me. Only as the cloth came down on my face and the rope tightened about my neck did I begin to struggle.

In vain, I grappled with the huge hands holding me. As darkness began to descend, I knew I had to fight harder for my life. I knew I had to fight for Joshua and perhaps for Peter, as well.

Chapter Eighteen

I don't know how long I lay unconscious. I opened my eyes, realizing that I was still near the brook, and Peter stood over me. Immediately, I stiffened.

Even as I sat up, I felt Peter leaning down next to me. My vision blurred.

"Darling, are you hurt?"

I struggled to sit up further. His arms went about me, those wonderful arms which held me and caressed me.

I stared at him. Finally, I spoke, my voice hoarse, "I'm—fine, Peter."

He drew me to him. "I heard your scream and I—I ran."

Grimacing, I sat up fully. My head felt as if it would explode. My lungs ached with each breath. "Did—did you see anyone?" Grateful for his support, I leaned against him dizzily.

His lips kissed my brow. "No, love. I didn't. I heard someone running through the underbrush as I came up, but I saw no one." His hand brushed away the loose hair on my forehead. "Do you have any idea who might have attacked you?"

I stared at him a moment before shaking my head, and I winced with the movement. "No. I saw nothing. I didn't hear anyone behind me until it was too late." Tears choked my voice. "Oh, Peter, why is this happening to me? Doesn't Terrah realize I only want to know my father? I only want to know who I am. That's all I ask." I sniffled. He drew me closer.

"You really think Terrah is behind everything happening to you?"

I stared at him. "Yes, I do. Unless you know something I don't know."

Peter shook his head, but I had the horrid feeling he did have information he wasn't giving me.

"My poor Elizabeth. If only I could do more to help you. If only you would come away with me."

I sighed and looked up into his eyes. "What are they afraid of? I don't know anything yet—except—" I stopped and saw Peter's brow furrow.

"Except what, dearest?"

Pursing my lips, I shrugged. As before with the fire, I had no idea who might have attacked me. I guessed it was David—or Peter—but I couldn't be certain. I stared up into his huge blue eyes so full of concern for me. Did he really mean that concern, or was I being a fool? I loved Peter Parkisham and tried to trust him. Why then did I feel reluctant to tell him what I knew about the bank?

"My sweet Elizabeth." His voice was husky with emotion. "What is it? Why are you staring at me so accusingly?"

I shook my head, ever so slightly. Again, I felt the pain. If he was so quick to perceive my suspicion, perhaps he had a reason to fear it. My stomach tightened with the agony of my doubt.

"Elizabeth, you must tell me what you know. I've been honest with you. Please. We must find a way out of this dilemma."

I took a deep breath, feeling a heaviness on my chest. Quite slowly, I began. "It's—it's about the bank."

"What about it?"

I wet my lips, feeling the dryness there. Once again, I felt my head pounding in agony as I tried to inhale. Peter watched me, waiting for my words.

"I know Terrah has embezzled money from her father's bank. And she—" Once more I licked my dry lips. "I suspect she or David killed Tilly, killed Mr. McCrae, and set the fire."

"Darling." He held me tighter to him. "Suspecting things like that won't help." I could feel him tense. "Have you any proof?"

I nodded and glanced up into his eyes. Did I read fear there? "I saw some of the bank account books." I closed my eyes, trying to block out the tension I could feel from Peter. "It was when I searched for—the old family Bible. I had seen it there once before and wanted to look at it again. The Bible was missing, but when I opened the drawer, I found the rows of numbers from the ledger. I copied them because they seemed to indicate something illegal was happening, and I believe the fire at the bank has proven me right. David wasn't with us the night of the fire. He could have gone into town earlier to set the fire."

It was Peter's turn to gasp. "Do you realize what you're accusing David of?" His voice was harsh.

I pressed my lips together and nodded.

Tears came again to my eyes, streaming down my cheeks.

"I can't be sure, but I believe Terrah suspects I know

about the bank," I said. "I'd destroy my proof if she'd tell me who my father is. If you want to tell her, you can do so." I held my breath as I waited for his reaction.

Peter was aghast. "Why do you ask me to do something which might betray you?"

I shook my head, relieved he felt as he did. "It doesn't matter. I think she already knows. How she knows, I'm not sure, but I'm sure she does."

"Oh, Elizabeth," he murmured in sadness as I nodded. "Don't you realize how ruthless your cousins can be?"

"But—"

"Come away with me, my love. Come now. Today. We can elope and no one will know. It will be just you and me. I'll protect you. I promise. Once we're married, they wouldn't dare hurt you. Alexander would realize he can't get me to marry Terrah and he'll back down."

Indecision made me waver. I wondered if they would back down. I doubted it. I did love Peter, despite what I suspected. I wanted to be with him.

"What about my clothes?"

He hugged me closer. Apparently, he felt I succumbed. "We can send for them after we're married. Or I'll buy you new ones. I've money saved. I—"

Tears continued to trickle down my cheeks as I shook my head. The pain, both external and internal, ached intensely. "Please," I whispered, "give me more time, Peter. I must—find out who I am."

"But how?" Peter seemed amazed at my persistence. Again, I shook my head. I didn't know. I just had confidence I would. If I stuck it out long enough, someone would have to tell me something soon. Peter took my hand. "You've been here over a month already. You've learned hardly anything. Who's going to tell you more? Hayward can't. Terrah and David won't. I haven't been able to find out anything. Please, my darling. Come away with me before someone hurts you." Tears were in his eyes now. "Darling, you must—you must forget your search. At least for now. To search is useless. It doesn't matter who you are." He touched my hair ever so gently, sending shivers through me. "I love you anyway."

I steeled myself. "It matters to me."

Peter continued touching me, stroking me. I felt myself sinking into his arms, caring about nothing but being with him. The pain of the past few moments disappeared as he caressed me.

"Please, my love, I beg you. Leave with me. Today."

"I can't," I cried, forcing myself to pull away. "Joshua—"

"Hang that farm boy!" he cried suddenly as he released me. "He means nothing to you and you know it. It's me that you love."

I stared at Peter in astonishment. I had never seen him act like this.

Seeing the stunned look on my face he calmed down. "Oh, Elizabeth." He took me into his arms once more. "I'm sorry for all that's happening to you. I wish I could do something more to help you. Truly, I do. I'm sad to see your friend, Joshua, seems to have developed an attachment for Terrah. As so many other men seem to." His voice seemed to break. I wondered if he wasn't jealous. My heart strings seemed to tighten. "He doesn't love you the way I do. God knows where I'd be without you."

I stared into his blue eyes, trembling, wondering how he knew about Terrah and Joshua. "Anyone would be infatuated with her. She has money and dresses well. I certainly don't. I never could. I don't have the ability to sway men the way she does." I glanced up at Peter again.

The way he looked at me tore deep into my gut. "Even you are swayed by her. Your father would never allow Terrah to marry anyone else. He needs her to marry you. I don't know who's doing the manipulation—him or her—but they seem to both want this." I choked back my tears. "You told me yourself. Your father wants her to marry you." The pain in my throat made it increasingly harder to talk. "Besides, she intends to become the mistress of Parkland."

"Has she said that?"

"Oh, Peter, don't be naive. I can see it in her eyes each time she talks about Parkland. I'm surprised your mother's life isn't in danger."

He stared at me. "No. She would never hurt my mother." He seemed to be blocking the thoughts coming to him. I was astonished when he bent once more to have his lips meet mine. "Oh, Elizabeth, I love you. Terrah won't hurt my mother, and she won't hurt us—not once we're away."

Tears veiled my vision as once again I lost myself in the loving touches of my darling.

"Peter, there's no sense in this. There's no use in this."

"You're wrong. The use is," he said, his voice barely audible, "that I refuse to live without you."

His hand loosened the laces on my bodice. He teased my nipples, bringing them alive, exciting them. I wanted him and yet I felt scared. It was one thing to be with Peter, to make love to him as before, but now Joshua was here. It felt as if I was betraying my friend. He pulled me to him. His breath touched my ear and warmed it. "Don't you understand? After what has happened, we must leave this godforsaken town. Tonight at the latest. By my faith, Elizabeth Larabee, I love you and only you. I want to be with you forever."

His kisses bruised me as they had at our first meeting by the gazebo. His mouth tantalized me, creating a need so great I could hardly stand it. My whole body ached for him and yet I could not forget my terrible suspicions.

"I will make plans for us to leave tonight."

I shook my head.

"My fear for your life drives me insane. It's been so long since—"

"Peter, it's only been a few hours since this morning."

"That farm fellow—"

I pulled myself away now. "Don't talk about Joshua like that. He might be infatuated with Terrah, but he's still my dear friend. I cannot abandon him."

"And I cannot abandon you." His mouth met mine once more, fevering me to a passion out of control. His kiss now gently searched out the hidden caverns of my mouth. His hands touched my naked skin, setting me on fire and once again erasing my pain, my doubts.

Swept away by his emotions, by his need for me, I nodded slightly.

"You'll come away then," he whispered.

"Yes. No. I mean. Oh, Peter." I looked up into his eyes. How easy he could make me forget my promise to myself, my determination. I couldn't let him do it.

Confusion once more took hold of me. "I don't know." My tears returned. I had to pull myself away from him before I ruined everything for myself.

Without Peter's hands about me, I felt cold. Hungry now for his caress, I touched him. I felt the hardness of his body as I tried to recapture the passion I had felt a moment before. My heart was torn between my desire for him and my desire to know who I was.

I stared at Peter and realized my passion had gone.

Where? Why?

Slowly, I began to relace the front of my dress. "I can't think about this now, Peter. My head aches dreadfully. I need to rest."

"Then come to Parkland with me. You'll be safe there. Alexander will never know the difference. I can hide you in the attic."

I shook my head stubbornly. "Danger or not, I must return to Jerseyhurst."

"But Elizabeth!" His voice held despair. "Don't you see—"

"My cousin will do nothing to me. Certainly not for the rest of the day. I'm going back to rest and—"

"And you'll meet me tonight?" His voice contained hope.

I looked directly into eyes, bluer than the sea. What did he truly think? What did I read in them? I couldn't tell, but I feared he was involved with Terrah more than he was willing to admit to me. "I don't know yet, Peter. I must think." I sighed, seeing his sad look. He had a certain power over me. Surely, he knew it. The same ache he felt, I felt also. "Very well. I will meet you tonight by the gazebo. I'll—give you my answer about leaving then."

Peter sighed. "If that's the best I can hope for, then, I must settle for it." He picked me up into his arms.

"Wait! What are you doing?"

"Isn't it obvious? I'm going to carry you back as far as I dare. You'll need all your strength for tonight—when we begin our journey."

"Peter," I sighed and felt his kiss on my brow. I could only wonder at his sudden determination to make me leave. Was it fear for me or was it more? Did he know something? Tonight—tonight, I would have to make the right decision.

I lay on my bed, staring up at the ceiling as I tried to think.

Glancing over to the chair, I looked again at the red bandana hung there. It had been in my room when I had returned just now. The bandana was the same one—or similar—to the kind Tilly had worn. Attached to it came a note: "The same'll happen t'you, if you don't leave now." I knew that referred to Tilly's death.

The handwriting looked crude and illiterate. My first thought had been Rose, but Terrah or someone else could easily have pretended. I tried to think.

I had few hints to help me understand what was going on. Then, I recalled the book—my aunt's diary—I had found upstairs.

Hastily, I rose from the bed and pulled the book from the drawer in the nightstand. I half expected to find the diary gone, but it was still there. Uttering a prayer, I kissed the old leather binding. This would help me. It had to help me.

Yes, it definitely was a diary written by my aunt.

But even as I read my disappointment grew. I realized the story here was about her first years in coming to Illinois, to Jerseyhurst, in marrying my uncle. My heart ached as I came to the final pages. Nothing. Other than a few comments of how difficult Terrah's birth had been and what a tiresome child she had been to raise, there was no indication of what had truly happened to her. No mentions of her being locked in this room or fearing for her life. No mention of my mother and her friendship with my aunt, or of my father.

Totally disappointed, I closed the volume and placed it

313

back in the drawer. I was no nearer to finding out who my father was or to finding out who had killed Tilly than I was when I first arrived. Maybe Peter was right. Maybe I just wasn't ruthless enough for them.

I paced back and forth, standing for a moment at the window and then returning to the fireplace. I didn't know what to do. Would I lose Peter if I didn't leave with him tonight? Should I even trust him? How did I know he wasn't the one who had tried to murder me on those many occasions. And what of Joshua? What would he think if I left here with Peter? Did I dare hurt him that way? No matter how infatuated he seemed with Terrah, I couldn't let him down like that. I had to help him.

Once more my heart felt skewered. I had sold the farm and had no farm to return to. I had no place to call home. Joshua had promised me a home with him—an honorable home and an honest life. On the other hand, would Peter ever be able to really marry me?

If I doubted Peter as much as I did, could I really be in love with him? The proof was in the pudding, my mother used to say. If I loved him, I wouldn't doubt him.

It wasn't fair. All these confusing thoughts were not fair. Mother had also told me that the more you loved someone, the more of their faults you saw. I saw many of Peter's faults and still loved him, yet didn't know if I could trust him.

A knock on the door startled me. Just by the authoritarian sound, I knew who it was, but I asked, nevertheless, "Yes?"

"It's Terrah."

My heart skipped a beat. It was almost as if my fears had communicated themselves to her. I heard my voice trembling despite my desire to remain calm. "What do you want?" I asked, seeing my hand shake as I hastily folded the red bandana into the drawer of the desk. Even if she had sent it, I did not want her to know how it had upset me.

"I must talk with you, Elizabeth." The knob turned but the door would not open for her.

Swallowing hard, I proceeded to move the chair from the door where I had placed it.

"Why, Elizabeth, my dear, whatever is wrong?" She swept into the room and eyed the chair. "You look like a frightened little rabbit."

I glared at her. I had been trying so hard to hide my fright.

"Why do you have that thing in front of the door? Don't tell me David acted like a bad boy again."

"Yes, I mean no." I licked my lips as I tried to think. Terrah was a queen at unnerving people—me especially. "I don't think I have to explain my fears to you."

"No?" Terrah raised her brows. "Why not? You shouldn't have anything to fear, my little Kansas cousin."

I stared at her, hating her superior tone. If I had been stronger, I would have thrown her out of the room.

Terrah sat down, uninvited, in the only chair. "As a matter of fact, I've just spoken with Peter. He believes I should talk to you."

My stomach tightened. "And what did he tell you?"

Terrah gave me her cat smile again. My irritation with her rose. "You're really lucky he was nearby and could help you home, aren't you? He says you didn't see who attacked you."

"No, but I have a fair idea of who it was."

"Do you? Do you really?" The sarcasm in my cousin's tone nearly broke my calm. "Have you considered it might have been Peter, himself?"

315

I felt my eyes widen. Of course I had considered it, but it shocked me that she would say such a thing.

Terrah continued sweetly. "I really don't think you know your menfolk as well as you might like." She paused. "Peter considers you his possession. After all, he has enjoyed your country charms on several occasions. I don't think he likes the idea of your farmer friend coming to take your attentions away."

"That's not true!" I cried, confused.

"What's not true?" She smiled at me. "Do you mean you and Peter aren't lovers or do you mean Joshua hasn't tried to reclaim your affections?"

I struggled to control myself as my fist clenched at my side. "Joshua—has never lost my affections."

"That's interesting. And are you sure of him?"

"Of course I am. Joshua and I have known each other for years. We grew up together."

Her silvery laugh grated on my nerves. "So did Peter and I. But I don't profess to know him." She paused and shifted her considerable weight in the chair. "You're luckier than most, darling cousin. Most women never really know their man's true affections, which is why you have to keep them in suspense. But I guess with you simple folk—"

"If that's all you came to talk about, you can leave."

Terrah's eyes narrowed. "No, Elizabeth. That is not all I want to discuss."

"Well, then say what you came for and leave." I waved my hand toward the door.

"Very well." She cleared her throat. "As you know, my party at Parkland will be next week."

I nodded impatiently.

"I merely wondered what costume you would be wearing?"

"Costume?" I stared at her. I had already been planning a dress with material I had bought the other day with the money she and my uncle gave me. That was, of course, assuming I stayed.

"Yes, of course. It is a costume ball. Didn't you know?"

I shook my head in amazement. I should have known. Terrah, David, and Alexander had done nothing but speak of the ball for weeks now.

"Peter and I," she said, watching me, "are going as Romeo and Juliet."

My eyes widened. I was too surprised to even bother to hide it. She laughed slightly and continued. "But, of course, there will be a different ending to our story."

"What do you mean?"

"Oh come. Surely you know the story."

I nodded.

"Well rather than die that night, Peter and I plan to marry. Right at the ball."

"Marry?" The word stuck in my throat. I could feel my blood running cold. "But I thought—"

"That we would only be announcing our engagement?" Terrah smiled. "Sorry to disappoint you but we've changed our minds. No. The wedding is next week as well. There seemed no sense in having two huge gatherings. I think the ceremony will do fine if we have it just before the dancing."

I continued to stare at Terrah as she went on. My heart had turned to ice. "Your farmer friend from Kansas goes as Othello. I thought perhaps you would like to appear as Desdemona. You do know who she is, don't you?" The apple red in her cheeks heightened. She seemed to be having great fun goading me.

"Yes, I know who she is," I said curtly.

Terrah stretched slightly like a satisfied cat who had cornered a mouse. "Would you prefer something else? After all, Desdemona was killed by her jealous husband."

My head still ached from this morning. Was Terrah telling me that Peter had tried to murder me? Or Joshua? No. It was inconceivable that either would injure me. I realized now my love for Peter was too strong. I could not, would not believe he had a hand in anything to harm me. But then how well did I know either Peter or Joshua—for all the time I had spent with them? I shivered.

"My. My. You've suddenly become quite pale. Shall I have a powder sent up for you?"

I met her eyes as boldly as I could. "I'm fine. I don't feel ill at all. And I have no trouble going to your costume ball."

"Fine." She stood. "I shall arrange for your costume."

I nodded and opened the door. Would I even be here for the ball?

"Tell me," I asked as Terrah stepped to the door. "Who is Alexander going as?"

"Oh," Terrah paused, "I believe he's going as Iago." Her hand touched the knob then. "You do plan to be here for the party? Joshua would be so disappointed if you left beforehand."

I gathered my courage. "That depends on you, cousin. If you tell me—"

"There is nothing I have to tell you, Elizabeth. No, it all depends on you. You give me whatever supposed information you have. Then, I will consider telling you what I know."

She exited then, closing the door firmly behind her, leaving me alone in the room to stare at the blank wood of the door.

Chapter Nineteen

Sleep refused to come to me. As desperately as I tried, I could not rest, nor could I think. I still had no answer to the question Peter had asked me. Did I dare run away with him and risk never finding out who I truly was?

My mind continued to play with the problems until I heard pebbles at the window. Rising from the bed quickly, I went to the window. My eyes widened in astonishment. I couldn't believe Peter stood there!

Wasn't he afraid someone would see him? Didn't he care?

I motioned him away but he refused to leave. Smiling up at me, he motioned for me to come downstairs.

True we had planned on meeting tonight but not until later and then at the gazebo.

I dressed quickly in the navy blue poplin. The clock struck eleven as I hurried down the stairs, shoes in hand. The darkened hall made me nervous, but I had long ago realized the lack of light meant nothing. Terrah did not like to spend money on lights, and only a few gas lamps dimly guided the way down the long corridor. Briefly, I considered taking the back stairs. I had never investigated them as I had promised myself. Even as I thought about it, shivers ran up my spine. It was not something I wanted to do in the darkness. Besides, Peter was waiting for me. I would look at it in the daylight.

I waited a moment more, listening. No other sounds came from the house. Reaching the butler's pantry which led out toward the covered walk for the kitchen, I stopped short. There were lights glowing dimly in the outer kitchen. Was Rose baking at this hour? I found it hard to believe. I was sure the girl was spying for my cousin.

My breath seemed to come quickly. I could no longer see Peter. I assumed he, too, had noticed the lights and retreated to the woods. I didn't know if the lights had just come on or if they had been on for some time, but I did not like it.

Still in the shadows of the house, I paused. I walked forward toward the kitchen. If Rose was there at this time of night, I intended to confront her. I hadn't thought myself to be so bold, yet I was tiring of her snooping. She had no reason to hate me. Perhaps if I talked to her, I could make her understand my feelings. I approached the separate outside kitchen.

My heart squeezed tighter as I approached the kitchen windows. The brush and twigs snapped beneath my feet. I hesitated and then realized if Rose was in the kitchen, she had probably already seen me. Taking a deep breath, I peered over the ledge.

To my amazement, especially knowing my cousin's penny pinching ways, the room was empty yet the gas fires glowed dimly. Had someone been there? Or was it just a mistake that they had been left burning?

Puzzled, I pulled away. There was still the possibility I was being watched. I didn't know what to do. If I decided to join Peter as I wanted, I had to be careful. My throat constricted as I glanced toward the big house. No lights.

After several moments, I decided I would have to sprint across the open yard, through the path of light made by the kitchen. My only other option was taking the long path which eased around to the road. But that would make me miss Peter since I was sure he was waiting for me by the clearing.

My heart raced as I ran across the yard.

Reaching the trees on the other side, I paused. My breath was coming hard. I continued to watch the light from the kitchen. I still found it hard to believe no one was there, and I half expected to see Rose's sour face appear, ready to begin her spy mission, but nothing happened.

My breathing slowed to almost normal. I now turned toward the shortcut which led through the valley and toward the gazebo near Parkland.

Where was Peter? He had been the one to throw the stones, hadn't he? Yes, I felt sure I had seen him. Why hadn't he waited for me? Tears came to my eyes. He knew how I hated walking this spooky path at night.

Behind me, a branch snapped.

I whirled about. My heart thudded as my dress caught on a twig. No one was there, but suddenly, I felt a heavy hand on my shoulder. Gasping, I had no time to think before the man's lips met mine in a hard, bruising kiss.

I pulled away my hand and was ready to slap the man. It was David!

He caught my arm and smiled. "You did come out to meet me, didn't you, Cousin Elizabeth?"

I glared at him as he raised his brows a bit. The moonlight seemed to glint in his evil eyes. I shuddered. Could I have been wrong before? Could it have been

David I had seen?

His lips came down toward me once more, and my stomach tightened as I feared the worst, but his mouth did not touch mine. Instead, his hands grasping my shoulder suddenly lost their grip as he fell to the ground. It was Peter I stared at now.

"Peter! Did you— How did David—" The unanswered questions tumbled from me. Peter took my hand as my fright slowly calmed. "Oh, Peter." I put my arms about his neck. I was so happy to see him.

"I'm so sorry that happened, my love. I don't know how David knew we were meeting, but you must see now how important it is for you to leave with me. Tonight."

I glanced at the still form of David. His breathing was heavy, as if in a deep sleep. I knew he was not dead.

I found speech impossible for the moment. I hated what I was thinking, and yet it seemed the only way David would have known of our plans was for Peter to have told him. But why? I looked up into Peter's lapis blue eyes and, despite my fears, felt his love.

Taking my silence for agreement, he took me into his arms. "Are you ready?" His lips nuzzled my neck, sending delightful shivers up and down me. He knew how to get me, damn him. He knew now what made me tingle with desire.

I tried to fight the warmth slowly creeping up. "Ready for what?"

"To leave, darling. I have the carriage."

With an effort, I pulled back and sat down on the rock nearby. I sighed and felt the effort of denying him and myself coursing through me. I had to do it. I had to deny him or I would never learn the truth. Even I could hear the sadness in my voice as I told him, "No, Peter, I am not going with you tonight."

In the moonlight, I could see his figure stiffen. His blue eyes widened in surprise. I said nothing more.

"Elizabeth, my love, you're joking with me. I fail to understand—"

"Why didn't you tell me it wasn't just to be an engagement announcement next week but a wedding? Why didn't you tell me you had agreed to marry her at the party. Am I nothing to you?"

"Elizabeth, you are everything to me. That's why it's so important we leave town." With the helplessness of a little boy caught with his hand in a cookie jar, Peter glanced down. His fingers spread apart as he stared at his hands.

"What exactly did Terrah tell you?"

"She told me you were planning to marry at the party. She made it clear to me you've been in on the plans all along."

There were several moments of silence before Peter spoke again.

"Elizabeth, my sweet passion." He reached for me but I stepped back. The pitiful tone in his voice would have drawn my tears if I hadn't been so determined. "My love," he continued in his trembling voice, "you must understand. Please. I love you, Elizabeth. I do. Only you—" He reached out again to me. For a moment I hesitated, allowing his touch.

It was my downfall. Unable to push him away, I felt my brittle resolve crumble into tears. I let his hand remain on mine, warming me with its touch while the rest of me felt cold. I wished I could just forget everything. I wished I could absorb myself into Peter's arms. Picking me up into his arms, he carried me toward the gazebo, nearly a ten minute walk further along.

"Don't you see?" he whispered. "Don't you understand? That's why I want us to leave now. Tonight. That's why—" His voice seemed close to breaking now. "What I feel for you is more than just desire. Please!" He tugged at me, pulling me forward into his arms.

I grudgingly allowed myself to be manipulated, wanting him, and yet trying to keep cold control of my feelings. As his arms engulfed me, I felt his tears against my cheek. My resolve melted as I feared it would. "Oh, Peter—" I responded to his kiss with a fervency matching his own. My mind was awhirl with only one desire: to make Peter mine, to know him one more time. His hot breath was on my brow, on my neck.

"You'll come with me now?"

It was my turn to cry. "Peter, I need to know—can't you understand?"

His quivering hands had already unlaced my bodice. As he drew me to the ground I realized a blanket had already been placed there. For the moment, I was angry at his planning, and then I lost myself in the joy of his touch, the nerve-thrilling probing as his body met mine. I gave no other thought to the worries of the moment. We were away from the house, away from all the problems. Peter was mine. He belonged to me, no matter what Terrah said or did.

Time seemed to stand still for us, but I knew from the passage of the clouds over the moon that time was passing all too quickly. Our lovemaking had been the best, yet I still had my doubts. Silently, I lay in his arms several minutes. My head rested against the dark hairs of his chest.

"Do you know that I love you?" he whispered.

I nodded, not wanting to break the moment with speech.

"Do you also realize how much I need you with me? Without you, I am nothing."

I nodded again, wishing he wouldn't talk so.

"Then tell me you'll come with me tonight." His hands touched my breasts, gently and playfully stroking my nipples into erect excitement.

I gasped with the pleasure and torment. "Peter—I—" I pulled away, then, reaching for my skirts and petticoat. "Peter, I've told you. I cannot come away with you tonight. I must find out who I am."

"Hang it! You may never find out."

"Yes, I will. Somehow, I'll find out. I thought you were going to ask questions for me."

"Oh, blast! Elizabeth, I did. I tried. No one seems to know anything except Alexander and maybe Harriet, but neither will say anything."

"Harriet?" I realized my fears about his half-sister were accurate. "Do you think she took the papers?"

"My sister?"

"Who else would Terrah get? Your sister's been out of town for years. Obviously, Mr. Dunn and the boy wouldn't know her."

"But Harriet—"

"Have you checked her room? Have you—"

"Damn it, Elizabeth. No, I haven't. Honestly, love," he pleaded, "it would be so much safer for you, for me, for us to leave now. Your search has to wait."

I felt my eyes narrow. "If I wait, I'll never learn. Peter, I can't leave. I feel that—that—I'll learn something very soon."

"But what if you don't?"

"I will. I feel it. If you loved me as you say, you'd help me."

"Elizabeth," he hissed.

"What?"

"Lower your voice."

"Why?" Peter didn't understand what it meant to know who I was. He was as bad as Joshua, and yet I had expected more from him. Maybe that's why it hurt more.

I stood, leaving the blanket. "Elizabeth." He tried to bring me closer again. I pulled away, stepping on a twig. "I swear. I'll find out for you—if we leave tonight."

I shook my head.

"Please, Elizabeth. You'll condemn me."

"Condemn you?"

"Darling, if we don't leave tonight—if I'm here next week, I'll have no choice but to marry that cousin of yours."

"Why can't you simply refuse?"

"I can't." He moaned. "You don't understand Alexander. I can't. Please. Come away with me. Don't do this to me."

"If you were honest with your father, with Alexander—"

"Christ!" His hand shot out, gripping my arm. "You aren't going to do this to me, Elizabeth. You led me to believe you'd come away with me. I have the carriage. I—"

"You're hurting me." I felt the tears come to my eyes as I tried to pull away.

Abruptly, he released me. "Elizabeth, my darling. I want you—not to hurt you. I fear for you. What happened tonight with David can happen again."

"What do you mean?" The fear I felt earlier was realized now. Peter had told David. They had arranged this between them—to get me away. I was sure of it. I could feel my breath coming in gasps as I tried to control my fear of Peter. I had never expected this from

Peter and yet, perhaps I should have. With violence such as he now showed me, couldn't he easily have been the one to attack me on those occasions before?

I stared at him. It was hard for me to conceive that he could want to hurt me.

"Why?" I asked. "Why should you fear for me?"

"Because your cousin's attempt this afternoon failed. Because obviously, she doesn't like the questions you've been asking about your parentage, about that black—"

"That black was Tilly, my mother's nurse," I snapped.

Shrugging, Peter said, "Her name doesn't matter. What matters is that your life's in danger."

"But I—"

"Elizabeth, whatever proof you think you have, I'm sure Terrah will find some way to discredit it."

I felt myself go white. He was right. "She can't." I tried to deny my fears. "Please, give me a few more days. The ball isn't for another week yet." I took a deep breath. "It's Saturday today. If by—Thursday, I haven't learned anything more than I know now, I will go with you. I'll be able to tell Joshua then, too."

He frowned. "Must you tell him?"

I nodded. There was no question of that.

"Tuesday, then."

"No. That's not enough time. Wednesday."

Peter's arms went about my shoulders. "Oh, Elizabeth," he groaned, kissing me passionately and melting our bodies together to create the heat it seemed only the two of us were capable of. "Very well, we shall try for Wednesday. I only hope—" His head jerked up.

"What?" I could feel his heart pounding, I could hear it as I leaned against his chest.

"Did you hear something?"

I shook my head. My senses had been full of him. I had

heard nothing. There were tears in my eyes and a tightness in my chest as I touched his cheek. Why did I feel so overwhelmingly sad? "Wednesday. And if you check Harriet's room, if you find anything before then, you'll contact me."

He nodded. "But I doubt Harriet will still have the papers. If Terrah or Alexander wanted her to get the papers, they'll have them hidden already." He held me as if he wanted never to let me go. His lips grazed my cheek again. "Please, my love, do take care. I want you to remember how very much I love you."

I inhaled deeply the night odors, his masculine scent. Every second with Peter was precious to me. I still did not understand how I could love him, and yet I did. Our parting kiss was a lingering one. It would have to suffice until Wednesday. "Good-bye, Peter." I turned quickly then, not wanting to see his sad eyes as I ran back toward the house.

At the edge of the woods I paused. My stomach tightened with fear as I inhaled and tried to steady my nerves. The kitchen lights were out. I hadn't noticed David on the way home. Had he recovered? Had he followed us after all? Had he overheard our plans to leave?

I waited a moment and then ran toward the back of the house. The door was unlocked as I had left it. Again, I thought of David. My mouth was dry with fear. Peter wasn't about to protect me now. I saw no one about.

Without hesitation, I made my way up the stairs and to my room. Bolting the door with the chair, I lay down on the bed, breathless and worried. I had to find out something soon. There was no way I could leave without learning who I was. Peter would have to understand.

Chapter Twenty

But nothing did come to light in those next days. I heard not a word from Peter. And when Wednesday arrived, it scarcely seemed possible that my time had run out. I was going again to see Peter, but not without a heavy heart. I knew he expected me to leave with him that night. It seemed I was fated to disappoint the men in my life—first Joshua, and now Peter.

As I made my way to the gazebo, the darkened woods were illuminated only by periodic blasts of lightning. In the glare, the tree trunks stood out like dead things—wretched and cursed. I hurried on, trying not to think.

Being without Peter these past few days had been difficult for me, especially since I knew he was often at the house to confer with Terrah about plans for the ball. I hadn't dared attempt to talk with him, and yet how I longed for the sound of his voice.

As I reached the depth of the woods, I shivered and put my hands to my shoulders. I should have brought a warmer wrap, but I hadn't thought of it earlier. The wind picked up and howled in my ears. It sounded like the wail of a demented woman in agony. For just a moment, I longed to return to the safety of my room, to pull the covers over my head and hide until the storm had passed. But I had to see Peter tonight. I had promised him.

My hands shook as I continued to push away the swaying leaves and resolutely continued my walking. Any moment now, Peter would come out of his hiding place. I knew he had to be along the path here—somewhere. He would surprise me as he did the last time. He would save me from the torment of the storm, from walking alone. I would be safe in his arms. I turned about briefly. There was no sign of any other human near me.

Surely, he would be here tonight. He had agreed to Wednesday. Today was Wednesday.

I felt sickness in my stomach. I had eaten precious little at dinner. I didn't know if it came from my worry about meeting Peter now or from the disgust I felt at the way Terrah was leading poor Joshua on. At dinner, they had sat together, talking—no, impolitely whispering, as if they were alone in the world, as if they were lovers. But I was sure that could not be. Joshua, who had been reluctant even to kiss my cheek when I had left Kansas, could not be Terrah's lover and yet—my fears invaded my thoughts. I was so afraid Terrah was only using him to somehow hurt me.

Oh, where was Peter? He had promised to meet me halfway.

Surely, I was more than halfway now. This was the only path he would be taking. As the wind whistled through the leaves, I felt chills go through my body, beneath my thin shawl. But I knew the best thing I could do would be to continue.

I would wait near the willow. If the rain started, I

would go straight to the gazebo. Yes, the gazebo would be the best place. Peter would be sure to look there.

The first drop fell on my brow. I glanced up to the sky but could see only thunderous dark clouds looming above me.

Raising my skirts, I ran as best I could down the path, past the cliff, and up the hill toward the white iron gazebo. In the thunder and lightning, the gazebo was illuminated from behind, giving it a ghostly aspect as the flashes continued. How different it looked from the first night I had seen it.

For a moment, I thought the gated door was locked, but it was only stuck. Sneezing, I stepped inside just as the downpour started. Thankful for the blanket which Peter had left from our last encounter here, I huddled in the shadows. I prayed Peter wouldn't get caught in the rain and that he would come soon—very soon. I longed to have him hold me, love me, comfort me. I jerked my head up as fear tightened my stomach and nausea suddenly overwhelmed me. Had I heard something? I straightened. Was that Peter coming?

Dropping the blanket, I left my corner and ran to the door of the gazebo.

The rain continued, unabated. It soaked through my gown. I had no choice but to return to my corner and huddle for warmth. The rain continued to pour down as heavy as bullets. Where was Peter? There was no sign of him. He had promised to meet me tonight.

For just a moment, I forgot my determination to ask him for another few days. I felt so close to learning something and was so frustrated by the elusiveness of the information. If only I had a few more days, but how could I ask Peter for that grace if he wasn't even here? I realized then how many times I had done this—telling myself in a few days I would make a decision. Tears came to my eyes. Maybe he was right. Maybe I was deluding myself and the information would never come to me.

I glanced toward Parklawnd. The house was in darkness just as Jerseyhurst had been when I had left it.

I wiped away my tears and tried to calm myself. Peter might be a dandy, he might have had other women, but I believed him when he said he loved me. I wanted to believe him. He would meet me. Unless he were deathly ill, I knew he would come. Perhaps even then he would attempt.

My mind whirled as I tried to think. Had I heard anything about Peter's being ill or called out of town? No, I was sure he had been at the house only yesterday morning. But then I had been in my own little world since Sunday, sorting out my emotions about Peter and Joshua and attempting to piece together all the clues I had come up with. Had Peter found something in Harriet's room? Had Alexander learned he was helping me?

Again, I lifted my eyes toward the path. No, there was no one coming. I tried to keep my eyes open but could not. Well, if I dozed a moment or two, Peter would surely wake me when he came.

The sound of thunder booming jerked me alert again. I opened my eyes. What time is it? Tears once more started in my eyes. I wiped them away with the corner of the blanket, realizing that Peter was not coming. I could not return to Jerseyhurst until the storm had abated. Cursing and crying, I pulled the blanket further about my slender shoulders. I tried to control my fears as the mist swirled about me.

Just before I dozed off again, I realized that Peter had

332

been right. I should have gone off with him last week. I was a fool to have stayed so long, but now that I had, I would not leave until I learned something more.

I woke with the first rays of dawn and moved from my cramped position. Raindrops and dew sparkled on the grass about me. The storm had stopped. I could see a rainbow curving over Parkland. I could only hope it was an omen of hope for me.

I glanced toward Peter's home. It was still dark.

My heart ached as I stood. Why hadn't Peter come to me? Tears shimmered in my eyes and veiled my vision. I would have to return to Jerseyhurst. It wouldn't do for my cousin to know Peter and I had talked about leaving. I let myself out of the gazebo and heard the creaking of the door shutting itself as I hurried along the now muddied path. There had to be a message from him today.

I hoped to get to my room unnoticed, but I realized it would be impossible. Rose was already up and bustling about the kitchen. She had taken over her mother's duties with a sullenness which made everything she did seem distasteful to me.

Rose stopped mid path from the kitchen to the house as she saw me coming. I could feel her piercing stare and knew there was no way I could turn back to hide.

"Morning, Rose." I tried to keep my voice light.

"Morning," Rose grunted, still staring at me. "You's up mighty early—or mighty late."

I felt color rise to my cheeks. "Early. I went for a walk to the old house in the woods."

"Oh?" Rose raised her brow. "Were it nice there?" She glanced at my muddied hem.

333

I pressed my lips together. "As a matter of fact, it was rather sad. Excuse me." I brushed past the girl and hurried up the stairs. Thank goodness both my cousins were late sleepers, I thought, though I didn't expect my secret to be kept very long.

There was fresh hot water in my pitcher. I was grateful for that but also bothered by it, since it meant Rose had been in my room this morning. I freshened my face. I glanced about. Well, my mother's locket was already gone. Other than the gun and the paper, I had nothing else of value here.

I looked at the fireplace. Was it my imagination or did the brick which hid my treasures look different—out of place. Surely—

I crossed the room in two steps.

The brick came out easier than I had expected it would. My fears increased.

Carefully, I set it onto the wooden floor and peeked inside the hollow space. I could see nothing. I put my hand in. The blood colored my face as it rushed to my temples. Where was my gun? Where was the paper with the numbers? Where was the red scarf Tilly had worn?

My whole body trembled as I pushed my hand in deeper, feeling edges of brick scraping at my hand, feeling cold and clammy dampness of the chimney flu, feeling the cobwebs which had gathered here over the years. In revulsion, I pulled back slightly. It was then I touched the steel of Zebulon's gun and breathed a sigh of relief. The gun had somehow shifted to one side. But wait. Next to the gun I felt something else. It was a parchment, but it wasn't the sheet with the numbers on it. No, I had folded that flat. This one was crumpled and rammed into the back of the space.

Curious, I tugged gently at the parchment, pulling the page forward. I hadn't noticed anything in the space before then, but I hadn't checked very carefully.

It wasn't hard to recall the day I had hid the gun, the day David had attacked me. It had also been the day I first realized I loved Peter Parkisham. How could I help the tears which came to my eyes? I could not understand where he had been last night. Was Terrah right? Had he already lost interest in me?

The yellowed parchment resisted my efforts to free it. I grew more impatient.

Hearing steps in the hall, I paused and spun about quickly to hide the empty spot in the fireplace, should anyone come in.

No one opened the door and yet I felt in those few moments as if I were being watched. Fear drained me of any feeling as I continued to stare at the closed door.

Only then did I realize that I still held the paper in my hand. My eyes glanced down at it. "I hate her," it read. Below it then was, "I am Geo." The rest had been torn off, either as a result from my own struggle or earlier.

"Georgina," I whispered, staring at the parchment as I whispered my aunt's name. Suddenly I knew, as if she herself were reaching out to tell me from her grave. She had not committed suicide as Tilly wanted me to believe. She had been murdered.

I moved the chair under the door so I wouldn't be disturbed. With even greater care now, I removed the rest of the aged paper. I winced as it cracked and broke in my hands.

When I had unfolded the rest of the page, being as delicate as I could, I found myself staring at the paper without even reading it.

In my hands I held a letter to my aunt from my mother. My mouth went dry. There was no signature, but I recognized the small, neat penmanship which Mother had pushed me to learn.

Trembling, I once more braved whatever dead creatures lay in the hole to see if I could find anything more of the letter, but no, there was nothing. Wishing and hoping, I touched each side. Nothing. Nothing but my gun, the sheet of folded papers, and Tilly's scarf.

It took tremendous effort for me to read what I held here. Sitting down on the bed, I closed my eyes a moment as my heartbeat throbbed with such intensity that I could not have spoken a word, even if my life had depended on it.

As delicately as I could, I touched the page, spreading it flat on the surface of the bed. Some of the ink had faded with time, but it was still possible to read.

My dearest sister, Georgina:

Though we have only met a short time many years ago, I feel I can write to you. In fact, I feel you are the only person who I can turn to for help. My brother will not assist me. You must.

Perhaps you know—or if you do not, I now tell you unashamedly. I was with child when Zebulon and I left Aberdeen. The child is not my husband's. Though he has cared dearly for Elizabeth and me, there is still a longing in my heart to see things right. I have written Hayward, telling him of Zebulon's untimely death, of my need for money. I have received no reply.

Georgina, dearest sister, I confide in you. I would not be writing to you if not for my desperate situation, for need of funds for Elizabeth's schooling. She is a gentleman's daughter and must be educated as such. She . . .

The next section was illegible due to time or tears, I could not tell which. It continued:

No one has seen fit to send me word of Andrew. Pray tell me, is he alive and well? I beg of you. Talk with him in private. Tell him of his daughter and her needs. Tell him . . .

I numbly stared at the paper in my hand. I had found it. I had my answer and yet, I felt nothing. Rereading the last paragraph, I felt shivers go through me. Andrew, not Alexander. When my uncle had talked about the Parkisham fellow, he had meant Andrew!

Relief and happiness mingled with confusion. It all made sense now. Dizzily, I closed my eyes, the paper still in my hand. The picture had been changed the night of the party. The way Harriet had regarded me so strangely. And Peter. He had said Alexander had had no money until his uncle, Andrew, had died. I pressed my lips together.

At first I could not understand why Terrah and everyone wanted to keep this knowledge from me. Then, as I lay back on the soft pillows, the answer came to me. If I was Andrew's daughter, if he truly had been my father, then his estate or his home of Parkland could be mine.

Shivering, I finished what was left of the letter.

If, my dearest sister, you or he doubt my word, and I pray for our daughter's sake he does not, then my tale may be verified with a letter I have left with a lawyer, Meredith McCrae. His instructions are to show them only to Andrew, or to Elizabeth, should she one day return to Aberdeen.

The letter ended now, torn off raggedly, perhaps as if in a struggle. I saw my aunt had scrawled something on the bottom. I realized it was what I had seen before: "I hate her," and "I am Geo." I wondered whom she hated—my mother or her daughter? Tears blurred my vision as I realized my mother must have guessed I might one day come here.

"Oh, Mama!" I pressed the yellowed paper to my heart. If only she had been honest with me! If only I had found this earlier! I glanced again at the scratched wall. No, I had no certain knowledge of my aunt's demise, but I couldn't help wondering if it had something to do with this letter.

Had Andrew, my father, been dead then? Had my aunt tried at all to tell him? I doubted Terrah, bent as she was on becoming mistress of Parkland and on joining the two lands, would have allowed that. It would not have surprised me to learn of her assisting her mother—and Tilly—to their deaths. Terrah, it seemed, would do anything rather than let another inherit.

Aching tears seemed to tighten my throat and scorch my cheeks. The irony was that I wanted nothing of Parkland—except Peter. I wanted only to know who I was. My cousin and her paramour could easily have had Parkland. They need only have told me the truth. I sighed. They probably assumed I was as greedy as they were.

Sniffing, I recalled the reason I had opened the brick.

338

The gaping hole still stared at me.

I rose slowly and returned to the fireplace wall. Shivering, I refolded the yellowed paper and replaced it there. Then, satisfied it was safe, I placed the gun and my other treasures atop it. I fitted the brick back into the facade.

It took an effort for me to wash. I had thought I would be ecstatic at learning who my father was, but now I felt only that I could not be happy without Peter to share my joys. As I changed my clothes, I knew. I would have to get a message to him somehow. I wanted him to share my happiness. I could be with him forever now.

Sounds from the hall told me the others were awake. Breakfast would soon be served.

Glancing in the small mirror, I grimaced. My bloodshot eyes betrayed my restless night. But there was no help for it. I would have to make up some excuse.

David and Joshua were already at the table, talking about farming methods. My cousin's knowledge astonished me. It also surprised me that for all his lack of grace, Joshua seemed to fit into the world of Jerseyhurst better than I did. It was almost as if he had lived here for years.

Without waiting for the maid, I poured myself some coffee.

Neither man seemed to notice me, which was just as well. I was aware of my hand trembling as I drank the stimulating brew. For just a moment, I closed my eyes, inhaling the steam and aroma of the freshly brewed drink. I knew I would need all my wits about me to get a message to Peter. I wished I could get to him, myself, but I didn't dare. He hadn't deserted me. I was sure of that. Somehow, I would let him know what had happened, what I had found. Together we would escape the clutches of Aberdeen.

My moment of contemplation was a moment too long. My eyes flew open as the rustle of a silk gown alerted me to Terrah's presence. I turned and saw she wore a low-cut pink morning dress with burgundy trim. It highlighted her ample features—something which Joshua seemed most appreciative of. My stomach knotted.

"Are you all right, Elizabeth, dearest?" Terrah asked me in her honeyed tones.

I drew a quick breath. Then, slowly I sipped more of the coffee. "Yes. I'm fine," I said, unable to meet Terrah's eyes.

"Are you, Beth?" Joshua seemed to notice me for the first time since his arrival. "You look dreadful. Could you be ill?"

Rose had come in now to serve Terrah's coffee. Studiously, the black girl avoided my empty cup. It was obvious, I think to everyone, that I needed more of the stimulating Turkish drink.

I forced myself to smile at Joshua. "Truly, I'm fine." With difficulty, I turned my attention toward my plate. I realized Jerseyhurst had changed him. It had only been a few days and yet he was different. I wondered if I even knew him anymore.

"My dear." Terrah's hand was on my shoulder. "We must take care of you. It wouldn't do for you *and* Peter to be ill for the party."

It took all of my effort not to jerk away from Terrah's cold hand. "Peter's ill? What's wrong? Will he be well soon?"

Even as I said it, I knew I had made a mistake. Terrah's eyes met mine boldly. She smiled sweetly at me.

"Yes, I assure you. Peter will be well in time for the party. I doubt, however, that he'll be about much before then."

We stared at each other, neither speaking.

"I didn't hear that Peter was ill," David said, breaking the tension between us.

Terrah released her hold on me but continued to stare in my direction. "Yes. He's been ill since yesterday morning. Alexander sent a messenger over just this morning."

I tried to catch the gasp which had come to my lips, but it was too late. I realized then as I glanced at my cousin that we *had* been overheard. Somehow Alexander and Terrah had found out about our plans. I glanced toward Rose at the buffet counter. She refused to acknowledge me.

"Not hungry, Elizabeth?" Terrah smiled. "Surely, if you're not well, you should have more than just coffee."

Mutely, I shook my head.

"Oh, come now. You must eat. You won't enjoy the party if you aren't in good health, and after all, I do so want you to enjoy it." Terrah motioned to Rose and then smiled at Joshua as well.

"You can give Mr. Harmon another helping too, Rose. Someone as big and strong as he is needs plenty of food."

Joshua flushed but offered Rose his platter without hesitation.

I stared at the food on my plate. No, it couldn't be poisoned. Terrah had taken some of the food, herself. Peter was right: I was scared for my life. I should have admitted it to myself before this. My throat was dry as I recalled how Peter had begged me to leave with him. We

341

should have left. If only I hadn't been so foolish and so stubborn. I had known Terrah was desperate. I bit my lower lip. I wondered if there was any way for me to reach Peter.

"Good food," Joshua mumbled. "Aren't ya eatin', Beth?"

Nausea welled up in my stomach. I shook my head. "Maybe I'll feel like eating later." I pushed the plate from me. "Right now, my head aches."

"Poor cousin," Terrah cooed. "I'm so sorry to hear that. Shall I bring you one of my mother's powders? She used to get a lot of headaches, too."

I stared at her. How much did Terrah realize I knew? What had Peter told her? I was aware of my hand grasping the edge of my chair as I stood. "No. No, thank you, Terrah. I have something of my own."

A smile played on her lips. "Just as you wish." She turned away from me and resumed her meal. She smiled at Joshua and David as if I did not exist.

With a sinking heart, I left the room. I had to get a message to Peter. I glanced back into the dining room. Of all the people at Jerseyhurst, Joshua was the only one I could trust. If only I could see him alone! I put my hand to the cold bannister. Closing my eyes for a moment, I swayed dizzily. My head pounded unmercifully. I had to think. Dare I try to leave on my own?

No. I knew I would not get far. How could I leave, knowing Peter was being held captive, too. It was the only obvious reason for his not meeting me, for his "illness." Guilt filled me. I had done this to him. I had gotten him into this mess with my stubbornness.

A huge hand touched my shoulder. Startled, I spun about.

"Gosh, Beth. You looked so strange standing there. Are you sure you're all right?"

I forced myself to smile up at Joshua, feeling a rush of affection for him. He was my friend, still. He was the Joshua who had stood by me through my mother's death. Swallowing hard, I knew I had to speak with him. This might be my only chance.

"Joshua dearest, I need your help."

"'Course, Beth. You know I'll do what I can for you." He glanced awkwardly down at his feet. He hadn't changed. He was my Joshua, still.

Ignoring his embarrassment, I touched his hand. "Joshua, I need you to take a message for me."

"Message? To whom? 'Bout what?" Joshua was staring at me strangely now.

I swallowed again. Blood was rushing through my ears, and I felt I might double up with the nausea which had suddenly attacked me. If he failed me . . . but he wouldn't. Joshua was my friend. "Joshua, you must see Peter alone; you must tell him that I know who I am."

"You do?" His eyes widened like a child's. For a moment, I thought I saw astonishment and then what — horror? If I saw it on his face, it quickly disappeared as a grin spread over the corners of his mouth. He gave me one of his huge bear hugs, squeezing me so it almost took my breath away. "Gosh Beth, that's wonderful. It's what you came for. Now—"

It cheered me to see him happy for me, but I needed his help. I needed his promise. "Yes, Josh, I know. And it is what I came for, but I need your help now. I need you to let Peter know." I touched his cheek.

The sadness which came to his face hurt me. "Oh, Beth. But why? Why can't you just go now? I'll take you back to Kansas. I—"

"Please, Joshua. I'll explain it all to you one day. I will go, but Peter must be told. Please. Tell me you'll do it." I was on the step now. The agony in my stomach and in my head was almost unbearable. "Will you?" Tears came to my eyes. I could not hold them back."

"I guess but—"

I threw my arms about his thick neck. Kissing him on the cheek, I felt my tears touch his skin. "I knew I could count on you. Please. Tell Peter what I said. Tell him I will wait for his word."

"His word?"

I nodded.

"Will you be leaving with him, Beth?" Again the sadness was unmistakable. I hated hurting poor Joshua so. He would be hurt later, with Terrah, too. I couldn't think of that right now.

"I don't know yet, Joshua. I just need to talk with Peter." My throat tightened. "Please, Joshua. Help me. I will tell you later—everything."

He stared at me as if seeing me for the first time. "Will you help me?"

Finally, he nodded.

I kissed him once more. "Come to my room when you've told him, then. I must rest or my head will split."

Slowly, he nodded. He released my hand, and I dragged myself up the stairs before I could disgrace myself. I did not hear my cousin step out into the hall.

Only as I reached the top of the stairs and paused for a moment did I see Terrah talking with Joshua. Only then did I see him smiling at her.

My heart chilled, but just for a moment. I knew Joshua would not betray me. He could not.

Chapter Twenty-One

I returned to my room and sank down on the bed. Peter would be told what I had found—or rather that I had information. I knew he would come to me as soon as he could. I knew no matter what had detained him before, he would arrange for our departure tonight. Yes. I would go with him tonight. I cursed myself for having been so stubborn before. I almost wished he had thrown me over his shoulder, cave man style, and taken me away from here, but then I wouldn't have learned what I now knew.

I laid my head on the feather pillows and closed my eyes when I heard the distinct rustle of silk near the door. My heart pumped the blood to my brain as I forced myself to sit up in time to see Terrah enter my room.

"Don't you ever knock?"

She smiled at me. "Oh, cousin dear," she cooed. "I merely came to see how you were feeling. You looked so poorly. Poor Joshua was worried about you."

I stared at her. I could believe that Joshua was worried about me. I doubted that she was.

"You didn't come just to tell me you worried about me."

Her smile was slighter this time. "Ah, cousin, you're becoming more intelligent with each passing day."

I made no comment.

"If you can stir yourself, I have something to show you."

"What?" I felt a tightness in my gut as I stared at Terrah.

"Now, now. Don't sound so suspicious. It's a surprise."

"Tell me. I don't like your surprises."

Terrah shrugged. "I think it's better that you see this."

She held out her hand to me.

"Where are we going?" I asked, standing and allowing her to lead me out the door and into the hall.

"There." She pointed toward the back stairs. I glanced back at her.

"Well go on. I'm not going to push you."

I studied her a moment. It wasn't something I would put past her. Nevertheless, I went ahead. I started down the steps, feeling them sag as if they would not take my weight. Cobwebs were all over the stair corners, and I was sure I saw a few spiders about. I itched just seeing them.

"Stop there." She indicated the landing where I now stood. We were not quite on the first floor yet but close to it. I realized then there was a door here. Cobwebs in this part of the stairwell were thicker. How many times was this room visited? Shivers went through me. Surely, my cousin wouldn't imprison me here.

"Well, open the door."

"Why?"

Her sweet smile nearly caused the bile to overflow my stomach. "Open it, Elizabeth. It's a surprise."

346

My hands trembled as I put my fingers on the knob.

"Oh, come now." Terrah stepped in front of me, impatiently. "There is nothing to hurt you inside. Trust me." I stared at her. Peter told me to trust him, too. So far I hadn't and had been wrong. But there was no question when it came to Terrah. She was not to be trusted.

Her hand went over mine as she opened the door. The creaking of the hinge sent chills through me as it opened. Immediately, I heard the wail of a baby and stared at the figure in the dim light.

The child who cried looked to be over three years old and yet still sounded like a newborn infant. I stared at the almond-shaped, blue eyes and rounded face. More important, I stared at the blond hair—the same shade as Peter's.

Questioning, I glanced at Terrah.

I wanted to wipe the smug smile off her face, but all I could do was stare.

Her voice was soft. "Now you know why Peter cannot wed you, cousin. His being a bastard is one thing. But if the town ever learned what he was doing to his child, they wouldn't like it."

My gaze shifted back toward the child. Horrified, I stared again at my cousin. "What he's doing? What about you? She's obviously yours as well."

"Yes, the child is mine." She paused for effectiveness. "Mine and Peter's."

I reached my hand out to touch the little girl, trying to tell myself she wasn't real. "This baby isn't Peter's."

"Oh, come, Elizabeth. Surely, you didn't think your Peter was a saint."

"No." I took a deep breath. "I know he's no saint."

The idea of Peter and Terrah was more than enough to nauseate me. "But he'll have to tell me the child is his before I'll believe it."

Terrah gave a sour laugh. "Do you think he'd admit it?"

The child reached out for me. I saw the deformed hand. "Does he know you keep her here, like this?"

"Of course, he knows. He also knows it's his duty to wed me."

"Why don't you care for her properly?"

"All her needs are being met. Even so, she will probably die shortly."

I stared at her. "You would let your own child die?"

Terrah shrugged. "It was Peter's decision. Not mine."

I felt myself gag. I couldn't believe Peter would be so callous. And yet I had nothing I could say in his defense. What did I really know of the man I supposedly loved?

Unable to take my cousin's haughty looks anymore, I pushed past her. I heard her laughter echo in my ears as I ran to my room.

Tears were in my eyes as I reached the wedge room. I could not believe that Peter knew what Terrah was doing. All the stress of the past few hours erupted into the wash basin bowl.

My head ached dreadfully now. After a few minutes, I washed my face with the coolness of the water left in the pitcher.

I turned toward the bed, thinking I would lie down when I heard the distinct click of the locking of my door.

In horror, I stared at it as footsteps faded in the hall.

Pulling and tugging at the door, I cried out in rage and fear. It was all in vain. My cousin had indeed locked me in. Pounding on the door, until my hand hurt, I shouted.

No one came. No one spoke to me.

Tears rolled down my face and I sank to the floor.

The hot muggy air seemed to vibrate about me as I stood at the window, staring out toward the forest path, toward the cliff. The sun would be setting soon and taking with it the glorious reds, golds, purples, violets, and blues which preceded the day's end here at Jerseyhurst. The cliff was beautiful. Far more beautiful than anything back in Kansas. I would miss it—if I ever managed to leave. The dying rays of the sun began to slant toward the window.

Lifting a white gauze-covered arm, I dabbed the sweat from my brow. The loose Roman gown, with the cowl neck and clinging toga wrap representing Desdemona, flowed about me. It revealed far more than I thought proper. Knowing Terrah, she probably thought if I had revealed myself to Peter, I could do so with her guests. It was one thing for her to torment me privately. It was another for her to expect me to wear a gown such as this in public.

Pacing back to the door, I tried the handle. It was the twentieth time today. It remained locked, as it had been since breakfast Thursday, since I had been treated to the discovery of Terrah's child. My stomach tightened now even as I thought of the poor innocent, but I could not consider her Peter's. Terrah was lying. She had to be. Yet the infant had Peter's coloring. Once again, my stomach threatened to revolt.

All my meals, of which I ate very little, had been brought up here by Rose. The way the black girl looked at me, I couldn't help but think that she, too, gloated.

I recalled Terrah's explanation for my imprisonment. Because of my unhealthy habit of wandering at night, she had thought it best for me to be locked in. I needed, she said, to be "looked after." I could still hear those honeyed words. She did so want me to enjoy the ball.

It had taken all of my effort to keep calm. I knew her real reason for locking me up was to keep me from seeing Peter. Was he being watched as closely as I was? Once more I blamed myself for not listening to him before, for not leaving when we had the chance.

The knock on the door startled me. No one knocked anymore. They simply unlocked it and opened it.

"Yes?" I turned and stared.

"Are you dressed, Beth?"

"Joshua! Oh, Josh!" I ran to the door and tried the handle again. "Joshua, you must help me."

Even as I began my plea, I heard the key turn in the lock. He must have known of my imprisonment, and yet he had done nothing to help me.

My heart raced as the door swung open with a creak. Joshua stood there wearing a magnificent, Moorish style robe, such as the kind I imagined Joseph and the coat of many colors he wore. His dark blond hair was covered with a white turban. The tan of his skin, still dark from his daily work on the farm, had needed no additional darkening.

His mouth opened as he saw me, too. I could tell he was surprised at my costume.

"Joshua, I need your help."

I saw something then in his eyes which bothered me. "Joshua?" He blushed then and I told myself the look I had seen was merely embarrassment. But I felt myself grow cold as he continued to stare at me. This was not the

350

man I had grown up with. A sense of being hopelessly lost pervaded me. If Joshua wouldn't help me, who would? I pulled back and turned to the window.

"Do you like my robe? Terrah said I could keep it."

Numbly, I nodded. He continued to stare at me. "Gosh, Beth, I never realized you could look so nice."

I forced myself to smile at the compliment. "Joshua, why don't we take a carriage ride before we go to the party. It's such a nice evening and I could use the air," I said as calmly as I could.

He shook his head. I did not like the look in his eyes. "It's time to go to the party. The carriage is ready. David and your uncle are waiting."

I swallowed hard. Yes, the carriage to take us over to Parkland for the ball, where I would pretend to have a good time. And what then, after the party?

"Why didn't you come to see me after you delivered the message to Peter? Didn't you see him?"

He stared woodenly at me. "I gave him your message, Beth. Only he had no answer."

"None? He didn't say anything to you?"

Joshua glanced toward the hall. No one seemed about. "Beth, I couldn't get to you." He hesitated. "What's happening? I don't understand this. Were you really so sick?"

"Oh, Joshua." There were tears in my eyes. "I'll explain it later." My voice choked. "But tell me what Peter said."

He hesitated. "He said he'd see you tonight."

"Tonight? Before the ball?"

Joshua shrugged. "No, I don't think he meant before. Must be he meant after."

I nodded then, realizing that Joshua did not know.

I placed my arm though his and took one last glance at the room. Briefly, I wondered if I should take Zebulon's gun with me, but in the skimpiness of the costume, there was nowhere for me to put it. Besides, it was too late for that now. If Joshua had told me the truth, then I had nothing to worry about. I turned to him.

"Joshua, you were alone with Peter when you told him, weren't you?"

He reddened. "Gosh, yes, Beth. It's what you told me to do."

I stared at him. I did not recall giving him instructions to see Peter alone. Was he mistaken or was my memory at fault?

I felt suddenly positive that Joshua was lying to me. It chilled me to the bone. There was no one, now, that I could trust. I was alone.

Shivering, I allowed Joshua to help me into the carriage.

I sat down on the padded cloth seat and forced myself to smile at David. His lewd grin disgusted me. I glanced at my uncle who had his head leaning against the frame.

"Don't mind him," David said sardonically. "He'll come to in time for the party. He's got a great ability to snap out of things, just like that." He snapped his fingers in front of my face, startling me.

I forced myself to calm down. I clung to the hope that I would get through this party, and then Peter and I would somehow make our escape. If only we could do it before midnight, before the wedding, we would be safe. I bit my lower lip. I did not want to think about what was to happen this evening.

The drive took only five minutes, but we slowed as we

reached the main entrance to Parkland. A line of carriages already extended to the road. Gas and candles lit the house with a fairy-tale glow that showed impressively against the twilight.

I reluctantly accepted David's hand as I descended from the carriage and stood for a moment staring at the mansion, taking in its beauty. I also understood—to a point—why Terrah coveted it over Jerseyhurst. If I were to inherit, this would be mine, I thought. Then I dismissed the idea. I had only wanted to know who I was. Now that I knew, I wanted only Peter and my freedom.

Colorful costumed figures milled the lawns, halls, and rooms, among them several other Shakespearian characters. I paused and tried to guess who they represented and why. It was a game to me, just as this whole evening was a game—a game in which the odds were rigged hopelessly against me. Yet I refused to admit defeat.

As Joshua helped me up the stairs, I was aware of David who was following me close behind. I panicked for a moment, thinking he had been assigned to watch me. If so, I never would be able to find Peter and plan our escape. Beads of sweat touched my brow. I turned to find David had disappeared. Thank goodness.

"Joshua, dearest, I think I'll go to Harriet's room with the other women and freshen up."

"You look fine," he said, refusing to let go of my arm. "Besides, Terrah wouldn't like that."

My blood froze. "What do you mean, Terrah wouldn't like that?"

He refused to meet my gaze. "I told her. I'd take care of you."

I stared at Joshua, not believing what I had heard. The pain going through me was like a hammer smashing my heart. "Take care of me?"

"Yeah." He shrugged. "You know, see you don't get lost. This sure is a fabulous house. Looks a lot bigger than Jerseyhurst."

I refused to be diverted from the subject. "You mean she asked you to see I don't speak with Peter. Is that it?"

Joshua didn't answer.

Nausea overwhelmed me. I turned away for a moment as I tried to swallow it down. If he was in love with my cousin—or thought he was—perhaps he didn't know what she had planned that night. I put my hand out to him, trying to keep myself calm, trying to think. "Joshua."

"T'aint no use t'beg me, Beth. I promised Terrah."

I took a deep breath and nodded. "Just tell me one thing."

"What?"

"Did you really give Peter my message?"

He stared at me a moment and then nodded. "Sure. I wouldn't lie to you."

"And were you alone when you told him?"

Joshua glanced down at his rough hands. "Gosh, Beth."

I took a deep breath. "Who was with you?"

"Well, just his daddy."

I felt as if the blood had been squeezed out of me. I shivered with the violent cold overtaking me. Alexander had been with him. Alexander knew. That meant Terrah was aware of my knowledge.

"Honestly, I couldn't help it."

I saw tears in his eyes. Suddenly, I felt sorry for him. I felt more sorry for him than myself. I wondered how he would take Terrah's betrayal. From the large ballroom, the strains of music began to encircle us.

"It's all right, Joshua." I sighed. "Come on. The music's starting."

"You're not angry with me, Beth?"

I sighed. "No, Joshua."

"We're still friends?"

I swallowed my disappointment. I nodded and understood now why I could never feel the passion for him I felt for Peter. Peter, at least, took command of some situations, whereas Joshua, it seemed, always let a woman lead him.

"And you won't leave me tonight? Terrah would be awfully angry with me, if you do."

"No, Joshua. I won't leave you." I was past caring whether I lied to him or not. "You really like Terrah, don't you?"

His stare unnerved me. There was a moment of silence between us as the music grew louder. "Sure do." I could barely hear his words. I wondered how he would react if he knew what I knew about my cousin, if he had any inkling of the child she had hidden. A chill ran through me. As the music grew louder now, reaching my ears, I recognized the melody. I felt myself grow faint. It was the wedding march! Terrah had told me she planned not to be married until midnight!

My stomach tightened and I looked at Joshua. "It seems we're both destined to be disappointed in our loves."

"What do you mean?"

I pursed my lips. "I think we'd better go into the main ballroom now."

Lacing my arm through his, more for support for me than for him, I held my head high as I walked with Joshua

355

through the room to a pair of chairs. Looking up at the wall above the fireplace, I saw the portrait of Andrew Parkisham, my father. Tears came to my eyes as I realized for the first time that I would never know my father, and he would never know me. I could only hope he hadn't been as evil as his brother. I could only hope he had been someone I could be proud of.

Chapter Twenty-Two

The ballroom was suddenly hushed, but every so often someone would audibly ask his neighbor what was happening. Seated in the corner near heavy blue-velvet drapes, I didn't have to listen to know the answer. My heart ached for myself and for Joshua. The sadness which overwhelmed me almost prevented me from seeing Terrah as she floated down the staircase, wearing a white Juliet dress of watered tabby, seed pearls, and a mesh veil. The puffed sleeves accentuated the tightness of her bodice and the fullness of her skirt.

Grudgingly, I had to admit that Terrah looked breathtakingly lovely.

Joshua's grip on my arm tightened. "What's happening?" he whispered.

I shook my head, unable to speak for the tears tightening my throat. Peter now descended the stairs. I saw him hold his head proudly and stiffly as he looked straight ahead. I don't know if he saw me. I hoped he did. As Terrah had told me, Peter wore an Italian renaissance costume of Romeo. The costume was of blue and white velvet trimmed with gold. In the renaissance fashion, he wore white hose. He was a Romeo. My Romeo. I didn't know if I should be angry or sad. Wasn't there any way he could have gotten out of this? He must have had other options. I couldn't help recalling all the times he had begged me to leave with him. Was I at fault for keeping him here?

Alexander Parkisham followed closely behind, wearing a similar outfit which only seemed to heighten Alexander's crudeness. I could not believe he was my uncle. I thanked the lord he was not my father.

My lips silently formed Peter's name as he passed directly opposite me along the makeshift flower-strewn aisle. He seemed to glance my way for the briefest of moments. I wanted him to understand why I hadn't gone with him that night. I wanted his forgiveness for not leaving with him, for allowing him to be caught in the deadly web spun by Terrah and Alexander.

He could still leave with me tonight. If we could escape we could be together forever. I told myself it wouldn't matter if he was married to my cousin. In my heart, he was and would always be married to me. As long as we were together, it wouldn't matter.

He had passed me now. He continued to hold his head high. He seemed to see nothing but the altar. As Alexander continued to follow closely behind, I stared at him. It was hard to see, but I wouldn't be surprised if the odious man held a gun to Peter.

My eyes prickled with unshed tears.

I glanced across the room and saw David standing by the door, almost like a sentry. For just a moment, our eyes met. As the leering smile spread across his face, I knew he had read my mind. Any escape that night would

358

be useless.

I looked back at Peter. Was he acting? It seemed as if he was in a daze.

Joshua's insistence broke my own thoughts. "Please, Beth, tell me. Why is it so quiet? What's happening?"

"Don't you understand?" My eyes narrowed in irritation. "You've been used, Joshua. Terrah doesn't love you. She used you."

He stared at me wide-eyed, disbelieving.

"Yes, Joshua," I hissed. "My cousin, whom you profess to love, is tonight marrying the man whom I love." I felt a sharp pain in me as I saw the pain in his eyes. I hated to hurt him this way, but I had to tell him.

Joshua still continued to shake his head. "No. Terrah said she loved me. Terrah promised we'd be together." He rose and took a step forward, toward the alter, forgetting me.

"Don't be foolish!" I grabbed his arm, hissing. "She'll only laugh at you. Step back."

Reluctantly, he returned to his seat. The attention, which had momentarily turned toward him, returned to the couple up front.

"Listen to me, Joshua. You and Terrah can still be together." He stared at me. "If you help me meet Peter as you promised." My words were cut off by the look in his eyes.

"Beth, I can't do that. I told Terrah I'd take care of you."

I stared at him as a chill went through me. What did he mean—take care of me? Why was he being so unbelievably stubborn, so thick headed! Why couldn't he see what Terrah was doing to him? "Joshua!" I hissed.

The couple in front of us turned about, glaring. I was

forced into silence, forced into watching Peter go through the sham ceremony. One of the women near the altar was dressed as a harlequin. How fitting, I thought, and felt a hysterical laugh rise within me.

The minister spoke of the sanctity of marriage and of the lovely couple he was joining in that holy state. My stomach turned. If he only knew what Terrah was really like, and what a sham he was taking part in.

I scarcely realized the ceremony was completed until I saw Peter give Terrah a chaste kiss on her round cheek. Everyone but Joshua and myself applauded. The newly married pair crossed the floor and left the room. The orchestra struck up a waltz, and people about me were choosing partners. I didn't even notice David had come up to stand in front of me.

Joshua, with tears in his eyes, still stared at the door where Terrah and Peter Parkisham had gone. I knew what he was going through. I could hardly believe it myself.

"What's wrong with your little friend, cousin?" David leered.

I glanced up at him and glared. "You should know," I responded, hating my cousin even more at this moment than I had ever hated him before. It was one thing to attack me, but quite another to take advantage of Joshua's naïveté.

"Should I?" His huge hand gripped my shoulder. "Explain it to me while we dance." His eyes roved over my scanty costume.

"How can I dance with you or anyone when your sister is having Joshua act as my bodyguard?"

"Like this," he said, pulling me roughly toward him and whirling me into the throng of swaying couples. I tried to push him away but could not extricate myself from his grasp without causing a hideous scene.

"You should be grateful to me," he sneered, the smell of whiskey on his breath.

"Oh?"

"Of course. If I hadn't insisted, Terrah would never have allowed you to come to the party."

"Gratitude is hardly what I am feeling at this moment."

He allowed his hand to slide beneath the loose-hanging back of my dress.

"Leave me alone, David." I managed to free myself and stepped backward toward another couple. David grabbed me before I could fall.

"You'd better change your mind, little Elizabeth. It could be your last chance to be with me."

I felt my eyes narrow. "I don't believe you would ever miss a single opportunity to torment me."

David shrugged.

"Since I am thirsty, I'll let you free now. But remember," he said, blowing me a kiss. "Joshua's not the only one who will be keeping an eye on you." He grinned. "Enjoy your ball, dear little Kansas cousin. It will probably be your last."

I stared after him, surprised he had given up without a bigger fight. I glanced at Joshua and saw that he was looking in another direction.

I moved quickly. If I wanted to leave, this was my chance. I had to find Peter. I slipped past the dancers into the wide hall. There was no sign of either Peter or Terrah.

I found myself in the great hall that was used as a banquet room. More spacious than the halls at Jersey-hurst, it now had table after white-clothed table laden with meats: roast duck, chicken, beef; and sweets: German chocolate cake, a three-tiered wedding cake, strawberry tarts, fruits, and every conceivable delectable. I paused, recognizing the breads I had seen Rose make the other day. I wondered briefly if I should take something for my trip. But I was more concerned about getting out of here.

The one thing I wanted to do before leaving was go up to Harriet's room to see if my mother's locket was there. That and the silver brushes were the only things of Mother's I had left.

Glancing up the stairs, my hand on the rail, I wondered which of the rooms belonged to Peter. Even during the time I had stayed here to recuperate after the fire, I had not found out.

My lips were dry. I looked back for an instant and saw a gleam of red hair making its way through the crowd. David must have noticed I was missing. I didn't think he had seen me on the stairs yet. I had to hide somewhere quickly.

I saw a door on the other side of the hall ajar and hurriedly left the stairs. I could feel the tightness in my chest as I reached the door.

For the briefest moment, I listened. There seemed no one about. I pulled open the door. The room was empty.

Shutting it behind me, I lit the gaslight at the side of the door. The room sprang to life. I realized then that this was the parlor which Alexander used as his study. The huge leather chair which he had interviewed me from that day was again turned toward the fireplace. I couldn't see if anyone was sitting in it and tiptoed about, but it was empty. I sank into the chair for a moment, trying to catch my breath, trying to calm my fear and get up my courage to continue.

My heartbeat quickened as I glanced up into a portrait of a younger Andrew Parkisham. Yes, he was handsome. I could see how my mother might have fallen in love with him. Perhaps it was my imagination, but I was sure he must be smiling down at me.

I stepped forward to examine the painting. This was my father! My father! I wanted to shout it out even as I reached up to touch the canvas. His eyes were the same blue as my mother's, and his cheeks were dimpled in a slight smile. I could see why my mother had fallen in love with him. Tears were in my eyes. Had he known about me? Had my aunt been able to tell him? My hand rested on the frame now, vaguely aware of the uneven edge.

My attention diverted, just for the second, from those deep blue eyes. I realized the rough edge of the wood wasn't wood at all. It was a paper of some sort.

Blood rushed so quickly through my lungs and pounded so fast in my ears it was almost impossible to think. What was more logical than to have the papers from my mother hidden in the portrait of her lover?

I knew who I was now but even so, I could hardly believe my luck at finding them. Gently, I pulled them out of the hollow space in the frame. My heart leaped like a horse jumping over a fence. Yes, I recognized my mother's neat handwriting again.

Quickly, I scanned the papers. These were written by mother. They were the documents which my mother had given Mr. McCrae.

My hand trembled as I read the papers.

Dearest Daughter:
    If you're reading this, you will have met my dear

363

friend, Meredith McCrae, who will assist you in your quest. I am sorry I could not tell you before about your father, Andrew Parkisham, but the time never seemed right.

I was probably wrong for leaving Andrew. Indeed, I never forgot him and I doubt he ever forgot me. He had promised me—many times during our love—that should I ever have a child, it would inherit above all else. You, my darling, are his child and you should inherit whatever Andrew has, since I know now that he never married.

My dear friend Meredith will help you fight since I know Alexander, Andrew's brother, will not be happy at seeing you. In fact, I expect him to put obstacles in your way. It would be just like Alex. Meredith has agreed to see that Andrew's last will is followed. Do not worry. You are a gentleman's daughter and your father loved you—despite the fact he never married me.

Again, my darling, forgive me for not having been truthful with you before.

Your loving mother,

Margaret Swanson Larabee.

Here was the proof I needed, if ever I should want it.

My hands trembled as I folded the papers into the belt of my costume. Once again, I was sure I saw Andrew smiling at me. Now, if only I had my mother's locket back. I looked about. It probably would not be here in the study.

I looked away from the desk when the red paper flagged my attention. A train ticket? Was it proof of Alexander's trip to Kansas? I didn't need any more proof, but I picked up the paper anyway—and felt it flutter from my hands in astonishment. No, I could not believe it. The ticket was made out in Joshua's name, and it was dated two days after I left Kansas. At first I could not understand. Had Joshua been here all this time? Where had he been? Why would he have been here?

My heart constricted in a spasm as I thought of all the times when I was sure I had seen him and then told myself it couldn't be so. I continued to stare at the ticket.

Perhaps they had sent him a ticket to come for me when I was ill. Perhaps he had been unable to come. Yes, that had to be the answer. I put the ticket in my belt as well.

Noises outside the door made me stiffen. I realized I had been in here too long, and I still needed to find the locket before leaving.

Going to the door, I waited a moment. There was a burst of loud music and the sound of clapping hands when I stepped out of the room into the hall. Shutting the door behind me, I was glad to see the passage was empty. Then, clutching my hands together to control my helpless anger, I realized why they must be applauding. Tears again sprang to my eyes. The new couple must have just returned to the ballroom. I had lost my moment to speak with Peter. Even from where I stood in the hall, I could see guests surrounding them, congratulating them. Peter was there, within my sight but forbidden to me. I longed to reach out and touch him but could not.

I stared at them. Should I leave now? Should I forget Peter? My heart ached. I knew I would always think of him. I even contemplated asking Joshua for money, but no. The leftover money from the sum my uncle had given me for the dinner dress would have to do. It was enough to get me to Chicago but not back to Kansas. Perhaps that was best. There was nothing left for me in Kansas.

My hands trembled as I began to climb the stairs. No one would be up there now—not with the new couple downstairs. If my mother's locket was anywhere, it would be in Harriet's room. I had thought Harriet was my friend, but then it seems I had made a lot of false assumptions during my stay in Aberdeen.

Reaching the top of the stairs, I closed my eyes. I tried to recall which room was Harriet's; panic rose up in me. Was my mother's locket so important? An overwhelming instinct of danger made the hairs on my neck rise. I choked the bile which had risen in my throat. I should go back down. I should flee Aberdeen tonight, before it was too late.

But even as I stood there, I knew, I would never forgive myself if I didn't make at least one effort to find the locket. I knew, too, I had to somehow say good-bye to Peter. Peter was the only man I would ever love, just as mother had loved only Andrew.

I advanced cautiously down the hall. I paused a moment at the second door. The only sounds were from below.

Cautiously, I tried the door. Locked.

I tried the next one, and then the next. All were tightly fastened. I didn't know if the doors were locked because of the party or because of me. It was almost as if Terrah had guessed my goal. She had second-guessed me so many times, it seemed.

I bit my lower lip. I had to admit defeat, here as elsewhere. Wiping away the tears which had formed, I started back down the stairs.

Joshua stood just within the doorframe of the

ballroom. His jaw was set in a firm line as he watched the new couple dancing. Suddenly he turned to me. I didn't like the way he looked at me. Was he angry with Terrah or with me? "You shouldn't have gone off like that. You should never have left Kansas, Beth."

I swallowed hard and had to nod. For once, Joshua was right.

"Where've you been?" He stared at me strangely.

"To fix my hair."

"Well, it don't matter," he said, frowning. "I have a message for you." He jerked his thumb toward Peter who had stopped to speak with his father-in-law and Alexander. I didn't want to take my eyes off him, but I had to turn to Joshua.

"A message from Peter?"

He nodded. "I went to congratulate him."

"And—"

"He said to tell you he'd be by the gazebo in an hour."

I swallowed hard, incredulous at my good fortune. "An hour? Can't I have more time? I need to get some of my things. I need—" My voice came out in a hoarse whisper as I realized Joshua had that strange look in his eyes again.

"I'm just passin' on the message."

"Never mind. Thank you, Joshua." I touched him gently again. "Josh, I want you to know I'm grateful for all you've done for me." My voice broke. "I don't think I'll ever forget you. I hope you find some happiness."

He grunted and said nothing. He didn't meet my eyes.

I pressed my lips together. Perhaps I had said too much. I edged into the room and tried to get Peter to look at me. He did nothing to acknowledge me. It was probably better if he didn't and yet I wanted so badly to see his eyes.

The dancing had started up in earnest now. Mr. Dunn, dressed as Ichabod Crane, strolled over toward me. I was aware again of David's watching me, but I no longer cared. If Peter had managed to get a message to me, then everything was going to be all right.

Stiffly, Mr. Dunn bowed. "I'm surprised to see you still with us in Aberdeen, Miss . . ."

"Larabee." I flushed, filling in for him. "Elizabeth Larabee, Mr. Dunn."

He grimaced. "So you said."

"Tell me, Mr. Dunn. Do you recognize anyone here? I mean, do you see the other girl who claimed she was me?"

"Or whom you claim to be?" Dunn glanced about the room. Harriet stood a few feet away talking with her brother. Her costume of Rapunzel suited her well. "No, miss. I do not."

"Are you quite sure?" I glanced once more at Harriet.

"I am. Quite sure. But I've not come here to discuss that. Would you care to dance?"

David had taken up with Harriet. Probably he had supposed I would be well occupied with the lawyer. I glanced about the room. Joshua had disappeared. If ever there was a chance, it was now.

"I—think I had best get some air. I've a headache."

Mr. Dunn stared at me, obviously hurt and then turned away without a word. I looked around once more, steeling myself as I saw Peter dancing with Terrah. For a moment, I wondered if he wasn't having a good time, but no. It was all an act on his part. It had to be. He loved me, didn't he? Suddenly, I again felt unsure of his affections.

Quietly as I could, I eased myself into the hall. I

grabbed a strawberry tart and then hurried out the back way. No one was about. No one, it seemed, had seen me leave. But I knew it wouldn't be long before someone saw me missing.

The ground was soggy with moisture as I ran past the gazebo, past the willow, glancing briefly at each. It was impossible not to think of the happy moments I had spent here. Well, there would be happiness away from Parkland, away from Alexander and Terrah. I had to hurry to get back to Jerseyhurst, to get together what I wanted and to change my clothes before meeting Peter. I could not very well travel in this costume nor did I expect him to travel in his.

A ripping sound made me grimace as I realized that I had torn my costume on a loose limb. It didn't matter. I freed myself hastily. I'd be back at Jerseyhurst soon. Once there, I would change to my travel clothes and quickly pack a few of my dresses. Then, I'd return to the gazebo and wait for Peter to come. He had told Joshua. I knew he would come.

Hurrying along, I knew I hadn't much more than a few moments, not only because Joshua had said an hour but because I couldn't let Terrah find out I was gone.

The thought of Peter seemed to give wings to my feet, and I forgot how I hated this part of the forest. I reached the clearing in no time and saw the outline of Jerseyhurst silhouetted against the full moon. Again my heart quickened. The house was dark, and yet it seemed I had seen a light on the third floor. No, that couldn't be. It was only my fear and a shadow from the moon.

It took a second of standing there, shivering, before I could move forward. I had the feeling of being watched, but no one was at the house. All the servants were at

Parkland, helping with the party.

Taking a deep breath, I told myself, "It's the last time you'll have to go in there." Gritting my teeth, I started forward. Of course, what I feared was probably imagination. After all, no one knew I had left yet. No one would come after me. I would soon be away from all of this; I would soon have Peter's arms around me to comfort me.

With relief, I reached my room. As quickly as I could, I shed the costume, leaving it on the floor.

It took but a moment for me to dress in the black bombazine for travel and to pack the small portmanteau with a few of my clothes, two changes of linen, and of course my mother's brushes. I was sorry I had not found the locket. The rest of my garments remained in the armoire. I would just have to trust Peter to purchase more clothes for me. As it was, the baggage would be difficult to carry along the forest path. I remembered suddenly how I had dragged the case from the train station, so full of expectations then. How things had changed!

My mother's papers from the lawyer fell to my feet as I picked up the costume from the floor. I had almost forgotten them, and they reminded me of the letter to my aunt, of the proof of Terrah's embezzlement and of the gun.

Crossing the room, I stood in front of the fireplace. I stared and felt the color drain from me. The brick wasn't right. Something was wrong, dreadfully wrong.

Unable to control my fears, I yanked the loose brick from the wall, throwing it to the floor with a thud.

The space was empty! I shoved my hand in, remembering the last time when I had thought everything was gone. Nothing!

Frantic, I stepped back and counted the space. Six by six. I couldn't believe it. Everything had been there earlier. When had my cousin found them? I had been so careful, so very careful. Shivers went through me. All I could do was stare at the empty space.

I felt the paper in my pocket. I realized that all I had now were the papers from the lawyer. Well, that would have to do. I really didn't care about Parkland, about my supposed inheritance anyway. All I wanted was to be away from here with Peter.

Tucking the papers into my bag, I threw my worn cloak over my left arm and took up the portmanteau.

I struggled with my heavy burden to the top of the stairs and paused. Had I heard a sound below or was it my imagination? Perhaps it was the baby crying. For a moment, I thought about taking her, but there was no way I could carry her and my luggage as well. I would just have to tell Peter about her and make sure something was done. I could not believe he knew what Terrah was doing, nor could I believe the child was his.

I listened again but the sound wasn't repeated. My imagination was much too active. I was too tense. I had to get out of this house, away from all the grief that Jerseyhurst represented for me and for so many others.

The grandfather clock in the hall struck eleven. Was it that late already? Sweat broke out on my brow. Peter would wait for me. I was certain of that.

But I would never get to the gazebo in time with my portmanteau. I opened it quickly. My mother's silver brushes from Andrew—from my father—lay on top. These and the paper were the only things of real importance to me.

371

Emptying the case, I closed it once more so that it contained only those essentials and one change of clothes.

With the portmanteau lighter now, I turned. The gaslight in the hall flickered a moment and then went out. I stood in the darkness for a brief second, saying a silent good-bye to the house where my mother and then I had known so much misery and so much happiness. I said a silent prayer for Tilly's soul and for my aunt's. I still believed my cousin had murdered her mother, and it had something to do with me, but I probably would never be able to prove it.

The woods seemed darker, more dangerous than they had before. I was aware of my heart racing, of the blood pounding in my lungs as I tried to hurry along the path. The sensation of life was suddenly strong within me. Peter loved me despite the sham of his marriage to Terrah. And for Peter, I would risk anything.

I reached the clearing by the gazebo. Where was Peter? There were still people at the house. I knew that from the sounds, yet I could see no one as I glanced toward Parkland.

Then, from near the willow, someone moved. My heart leaped when I saw the white costume. He hadn't even bothered to change. I dropped the bag I carried and began to run toward the figure.

"Peter!" I called. "Peter!"

I took several more steps forward, then I stopped and stared. It wasn't Peter who awaited me, it was Terrah. I felt my heart race. In her hand was a gun.

"Yes, you can stop there, Elizabeth."

I continued to stare at the gun. "Where's Peter?"

Her laughter floated across the space toward me. It sounded almost like a hawk's cry, a hawk who had caught its prey. "My darling husband is dancing with his sister right now. He knows, of course, that I've come to meet you."

"Does he? Does he really?" I stared at her. So Peter had set me up for this. He was part of the plot to harm me. My voice barely came through. "Does Joshua know you're doing this?"

Again, she laughed. I started to go toward the house. I would find safety there, if nothing else. And I would find Peter and Joshua. The gun went off once. I started. "No, my little cousin. You're not leaving me now. The fun is just getting started. Stand where you are. I want a good shot. And don't think Peter's going to save you. He won't. No one will. Peter's been my lover since you came to Aberdeen and so is Joshua. I've known everything you've done and everything you've said to him. He's mine. I have control over him and your farmer friend. I told you once cousin, you don't know your men well. And don't worry, no one will hear the gun. The music inside is too loud."

My blood was cold as I felt numbness going through me. This wasn't happening to me. I shook my head slowly. "Do they know you plan to murder me? Do they know you killed your mother and Tilly. Did they know you embezzled money from the bank and started the fire? What would your precious minister and town society think of you and your baby?"

She smiled at me. Her voice was as seductively soft as the silvery moonlight that played on her fair hair. "I didn't kill anyone, Elizabeth."

My voice scratched in my throat, but I had to know. "Who then—who killed them? Who attacked me?"

She laughed. "Does it really matter? You're going to die anyway. In a moment you'll join your precious Tilly."

I forced myself to meet her eyes. "I know who my father is."

"Good for you. I'm surprised that with your tenacity, it took you this long to figure it out."

I glanced again toward the house. Someone had to come out. I tried to edge closer to the light.

"I said, don't move. I won't hesitate to shoot you now—though that isn't what I've planned."

I took a deep breath, trying to hide the fear in my voice. "What do you plan to tell Joshua?"

Terrah shrugged. "Nothing. After all, one Othello killed his Desdemona in jealousy. When poor Joshua realizes you were in love with Peter, he'll have a fit and shoot you. That is, of course, if anyone misses you."

I gasped. "No! No, you wouldn't blame it on him."

"No, she won't blame it on me!" I heard Joshua as he emerged from a tree. I stared at him and moved toward him, thinking he had come to save me. I realized with a horror he had Zebulon's gun. How had he gotten it?

"Stay where you are, Beth. I sure didn't mean it to come t'this. I didn't want to harm you. The attacks were meant to scare you away. You were too stubborn. Too stubborn for your own good."

"Joshua! You!" My mouth went dry. "You were the one to attack me—at the brook, at the bank, in the house?"

He gave a curt nod.

Terrah's laughter rang in my ears. "You didn't once

374

suspect, did you? Joshua's been helping me for some time now. Joshua's a lovely boy." She stepped over toward him and draped her arm about him. I could only stare numbly.

"How did you know about Joshua before I came? How did you get him to help you? I don't understand."

"It's all so simple, cousin. It was Joshua who rigged the carriage that killed your mother. You were supposed to die with your mother. When you didn't, he tried to persuade you not to come here. You wouldn't listen to him."

Stunned, I could only continue to stare.

"Joshua! Joshua, I thought you were my friend."

The moonlight shimmered, showing tears in his eyes now. "I was, Beth. Truly I was. But Terrah has helped me so much. Do you remember when my farm was in trouble? Well, the bank refused to lend me money. I happened to meet Miss Terrah in town then. She asked questions 'bout you and yer Mama." I heard a sob from him. "She and I—we became friends, if you know what I mean. I agreed to help her for saving the farm and because she said she'd marry me later—after you were dead."

"Spare us the details, farm boy," Terrah said impatiently. "Just do your job and you'll be rewarded."

"Can't be."

Terrah turned toward him, and I felt a moment of hope. "Can't be," Joshua repeated. "You were to marry me. You promised. You're married to this Parkisham fellow, now. You lied to me. I ain't doin' nuthin' more for you."

I stood there, horrified, watching. For once, Terrah seemed to be at a loss. "You must kill her. I'll see you

375

hang for killing Tilly and McCrae. If you had been true to me, you would have done this fool girl in a long time ago! You would have destroyed her at the brook, or in the bank; none of this would be happening. I would have married you. Truly, Joshua. I would have." Even through her honeyed tones, I could hear her tension.

They both had guns, and it seemed they were at a standstill. Taking advantage of the momentary confusion, I began to run. I had to get to the house. I had to get to Peter.

"No! You can't go to that house!" Terrah cried. I didn't hear anything more but felt a sharp pain in my right arm as I stumbled forward onto the soggy ground. There was a cry, and I thought it was mine, but I knew I hadn't cried out. I heard the cry again and twisted my body to see. Terrah had fallen. She still wore her wedding finery, but it was stained now with mud and blood.

Joshua stood over her with his gun. In horror, I stared at him as he bent down over her. In the moonlight I could see him sobbing.

I forced myself to sit up as I tried to—despite my pain—edge back toward the house.

The sound of footsteps made me rejoice. Joshua looked up away from Terrah and toward me. "I had to do it, Beth. She betrayed me."

"Joshua." I felt the tears in my own eyes. "Joshua, I understand. Please, Joshua. You have to help me. Get Peter. Bring him here."

Joshua shook his head. "You know about me now. I can't have you tellin' people what I did to that black and the lawyer fellow. Can't have you talkin' about what I just done t'Terrah."

He moved toward me. There was no way I could move

376

fast enough. The pain in my arm and in my side had paralyzed me.

Joshua came up to me, lifting me in his strong arms— those arms which I had once loved. He had been my friend. He had helped me. I couldn't believe this was happening now.

"Please, Joshua," I pleaded. "We're friends."

"Yeah, Beth. I know." He hung his head, but he didn't let go of me.

The footsteps I thought I had heard now were closer.

"Help!" I called out. "Help!"

Joshua put his huge hairy hand over my mouth. The tears still shimmered in his eyes as he slowly carried me toward the cliff. "Don't ya understand, Beth? I can't have ya screaming out like that. I don't want t' do this, but I gotta."

"Please, Joshua. Think of all the wonderful times we had together back on the farm. Think of how you helped me with the water when we had the drought."

"Hey! Hey! What do you think you're doing?" I saw the other figure emerge from the clearing. The white costume this time told me it had to be Peter. "Drop her, Harmon! Drop her now!"

Joshua refused to let me go, but he turned now toward Peter. I felt him go for Zebulon's gun.

"Peter, be careful! He has a weapon. He has—" A shot rang out. I closed my eyes, unable to watch as Peter seemed to fall.

"Harmon, you won't get away with this. I've got the constable coming now." Peter stopped a moment, and in the moonlight I could see the horror on his face as he saw Terrah's still body.

Joshua aimed again but missed as Peter ducked. In the

distance the constable and others were crashing through the woods now.

Realizing he had no hope, Joshua let go of me and I fell to the ground. He ran down the hill just as I had that Sunday when Peter first kissed me. My heart went to my throat as I saw him jump the cliff. His scream seemed to echo through the whole valley as the men ran to the edge.

Peter came quickly over to me and picked me up in his arms. I buried my head in his shoulder and felt my tears stain the white velvet. "Oh, Peter, why did this all have to happen?"

He stroked my hair. "Oh, my darling." His lips brushed my brow. "If only you had trusted me before." I saw tears in his eyes. He held me to him as I saw the men move away from the cliff.

"Let me take you back to the house."

"But there's so much we need to talk about. So much I want to tell you."

He touched me gently. "Later, my love. I must talk to Alexander now. Now you know who you are, we had best see this thing through."

I put my arms about him and allowed him to carry me through the gardens. Those who had been left from the party gathered about in shock. The wedding had turned into a funeral, and I felt I was to blame.

I lost consciousness.

Chapter Twenty-Three

I believe it was somewhere near dawn as I opened my eyes again. Peter was at my bedside, watching me, studying me. At first I thought it was Harriet's room I was in, but the furniture was too masculine, too much like my Peter.

I started to sit up.

Immediately, Peter took my hand in his. "No, my darling. Don't move. You've been injured, you know."

I opened my eyes and stared at him. I still found it hard to understand how Joshua had kept his affair with Terrah from me for all this time. I found it hard to believe he would have tried to hurt me.

"Oh, Peter. He was my friend." I sobbed on his shoulder as he hugged me to him.

"I know, darling. I know." He paused. There was a moment of silence. "I must tell you about Alexander. He confessed to me—he murdered Andrew for his fortune. When he learned you existed and that your mother needed help, he and Terrah went out to see you. Terrah started up with Joshua then. Alexander feared once you learned who you were, he would lose everything."

I tried to protest. "But I didn't want anything. All I wanted was to know who I was. All I wanted was you."

Peter held me to him again. "I know, but neither Alexander nor Terrah could believe it. They thought all their schemes of merging the two lands, of taking over the bank, of their love relationship would be ruined by your being here."

"What will happen to Alexander? What about my uncle and David?"

He stood and walked to the window. His hands were behind his back. "Nothing will happen to Alex. Nothing can. He's dead. He hung himself late last night after the last guest had gone home after the farce wedding."

"Farce? You mean it wasn't real?"

"Oh, Elizabeth, darling, you know I wouldn't ever have married Terrah—not like that, not with the love I felt for you."

"But I saw a ceremony. I saw—"

He crossed the room toward me again. His lips touched mine. "Let's just say the minister owed me a favor. The words he used were not the correct marriage ceremony."

"It wasn't valid?"

Peter shook his head.

"And what about the baby?"

Peter looked at me blankly. "What baby?"

I told him about Terrah's baby, pathetically deformed and kept locked away. Peter took my hand. "It's not mine," he said. "Obviously it's Alexander's." He looked grim at the knowledge of Terrah's cruelty. "We'll have to see that she receives proper care."

"Oh, Peter. I should never have mistrusted you. I should have gone with you when you asked."

"No. You were right. You had to find out who you were, and now that you know, we don't have to leave. Alexander left his brother's will on the table before he hung himself. All this land, this house is yours."

I was silent for a moment, trying to digest my changed circumstances.

"And what about you? What about Harriet? Your mother? My uncle?"

He took my hand in his and kissed each finger separately. "Harriet is returning to Chicago. She admitted having helped Alexander. Mother has a small income which she brought to the marriage. I think she'll be much happier without Alexander, but your uncle will take quite some time to recover from the death of his daughter. David's disappeared. No one knows where he is. I think he ran off with Rose."

I sighed. I had never meant to cause such pain and turmoil. "What about you?"

He touched my cheek gently. "What happens to me depends on you. I can leave and try to make my own way somewhere else, but I don't want to. All I want to do is be with you."

There were tears in my eyes as I put my arms about him and felt myself choke as my throat tightened. "And all I want to do is be with you. How soon can we be married?"

He laughed and kissed me tenderly. "I was hoping you'd make an honest man of me."